Cymberie is
She enjoys
Adult Educa
lived for thirt
is set, in a se
on the Nationa ommon land where
she used to walk her Irish setter.

She has written primary literacy non-fiction for Collins and Oxford, on subjects as diverse as improving the environment, castles, scaffolding and Archimedes, and it was the research for these that first got her hooked on historical research – *Cymberie* is the first historical novel she has written. She also writes poetry, and was one of the founders of the Essex Poetry Festival. She is currently coordinator of Chelmsford Writers.

Maggie was born in Trinidad, and lived there and in Tobago until she was ten, when her family moved to England. She is married, with two sons.

For Lena.

CYMBERIE

Love -

MAGGIE FREEMAN

Maggie

Indigo Dreams Publishing

First Edition: Cymberie

First published in Great Britain in 2012 by:
Indigo Dreams Publishing Ltd
132 Hinckley Road
Stoney Stanton
Leics
LE9 4LN
www.indigodreams.co.uk

ISBN 978-1-907401-81-7

British Library Cataloguing in Publication Data. A CIP record for this book can be obtained from the British Library.

Designed and typeset in Minion Pro by Indigo Dreams.
Map on cover reproduced by courtesy of Essex Record Office.
Author photo by Derek Adams

Printed and bound in Great Britain by: The Russell Press Ltd.
www.russellpress.com on FSC paper and board sourced from sustainable forests.

Thank you to Kathryn Heyman for mentoring me in writing this, and to Laura Morris for her encouragement and belief in it. Many thanks too to Steve for his continuing support.

CYMBERIE

1

Elaine was climbing the track to Cymberie. The leaves of the oaks swayed above her head and sang; the mossy bank was velvet beneath the soles of her feet. A cock crowed some way away. She could just hear the voices of the men in the harvest field, the swish of their sickles through the stalks of ripe wheat.

She was sweating slightly. A horsefly settled on her cheek and she slapped at it. She felt scared on her own, incomplete, as if there were only half of her here. Will Samuel be safe with Mistress Margery? she worried. He'd almost leapt from her arms into the hedged garden of hollyhocks and pink crawling babies, he'd settled by a cabbage sucking a stone. Margery had said: Don't concern yourself about him. I'm used to caring for infants. Trust me.

I've no choice, Elaine thought. I have to have money. But this – this thing I've said I'll do today – I can't bear to do it.

The moss came to an end and she stepped down on the track. The earth was warm, the pebbles hard but they didn't bother her; she'd walked barefoot for months, ever since March. She skirted round the horseshit. What will Cymberie be like? she wondered. She had never been to the house before. She'd heard tell of it in the village, how huge it was, with its many windows paned with glass and white swans floating on the lily lake. A tall fountain showered silver water, people said, and the kitchen overflowed with food: roast venison and quail, gingerbread and marchpane. It was two days since she had eaten even plain stale bread.

If only it were not him, she thought, if only it were some other man. I could bear to do this for any other man. I could manage it. I wouldn't mind. But him...

She stretched out her arm, looked at how thin her wrist had become, saw that the skin had sunk into the fan of bones in her hand. That it was almost translucent. She had to have food. She wouldn't have cared for herself, wouldn't have minded if she lived or died, but Samuel – he changed the matter.

In the palm of her left hand was the scar of the cut she'd got when her husband Thomas's chisel had slipped. She'd been working on a carving of Cupid and he had leant across to neaten a feather on the young god's wing. She had turned to kiss him; his attention wavered. It was her fault, truly, not his. The cut had healed well. It was the last relic of his love left on her body, and she kissed it.

At the top of the hill the woodland came to an end. The great oak at the edge spread its branches over the level scythed grass; Elaine stayed in its shade. Solid in front of her stood Cymberie, a block of dull brick beneath a steep slate roof. Octagonal chimneys twisted into the sky. Smoke rose from one of them, blue smoke that drifted toward her. Apple wood: she recognised the sweet smell instantly, and grieved for the tree that had been felled for fuel when it might have grown on to provide food. Crisp apples, red-skinned, yellow-fleshed, running with juice; her mouth ached with longing for the taste. All she'd had to break her fast this morning were a few currants she had snatched from bushes at the side of the road. Her belly rumbled and she hoped it wouldn't when she was with him, when his head lay close against her chest.

I can't do it, I can't do it, she had said to Mistress Margery in desperation this morning, as if it were something that could be avoided. I don't know how to do it.

Nothing could be simpler, said Margery, who had arranged it all, who was going to take a half share of her payment in return for looking after Samuel. Anyone can do it. It's instinctive.

Elaine stepped out into the July sun and half-closed her eyes against its dazzling brightness. The heat burned through her bodice, into the linen shift next to her skin. The scent of lavender gusted toward her from bushes that rocked in the breeze like grey waves of the sea. Bees hovered over them, sucked nectar from the flowers. The garden hummed. White butterflies flapped. Up in the blue sky larks sang their high song.

This is a voyage I am setting out on, she thought. Exploration of an unknown land. I'm afraid of what I may find.

The leaded casements of an upstairs room were latched open. But no-one was around. No gardener was trimming the low box hedges, or carrying water to the fountain that was parched dry. The marble statue in the empty pond glared in the sun.

I wish I were made of marble, she thought; if I were made of stone, if I didn't have feelings, this would be easy. How easy to be a statue here in the sun where no-one is weeding the borders or sweeping the gravelled alleys, no-one is anywhere at all.

The house seemed uninhabited, unreal, a mirage in the heat. But its main door beckoned her on, its massive oak door with arched moulding, set in a square frame. A huge keyhole that when she bent to it, she found was blocked, so she couldn't see through. She tried the latch but the door didn't budge; it must have been locked, or bolted on the inside. There was a great bell but she didn't ring it. This isn't the right door for me, she thought, this entrance is for the fine folk, there will be a small door somewhere for people like me. She released the latch as quietly as she could and followed the path under the gloomy hollies at the side of the house until she came to a cobbled yard, where there were stables: the stink of horses. Black hens pecked between the stones. Straw; tufts of grass, dog shit. A ginger cat snoozed on a ledge. Housemartins swooped low on purple wings down from their mud nests under the eaves, almost colliding with her.

The house walls here were of stone, and clearly older than the brickwork at the front. The windows were arched rather than rectangular. A plain door stood wide open at the top of two steps.

Elaine peered in. A long passage paved with stone and deep in shadow lay before her like a lime-washed cave. She hesitated; combed her hair with her fingers and coiled it up neatly, shook her skirt, pulled her sleeves down to her wrists, squared her shoulders. 'Good morrow,' she called out.

There was no answer. She entered, stood still a few seconds for her eyes to get used to the lack of light. The flagstones were cooler under her feet than the stones outdoors. A fustiness hung in the air, a smell of damp though it had not rained in days. Muddy clogs of various sizes were spread out in pairs on a low rack; a few sacks, a worn bridle and an axe hung from hooks on the wall.

'Good morrow?'

No reply. She stepped past several closed doors. Her feet made no sound. The whisper of her linen skirt seemed like thunder in the silence; she held it up to try to make it quiet. Birdsong seeped in from outside.

The door at the end of the corridor was ajar, letting in a sliver of light. She knocked on it but there was still no response. Again she called out, 'Good morrow,' then gently pushed the door open and stepped through.

She was in the kitchen. It was empty of people but full of the fragrance of food. Flour spotted the stone floor. Soot-black pans stood on the unlit grills below the window; baskets of onions and feather-flecked eggs slouched beside them. The oven door hung open. A kettle simmered by the fire, which was very low, almost all ash. Someone will have to relight it if it goes out, Elaine thought, I will save them the effort; and she placed two fresh logs on it from the stack at the side. A little thud; a puff of grey punctured with sparks. It's so quiet here, she thought. All the servants must be down in the harvest fields, they will be cutting the wheat. Raking it into stooks, to dry while the fine weather lasts.

The top of the scrubbed oak table was covered with a white muslin cloth weighed down at the edges with scarlet beads and swarming with those little black beetles she didn't know the name of, that when they sat on your bare arm nipped through the skin and brought a bubble of your red blood to the surface; also with iridescent green flies. She lifted a corner of the cloth and saw pies and bread – huge meat pies glossy with egg glaze and ornamented with leaf and corn-sheaf shapes, beef gravy oozing brown under the lids, blackcurrant pies where the pastry was stained purple, and great loaves marked with crosses on the top, sprinkled with caraway seeds – they were cooling on racks – and pasties with thick crimped edges where the pastry swelled with chunks of lamb, turnip and onion. There was a vast round cheese there, with just a wedge out of it: how she longed to cut a slice with the knife at her side. She couldn't help but imagine the cheese crumbling in her mouth, its salt filling taste.

But all this belonged to Sir Richard Belvoir. She couldn't touch it. Not when he had done that to Thomas. She lowered the cloth. Her mouth was dry; she longed for a drink. She looked at the beer-barrel, touched her mouth with the side of her finger, licked her lips. But she turned away, lifted the latch on the inside door of the kitchen, and stepped through.

A short passage, a precaution against the spread of fire, took Elaine into the new part of the house. There she stood in the octagonal-fronted entrance hall, which rose to the full height of the house. Cool tiles underfoot, patterned ochre and red. Tall windows on each side of the wide entrance door, fragments of scarlet and blue stained glass among the small leaded panes. The walls were vivid with painted green forests where hunters with spears pursued wild boar and deer, their dogs running beside them, tails in the air, and there was a church in a valley and a thatched timber house and a well with a child carrying water, Morris Dancers and a woman in a low bodice played a serpent under a tree, enticingly –

A fly buzzed against the glass. Elaine looked round her with awe. This was such a big space. It was so quiet here, so strange. This painted world. This empty place. She didn't belong. She wanted to take flight.

A staircase rose square to the first floor. Every banister was sturdy, ornamented where the oak bellied with the talbot that was part of Sir Richard's coat of arms, or the rose that was his wife's, and examples of strapwork and moresque. Pleasing enough carving, Elaine conceded, but heavy, a long way from being as skilful as Thomas's. Dear Thomas had been a master craftsman, his work airy, full of pinnacles and light. When shortly after they married she found herself with child he patted her belly and said, come, sweetheart, let's walk south and make our fortunes. They said farewell to their families. He carried his tools; she carried their clothes and their bedding. How certain our future felt then, Elaine thought wistfully, as we strode side by side over the hills and the valleys unfolded in front of us. We knew we would do well. We were skilled craftsmen, imaginative, sure of our art. We would carve you a statue as perfect as any of Michelangelo's. Hadn't we pored over woodcuts of his work?

Cymberie had been just one of the houses where Thomas had hoped to find work. Sir Richard Belvoir is courteous and hospitable, he'd been told, and generous to craftsmen.

The mantelpiece in the entrance hall was carved oak too. Above it hung a heavy painting in a frame that gleamed with gold: a portrait of the family. There was Sir Richard: Elaine recognised him at once, his thin build and his height, his hooked nose and green eyes, even though in the painting his beard and hair were still brown, not streaked with grey as they had been at Thomas's trial ten months ago. There, next to him, that had to be his wife. Both beruffed and bejewelled, they stared out over the heads of their daughter and son. The children were wearing ruffs too. An African grey parrot perched on the son's left wrist; he held a toy boat in his right. The daughter held an open book. Milady had a straight mouth, a reddish nose and a great string of pearls coiled around her neck. The embroidery on her bodice was picked out in gold leaf, as it was on Sir Richard's scarlet doublet. He had a slight smile; his arm was round his wife's waist.

How long ago was that painting done? Elaine wondered. Everyone in it is innocent and full of hope, just as Thomas and I were, walking south. There's never any way of telling what will happen. Perhaps it's as well. You'd never be able to feel joy if you knew what the future was going to be.

She crossed her arms defensively across her chest. She longed to leave the house but she had to go through with this. She had no choice. In spite of all the wool she had spun, she was still deep in debt to Mistress Margery, for helping her when Samuel was born, and afterwards for giving her advice when she didn't know how to look after him. She had to do this so she could pay Margery back.

Elaine wasn't accustomed to stairs. Climbing them was a bit like climbing a ladder. Her heart was thumping with fear, and to calm herself she imagined she was back in her father's orchard, climbing up into the branches of a pear tree. The ladder was wide at the base, narrowing toward the top, the rungs sturdy, the wood warm under her hands. It was green at the top among the rustling leaves, dusty-smelling. The fruit she lifted off in her hand was hard but when she bit into the flesh it was sweet and juicy, filling, thirst-quenching.

July now. Two months till the pears would be ripe. She hauled herself up the stairs by the banisters.

At the top was a long gallery, the wide irregular floorboards of which glistened with polish. Tall windows overlooked parkland and the tiled roof of the kitchen; portraits loured in gilt frames. Closed oak doors were solid and secret. Just one was part open, and through the crack drifted the fragrance of rushes and sweet herbs. That room's in use, Elaine thought. Maybe that's his room. Maybe he's there.

Her legs ached so much to carry her downstairs that she had to grab hold of the door frame. 'Good morrow, sir,' she called tentatively.

'Who's there?' It was a man's voice, but weak, she could barely hear it.

'Mistress Fisher.' Her throat was dry; the words came out all hoarse.

'Don't mumble, for God's sake.'

'Elaine Fisher, sir. I'm your nurse, sir.'

'Show yourself, damn you.'

'Yes, sir.' She went in and her feet released the scents of the herbs with each step she took toward the bed with its carved posts and canopy and curtains of scarlet and yellow silk, the great bed that compelled her forward as if it were a powerful lodestone that overcame every inclination of her mind and body.

It was the first time since that terrible day in the courtroom that she had seen him. His beard and hair were now all white; there was no trace of brown in them any more. His face was gaunt and yellow against the linen pillow. His cheeks were sunken, his lips a thin pale line. His creased, unbuttoned shirt fell open to reveal a scrawny neck. Gone were the wide lace ruff and black damask gown with its fur lining and belt of gold, that he had worn that November day. Can it truly be him? she wondered. 'Sir Richard?' she asked.

He looked at her. Dark circles smudged beneath his yellowed eyes. His illness had made him into a weak old man teetering on the brink of death.

She picked up her skirt between finger and thumb, bobbed him a curtsey.

'Wash,' he commanded, his thin voice still spiked with authority.

She looked around. In front of one of the windows, on a marble-topped table veined with pink, rested a silver basin filled with water. She dipped her fingers in it and swirled them around. The water was almost blood-heat from standing on such a hot day.

'Your breasts,' he hissed.

Sick came up in her mouth; she swallowed it down. There was a buzzing in her head, as if a bee had crept in one of her ears when she was out in the garden, and were now crawling around in her brain. She was sure she was going to lose her balance and fall. But she was determined not to let him see her fear. She had to do this. For her baby's sake, she had to earn the money. Her body was as much at her son's service as when she carried him in her belly. So Samuel could survive: that was why she had to do this. Give me courage, Lord, she whispered. Give me courage. Please.

She cupped her hand and scooped water up into her parched mouth, wiped the dribble from her chin, slowly untied her ruff and carefully laid it down on a wooden chest. She undid her bodice, laid it beside the ruff. Then she undid the ties of her linen shift, bent forward over the basin to wash her breasts. She could see them reflected, white and full, with distended brown nipples. She thought: they look as the goddess in the garden's must, after rain, when the pool's full. Shimmering. They're stone. They don't belong to me. They can't feel.

But her face behind them was thin and scared, child-like. She was ashamed of it and bit her lips to redden them.

'Use soap,' he ordered.

The ball of soap at the side was scented with spices she didn't recognise, that she thought must have come from the Indies, cardamom and cinnamon she murmured to herself, because she loved the sound of the words, and she imagined a spice-laden galleon in full sail sweeping home over the blue oceans as she lathered under her arms too, to get rid of the sweat smell. White foam on her fair skin, like clouds. She rinsed it off. Or maybe the spices have come overland, she thought, on the backs of camels, from Samarkand.

When she turned round she couldn't avoid reality. She clasped the slit in her shift closed. She felt the milk rise in her left breast, hover on the tip of her nipple and fall to her skin. 'I don't know how to do this,' she said, flushing.

The man inched up into a sitting position and the effort exhausted him. He gasped for breath. Sweat beaded his ashen face, his eyes were glazed, and Elaine suddenly panicked. Suppose he dies right now, she thought, how terrible that would be. I'd be left with no possible way of paying off my debt to Mistress Margery.

No way of buying food.

I can manage it, she thought. It's only a kind of nursing. 'He has a lump big as a turnip in his belly,' was how Margery had explained it to her. 'The physician he consulted in London told him that his only chance of recovery was a diet of breast milk.'

'Will that help him?' Elaine had asked.

'Only the good Lord knows.'

Elaine climbed on the bed beside the sick man. His sheet smelt of stale urine; a bitter stink came from his mouth. She thought again: I can't do this. Then she thought: just a short time and it will be over. She puzzled how to position herself: whether to pillow his head in her lap. His eyes were only a slit open; he seemed barely conscious. His skin was cold, waxen, a little sticky. If I imagine you as a block of wood, she thought, wrinkling her nose, then I can bear to be next to you. If I pretend you are a piece of white lime clamped to a bench, and that I have beside me a range of chisels in a leather roll. Then I'd square your mouth as if it were a mortice. My nipple the tenon. We'd slot together like the timbers of a house frame. If I were made of wood, this would be easy.

She wanted to be a block of wood. She wanted not to be flesh and blood. She wanted not to be soul or spirit or mind. She wanted not to feel. She wanted to be stone like the statue in the garden.

She did it all of a sudden. It was the only way she could do it. She leant forward, grabbed his shoulders and heaved his head toward her, thrust her nipple in his mouth. He turned red, gasped for breath, spat it out. Her milk spilled on his face. It's so thin, she thought, it's not thick like cow's milk, how can it do anyone any good?

'Don't – suffocate – me,' he hissed, and this time she lifted his head more gently, held her breast away from his nostrils with one finger. He sucked once or twice. Sucking wasn't a natural action for him, as it was for her baby son. It was an effort for him. His beard prickled her chest, his moustache her breast. She could feel how weak he was. Little Samuel was a Hercules in comparison.

He sucked again. She could feel his teeth and his tongue. It was so odd, looking down at a stranger, an adult sucking at her breast. She thought: I must remember how free I will be afterwards. With the money he pays me, my debts paid, I won't be tied any more to the village. I will be able to walk north, carrying Samuel on my hip home to my family. Or maybe, if I can keep the old man alive long enough, I'll earn enough to buy back Thomas's tools that he had to sell to buy us both food, and then I can practise his trade. Because she had been his apprentice and he had taught her all he knew about carving wood. You have an aptitude for it, my sweet heart, he had said, offering her a chisel, blade first; and he had given her his knowledge freely. Adam and Eve she had carved without a figleaf to cover their shame, supporting the mantelpiece in the main bedchamber of St Bede's manor, the Prodigal Son feasting on the fatted calf she'd carved at Olaf's hall.

Her shoulders ached; she flexed them. This is what a baby does, she thought bitterly. It's what a lover does. She couldn't stop thinking of Thomas, how he'd kiss her breasts back in the gold days of their marriage. His hair was soft and brown, she'd twist her fingers in it and sometimes he'd cry out because she pulled. Thomas, Thomas …

Sir Richard Belvoir had been the judge who had sentenced her lover to be hanged by the neck until dead. She couldn't forget that. This was the man sucking at her breast.

This isn't a man, she thought, don't be fooled. This is a block of wood.

Block of wood. How she loved trees. The rustle of leaves

around her forest house gave shade and protection by day and by night.

Thomas had been hanged from a scaffold of oak. Oh, she loved to carve oak, she loved the swirling grain of the wood, though beech were the living trees that she loved most of all, she loved their smooth trunks and cathedral grandeur, the slow unpleating of their leaves in spring, the brightness they brought after the dullness of winter.

It had been winter since Thomas was hanged. It was July now, and it was still winter.

The old man let her nipple slop out of his mouth and lolled back. She covered herself with her shift. 'Don't hold yourself so stiff,' he said.

She didn't reply. Tears were pricking her eyes.

'Tint,' he said.

She couldn't focus on what he was saying.

'Tint,' he said again.

She didn't know what he meant.

'Uh,' he said, waving a hand.

She didn't know what he wanted. She didn't belong here. His world was as different to hers as if the dust that had made them came from separate stars.

But she had to be obedient to him. She looked around.

On the carved court cupboard he'd indicated were a dozen leather-bound books with gold markings on the covers. Three silver-gilt bowls, a huge silver platter, several silver plates, two wineglasses and a cistern of water with a jug standing in it. Guessing, she picked a book at random and brought it to him. He shook his head. She took it back and tried again, poured some of the contents of the jug into a glass and offered it him.

'You,' he grunted.

'Me?'

'Uh.'

'You want me to drink it, sir?' Her thirst was suddenly like a lion in her throat and she gulped at the Spanish wine but it was so sour that she grimaced.

'Honey?'

'No, sir.' Better if the drink were unpleasant. Nothing must be good here. Everything had to be bad. She downed her glassful in six gulps.

The tint wasn't good but it was good to drink from a glass, she had never done so before, such a delicate thin glass as this was with its slender stem and the green snakes, the ivy leaves that coursed up it. She had only ever drunk from pewter or earthenware mugs before, ale or beer or cider or boiled water, never this strange tint that was so sour and thirst-quenching. She tipped back her head and let the last drops fall in her mouth.

'More,' he said.

'I can have more?'

He closed his eyes and she took that as assent and refilled her glass, then thought suddenly that he must have meant that he needed more of her milk (he had had very little, as far as she could tell, and he was paying her well, she didn't want to sell him short) and so she swallowed her wine quickly, rinsed the glass in the water of the cistern and replaced it on the cupboard. Her head was feeling unaccountably swimmy but she climbed back on the bed and pulled him toward her. But he had fallen asleep, or was reluctant to move, and she was perplexed as to what to do. 'Sir,' she said, 'your doctor said –'

When Samuel was born his skin had been yellow and all he wanted to do was sleep his life away; he wouldn't feed and she had been desperate until Margery told her to flick the sole of his foot hard with her finger to keep waking him up so he would suck and drink enough milk to grow stronger. And that had worked. Samuel drank; now he was a fine baby. Nearly eight months old. He could sit up; he'd be crawling soon.

Elaine couldn't reach the soles of Sir Richard's feet, and so she flicked hard at the lobe of his ear. He lifted his hand as if to swat a fly and opened his mouth as if to swear. She popped in her nipple. Startled, he sucked. Two or three sucks, and then his head dropped back. He half-opened his eyes; they were green slits. He looked up at her. 'Morrow,' he said.

Elaine walked back to the village along the lane through the woods. Inside her bodice, inside her shift, between her breasts was a pasty she had stolen from the kitchen table. The pastry crumbled at the edges with each step that she took. A crumb slipped over her belly, skidded down her thigh. She didn't know if she could be hanged for stealing a pasty.

She climbed over the bank and into the woods where an old holly tree drooped its prickly leaves to the ground, solid and secret as a bell. She crawled inside and picked the pasty out from between her breasts. She devoured it slowly, painstakingly within the evergreen darkness of the holly tree. The exterior of the pastry was dry except where it was damp with her sweat, the filling was moist with gravy. She didn't know when she had last eaten meat. She was afraid of the crumbs, in case they were evidence against her. She picked every one out of her cleavage and ate it. She dusted round her mouth and licked her fingers. She loosened the waistband of her skirt and shook it. Then she scrambled back to the lane.

Hazels overhung it here, and the nuts that squirrels had dropped lay like bright opals among the dried mud and the horseshit. Greedily she collected them up and inspected them. Most had holes chewed in them, but a few were intact and these she stored in her pockets. She would crack them open later, at home. They would make a good supper. She tipped back her head and saw many hazelnuts still on the trees. Tomorrow, she thought, I'll cut myself a hooked stick so I can pull down the high branches.

A man's voice was drifting up to her on the breeze from the far-off harvest field. She didn't know the song he was singing. Someone was accompanying him on a rebeck. And then suddenly a whole band of people joined in the chorus, an explosion of voices.

I wish I were home, Elaine thought. There, I'd be joining in the harvest with my family. It'd be hard labour but there'd be jugs of ale and bread and cheese and I'd be working alongside the people I grew up with, there'd be that satisfying sense of sharing a common purpose. Getting in the ripe grain before the rain came. Back-bending raking and watching the heaped white clouds sweeping in from the west across the blue sky, plumping in threatening masses. Muscles would ache; hands blister. That absolute necessity of life: if the grain were not harvested in time, villagers would die from lack of food during the winter.

But here she was an outsider. A masterless woman. She didn't belong. She was her own self, with all the vulnerability that implies. Her loyalty was just to her infant son.

And to Thomas. She would never forget him. She'd seen him hanged one blood-red sunrise. The twenty-ninth day of November. When the cart lumbered off and he was left dangling from the scaffold, she reached up to put her arms round his ankles and she swung on his legs so he would die quickly, so he wouldn't suffer. He had had no-one else to do it for him. They were both strangers there. He had asked her to do it. He was very afraid. 'I'm afraid of the pain,' he said. 'Pull on my legs so my neck breaks quick. Do this for me, Elaine.' His piss ran all over her hands. 'Christ have mercy,' she had said, and walked away in a haze all heavy. She didn't wash her hands. The baby kicked inside her belly. She didn't look back. That whole day she walked by the hedgerows, gathering threads of sheep's wool that were caught on the thorns. It had been a grey day, very cold. A fierce wind. She wore his leather jerkin for warmth. It didn't meet over her belly. 'Let the baby not take cold,' she had said.

He had been hanged without his shirt because the hangman had wanted it. So cruel, so cold in nearly December. His body was cut down. He was thrown face down in a rough grave that had been dug north-south, the wrong way, in an outer part of the churchyard that was cut off from the rest by a ditch. She didn't know if it was holy ground or not. She thought that the unmarked graves he lay among must be those of criminals and usurers and strangers to the parish.

When she had gone there the next morning the fresh earth was crisped with frost, the low sun glittered the ice crystals as if they were jewels. 'Thomas,' she'd said.

She couldn't cry. 'Thomas,' she said again.

'Why?' she said. 'Why did they do it?'

'Thomas, I love you,' she said.

She span the wool she'd gathered the previous day. She didn't have a wheel, she'd left that behind when they moved south, she used a spindle made of a stick and a stone. She had walked to the village and sold the yarn to Mistress Margery, who spoke kind words and gave her money for a loaf of bread.

'Thomas,' Elaine said. She was standing in the July sun by the hump of his grave which was partly greened over now with grass and with weeds. 'Thomas.' The two of them had always been honest with each other. 'This is what I have just done,' she said, and hesitated. Should she tell him? But she had to tell someone who would understand the horror that she felt. And if he couldn't hear, so much the better. Saying it out loud would put it outside herself. 'I have fed the man who ordered you to be hanged,' she said. 'I have let him nurse at my breasts.' She touched the front of her bodice. 'I am being paid. The man who ordered your death is paying me to save his life.'

She said, 'I have to do it, Thomas, for your son. Our son. For Samuel. So he can survive. I don't see any other way.' She sank on her knees in the dry grass. The knapweed flowers made a purple haze around her. 'I wouldn't do it if I could think of any other way. I wish you were here, Thomas. I need to talk to you.' Her eyes stung. Sweat's running into them, she thought; she was so used to not crying. She rubbed them with her hands. 'I don't know any other way to earn enough money,' she said, 'not without the tools and you sold those. I said not to sell them –' But when she'd kept fainting he'd said she had to have more varied food or he would lose her. And then, when he'd sold the tools, on his way home he went to the inn for a drink. The murder had just been committed and the men had robbed him before they handed him over to Sir Richard, swearing he'd done it.

'They gave me the money, though, Thomas,' she lied. 'I ate well for a long time.' The truth – the near-starvation of that terrible winter, the near-freezing to death when she'd been too weak to fetch firewood – she had never told Thomas about that. She couldn't have borne for him to know it. Mistress Margery had been the only person who helped her.

She said, 'Don't be angry with me, Thomas, or jealous. Don't mind what I'm doing, will you? I can manage it, it's easy work. What I'm doing – it's just appearances, it's not real. It's just pretence. We have to pretend, Thomas, that's how life is. We couldn't survive otherwise.'

She sat back on her heels and kept so still in the early

afternoon sun that a thrush flew down right in front of her and began pecking at his grave. She noticed small spiders now, spinning webs between leaf-blades and stems, and black ants marching busily in and out of their nest, and two snails curled up copulating, and a beetle with vivid green wings. The whole of creation is so rich and random, she thought, so painful and purposeless.

The thrush bobbed its beak, detached a snail from its mate and cracked it open on a gravestone; that sharp little sound, and all that was left were fragments of its shell. The glisten of its slime.

A stone thudded down by Elaine's knee. A pluff in the dry earth. She recoiled in shock, then grabbed it and jerked up, ready to hurl it back at whoever had thrown it. But she couldn't see anyone. No-one at all. Over there was the church with its tall tower, its stones shimmering in the heat. There, the yew trees casting dark shadows across the path. There, the lych gate where they rested the coffins. There, the gravestones. But there was no sign of man nor woman. She stared around, let the stone fall from her fingers.

Wasn't everyone in the fields? Who would want to throw a stone at her, and why? Was it because she didn't belong here, because she was an outsider and they didn't want her filching the food from their mouths?

Then the brim of a black hat appeared at the corner of the brick base of the lych gate.

So that's where you're hiding, she thought. Very well. She dusted her skirt, shaking off the grass and the leaves, keeping her eyes on the gate, and then stepped all nonchalant toward it, jumping the ditch. She was humming *Summer is a-cumen in* under her breath, the sun gleaming in the darkness of her hair. A half brick lay at the edge of the path. She picked it up and studied it. Little stones were embedded in the clay and it was cracking, but it would do fine to hit someone over the head or in the codpiece with. And he was still there, still hiding, that gentleman with the black hat, thinking he was invisible. It had to be him who'd thrown that stone.

'Don't do your business there, sir,' she said loudly. 'Go further away from the road, where passers-by can't smell the stink you make.'

A pause, and then the man bobbed up. He was dressed severely in black with a narrow yellow ruff, and his face was bright red. His breeches were perfectly buttoned. 'I w-was n-not, M-mistress El-laine,' he stammered. 'You kn-now I was not!'

'Master Candlemaker – what are you doing here away from your shop?' She was astonished to see it was him. He was a respectable man as far as she knew, a hard-working, successful tradesman; someone who kept himself to himself on the whole. You wouldn't see him gossiping in the Talbot's Arms, or with the old men on the bench in the village square, or swigging ale at the archery butts. A bachelor, he lived with his mother in a biggish hall house. He was a Puritan, the gossip went, more likely to be found poring over the pages of a Bible than throwing stones. Maybe he tried to live by the rules of his faith. Certainly it had been he who had had the kindness to walk out to her forest house all those months ago and tell her of Thomas's arrest for the murder in the inn.

'N-no-one buys candles on a fine summer day,' he said.

'I'm surprised you're not helping with the harvest, then.'

'Why aren't you helping there yourself, Mistress Elaine?'

'I had another task I had to do.'

'I know what it was,' he leered at her suddenly. 'I know what you were doing. I heard all about it, Mistress Elaine.'

She flushed angrily. 'There's nothing improper in it.

Nursing is an honourable occupation. Tell me, why did you throw that stone at me?'

'A s-stone? M-me throw a stone? At you?'

'Yes. When I was kneeling by my husband's grave.'

'I – I wanted to distract you.'

'What do you mean?'

'M-mistress Elaine.' The candlemaker took off his hat and combed his greasy blond hair up on end with his fingers. 'Truly, I was s-simply c-concerned to see you there. T-talking to the dead. They say in the village that grief for your husband has made you go mad. There's s-some – I'm not one of them – some might say you're talking to a soul in hell. They might say it's a sign you're a w-witch.'

'Are you suggesting that my husband is in hell?'

'He was g-guilty of murder. He was hanged.'

'He was *found* guilty of murder. Only because lying bastards accused him of it. He never killed anyone. Thomas was a loving soul, gentle as a feather. He was completely innocent of any crime. He's a saint in Heaven, I know he is. There's no place he can be but Paradise.'

'Yet three men swore on oath they saw him stab Guy Trebcott.'

'That doesn't make it true.'

'Three voices against one, Mistress Elaine.'

'Three liars against the truth. Why didn't you speak up for him? You were in the inn at the same time, weren't you? Just because he was a stranger here …' She stopped, sharply reminded of her own vulnerability. What if this man were to spread rumours in the village that she was a witch? If people believed him, it might not be long before she found herself tied to a stake, with flames lapping at her ankles and smoke swirling in her face, and dearest Samuel would be left a starving orphan farmed out into servitude.

It's only two months, she thought grimly, only two terrible months of breast-nursing Sir Richard and if I'm frugal I'll have settled my debt and will be able to leave this accursed village. So glad I'll be to shake its dust from my feet.

She sighed extravagantly. 'You must forgive me, sir,' she said. 'My grief – sometimes it overwhelms me, it has to find expression. I am certain my husband's soul has risen up to heaven. When I speak to him, I am addressing one of the saints.'

'S-sometimes, Mistress Elaine, I imagine your husband and I have changed places.'

'What do you mean?'

'Sometimes, Mistress Elaine, I imagine myself to be lying in your bed, in your husband's place, on your bed of straw at night. I think of you at my side. I think of our bare skins touching …'

She shrank away from him. 'I'm not a whore, sir. If you think that you're mistaken. I'll always be faithful to my husband, that I swear. I have to go now to fetch my son.'

He had to check some beehives on the hill, and she walked on into the village alone, head down, brooding, her day darkened by this new and unexpected threat.

Then Elaine reached Mistress Margery's sunlit garden and looked up. It was jammed full of golden marigolds and purple cabbages, tall hollyhocks and plump babies in woolly bellibands with bare legs and bottoms, all chortling or crying in the dirt, sucking pebbles or stuffing daisies in their mouths. She spotted Samuel at once, swooped down on him and gathered him up. All of a sudden he was screaming with hunger – why hadn't she been here sooner? – and she fumbled her bodice and shift open, laughing at him, and he launched himself at her breast, and then there was silence. Just the rush of the milk and the slight slurp as he drank, and his warmth against her body, and the way his little body and hers fitted so snugly together. The way he closed his eyes, the curl of his dark eyelashes on his pale cheek. The way his hands clenched and opened and stroked her. The joy of that simple trust and primitive belonging: it filled her with utter delight. The weight of him in her arms: he was growing so heavy. 'You make everything worthwhile, Sam,' she whispered to the perfect shell of his ear. The contentment he gave her outweighed all her problems.

'Elaine!' That was Rosamund, the butcher's wife, nursing her little daughter, calling from the rose arbour. She shuffled along to one end of the bench and patted the free space. 'How did you get on this morning? Tell me about it! What was he like, the old man?'

Elaine sighed into the pale scent of roses beside her. 'Oh, it's good to sit down.' She wriggled her feet in the air and switched Samuel to her other breast. 'It's a long walk from Cymberie.'

'I was going to do it, you know. Margery asked me first but then Ralph wouldn't let me. I told him there's no harm in it, you know Sir Richard's a real gentleman, I said, and it's well-paid, the job, I said. I can save up and buy a new blanket for our bed. I'm not having any man sucking at my wife's bosom, he said. What would people say about it, now I'm churchwarden? he said. Don't think I'll waste the money, I said, don't think I'll fritter it away on clothes. Though what I truly wanted was to buy a beaver hat. Wouldn't you like one, Elaine? But Ralph put his foot down. No, he said, I know what that family is like, one thing will lead to another and you'll end up in bed with him. Like son, like father, he said, I'm not paying for the upbringing of one of that old man's offspring, he said, not for all that he's a knight. I told you what happened to Betsy, didn't I, Elaine? My cousin that is married to the miller over Epping way?'

'Um –' She was only half-listening; she was counting Samuel's tiny fingers, marvelling at the way they clutched hers.

'Betsy had this fine plan to outwit him. You see, he'd sworn to marry the first woman who bore him a son, and of course everybody wanted to see if they could, naturally they all wanted to be mistress of Cymberie.'

'What?' Elaine could not reconcile Rosamund's gossip with what she had seen at Cymberie; it was a world away from the order and dignity of the place. 'Surely Sir Richard was already married?'

'No! Don't be absurd. Not the old man! It's Gabriel I'm talking about.'

'Gabriel?'

'Sir Richard's son.'

'Oh. Does he live at Cymberie?'

'Mary mother of God! Don't you know anything? Do you walk round with your hands over your eyes and your ears? When Gabriel's mother had her accident he blamed his father for it and went off adventuring. Exploring. They say he's become captain of a small warship.'

Elaine blinked. 'There's a family portrait in the hall at Cymberie and the son looks about twelve.'

'Oh, he's older now,' smirked Rosamund. 'He certainly is. He's quite a lad. So good-looking. He was the apple of his mother's eye. He went to court and had an audience with the queen, and she complimented him on his choice of clothes. He rode around the county in them, afterwards, to show them off. He was so good-looking with his dark hair in ringlets and his great ruff with sapphires glittering in its folds. He wore a black and white doublet and magical silk stockings embroidered with spangles. He has such beautiful legs, I wish you could see them. Elizabeth was in the yard when he came riding past her house.'

'The queen was in the yard?' Samuel was drinking more slowly now, and Elaine swapped him back to the first breast, and tickled him gently under the chin, and kissed his dirty toes.

'No, you fool, my cousin Betsy. Haven't you heard a word that I've said? It was a June afternoon and they lay in the long grass under a haze of cow parsley. Aunt Meredith was furious when she found out. Betsy said, Mother, just trust me, wait and see, in nine months time I'll be mistress of Cymberie and then you'll see the sense of it. But all she ended up with was a daughter –' Rosamund sighed – 'and she had to make a quick match with the miller in Epping. Such a waste.' She put her baby on her shoulder to burp her. 'He went to bed with all the pretty girls round here, Gabriel Belvoir did, Elaine, and not one of them had a son. They all had daughters. It must have been some kind of witchcraft he put on them. There, there – oh, a pox on it!' A stream of yellow diarrhoea squirted from her howling baby, and she held her at arm's length as she went to dip her bum in a bucket of water by the door of the cottage.

'I met the candlemaker on my way home today,' Elaine remarked when she came back.

'The candlemaker?'

'The man with the candle shop. Tell me, is he the same kind of man as Sir Richard's son?'

'What? Walter Vernon? You can't compare them. That hangdog, yellow-faced misery! He dresses worse than a slug-bitten peapod!'

'I mean, does he sleep with all the girls?'

Rosamund rocked with laughter, the rose thorns of the arbour catching in her hair. 'Walter Vernon sleep around! Where on earth did you get that idea? He's as strait-laced as they come.

He's never touched a woman in his life. I'll bet he doesn't even know what his thing is for, apart from pissing!'

Samuel let out a fat belch, and Elaine buried her face in his chest; Sam pulled her hair with his plump little fists. 'You let go, sweetheart, or I'll gobble you all up for my dinner.' She swung him down and blew a raspberry on his bare tummy; he giggled and she lifted her head. 'Rosamund, I'd like to go and help with the harvest, but I don't know how people would feel about it. What do you think?'

Rosamund pursed her plump lips. 'You want the truth?'

'That's why I asked.'

'They'd say a foreigner was coming in and stealing their food. Do that and you'll be stirring up trouble for yourself.'

Elaine nodded. 'That's what I thought.' She sat still for a moment, letting her dream of using the gleanings to make a flour and water pancake evaporate. She wished with all her heart that Rosamund might offer her some steak, or even some beef dripping, or tripe, but the butcher's wife was so used to plenty that she didn't think. So she stood up and said, 'I'll get on home then.'

Elaine trudged up into the low hills north of the village, hills made of gravel and of no value for farming, hills grown over with scrubby birch and oak, sloes, crabapple and hawthorn all intertwined with brambles and honeysuckle vines. Her path wound its secret way between them. An occasional late flower scented the hot air in the still shade, and the sun gleamed bright green in the leaf cover, filtering through to cast sharp dappled shadows on the trunks and the ground.

She was sweating, and Samuel was heavy, even though she had made a sling to support him from a rectangle torn from her linen sheet; he was hot at her side and she kept thinking: I can't manage, I can't do this any more, I can't take another step, not this and the walk to Cymberie and back, it's too much, and then Samuel emitted a light snore and she looked down at his face, his closed eyes, his dark lashes curved on his pale cheeks, that purity of baby skin, and that likeness to Thomas that was faint at first (she used to think he looked more like her father) but was growing stronger as he matured, so she felt as if she were carrying the three men in her life that she loved, and for their sake she had to go on, she couldn't give up.

Down in a dip there was a spring where water bubbled up through the leafmould and she laid Samuel under an oak without waking him and lay on her belly and put her mouth down to drink straight from the ground, closing her eyes and letting the cool water flow over her face to refresh her, lifting her head to breathe and lowering it again. The water tasted of the earth but she knew from experience that it was pure; no-one else came here. Thomas had found it – he used a forked hazel-twig to divine it – and he built their house on the hill above, where the ground was almost entirely gravel so that the floor was never water-logged, and the rain ran away from around it. She had been so glad of that in the winter, when a foot of snow lay for two weeks and then melted, and she stayed cosy and dry, having gathered firewood constantly in the weeks leading up to the birth.

It was last October that they came here. 'This place will be fine,' Thomas had declared, standing tall under the blue sky, gold leaves falling around him, tangling in his brown hair, gilding his shoulders as if he were king. The two of them levelled an area at the top of the hill, tied a vine to a post and, stooping, swung it round to draw a circle in the gravel, the autumn breeze sighing all the time around them, the falling leaves of the birches swirling around them. They held hands and laughed. Thomas cut tall posts which he erected in holes around the circle. Then he dovetailed in rafters in a cone shape. He thatched the roof thickly with rushes from down by the riverside, making a hood for the smoke to escape. Together they plaited twigs through the framework and daubed the walls with clay. He caught pheasants and hares, and a small deer, and they ate well. He built the frame of a bed and she plaited rushes to make cords for the mattress to rest on (she'd carried a flock mattress there on her back; they'd slept on it twelve chill nights in the open on their journey south) and when the rain came Thomas added on a porch, lowering the height of the entrance to make the place snug, and by the beginning of November the house was warm and dark and they lay side by side, their baby growing between them, and whispered their dreams while the fire crackled and outside the frost sharpened the stars.

When Thomas was hanged for the murder he had never committed and Elaine was left alone in the house on her own she noticed a gap where the moonlight shone through, fragile as a moth, and lying awake she would watch the moonbeam travel across the floor of the house. It was company for her. Something to depend on. Not like the midnight hooting of the owls which remained always alien and other, and scared her. Not like the scampering of light feet when she lay in bed, rats and mice after any fragment of food she might have dropped. She couldn't help worrying that they might bite her.

After Samuel was born, she had mended the moonbeam hole, caring most about keeping him warm.

Now she climbed the last few steps to the house, bent her head to go in, and laid the sleeping baby on the bed. She took the hazelnuts she'd gathered earlier from her pockets and sat cross-legged at the entrance to the porch, in the sunshine and the southerly breeze; the hill was high enough above the trees to catch it. She cracked the nuts between stones and ate the small milky kernels; they were sweet and tasted good. She swept up the shells in her hands and carried them over to the midden behind the house; and coming back she stopped to place her hand on the ridged bark of an old oak and feel the tree's great strength seep into her. For months the trees here had been the only adult company she could rely on, the only things that would listen to her, her only true friends. 'I want to go home,' she told the oak. 'Back north to my family.' She thought how her mother would make her up a warm bed underneath the rafters, how Samuel would sleep in the cradle that she herself had slept in.

But her debt to Margery tied her to the village, and her terror of being sent to debtors' prison – they locked you up in there and they wouldn't let you work and they never gave you any food: how could you buy your own food without money? She was scared of small rooms, enclosed spaces, cells, she was scared of starving to death. She was frightened of losing her child. He was the only thing she had left to love. She was scared of what might befall him without her to protect him.

At least here she would be able slowly to pay off her debt. And here there was always the possibility of a good future, sometime, if she worked hard for it. What she would truly like to do, still, was what she and Thomas had had in mind and talked over endlessly as they walked south, to do wood carvings for the big houses, and so make their fame and their fortune.

Just to make a living from wood-carving: that would be so good. She'd be happy just to make a living so she and Samuel had enough to eat.

Bees were buzzing on the heather on the slope below the house. Elaine sat with her back to the porch and stared out over the common land to the thatched roofs of the village and the stone church tower, the gardens and meadows and the wheatfields where workers were still busy, tiny as midges. The long plain lay beyond them. Sheep dotted the meadows. Smoke coiled up from chimneys.

A branch cracked in the scrub at the foot of the slope. It had to be something big down there; perhaps a stag. She fingered the knife at her waist, wondering if she was fast and strong enough to kill it. She thought of haunch of venison spit-roasted and licked her lips.

And then a man came into the open.

No-one ever came here. This was her and Thomas's secret place.

The man was wearing a black hat. He had on black doublet and breeches, a yellow ruff.

The candlemaker. Walter Vernon.

Sometimes I imagine your husband and I have changed places. The memory of his words filled her with horror.

He was climbing the gravelly hill on the path she'd worn smooth between the stunted bracken and heather. He was looking down, watching his footing. She melted back into the house and picked up the sleeping baby. She had to keep him safe. He whimpered; she put her hand over his mouth.

She didn't know what to do, where to go. If I go out, to hide on the common, she thought, holding Samuel tight, the candlemaker may be looking up; better to stay here. The only place to hide was under the bed. She slithered underneath on her back, pushing the baby ahead of her. The plaited rushes of the bed cords, so close to her nose, still smelt muddy from the river bank where she had picked them.

Samuel started to cry. 'Ssh,' she said, 'ssh,' listening hard for the man's footsteps as he hesitated in the porch. 'Mistress Elaine,' he called out. Then he came into the house. His feet rustled the gravel floor. What does he want? she thought. There's nothing to steal. It can only be me he wants. Will he attack me, will he rape me? Can I let him do that without attacking him back? I have my knife. I don't want to hang for his murder.

'Ssh, Samuel, ssh,' she breathed, and she gagged him with a fold of her skirt, muffled his mouth in the squash of the dark under the bed. 'Sssh.' She lifted her skirt away and the baby gasped for breath but he was quiet.

Not so the intruder. He was shuffling; he didn't lift his feet properly. The gravel rolled under his shoes. A sharp stone stuck in Elaine's back. She turned her head sideways. She saw the candlemaker's brown leather half-boots, scuffed at the toes. They had buttons at the side; a frond of bracken was caught in the left one. What did he want? The gravel pressed into the side of her face.

He stood by the bed. She imagined him scanning their possessions: the thin mattress, the torn sheet, the blanket; her spare shift hanging from a twig on the wall, Samuel's two petticoats, knitted bellibands and tailclouts that her sister had passed on to her when she started her journey south. Her green sleeves to go with this bodice. The griddle, the small cauldron, the axe. What would he steal? There was nothing she could manage without.

Imagine if he was angry at there being nothing to steal.

The ashes of the fire were cold, she'd not cooked food in days, but perhaps he'd see the flint hanging from a string on the wall. Don't, she thought, stiffening, don't set fire to the house, don't think of that. It would burn up in a flash. Herself and Samuel trapped under the bed. Her heart trembled, she was so filled with horror at the idea.

Go away she thought. The thought filled her whole brain and her body. *Go away.* She thought it so forcefully that the words hung tangibly in the air, he could open his mouth and touch them with his tongue, she felt. She tried to suppress her fear and her anger, to send out peaceful thoughts: it's a lovely day she told him in her head. You want to go out in the sunlight. You're not bothered about this woman and her child. There's nothing for you here. Go home. Go home.

The brown boots turned as if the man was about to leave, and she thought, it's worked! – and then the boots hesitated and turned back again. Samuel coughed and she smothered his face with a wad of her skirt. Had the man heard? He was very still. He was leaning forward as if to pick something up from the bed. One foot in front of the other. Perhaps he wanted the mattress, it was thin but it was good, and then he'd see her and Samuel trapped under the crisscross of the cords. 'Elaine,' he called. 'Elaine Fisher!' His voice wasn't strident, it was hesitant, questioning, full of doubt. She pressed her skirt even more firmly against Samuel's mouth.

Then the boots went out the door. She relaxed her grip on the baby. When he made no sound she panicked, my God, he's not breathing, I've suffocated him, I've killed him, and she ducked her face right close to his mouth, felt his hot scared breath on her cheek in the underbed dark. Thank you, thank you so much, Our Lady, Mother of Christ, thank you so much – wet tears on her cheeks, they made the baby's face wet.

But the candlemaker – where was he? What was he doing? There was no sign of his boots. He was not in the porch. There was no sound from outside. Was he sitting there, like a cat at a mousehole, waiting for her to come out? Sunning himself on the gravel, ready to pounce when the opportunity came?

If she stayed still, he'd make a noise. He had to make a noise.

She made herself count to two thousand, and then, when there was still what passed for silence in the woods – the rustle of leaves in the wind, crickets in the dry grass, the coo of a pigeon, a far-distant cock-crow – she slithered out from under the bed, leaving Samuel behind her. She stood up, sidled against the wall to the porch. She had to keep blinking; it was partly the tears, partly that her eyes, used to the dark, couldn't quickly attune themselves to the daylight. She stopped and listened intently at every step.

No sound. Had he gone or not?

She stepped into the porch. How bright the day was outside. How rich. Emerald leaves against a sapphire sky. Her toes, the soles of her feet hugged the small stones. Her hands were flat against the twiggy side of the porch. One twig, sticking out, scratched the back of her neck. She stepped into the porch entrance. Where was the man?

Perhaps, if he thought she wasn't there, he'd have hidden somewhere, planning to waylay her when she came home. He would wear a knife at his waist; everyone did. He imagined that he and Thomas had changed places; that's what he said in the churchyard, by the side of Thomas's grave. He would think he could take Elaine by force.

We'll be safe here, was what Thomas had said, building this house. No-one will bother us here, it's too out of the way. It had been a honeymoon house, where for six weeks they were happy.

But now the candlemaker was a threat.

She couldn't see him anywhere. He was dressed dark as a shadow, but that yellow ruff, his pallid face, mustn't they show up? She watched for any sign of movement.

A white flutter. She gasped in horror, drew back into the porch. Her heart thumped wildly. But it was just a butterfly, two white butterflies coming out of the wood and flitting over the bracken, dancing together up into the sky. A courtship dance, she thought; they'll soon mate.

A tug on her skirt. She thought she'd caught it on a twig and she looked down, not wanting to tear the fabric. But it was the baby. 'Samuel,' she cried, swooping him up in her arms and drooling kisses all over his little face. 'Baby, what are you doing? How did you get here? Did you roll, or did you crawl?' He started to cry. 'Are you thirsty, baby, is that what it is?' She slithered down against the side of the porch, in the shade, legs outstretched, undid her bodice and her shift. Samuel latched on to her right breast greedily, then settled down contentedly, steadily, rhythmically, as if nothing had ever been wrong, as if there were nothing ever to fear. His sense of security was infectious, it calmed her. This moment is good, she thought. This single moment. Never mind all the others. She stroked his head. How blond his hair was, almost translucent in this light. She twisted it between her fingers.

Sir Richard's head is bald on the top, she thought, with a skirt of white hair that's almost as fine as yours. He smells of piss and so do you.

She let Samuel suckle as long as he wanted and then warily, watching for the candlemaker, carried the baby down to the spring, where she sat him in the pool and washed him. It was a warm evening, there was no danger of his getting chilled. She splashed him with water, tipped handfuls over his head. He beat at the water with his hands, he laughed and wriggled. 'Sweetheart,' she said, kissing his nose and carrying him naked against her chest up to the house; laying him on the bed to knot on his clout, she wrapped his belliband around him and slipped his arms in the sleeves of his shirt. She pulled the sheet up to his chin.

Then she took the cauldron to fetch water for her patch of vegetables, the lettuce, peas and marrows that grew in the small raised bed she had built and filled with good earth she'd carried up from the valley bottom. The cauldron was small and she had to make eight trips to the spring. All the time she was on the lookout for a dark-clothed figure, a flash of yellow ruff. Every time a squirrel jumped from one branch to another, every time a pigeon clattered its big wings among the leaves, she jumped. But she saw no sign of the candlemaker. She ate a few lettuce leaves, drank water from the cauldron.

She hung her bodice and skirt up in the porch to air, lay on the bed, touched Samuel to make sure he was safe.

The moon will be up later, she thought, glancing toward the open doorway.

2

Elaine was climbing the hill to Cymberie. She'd left Samuel at Mistress Margery's and was quite light-footed, not weighed down; *this is the way to freedom,* she was thinking, it's not what I want to do but it's the best that I can, I'm taking control of my life; and she stretched out her arms in the still air to their full extent as if she were about to fly, to take off into the golden morning. She was wearing her green sleeves with her brown bodice; she'd combed her dark hair with her fingers, knotted it at the back of her neck. She was dreaming of the cool brick house with its wall paintings and carvings and stairs, and the table piled high with food, and the sick man upstairs who couldn't eat it, although it all belonged to him. The man she had to make better.

She pictured herself going into his room. The silver basin filled with tepid water would be on the pink-veined marble table. She would unfasten her bodice and her shift, take off her ruff and wash her breasts with the spice-scented soap. Then she would cross to the grand bed with its great curtains of scarlet and yellow silk, and would climb in and nurse the sick man and make him strong. Soon she would be able to pay Margery the money that she owed her. Then she would be free. It was that simple. There was nothing to fear or to hate. It was the unknown that had made her afraid. She knew what to expect now. She had to set the past aside, think only of the future.

She came to the end of the woodland and crossed the garden by the statue. One day, she thought, I'll do a carving like that, but in elm. I will chisel her out of the grain of the wood, her lips, her breasts, her thighs, the folds of her gown –

'What are you doing here?'

The sharp voice made her jump. She glanced around and saw in a vine-shaded arbour a woman on a stone bench supported by lions. A fat full-bosomed woman with frizzy red hair escaping from under her tight cap. 'Begone!' the woman shrieked across the empty pond. 'You have no business here!' She didn't get up; her lap and her legs were drowned in waves of lustrous velvet. She was like a mermaid emerging from a crimson sea.

'No.' Elaine shook her head, walked round the pond to explain. 'It's my task to nurse Sir Richard.'

'Huh, you're that poor fool, are you? You might as well spare yourself the effort.'

'What do you mean?'

'Sir Richard's too close to death for anyone to do him any good. Believe me, I've seen many men die, and I recognise the signs.'

'Is he worse than yesterday?' He can't be dying, Elaine thought, shaken. He has to live so I can pay off my debt. What would I do if he died? I'd have no hope then.

'He's pretty much the same. He won't last long.'

'He asked me to come today. I'll go on up to his room.'

'It won't do any good. He can't last more than a day or so.'

'But his doctor said –'

'London doctors, for God's sake. Prescribing breast-nursing so a filthy old man can die in an orgy of pleasure. What else could it possibly achieve?'

Elaine didn't reply. She knew how her son had grown strong on her milk; she suspected that it had helped protect him against some diseases; for instance he didn't catch the plague when there was an outbreak of it in the village in March; she herself had survived it a couple of years before, and didn't succumb this time. But maybe its effectiveness was only because he was blood of her blood. She didn't know. So she changed the subject. 'What are you making, mistress?' she asked.

The woman re-threaded her needle with silver-gilt thread and pulled it through the section of velvet that was stretched over the frame on her knee. 'An ear of wheat, see?'

It was precise, exact. The head was drooping under the weight of the fat grain, ready for the scythe, as the corn was in the fields. Gold thread glittered like the shimmer of sunlight. 'There's a sheep in this panel, beneath an apple tree,' said the woman, with justified pride in her work, passing the fabric through her plump hands. 'Here's a stag on a path, turned to face the hunters. Then, at the end, here, is Sir Richard's coat of arms.'

'What are you making? Is it a tablecloth, or a bedcover?'

'Good lord, no. It's his funeral pall. It'll go over his coffin.'

How definite and immediate that made the prospect of Sir Richard's death. Elaine shivered. I have to prevent it if I can, she thought. I need him to live so I can earn the money to set myself free. Head bowed, she walked on around the side of Cymberie.

Elaine was earlier than yesterday. In the kitchen, heat flared from the open oven; the burly cook was taking out the bread on a wooden paddle. His face was crimson, his hair slicked black with sweat. He tipped the loaves upside down on the table, tapped their bases to check they emitted the hollow sound that showed they were cooked. 'Pass me those pies, girl,' he snapped, and she handed him the tray of unbaked ones, the pallid pastry glistening with raw egg, and he slid them into the oven, slammed the door. The kitchen was immediately cooler. He took off his hat, wiped the sweat from his forehead with his sleeve. 'Who the hell are you?' he said. 'What in God's name are you doing here?'

'I'm Elaine Fisher. I've come to nurse Sir Richard.'

'Tch – that's a waste of time. Nobody can do anything for him now. He's too far gone. Swan's breast in a caper sauce I cooked him, and he just dipped his finger in the sauce and licked it. I fried him the sweetest little trout you've ever seen – caught it myself in the stream and slammed it straight in the pan – but would he eat it? Just a flake or two of its pink flesh, that's all. Such a waste, a waste – he was a good man while he lasted.' He shook his head. 'He's off to join his wife.'

'I'll see what I can do to persuade him to stay around a while.'

'No chance of that. He's halfway to Paradise or the other place already.'

'His doctor seems convinced that breast milk will cure his illness, from what I've heard.'

'Who believes in doctors? They set themselves up in fancy rooms and demand gold coin in payment, but they know no more than you nor me. And you – just look at you. You're such a skinny thing – how can you possibly do a grown man any good? You need building up yourself. Here, have a mug of ale.' He filled it from the barrel, passed it to her, foaming, in a pewter tankard. 'Have one of these cakes. They're stuffed with honey and marchpane. Have some cheese. Best Rochford milk that's made with.' He slashed a great hunk off the block and speared it on the point of his knife, waved it at her.

'That's for me?'

'Who else would it be for?'

She wiped the ale froth from her top lip with the back of her hand. 'Thank you.' She picked the cheese off the blade and bit into it. How wonderful it was, its sour salt taste, its crumbly texture, the feel of it dissolving in her mouth: and the cake was excellently sweet, with the cooked marzipan still warm and melting into the mix. 'I haven't tasted anything as good as this for months,' she said. 'Not since I left my mother's house in the autumn.' She'd had a yearning for something sweet ever since before Christmas, before Samuel was born, which she had never been able to satisfy. Now she ate very slowly, savouring each small bite. 'No-one will mind my eating this?' she said. 'No-one will say I stole it?'

'You take what food you want from the kitchen, girl,' said the cook. 'If anybody questions you, say you do it with Master Nathaniel's permission. It's feeding Sir Richard by proxy. Let me refill your mug.'

'I've had enough. I have work to do.'

'Finish your cake.'

'I've had sufficient for now. I'll put the rest in my pocket to take home.'

'For God's sake. There's masses of food here. No need to stint. Fetch a basket. You'll find one in the third room on your left, off the passage.'

A stone room, this, with an arched door, catching the fusty smell of the passageway. It had the feel of a very old room; she imagined ancient friars walking here in long corded robes. An earthenware jug stood by a shallow basin on a wide brick ledge; cheeses dangled in white cloths, great yellowed hams were suspended from sturdy iron hooks in the arched stone ceiling. Elaine opened her eyes wide. Such a richness of food. A mountain of orange fruits in a green-glazed bowl; what were they? She picked one up and sniffed it, cupped it in the palm of her hand.

'What's this?' she said to Nathaniel, going back, swinging a trug in her left hand, unrolling her right for him to see.

'An apricot. Taste it, it's good.'

Cautiously she bit in. 'Mmm,' she said. 'It's delicious. I've never eaten anything like it.'

'Eat it all,' he said. 'Harry Tuck, an old friend of the master's, grows them in his walled garden. He rode over with them yesterday as a gift for Sir Richard. But of course he isn't well enough to eat them. Give us that basket.' With his strong white hands he folded in a cloth, put in a great slice of plum cake and a bubbling pie, the top gravy-stained, which he took straight from the oven. Her eyes widened in amazement. 'Is that all for me?'

'No, it's not,' he snapped. 'It's for Sir Richard. How in the name of all the cows in Christendom can you feed him if you have no food yourself?' He didn't show any pity for this outsider, this refugee from the north, the strange girl with her odd accent, who was just skin and bone apart from her big milky tits which were the only thing about her that mattered, the only thing that had secured her admission to Cymberie. But maybe he felt some pity for her. He added a pound hunk of cheese to the food in the trug and folded the cloth over the top. 'Put it in the corner,' he said. 'Take it when you go home.'

'Thank you,' she said.

Elaine dropped the latch on the kitchen door and was swallowed up in the calm stillness of the entrance hall. Her bare feet welcomed the cool of the red and ochre tiles; old tiles pitted with dirt where the glaze had worn off. She traced the cracks between them with her toes. Inside the front door the tiles were worn concave and she thought they must belong to the ruin of an older building on top of which Cymberie had been built, an abbey it could have been that was destroyed on Henry VIII's command: these could have been the floor tiles of an abbey church, maybe, here could have been the entrance to the abbot's lodgings or the friars' dormitory. The kitchen and storerooms were definitely older. Life's like that, she thought, building up from the past and walking away from it, always climbing the stairs into the future.

Up past the wall painting of a bull being slaughtered. How had she missed that yesterday? Drops of its blood fell to fruit as crimson apples on the tree below. How succulent they looked, as if you could pluck them from the wall and eat them. She ran her fingers along the banisters, feeling the angular chisel marks in the oak, thinking how she would have carved them more smoothly. Climbing on up.

She came to a stop outside Sir Richard's door.

She thought she had schooled herself to accept what she had to do. She hadn't expected to be frightened. Yet here she was, nervous almost as on the first day. She smoothed her hair with her fingers, tucked a loose strand into the knot at the back, bit her lips. She raised her hand to knock at the door. 'Sir Richard,' she called.

He didn't reply and she called again. 'Sir Richard.'

Still no reply. The embroideress with the red hair in the garden, had she been right? She'd said he wouldn't last long –

'Sir Richard?' Foreboding made a heavy lump in her chest. Was he dead? Had her only chance of freedom escaped her?

She went in his room.

The rushes were sappy under her feet; some were mildewing and turned to slime when she stepped on them. The scent of green decay almost masked the stink of piss and shit. She scraped the sole of her foot clean on a floorboard. She crossed to the bed and Sir Richard was lying with his eyes a quarter open, slits of green pupils glassy. No sign of his recognising her. No sign even of his seeing her.

I am too late, she thought. Trembling, she picked up the

bony hand lying on the coverlet – no, it was warm, he was still alive – and she stroked it. Presently he turned his head toward her. 'Ann,' he murmured.

That was his dead wife's name. She bit her lip. 'I'll wash, and then feed you,' she said.

But the water in the silver basin was still scummy with yesterday's soap.

'Nobody has cleaned in here,' she said. Sir Richard didn't reply. She lifted the lid on the close stool with its embroidered seat; found the bowl was empty. 'Nobody's helped you go to the jakes,' she said; and when she pulled back the coverlet she saw the old man had shat himself. 'Ugh, that's not necessary,' she said, tight-lipped. 'Here – this hand-bell, it should be within your reach, not over on the court cupboard.' She put it by his limp hand; but she doubted if he was strong enough to ring it. 'I'll be back in one minute, sir,' she said.

She flew down the stairs, unbolted the front door and dashed into the garden, where the embroideress was stitching serenely, waist deep in velvet in her arbour. 'You've got to come,' Elaine shouted. She grabbed the crimson pall so it fell round the woman's ankles. 'You must come and help with Sir Richard.'

'What in heaven's name are you doing, you stupid creature? God knows what you'll have done to the fabric. Do you have any idea how much it costs a yard?' The heavy woman almost sprang to her feet, started to gather up armfuls of velvet.

'Leave that. You've got to come and help me. Sir Richard's dying. Nobody's looking after him; nobody's caring for him at all. He needs a fresh mattress.'

'That's nothing to do with me. He's not my responsibility. Look, you've unthreaded my needle, you've broken the silk.'

'You must help me.'

'Ask Mistress Phillis. She's the housekeeper.'

'Where is she?'

'She'll be at the harvest. I'm only here because a damned shire horse stood on my big toe.'

'Sir Richard must have a manservant. Where is he?'

'God knows. The old man got rid of all his personal servants when his wife died. Don't you know he's demented? He went mad with grief. He's locked himself away from everyone since her death.'

'He still has money?' That was all that mattered to Elaine.

'Oh, as for that, you ask my husband! He pays a terrible high rent for his land. Just pasture land it is, too, enough to feed a few cows and sheep, and he has all the upkeep of the hedges to see to –'

'You've got to help me. I can't manage on my own. There's no-one else I can ask. Come on, get moving!' Elaine prodded the woman's ample backside.

'God's blood,' the embroideress snarled; but all the same she folded the pall on the bench and limped indoors.

In the kitchen Elaine said: 'Help us, Master Nathaniel.'

'It's happened, then.'

'What?'

'He's dead.'

'No, no. I need someone to hold him while we change his bed.'

'Tuh. I'm no nurse.'

'You've got to help.'

'It's not my concern.'

'Who will help us then?'

He shrugged his great shoulders. 'Perhaps Master

Chibborne. The carpenter. He's strong enough.'

'Where is he?'

'He'll be at the harvest with everyone else.'

'You'll have to help us. We have to make him comfortable. Any longer, and it may be too late.'

In the bedchamber Nathaniel stood staunchly, legs apart, muscles tensed, with the sick man lolling in his arms like some giant's skinny baby, while Elaine and Mistress Winifred rolled up the soiled top mattress and tipped it out the casement window. They fetched a new mattress from another bed, smoothed a starched linen sheet across it. 'A fresh bolster cover,' Elaine said, 'and pillowcases. A fresh shirt.'

'God knows what Mistress Phillis will have to say when she finds you've filched things from her linen chests, Mistress Elaine. She keeps a rigorous inventory.'

'She should be doing this, or at least making sure that it's done. It must be part of the housekeeper's duties. Where can I find a broom to get rid of these stinking rushes?'

Nathaniel cleaned up Sir Richard's arse: a bit of male solidarity there, perhaps, keeping his master safe from the women.

Fresh water in the silver basin at last. Reflections of the sky and the trees trembled in it. Elaine was still shaking with the last of her anger at the way the old man had been treated. She took a deep breath, tucked her hair behind her ears, looked outside of herself.

The chamber was restored to order and quiet. She'd brought in sweet-smelling herbs: lavender and rosemary and rue.

'Now I can begin,' she whispered. She took off her ruff and laid it down. She took off her bodice. She undid the ties of her shift. She had damp patches on it where milk had spurted out in her fury. She washed her linen with the spice-scented soap, not wanting it to smell sour; then her breasts. She was not in a hurry. She had to be calm.

She settled herself at the head of the bed. 'We must get the barber to you, Sir Richard,' she said. She touched his white stubble. He was clean and neat; she had combed his meagre hair. She didn't feel repelled by him any more. His shirt smelled fresh from being dried over lavender bushes in the sun; it was crisp with starch. He was weak, though; too weak to suck. She cradled him in her arms, his head against her chest, and he fell asleep. Gentle snores. The rhythm of his breathing against her skin.

This familiar pattern, this matrix of loving: a man's head against your breast: caring, dependency. How can just being in this physical position make me begin to care about him? Elaine wondered. How can I put aside what he's done? She thought of what Mistress Winifred had said of his having gone mad since the death of his wife. You and me both, she thought, we have this in common. Maybe it's because you're vulnerable I can feel – what can I call it? This almost softness toward you. You can't speak, you can't hurt me. It's safe, you're safe too …

Since Thomas died all the love I've been capable of has been stoppered up, corked up inside my chest, my mouth, my eyes sealed with wax so no love could leak out. The concentrate of it a great lump that has swelled in my heart and grown heavy, weighed me down, made me lose my balance and stumble. It's beginning to leak out of me now, I can't stop myself giving it away. I have to find an outlet for it. It's not the same as my love for Samuel; Sam's a part of me, we're equals. But I need more than Sam.

Give love away to the helpless, that's easy, they don't make demands. What could be more helpless than you, old man?

A tiny spider – it was a grey good-luck money-spider – span a thread down from her hair, dangling out of focus in front of her eyes, and she felt the same sort of protective tenderness toward that. She put out her hand and let it land on the back among the thin bones, she shook it gently over the side of the bed so it could scurry away in a crack between floorboards. She closed her eyes; she was very tired. She hadn't slept well last night. She'd kept imagining she heard the candlemaker climbing the hill in the dark to her house with a flaming torch in his hand, had kept going outside to check.

Only the stars and the owls in the dark. Only the whisper of leaves, the cool touch of the breeze.

The spider-thread drifted into her dark head, but the cord was growing thicker; the tiny spider-body was elongating and widening, it was growing shoulders that were broad and strong from the hard physical work of carving, it was a man's body on a rope, she'd got her arms round his ankles, she was tugging with all her weight on them, and now his neck was broken she was running away, her mouth a wide O, her throat burning; when she glanced back she saw he was swinging, the wind was getting up, to and fro, to and fro the creak of the rope and the rattle of the pulley wheel, maybe a nail was loose; she had helped kill him, his piss was on her hands, the stink of it would be on them for ever and she couldn't stay and this stop, this emptiness, this shock made her hollow – there were people around and she couldn't show them, she couldn't let them see –

When she opened her eyes she saw that Sir Richard was sleeping more easily now. 'They told you Thomas killed the merchant,' she whispered. 'Why did you believe them and not him? Why didn't you believe him when he said he was innocent? Couldn't you read his honesty in his face, his eyes, his voice when he stood before you in the courtroom? You fool, you fool, why couldn't you see?'

A trickle of dribble slipped from the side of the old man's open mouth. Elaine wiped it away with a corner of the sheet, rubbed her eyes. Was your wife dead then, back in November, she thought, were you ill then, were you aware of the lump growing in your belly? Did you know even then, in the courtroom, when you condemned him, of your own death sentence?

She wriggled out from underneath him, laid his head on the pillow, pulled the coverlet up to his chin. She was filled with great sadness. She put the handbell by his shoulder so that when he woke he would feel the heavy bronze of it against him. She gave it him for the reassurance of it; she didn't think he'd have the strength to ring it. If you are going to get better, she thought, which is what I need for myself and Samuel, for our financial security, I will have to nurse you more often, just once can't be enough, you'll never build up your strength this way. If there is to be any chance of your surviving, I must feed you three times a day.

But what would happen about her being paid? She fastened her shift, put on her bodice and went to the kitchen in search of Nathaniel, but there was no-one there, he must have gone with his loaves and pies to feed the workers in the harvest field. She filled a pewter mug with ale from the barrel, lifted the cloth on her basket, broke off a third of the cheese and ambled with that and the remains of her honey cake out of the back door into the yard. The sun was hot, high in the sky, the shadows short; it must be about noon. No-one was around. The stables were empty. No jingle of harness, though the smell testified that the horses had recently been there. Clucking came from under a bush; a hen was hollowing out a place for herself in the brown dust.

At the front of the house Mistress Winifred had folded up her velvet sea and waddled away with it. Elaine sat on the stone bench in the shady arbour. She was bothered about this question of money – how much and when would she be paid? There didn't seem to be anyone she could ask. Would she be paid for the extra time if she worked for longer than was agreed? She had been asked to come in for only one session a day.

He is so weak, she thought. If I don't feed him more than once a day, he will die and I'll have no money at all.

She put her feet up on the bench, broke off fragments of the cake and the cheese and ate them slowly with sips of ale. She watched a black crow perch on the marble curls of the statue in the empty lake. Black and white. Black and white. If only right and wrong were as simple as that. Then you'd be able to make sense of the world.

How good it is sitting here, she thought, how much easier than helping with the harvest. She remembered how her hands always blistered from the rake and her feet and shins got cut by the stubble: but oh, she hated being alone, she longed for the companionship of the harvest fields. Working with other people. That sense of shared purpose – that losing oneself in the urgency of getting in the ripe wheat before it went to waste, racing the weather, the billowing rain-clouds, gathering in every grain so all would have food for the winter. Working with others was proof that something mattered. Who cared about an old man's lonely death?

Sir Richard's room was up there, to the right of the front door. She would hear the sound of the bell through the open window if he rang.

On the path beneath his window lay the stuff she and Winifred had shoved through it. She fetched a barrow and pitchfork from the stables and cleared up the rushes, wheeled them round the back to add them to the manure heap. The mattress was too heavy for her to move on her own, but she pulled it flat in the sunshine, fetched buckets of water from the spring and sluiced it off. *Whoosh* went the silver water, rainbows sparkling in it as she threw it, and up whirled the emerald horseflies, off of the shit.

'Ann,' said Sir Richard.

'Yes, sir?' said Elaine.

He didn't answer. He closed his eyes again. She nestled his head closer to her.

After noon, and very quiet. No birds were singing. The sun shone on the water in the silver basin on the marble table; it reflected its image up to the white ceiling with its elaborate cornice of talbots and roses. The image was bright; it shifted and shook. It never stayed still. Elaine straightened her legs.

She stroked the old man's head, his hair, his brow. *Poor you.* She touched the corner of his mouth with her finger; he opened his lips. She cradled his head higher to her full breast, and her milk dripped between his withered lips. He swallowed. You're at the end, she thought, my baby's at the beginning. My baby began at the end of his father's life.

She was sleepy; so sleepy now. The casements were wide open, the sky blue outside. The trees, out of sight, made a susurration like singing. A dragonfly came in, sipped from the silver basin, settled for a few seconds on the white-sheeted hump of Sir Richard's shoulder. She marvelled at it, the strangeness of the body, its four gauzy wings, the alienness of the antique lifeform. It flew out the window. There were house martins outside, they swooped steeply on curved purple wings after insects, chirupping. How good it must be to fly, she thought, to have no limits on you.

My dragonfly is too big for the house martins to eat, she thought.

The man in her arms stirred and she put her breast to his mouth. He suckled a bit. She started to sing him a song. It didn't have words. He fell asleep again. '*Who but my lady greensleeves*,' she sang.

Her shoulders were stiff. She settled herself more comfortably against the head of the bed, moving so he could suckle at her other breast. He was still asleep. She stretched her neck, tipping her head back, and noticed there was a painting under the canopy of the bed. Gaudy bright colours. A topless Europa, a gauzy slip of silk round her hips, was picking cowslips (done in gold leaf) in a grassy meadow while Zeus, disguised as a white bull with huge bollocks, nosed at her arse. How beautiful they were, she all soft pink flesh, brown-nippled, with ringlets cascading over her shoulders, the bull lumpy with muscle, oozing masculinity and strength. A cobalt sea lapped at the fringes of the meadow, and soon Europa would climb on Zeus's back and be carried across the waves to Crete, where the god would – did he rape the princess, or was she willing? Elaine couldn't remember.

This must have been Sir Richard's marriage bed, she thought. He must have slept here with his pretty young bride. If Cymberie was built then. They'll have climbed the stairs from the bawdy celebrations in the hall. Lady Ann'll have been nervous and shy when it came to being alone with him, when she laid her head on the white pillow and looked up she'd have been confronted with that. Zeus and Europa. Did they give her courage, did they frighten her? Or maybe she was too drunk, or it was too dark to notice and she saw them first in the cool light of the morning.

What sharp edges our personalities make between us, she brooded, her thoughts drifting away from the gods. We prickle and rasp against each other. We make demands. We want different things. Even when we want the same thing, the other person's selfhood can weigh on us, it can turn into an assertion of identity, of dominance. That essential separateness of each individual. The islandness of us –Thomas and me – I sometimes wondered if he was jealous of me. He was so generous, he shared everything with me, he taught me all that he knew. One day, it was the day I finished Eve on the mantelpiece at St Bede's Manor, he said, you haven't done that right, Elaine, and I said, I have, look, and I slipped off my clothes and put my hand where Eve's figleaf should have been, and he said, she's not carved like that traditionally, you make her look as if she's got her finger up her cunt, she's enjoying herself, she's not ashamed, look at the pleasure on her face, and I made him laugh, and we made love there, on the wide boards of the bedchamber –

Losing ourselves.

Sir Richard's nearly lost. He's nearly given himself up. Maybe that's why this is so easy. He's not himself. He's not fighting. If you don't fight you lose. You have to fight.

He stirred again and she got him to suckle at her breast; three sucks and his head fell back.

Sir Richard didn't speak in the late afternoon. Elaine dribbled milk in his mouth from a spoon. Nathaniel came back from the harvest, drew up a stool and sat by the bedside. He was pink with sunburn, had scratches on the backs of his hands, straw in the buttons of his doublet. 'Damn your eyes, Mistress Elaine,' he said. 'We were laying bets on him in the field. I said he'd have shuffled off to the next world by midnight. Put half a crown on it. It doesn't look such a sure thing now.'

'Ssh,' said Elaine. 'He can hear you.' But she wasn't certain that he could.

'I'll go and wring a chicken's neck,' said Nathaniel. 'A sweet little breast in a white wine sauce, maybe he'll fancy that in a day or so. Not as much as your melons of course, Mistress Elaine.'

'You have to fight, sir,' Elaine said to the old man when Nathaniel had gone. 'You can't let them win.'

When he'd fallen asleep she went down to the kitchen and took her basket from the corner shelf, unfolded the white cloth. That beautiful pie was still nestling there: she broke off a chunk of the soft pastry. Mmm, it was good, imbued with all the flavour of the gravy. She tucked the pie up again and set off home through the woods. But carrying the basket was a nuisance; it kept bumping against her leg and she couldn't walk as fast as when she was swinging both arms. So she left the lane and climbed up into the privacy of the woods, in the shadows beneath the heavy-leaved sweet chestnuts, sat cross-legged and bit a big hole in the crust of the pie so it was almost like a cup. She sucked out the gravy inside it, scooped out the steak with her finger, munching down the sides of the pie as she went – how delicious the meat was, how fine the pastry, how excellently the herbs complemented the flavour. She licked her lips, stretching out her pink tongue – with her finger pushed a flaky crumb on her chin into her mouth. She put the plum cake in her pocket and hid the basket and its cloth behind a hawthorn tree next to the path, to collect the next morning on her way to Cymberie. The cheese she ate as she strolled along, munching mouse nibbles of it with her neat white teeth.

'What kept you?' demanded Mistress Margery, ducking her head to come out of the low doorway of her cottage. 'Why are you so late?' Elaine was sitting there in the garden, on the bench in the rose arbour, as settled as if she'd been there for ever; she'd snatched Samuel up from the dirt, and he was feeding contentedly away, eyes closed, fists clenched, his entire world centred on his mother's breasts.

'I had to stay the whole day.'

'There's no call for that.' She was so sharp, Mistress Margery was, standing there red-faced from the heat, stinking of sweat in her shiny black bodice, her narrow pink ruff, plump hands resting on the bum-roll that padded out her stained skirt.

'The old man needed looking after. He's in a bad way, and he has no one to care for him.'

'My God, you're a fine one to talk about caring! Here am I, I've been looking after your baby for hours longer than we agreed. Didn't you take any thought for me? Don't you think I've got anything better to do than look after your brat? Your poor child was screaming so with hunger I've had to fetch milk from Mistress Vernon's cow. What kind of mother are you, allowing that to happen? Don't you care at all about your son?'

As if I wasn't doing this just for him, Elaine thought bitterly. As if I didn't love him with my whole overflowing heart. As if this wasn't the only way I know to make money, to build a future for him. She brushed back her hair nervously, trying to think how to reply. 'The old man is very weak,' she essayed. 'I felt he'd die if I didn't stay and look after him.' She looked down at Samuel, smoothed his hair, ran her finger round the pink curl of his ear. She loved him so much; she'd do anything for him.

'Do you expect me to give up my time freely to care for your child just because some old man is dying?' The woman still had her hands on her hips; her mouth was a red cave, opening, closing, her voice sharp as any dagger. 'Old men are always dying; that's the eternal cycle of life. But I still have to earn a living.'

'Yes, but – '

Margery stepped closer, rubbed her thumb and forefinger together under Elaine's nose. 'Payment. That's what I need. For my time. For the milk. You'll have to give me more. That's only fair.'

Elaine leaned back away from her, the baby following the curve of her breast like a limpet. What could she do? She depended on Margery; she couldn't work unless Samuel was safely looked after. 'I'll be paid more if I'm working longer hours,' she pleaded. 'I will pay you proportionately. There was no-one there today for me to arrange it with. But I will.'

'There's no need for you to fret about the matter. Mistress Phillis and me, we've been friends since we were so high. We understand each other very well. I'll talk to her about it, and get her to pay your wages directly to me.'

'No. No.' Elaine's heart sank. She could see the danger of this: she was likely to end up with nothing at all. What could she do to prevent it? 'You don't need to trouble the housekeeper,' she said as calmly as she could. 'I'd prefer to pay you myself.'

'If she gives me your wages, that way you'll repay your debt in half the time. It's high time you settled it. Lending money isn't my business; I'm not made of gold. I'm just a poor woman working hard to make an honest living for myself and provide for my family.'

Elaine didn't know what to say. She looked down at Samuel, kissed the top of his head. How much she longed for the simple weight of coins in her hand: that assurance of independence and power.

'You can't begrudge me the money you owe me,' Margery continued, aggrieved. 'Think how well I looked after you when your time came and your baby was born. And afterwards, when you were weak, when you didn't know what to do – you couldn't have managed without me.'

That was true enough; Elaine was happy to acknowledge it. But Margery's charges were much higher than those of the midwife in Elaine's home village, and the amount of her debt didn't make sense. It seemed to increase every time she checked with the woman how much she owed her now. Was it deliberate, or was it simple lapses of memory? Margery was illiterate too. The trouble with figures that were kept in your head was that they were subject to change, they were fluid and variable. How Elaine longed to be able to pin them down on paper, so they couldn't shift about, so she knew precisely how much she owed, how much she had to pay back. Those firm, fixed, desirable black penmarks. One shilling, she'd be able to write, if she knew how to write, or half a crown, or five shillings and elevenpence three farthings, and the figure would be the same in the morning as when she wrote it, it couldn't change. But she had never had the chance to learn to read or write. So she had to say humbly, 'I need some money to live on, mistress.'

'Of course you'll have that. As soon as you've paid off your debt to me. I have responsibilities to settle too.'

Elaine turned her head away; her eyes were filling up with tears. What could she do, what could she say? She was helpless. She detached Samuel from her breast and he howled. She put him on her shoulder to burp him, then when he was quiet she fastened her shift and her bodice. 'Make what arrangements you wish with the housekeeper,' she said. She tied Samuel in the sling at her side and set off up into the low hills and home. Presently he fell asleep, calmed by the steady rhythm of her walking.

And then, beyond the village, her nightmare was completed. The candlemaker joined her. Walter Vernon. He stepped out from behind a tree and started pacing along the lane beside her. He was all in black again, with his yellow ruff. He had combed his blond hair, he was less unkempt. His hat was in his hand. He was taller than her, his legs longer, so when she quickened her pace hoping he'd fall back he matched her without difficulty. Go away, she thought. I don't trust you. You who imagine you can change places with Thomas. You're not sleeping with me. You're not. I'll kill you if I have to. But she kept silent, hurrying on.

He didn't say anything either. He just strode along beside her.

She was panting, out of breath. Samuel was such a weight now, nearly nine months old. She yanked him up at her side. Then she got a stitch, a sharp pain, she had to stop.

Walter stopped too.

She looked at him. 'Any stones in your pockets today?' she sneered.

He fumbled in his breeches pocket. 'I brought you this,' he said. It was a beeswax candle. He held it out to her in his skinny, shaking hand. She stared at him. 'Take it. It's for you.'

It was a large candle, creamy-coloured, waxy-smelling. It was far finer than the candles her parents burnt on feast days on the trestle table in their hall. 'I can't pay you for it,' she said.

'It's a gift.'

'I don't need it.'

'Everyone needs light.'

'I have a stack of candles at home.'

'No you don't.'

'How do you know?' She was suddenly overwhelmed by the memory of his intrusion into her house. Her terror as she'd lain hidden under the bed hung in the long silence between them.

Neither of them said anything. Suddenly he leant forward and slipped the candle into the sling beside Samuel.

Then he turned and bolted back to the village. Slap, slap went his leather boots on the stony surface of the lane, retreating. She didn't glance back at his black back.

Walter Vernon's candle was thick, straight, tall. Elaine carried it in front of her, unlit, in her two hands, as if she were in a saint's day procession. She wanted it. There's no point in rejecting it, she thought, if I throw it away someone else will pick it up. They won't need it as much as I do. Why did he give it to me? Perhaps he's mad.

I could sell it, she thought. That would be best. But I don't want to. It makes me feel good. It makes me feel like a fine lady.

Elaine took off her ruff and her bodice, hung them in the porch of her house. She took off her skirt, turned the pocket inside out, slowly ate the slice of plum cake. How fat and moist the raisins were, how deep crimson the cherries. It was good not to be hungry.

The linen of my skirt will have absorbed grease from the mix, she thought, what can I do about that? She had only the one skirt. She had had two, travelling south, but she had sold one for bread.

She stood at the door in her shift to watch the sunset. A harvest sunset, the red sun hanging like a ball above the horizon, sinking to be swallowed beneath the earth. Dust in the air from the fields. Light on each particle, a distortion. Changing the view.

Now, in the blue-grey and darkening sky, a star shimmered. You could never see the stars as clear in the summer as you could in the winter. The cold is cleaner, she thought, but she loved the warmth and simple way of life of the summer.

She went into her house which was dark. Samuel was

asleep in the bed. She struck the flint and lit the candle. How tall the flame was; how pure. What a wide glow it cast. How strong it was; it barely flickered. She sat on the edge of the bed, hands between her knees, and watched it. She forgot everything; let her life be swallowed up by the flame.

3

Elaine stared out of the open casement, hands on the sill. She had been coming to Cymberie for a fortnight now; it felt so familiar. The garden lay below her with its straggling lavender, its low box hedges that needed a good trim, the empty pond with its bird-limed statue, the paving with ground elder and nettles forcing their way through the cracks between blocks. Nobody bothered to look after the place because they were certain the old man was dying. They couldn't have cared less about his son and heir, either, because he was thousands of miles away, tossing around in a captured caravel in the Caribbean, it was said.

Elaine had never seen the sea and she wondered if it was the same colour as the sky. Either that pastel blue at the horizon above the wavy green forest, or else that deep, deep blue at the zenith. She imagined the sky was shallow where it was pale blue. That was the area where the clouds were processing, puffy little white clouds, ornamental, not rain-bearing. Lots of them, she began to count them, twenty-eight, twenty-nine, but they kept on changing their shape, fusing with others or breaking into bits, silent and calm, as if there were some kind of reason or purpose or order behind what they were doing. The clouds are like the figures in Mistress Margery's head, she thought, when Mistress M is reckoning up my debt, they've got that same fluidity. There's no way you can ever pay back a sum as elusive as that. It's always subject to change, it'll always increase. Especially if the housekeeper is also taking a cut from my earnings, as no doubt she will.

Elaine needed to fix the figures somehow. If only she knew her numbers, she could have carved them in an oak tablet so they were immutable. Or she could have written them down, if only she knew how to write.

She glanced across at Richard and, seeing him sleeping, took one of his books from the court cupboard. She had only twice held a book before; she wasn't sure how to handle it. She stroked its leather binding. How smooth it was, and warm, with those little lateral bumps across the spine; she ran her fingers down them. She turned the book round in her hands. There was dust on the top edge; she blew it off. Then she opened the book. It was hinged like doors; the front and back doors opened and inside was the print. Black squiggles on ivory paper. She carried it to right near the window as if the extra light might help her decipher it. She studied the pages, the neat rectangular blocks of black print, the wide margins with just a few words in. She ran her finger along the lines. The words – they had to make sense if only you knew how to interpret them.

There were repeated patterns in the text that she recognised: small black dots were followed by a space and then by a letter bigger than the main text. So many *ſ*s; she marvelled at the way they curled over at the top, like shepherds' crooks. Some words had two crooks, like *feafon* and *firft.* She smiled to herself. You could catch twice as many lambs with those.

The text came in blocks like barges heaped high with hay and roped to each other, drifting down a cream river. After each block a break. At the beginning of each line following a break the first letter was always big. She searched for clues that would help her interpret the print. *Meffage* – that was a pretty word, almost symmetrical, with its repeated *e*s and *ſ*s – what could it mean?

She climbed on to the fourposter beside Sir Richard. It was the most comfortable place in the room. She sat there cross-legged beneath the seduction of Europa. The book was open on her lap, she was studying it. *Profeffed* – a strange word with three shepherds' crooks. *o* – there were lots of 'o's, like bubbles, or balls, or hoops. *e* was often repeated.

'Read to me,' said Sir Richard.

'What?'

'Read to me, damn it.'

'Heavens, sir, you startled me. Talking. You haven't said one word since the first day I came.'

'Read to me.'

'I can't, sir. I don't have the knowledge. Shall I fetch the priest to read to you?'

'Good God, no. I'm not dying yet. What day is it?'

'The ninth of August.' She didn't tell him he had been given the last rites eleven days ago, so he had no business at all talking to her, he should have been off climbing the stairs to the Pearly Gates, a golden halo glistening over his grey hair, a pair of angel wings flapping on his back. 'Are you thirsty, sir?'

'God, I could do with a drink.'

He was more than a little taken aback to have her undo her shift and raise his head to her left breast. He gasped with laughter. 'Brodbury – stupid fellow – doctor, filthy gown – he ordered this?'

'Sir, he's not so stupid. You were close to death. The only nourishment you have had these last two weeks was my milk. And look at you now. Strong as an ox.'

He struggled to sit up, but gave up, exhausted. 'I'm not ploughing any furrow today.' He waited a few moments to get his breath back, raised his eyes to her face. 'Have I truly been drinking your milk?'

'Yes, sir.'

'Am I paying you well?'

'Your housekeeper looks after that, sir.'

'Must have been in a desperate way.' His words were

slurring together.

'You were very ill, sir.'

'You can go now.'

'You don't want my services any more?'

'I don't steal milk from the mouths of infants.' He closed his eyes; he had fallen asleep.

Elaine closed the book and replaced it in the court cupboard, turned to rearrange the pillows so Richard was more comfortable, well-supported.

She had imposed a rigorous discipline on the sickroom: a clean top mattress and sheets every day, clean pillowcases, a clean shirt for the sick man. It had infuriated Mistress Phillis. 'For heaven's sake, don't you understand that I'm in charge of the laundry here?' she'd demanded, hands on her farthingaled hips, skirt and bosom trembling with indignation. 'Can't you see the problems you're causing me? I have to get Mistress Davis to light the fire under the copper every day to boil the damned stinking stuff. I have to send Eric out to fetch wood. Then who's going to polish the silver, who's going to make the soap, who's going to gather rushes? You've no idea how complicated you're making my life. All for no reason at all. The man's dying, he doesn't know what's going on, he doesn't give a damn about lying in his own shit.'

'It's such beautiful sunny weather,' Elaine was in the habit of murmuring, tipping yet another soiled mattress out of the window. 'The washing will dry in two ticks.'

Elaine loved the master chamber at Cymberie. She loved the cool panelling, the intricate high ceiling and the three casements with their panes of thick greenish glass, that you could latch open to admit the clear light of day. She loved the wide floorboards with their knots and cracks, on which she now scattered fresh herbs every day, also the silver basin with its tracery of snakes on the outside, so reflective within, and the ordered discipline of washing before she fulfilled her duties. The scent of the soap. She loved the books in the court cupboard and the secrets that were closed up inside them, which she was determined one day to decipher; she appreciated the skill of the unknown carver who had worked the oak bedposts, the lustre of the scarlet and yellow silk bedhangings.

Having overcome her initial revulsion, she had in the end become reconciled to the challenge of getting the sick Sir Richard to suckle, and was pleased when she saw his health begin to improve in spite of everyone around him still insisting that he'd be dead the next hour, the next day. Such a victory it was: one that gave her the possibility of escape from her poverty. Oh, and she liked the good food she was given, the freedom from hunger. She relished the quiet company of the men of the estate who climbed the stairs to his chamber in ones and twos, drew up stools, set their hats on their knees and watched her nurse the sick man, watched him grow stronger. They hadn't made the lewd jokes she would have expected. It seemed odd, breast-nursing witnessed as an entertainment, as a play; it hardly had the excitement of a tournament or bear-fight. Perhaps the men liked the calm of it too. The tenderness. The protection. When they went, they left behind them the sane stink of sweat and of horses. She had to sweep up the strands of straw that fell from their clothes.

'Go and look after your baby.'

'I'll go after you've drunk your milk.'

'Get me a beer.'

'After your milk.'

'How many days have I been doing this?'

'What?'

'You know.'

She counted up. 'Seventeen.'

'Thank God Gabriel's not here.'

'Gabriel?'

'My son. My god, he'd mock me.'

'Sir, it's what your physician ordered.'

'Elaine, I'm fifty-six.'

She persuaded him to suckle again. It lulled him; he forgot his embarrassment and shame. 'This is so comfortable,' he said, resting his head against her.

'Good.' She moved her hand to support his neck.

'Two days,' he said, 'and I'll be up and about. Then you can go.'

'Sir, will you teach me to read?'

'Why do you want to learn?'

'I want to understand writing, sir.'

'Well.'

'Please, sir.'

'Well, while I am confined to my chamber. While there's nothing of importance I can do.'

He sat in a loose red velvet gown embroidered with gold thistles, in a linenfold armchair by the window. Nathaniel had carried him to it, one arm beneath his shoulders, the other beneath his knees, and settled him there while Elaine stripped and made the bed. When the cook had gone she sat on a stool beside her master, a book open on her knees. 'Will you show me how to read this, sir?' she asked.

'Very well. Start at this page.' *The firre tree groweth very high and great,* he began, *having his leaves ever greene.* She pictured it in her head, the fir tree; it was one that grew at a crossroads just outside her home village. How many days she had played under it with her sisters and cousins, built stick houses under it, danced ring-a-roses round it. From its shade she had watched Thomas and her brothers at their longbow practice. How strange that the black squiggles of the print had the power to bring these memories back to her. She touched the letters lightly with the tips of her fingers, wishing she could absorb through her skin what they said.

'What are you thinking about?' he asked.

'Nothing.'

'Then concentrate.' He began to explain, to give her clues that would help her unravel the mystery of print.

Ten minutes he did it the first day; he couldn't talk for long. Sitting exhausted him.

The next day he asked for a pen. *Elaine*, he wrote. 'Now you try,' he said. The quill was made from the feather of a swan's wing; she dipped it in the ink horn and the black ink dropped in spots on the paper. *E*, she wrote, the point scratching. The barbs of the feather were stiff against her hand.

Then one day he was worse, he was barely conscious once more, groaning with pain. Elaine struggled to put a clean shirt on him, felt for the turnip lump in his belly. 'It is smaller,' she said. 'It is definitely smaller. You are getting better, I tell you.' But she couldn't truly remember how big it had been at first. She wished she had measured it against her hand so she could have been sure. She wouldn't let him sleep, in case he drifted off into that oblivion from which there's no return; she kept waking him to make him nurse. Uh, he said, pushing against her, uh; but she woke him again, pulled him to her breast. Listen, sir, she said, I'm not letting you escape me. I need you, I want you to live. Come on, you old devil, she said, suck, damn you, suck. You're not going down into your grave just yet, I won't let you.

What mattered to her was not just the paying off of her debts, she realised. This was the only sphere in her life in which she wielded any power. The power to deal out life or death, she believed. But yet she was infinitely substitutable. Anyone could have done this. All they'd have had to do was care.

Elaine stood in the churchyard by her husband's grave. It was evening; she was alone. Thomas, do you understand? she said in her head.

I couldn't do anything for you, she thought, I couldn't help you in any way. But I can help Sir Richard, and I will. I think I have the power to give him life. I have been powerless for so long, Thomas. Since your death. You, above all others, know what it's like to be a victim. To not be in a position to fight.

I ought to hate him with every fibre of my being. I know it. It's he who ordered you to be hanged. But I need to care. It's something rooted deep in me. I need my caring to be effective. I need to win.

He pays for my caring. It doesn't count. It's not love, Thomas. It may look like love from the outside, Thomas, but it's not, he's paying me.

All my caring for you was useless, Thomas, in the end. It ran away between my fingers like water. Like your piss.

She knelt down, pulled a few nettles from the ground. The fine summer weather had turned the heaped earth to dust, red flurries blew off it in the southerly breeze, they stung her eyes, she cried, she had to wipe them.

'His face, Thomas – you would love to carve it,' she said. 'His skin is lined like the grain of wood. He is so thin, so ravaged by his illness.' She had looked down on that face so many hours. She had imagined which chisel she would use to gouge out the corner of the mouth, the hollow cheeks, the torn lobe of the ear, which chisel to delineate the crooked nose, the heavy brows. She had imagined working that face in yew and oak and elm and lime; the different effects each wood would give.

She sat back on her heels. 'Thomas, you know how good it is when you are starting to carve a block of wood? The excitement of knowing that the sculpture lies somewhere within it, you just have to find it. You let fly with the chisel and mallet. Chips of wood everywhere. You know how determined you are then, how concentrated on your purpose, how you can't think of anything else?' That's how I feel about making Sir Richard better, she wanted to tell him. *I will succeed ...*

Her fingers were stinging from pulling up the nettles. She spat on them to cool the pain. Nettles were so vicious at this time of year.

'Mistress Elaine.'

She looked up. It was the candlemaker, Walter Vernon.

She froze inside, didn't reply. If she didn't acknowledge his presence, pretended he wasn't there, maybe he would disappear.

'Dock leaves.' He was holding them out to her; she ignored him. 'Take them; they will make your fingers better.'

'Thank you, sir.' Reluctantly she accepted them and rubbed her stung fingers hard until her skin was stained green. Six or seven times since he had given her the wax candle he had met her, seemingly by chance, always when she was on her way home from Cymberie. He had kept on giving her things. One day he gave her fat green hazelnuts he'd gathered, he emptied them out of his breeches pockets into her skirt. Another day he gave her a pot of honey which she saved until she got home; then she'd dipped her finger in it as she sat on the bed in the round house in the candlelight, and licked it, lengthways, all around. She gave Samuel a fingertipsworth to try and he loved it, wanted more.

'Tomorrow, sweetheart,' she'd said, 'too much isn't good for you all at once.' And she hugged the baby tight against her chest until he stopped crying.

Another day Walter Vernon had given her a thick slice of caraway cake, moist and sharp, that his mother, with whom he lived, had made. Another day he gave her a liquorice twig to chew, another a fat bunch of fragrant lavender tied up with straw. Today he had an earthenware bowl heaped high with blackberries. 'I'm collecting them for my mother to make comfits,' he said. He had been to the barber and he was neatly shaved, his hair was trimmed. The ruff he was wearing was a soft lilac, which suited his complexion far better than the yellow. 'Would you like some?' he said, holding out the bowl.

The blackberries glistened; there was a gleam to every globule and she itched to carve the intricate shape of the fruit on a grand scale, so that each would look like a bunch of grapes. A Bacchanalian scene, she thought she'd try, with a nymph dangling the grapes over the open mouth of a greedy satyr. They'd be at the edge of a cornfield, in the deep shade of an elm tree. A bas-relief in lime.

The scent of the blackberries rose up from the bowl, the smell rich, fusty-sweet as old velvet, and when Elaine took one and put it in her mouth it dissolved into juice, staining her finger and thumb purple, purple juice running on to her hand. 'Lovely,' she said.

'You're lovely,' he said. 'Will you marry me?'

'What?' She didn't think she could have heard right. She stared at him as if he were mad.

'Will you marry me? Will you be my wife?'

'Mr Vernon, are you seriously asking me by the side of my husband's grave if I will marry you?'

'He has been dead for nine months now, Mistress Elaine.

Do you think he'd want you to still be mourning for him? No, no man would, he would wish for your happiness. Would he want you to live on your own in the forest? No, he'd say go and live in the village with companions all around you. You think he'd want you to go hungry when a new husband would feed you? Of course not. He wouldn't want you to sleep on your own, he would wish that you had a good man to share the warmth of your bed.'

'You think you are that good man, Mr Vernon?' She was remembering what Thomas had said before his death. Afterwards, he said after his trial, in his cell, shivering, taking her icy hands in his trembling ones: afterwards, you know, when this is all over, don't mourn for me. I don't want you to do that. I want you to be happy. I love it when you're happy. The way your smile lights up your face. The way you get engrossed in what you are doing and ignore everything else. I love your happiness – Ssh, Thomas, she'd replied, don't, don't mention it, something will happen, I know it will, everything will be all right, you'll be pardoned, there'll be a happy ending, how can they kill you when you are innocent, when your baby will soon be born, when we are so happy, when life's so perfect?

'I have a profitable business, Mistress Elaine, and a good house, and I can provide for you well.' Mr Vernon's voice cut across her reverie.

She stood up. He was half a head taller than her. He would have been taller still if his shoulders hadn't drooped rather as if he were a melting candle. 'Thomas and I have a son, Mr Vernon. Do you expect me to abandon him?'

'Assuredly not. He will live with us both. I will bring him up with as much tenderness as if he were my own child. I will make sure that he is properly educated, and apprenticed to a trade.'

'Mr Vernon, are you serious?' This would resolve most of her worries for Samuel.

'Of course I am. Why do you doubt me?'

She couldn't ever forget that first day they met; the terrible fear that had possessed her then. Even though she now acknowledged there was no reason for her fear: his coming into her house had been quite natural, nobody's house had a lock on the door, you could go in and out, it was what everyone did, in and out without hindrance; it was the custom to shout out the house-dweller's name before you entered and he'd done that: 'Mistress Elaine,' he had called out as she trembled in terror under the bed.

'Mistress Vernon,' she said slowly. 'It sounds good enough. What would I be mistress of?'

'I'll show you.' They walked side by side down the dusty lane into the village. There was three foot of space between them; they were nowhere near touching. It was early evening and a few men were hoeing the lettuce, beans and cabbages in their gardens; they looked up and stretched their backs, rested their hands on the hoe handles and nodded good day, good day. Children were fetching buckets of water from the well and carrying them home, left arms outstretched to counterbalance the weight, water splashing silver over the bucket-tops. Fizz in the hot dry dust. Outside the bakery people queued, the fragrance of lamb pasties drifted down the street. An old crone sat in a doorway shelling peas into her apron while two bare-bottomed toddlers made lanes in the dirt at her feet and galloped their fingers along them. The smell of beef stew came from a substantial cottage that stood on its own in a side street. 'That's where I live,' said Walter Vernon. 'It would be yours if you married me.'

Elaine was impressed. The place was a small hall house

with the shutters of the candle shop on the right side of the doorway; she knew a screens passage would separate shop and hall and upstairs there'd be a solar, parlour and chamber combined, where in the winter she'd be able to sit and embroider, playing the lady, with her back against the warm bricks of the ponderous chimney that must have been added fairly recently, to judge by the state of the mortar, into the middle of the house. The low sun would slant from the south through the mullions, touch the fine wool of the new skirt she'd be able to afford. She would make this old linen thing she was wearing into sheets for Samuel's crib. 'It's a fine place, your house,' she murmured.

'So you will marry me?'

She hesitated, added a four poster bed to the furniture in the solar, imagined herself lying, arms straight at her side, next to a wooden Mr Vernon. Like dolls they'd be. The house without the marriage would be very attractive. But with? The prospect weighed her down, it deprived her of joy. Yet it would mean a secure future for Samuel; how wonderful that would be. 'I need time to consider the matter,' she demurred.

'Will you give me your answer tomorrow?'

'No, tomorrow's too soon.'

'Will you tell me by the end of next week?'

'Maybe. Maybe. I'll tell you then if I'm ready.' The end of next week seemed an eternity away. She didn't need to worry about it yet. Anything might happen in the intervening days.

'What do you think, Samuel?' Elaine said to the sleeping bundle in the sling at her side, putting her arm under his bottom and heaving him up; he was getting heavier all the time, it was becoming a strain to carry him back to their house in the woods at the end of a long day. 'What do you think about us marrying Walter Vernon? Living in a nice warm house with plenty of food:

it'd be good, wouldn't it?'

Samuel continued to emit little snores.

'Did you see the size of the garden? And the barn. We'll keep hens, you'll be able to breakfast on eggs every day. We'll have a couple of cows. It'll be so good,' she insisted; but somehow the thought of it created a heavy lump in her chest that was far more burdensome than the weight of the baby at her side. Then as she climbed the last hill to the round house all the memories of building it with Thomas came crowding back into her head.

Living there with him. Waking those fine October mornings to find him warm beside her: his breath on her cheek. Distant cockcrow, the sigh of the trees that sheltered them, the rattle of pigeons' wings, gold sun and chill air filtering through cracks in the walls. Snuggling into his bare body, his warmth and smooth skin that made her whole world secure, that protected her from all harm. Together they would always be safe, together they would make their fortune, that had been certain. She would slip from the bed and he would stick out an arm and grasp her leg, he'd pull her close, he'd kiss her round belly all over, her breasts, and he'd draw her back in, and later he'd get up, run downhill naked to wash in the spring. When he got back his nose and his lips would be cold; she'd squeal when he kissed her and he'd laugh.

Those days he was carving samples to take round to the big houses, to show off what he could do. A couple of biblical scenes, the Transfiguration and the women coming to the empty tomb, and a couple from classical myth – the Minotaur in the Cretan labyrinth, and Persephone being ferried across the river to the Underworld. 'Better to cover both the religious and the classical,' he had said. 'You never know what people's tastes will be like.'

'I'm not sure,' she said. 'The biblical scenes may not be

popular. They say this is quite a Puritan area. Think how the statues in the church have been defaced.'

'That's what people profess in public,' he said, 'but underneath they still hold all the old beliefs.'

She wanted him to use the Transfiguration as a sample as soon as he'd completed it. 'It's excellently carved,' she had said. 'They'll be able to judge your skill from that.'

But he'd demurred. 'There's no reason for haste,' he'd said. 'I need to be able to offer people a choice.'

'We must be careful,' she said. 'We're nearly out of money.'

That was when he had caught the deer. He skinned and gutted it, hung the joints up in a tree behind the house. But kestrels, owls and magpies tore at the flesh, foxes pulled one haunch to the ground and consumed it. So he hung it in the house, where he could barricade it in and there was no greater danger than rats, and for days the sweetish smell of raw meat permeated their dwelling. They feasted, they lay bloated on the bed. 'I feel sick,' she said.

When the venison was gone and the bones boiled up for soup they survived on oatcakes and barley. 'There are five big houses within a day's walk of here,' she pointed out. 'Please take your samples round. It's the only way to get a commission.'

The two of them worked side by side on the open gravel patch in front of their house. 'Pass me the quarter-inch chisel, will you,' she'd say, and he'd pick it up and hand it to her blade first; she'd take it in her left hand and use her right to guide it along the grain.

She'd been working on a cradle. He had found a fallen chestnut in the woods behind them and split it with an axe. The sides she carved like the planks of Noah's Ark, with windows from which peered pairs of dogs and cats and cows, mice and curly adders, hens and horses. Noah himself sat in a long gown, fishing from the stern. And the cradle hood was like a pair of angel's wings, curved over to guard any occupant and keep them safe from harm.

'That's beautiful,' he'd said. He was standing close, his shadow falling across her. The afternoon sun lit up the beeches and the birches; the few leaves they still bore burned gold. 'Elaine, you have such a touch. You can make wood flow like water. You bewitch it, I think. I have been carving ten years longer than you and yet next to yours my work seems heavy, stilted, dead.'

'No, Thomas, no! How can you say that? You are such a good craftsman. You have taught me so much. Look how neat your work is; it's immaculate. And you carve things in the old way, which is how people like them, they like that security, they'll pay you well. This – 'she gestured at the cradle – 'this is just for our baby. It's not for sale.' Which meant it had no value.

She'd fainted a couple of times. 'Do you think it could be because of lack of bread?' he'd asked, concerned.

'I'll be fine. Don't worry.'

The third time she fainted he took a blanket to the village without telling her, and sold it. He came back with three loaves of bread, half a cheese and a small cask of ale. They feasted again.

The evenings were drawing in. Sunsets were red, the twilights blue-grey. Often a mist would rise up and lie across the land below them. The village would disappear. He would stand beside her, watching, and fondle the back of her neck, under her hair. She would turn and encompass him with her arms, put up her face to kiss him.

'I want this to go on for ever and ever,' he would murmur.

'When will you start trying to sell your work?' she would ask.

'Soon,' he'd say.

'Not soon enough,' Elaine said to Samuel, sitting him down on the gravel by the round house. 'It wasn't soon enough. And then I had another fainting fit and he sold his tools for food without asking me first. I don't know what possessed him. Destroying both our potential livelihoods in one go. Hey, where do you think you are you going, boy, crawling off like that? Come back, it's supper-time.'

She undid her bodice and her shift and leant back against the porch. 'What's the matter, babe? Aren't you hungry? Auntie Margery has been giving you milk from a cup again, has she? That's so easy for you, isn't it? Come on, settle down, sweetheart, get down to work, don't fight me – concentrate.'

She fumbled in the pocket of her skirt for a slice of cheese and apple pie, unfolded it from its cloth. Pastry crumbs fell on the baby's head bobbing at her breast; she smoothed them away from his fair skin.

4

It was raining. A quiet rain that veiled the trees of the forest in a thin mist. It whispered on the surface of the leaves, it made them glisten, it pooled in the empty pond and polished the marble, it ringed the lying water. The whole world was grey and full of drips and trickling sounds.

'It's cooler today,' Elaine said. She closed the casement. 'You mustn't get chilled.' She soaped her breasts, rinsed them in the tepid water in the silver bowl.

Sir Richard was half-sitting up in bed, propped up against his pillows. His green eyes were wide open, he was watching her. 'You've got raindrops in your hair,' he said. 'They are like pearls.'

She picked up the white linen towel that hung by the bowl, and rubbed her dark hair up on end with it.

'You look a mess,' said Sir Richard. 'Use my comb.'

It was made of some kind of translucent mottled, slightly brownish substance, horn or whalebone she thought it must be. She dabbed at the tangle of her hair with it, afraid of breaking it, knowing it would be expensive to replace. She laid it down. 'Are you ready now, sir?'

'If you must. I can't believe this ritual is necessary any longer.'

'Sir, I don't want you to have another relapse.' She made herself comfortable at his side, pulled him toward her.

He pulled back. 'Elaine, your bodice is damp.'

'It's just the rain, sir. Summer rain; it doesn't hurt.'

'You must have worn a shawl or a cloak, walking here from the village.'

'No sir.'

'Why in heaven's name not? It's been raining for hours.'

'I was walking under the shelter of the trees, sir. My clothes are just a little damp, they won't hurt you at all.'

'It's not good for you to wear damp clothes. You'll get a chill.'

'Yes, sir. Will you suckle now, sir?' And off he went, with his eyes closed, nodding away at her nipple. She smoothed his thin hair and relaxed back against the pillows. She was thinking how the rain had shown up defects in the thatch of her and Samuel's round house; she had woken this morning to find the sheet and mattress sodden down by her feet. She would have to get fresh rushes and mend the roof as soon as she could. She'd carry the rushes up from the river in a great bundle on her back. They would be awkward; not too heavy. How good it will be when Samuel can walk, she thought, when I don't have to carry him all the time.

Sir Richard detached himself; she offered him her other breast. This was all a matter of routine now; she had long ago stopped feeling humiliated and resentful. Perhaps you could get used to any job. She liked the space that feeding the old man gave her to sit quietly in comfort and think about other things. She could write her name now; she wanted to learn to write *Samuel* and *Thomas*. There was a kind of magic in seeing one's name written down. The day she had learnt to write the whole of *Elaine*, right down to the final *e*, she kept writing it with a stick in the dirt on her way home. *Elaine* on the track, *Elaine* among last year's leaves, *Elaine* in the dust on Thomas's grave, *Elaine* in the damp earth by the spring, *Elaine* in the gravel outside the front of her house. 'See, Samuel, what your clever mother can do,' she'd said, and he crawled across, obliterating the letters, and made a grab for her stick.

When Sir Richard had finished she rinsed her breasts, fastened her shift and her bodice. 'Do you want to sit up now, sir?' she said.

'Of course.'

She helped him slide his arms into a black woollen gown, and fastened it over his shirt. 'Shall I get Nathaniel to carry you to your chair?'

'I can walk now.' He slithered his legs over the side of the bed and stood clutching the carved bedpost, the gown falling to skim his yellow-skinned feet.

'Will you put your arm around my shoulders, sir?' She slid her arm around his waist and together they shuffled the dozen or so steps to the chair. He grasped the wooden arms and lowered himself into it; she stooped to fold the gown over his bare knees.

'My dear, your clothes are still damp,' he said.

'It's a warm day, sir. It doesn't matter.'

'Call Mistress Phillis, will you.'

She hesitated. 'Is it anything I can do for you myself, sir?'

'Is there some dispute between you and my housekeeper?'

'No, sir.'

'Call her, I said. Tell her I want the key to Lady Ann's chest.'

'Yes, sir.'

Mistress Phillis's room was downstairs, in the old part of the house adjoining the kitchen. Elaine knocked fearfully at the door. She kept away from the housekeeper as much as she could, knowing how antagonistic the woman had become, angry at having the bother of organising the daily washing and drying of sheets and mattresses foisted on her. But Phillis Tewke had to be treated with respect. She was still in authority, she still paid

Elaine's wages directly to Mistress Margery.

'Come in.'

It was a stone room with limewashed walls studded with iron hooks from which hung keys of all shapes and sizes. The narrow arched window was latched open, and in front of it, where the light was brightest, Mistress Phillis sat on a stool, a sheet across her lap; she was engrossed in darning, making neat, almost invisible stitches. 'You,' she said. 'What in heaven's name do you want now? Have you run out of mattresses to hurl out the window?'

Outside, rain gurgled in a downpipe. A filly neighed across the yard. Elaine swallowed. 'Sir Richard sent me,' she said. 'He wants the key to Lady Ann's chest.'

'Ha,' said Mistress Phillis. 'So now we come to the real reason you're hanging round this house. Don't think you ever deceived me for one minute, miss, with all your airs of caring so much for the master. All that stuff and nonsense about clean sheets and shirts – utterly ridiculous. I've never heard of anyone making so much fuss about a dying man. Why? What's she doing it for? That's what I've kept asking myself. And now we know. You're a little thief. I should have guessed it. So you come and tell me this story of the master wanting the key to his late wife's chest, when he's never once asked for it since he gave it me for safe-keeping. You think I'll swallow that? You'll empty it while he's asleep, will you?'

Elaine blinked; decided to say nothing. She folded her hands primly together. Hooves clattered on the cobbles outside and she stared over the housekeeper's head at a stranger in a blue hat with a feather dismounting. Don't you know, sir, she thought, that Cymberie's reputation for hospitality and graciousness has all disappeared, since the old man took ill there's little courtesy shown to visitors here? You'll get bread and ale in the kitchen if you're lucky. I'd ride on if I were you.

'Well?'

Elaine turned her attention back to the housekeeper. 'The master asked that you should take him the key yourself, Mistress Phillis.'

'I want to finish mending this sheet. You take the key.'

'No, mistress. I'll go back to the master and tell him you're on your way.'

'No. Stay.' She fiddled with the great bundle of keys at her waist. 'Here, look in that little cupboard on the wall – there's a bunch of five keys hanging there; you'll find the key to Lady Ann's chest on that.'

Elaine didn't lift a finger. She was determined not to furnish the housekeeper with any grounds for accusing her of stealing. 'You bring it yourself, Mistress Phillis. I'll tell him you're on your way.'

'Lady Ann's shawl,' said Sir Richard. He had been sitting up for nearly half an hour and his head was swimming, he was getting tetchy and irritable. 'The blue one with the silken tassels.'

Phillis knelt in front of the great leather-covered chest with its iron bands, and inserted the ornate key in the padlock, turned it, slipped the lock from the loop, pushed back the hasp.

'Well, open it,' he commanded.

'It's too heavy.'

'For God's sake! Help her, Elaine.'

Together the two women lifted the lid, leant it back against the wall. It's not that heavy, Elaine thought, standing back, is the woman playing some sort of a game?

'The shawl's right on the top,' he said. 'Ann was wearing it the morning of the accident. It was her favourite. She left it in the solar, on the back of a chair, when she went riding. It was still there when I got home on my own. I didn't want to move it. Its being there made me certain she would be coming back. She's just gone visiting, I kept thinking, she'll be back any minute. Every day when I saw the shawl there I knew she was with me still, it comforted me, she'll be back soon I thought, she'll come in just as it's getting dark and sit by the fire, she'll pick up her lute and pluck it, she'll sing to me – she'll tell me what she's been doing – if it's been a sick churl she's been caring for, or a beast with a sore leg, whichever has touched her heart this time – Elaine, give it to me.'

'A blue shawl with silken tassels, you said, sir? Right on the top?'

'For heaven's sake. It's a simple enough request.'

'It's not here, sir.'

'Of course it is! I remember putting it in, and no-one has touched the chest since. Phillis, you know the shawl I mean, Lady Ann was always wearing it, get it out and give it to me.'

'It's not on the top, sir. You must have taken it out of the chest sometime. Perhaps you gave it to your daughter. To Ysabelle. I'm sure it was that. I distinctly remember, the last time she came to see you, when she rode away she was wearing her mother's blue shawl.'

'Don't be a fool! Do you think I wouldn't know if I'd given it away? It's my body that's failing, not my mind.'

'I'll look deeper down, sir. Perhaps it's buried under the rest of the clothes.' She burrowed her white paws in among the layers of heavy silks and wools and velvets, the purples, scarlets, blues and blacks that smelt of dried orange peel and elecampane roots, put in there to deter the moth.

'No.' Sir Richard stopped to draw in a deep breath. His shoulders were heaving with distress. He whispered: 'It must be on the top. I know it's there. It was the last thing I laid in that chest before I closed it up for good.'

'I can't find it here, sir.'

'Can you, Elaine?'

'There's no blue fabric with tassels, sir.'

'She must have stolen it, Sir Richard, that's what.' Mistress Phillis was on her fat little feet now, ranting, her smooth plump face convulsed with hatred. 'She's a filthy foreigner, she don't belong here. You shouldn't have trusted her. What more can you expect? She's a thief, she comes of a race of cattle-thieves, everyone knows all northerners are thieves!'

'Phillis.' Sir Richard's voice was quiet. 'You were with me when I put away the shawl. Do you remember? It was just eighteen months ago. No, less than that. Early February it was that Ann fell from her horse. April I packed away the shawl. Easter time. Good Friday I wore it round my shoulders all the day, mourning, weeping, wanting her with me for the springtime. Do you remember that, Phillis?'

'Yes, sir,' she said; what else could she say when his voice was so sad and compelling?

'I couldn't imagine how spring could come without Ann being here at my side. Spring, the time of rebirth. And her mouldering in her grave. It didn't bear thinking of. Then I knew I had to let her go. I called you in on the Easter Saturday, I opened up the chest. Ah, how her clothes still smelt of her then. That rose perfume she made every summer. I folded the shawl carefully, I laid it on the top. Mistress Phillis, I said, you are my witness, I am putting this away for good. I said, Mistress Phillis, I want you to have the key. I want you to keep her things safe from me. Keep the key safe, I said. Keep it safe. Keep it safe, let me let her go.' His eyes were watering, tears ran down his face. He didn't move to brush them away. He was sitting upright, very straight. 'The chest was securely locked, Phillis. And it's you I saw unlock it just now. You were the only one to have the key in all that time. I never asked you for it. If anything is missing you are to blame. I will not have you accuse Mistress Elaine. If I hear another word from you along these lines, you will leave Cymberie.' His face was ashen. You could see the bones of his skull. A vein throbbed at his temple.

Elaine was afraid that he was going to relapse. She didn't know what to do to protect him. She moved to the window but it was already shut. She could light the fire but that would take time to heat the room. She crossed to the bed and stripped off a blanket, tried to lay it over his knees.

But he pushed her away. 'Give me the key, Mistress Phillis.'

The housekeeper held it out to him; the ornate iron lay black in the white palm of her hand. He took it, closed his fist around it, looked up at her. 'Send Nathaniel to me,' he said. 'Quickly.'

Nathaniel lifted the old man into his bed. He was limp, in a state of collapse, he didn't say a word. Once his head was on the bolster he turned away and closed his eyes. 'What's the reason for this?' Nathaniel asked Elaine. 'He has been so much stronger lately. Has anything happened?'

'Oh ...' she said. She thought it was better not to mention the missing shawl. 'He felt poorly all of a sudden,' she said. 'I hope he'll recover.'

'Never fear, he's tough as an ostrich in the wilderness. He'll be fighting fit again in no time with your help, Mistress Elaine. Will he want supper?'

'Perhaps a light chicken soup. Nothing too heavy. He should be a bit better after he's had a rest.'

She sat cross-legged on the bed beside the old man,

watching his face, seeing the frown lines soften as he fell asleep. After a while a smile touched his lips. Is he thinking of his wife? she wondered. His fist loosened and the key fell on the linen sheet next to him. She didn't touch it.

She got up and crossed to the open chest and stared down at his dead wife's things. Such a richness of belongings. 'All I have of Thomas's is his son,' she whispered. How precious he is to me, she thought. Every day growing to look more like his father. I will keep him safe, she thought, make sure he has the chance to live a life more fulfilled than his father's. I must get Sir Richard better. I must get him to teach me to write *Samuel* so I can teach it to my son.

Soon I will be able to read whole sentences, she thought. She could read odd words now – God, tree, heaven, sun, moon, star, flower, house – she would run her finger under the line of the letters. Reading was listening with her eyes. A new skill. It was such a delight.

She lowered the heavy lid of Lady Ann's chest, fearing the damp would get into the clothes. She closed the hasp, slid the padlock through the loop, clicked it shut.

The rain didn't cease all day. It was restful. There was no washing that needed doing; Sir Richard was no longer incontinent. All Elaine had to do while he was asleep was to sit in his armchair by the window and to look at his books. She could recognise most of the letters. Those *ffs*, she knew now, made an *s* sound. Ssss, sssss, she went like a snake at the rain through the green panes of the casement.

She took the feather pen and the piece of old parchment she was using for practice, and wrote her name over and over again. *Elaine, Elaine, Elaine*. She thought, this would be a good time for carving if I only had my tools. She turned the parchment over and carefully drew a plump Cupid, modelling his curves on those of her son, giving him creases at the top of his belly, little angel wings. His face had the sly look of an older boy. 'But he's blind,' she whispered.

'I have to go now, sir,' Elaine said, fastening her shift and her bodice.

Sir Richard wiped a little dribble of milk from the corner of his mouth. 'Is it still raining?' he asked.

'That's why the light is so grey this evening.'

'Take a shawl.' He wriggled up the pillows a bit and unfolded his fist. 'Here's the key to Ann's chest.'

'I can't take anything of your wife's, sir.'

'She would want you to have a shawl, in order to thank you for your kindness to me.'

'Mistress Phillis will say I stole it.'

'Don't worry about her. She is in no position to accuse you when the odds are that she stole Ann's blue shawl. Though I will have to check that Ysabelle didn't take it. You need a shawl. Giving you one is in my own interest; I don't want you to catch a chill. How would you care for me then?'

'The damp won't hurt me, sir. I'm used to it.'

'Ann has a purple woollen shawl. It is plain, but it would suit you well, with your blue eyes.'

'Sir, I'd prefer not.'

'I command it.'

Elaine was walking tall and proud through the forest, the purple shawl over her head and shoulders, the points of the fine fabric flowing below her knees. The wool prickled her cheeks, kept her shoulders dry and warm. How grand she felt, like a lady. But she had to clutch the shawl in place under her chin, as she didn't have a pin.

Where the track started to dip she stepped up on the mossy bank; the moss was soft, like a sponge beneath her bare feet, a bit slippery. She jumped down from the bank and mud squelched between her toes, spattered the hem of her skirt. But she didn't care, all she wanted to do was to stare at her reflection in a big puddle, see what she looked like. The surface of the water was fuzzy with the circles made by the falling rain, she couldn't see herself well, she had to hitch up her skirt and step right into the puddle, the cool water washing almost up to her ankles, but her one thought was, *how good I look, how good* – and she stretched her arms wide so the shawl slipped off her head, and she gripped the edges so the shawl was like angel wings, and she ran, flapping her arms, up the other side of the dip in the track, over the top and down into another dip and up again, but she wasn't a bird, however much she flapped she didn't take off. She ran and ran until she was out of breath and then she started laughing, got a fit of the giggles and collapsed on a tree root, couldn't stop laughing.

It was so good. She felt as if she hadn't laughed like this for years. I just wish there was someone to share the joke with, she thought, wrapping the shawl tight around her, dead leaves and twigs caught up in the fine fabric.

She didn't go up to Thomas's grave.

Walter Vernon was not out watching for her. You're a fine-weather suitor, she thought scornfully, afraid to brave a drop of rain.

Margery scowled *Late again* and *Where'd you get that shawl?* at her, but she just grinned and whirled Samuel up in her arms and didn't bother to feed him straight away, but danced with him out of the village – there was no-one outdoors, they were all sheltering in their cottages, eating bacon dumplings and stew, the smoke from the chimneys hanging low in the lane. Samuel, startled by her behaviour, forgot to howl, and she whispered in the curl of his ear of the clothes she would buy, the silken sleeves and velvet skirts, when she'd made her fortune. The fine house they would live in, with a scarlet carpet on the table and a painting of Noah's ark on the ceiling above his bed – 'No, sweetheart, this is what I'll do, I'll carve an oak ceiling in panels and colour it red, green, blue and yellow, Noah's Ark and the flood waters with waves like the sea, and Mount Ararat and the dove on the top, the olive branch in its beak …' Samuel remembered to howl and she put him to her breast, wrapped the shawl round to support him and keep them both dry – 'I'll carve Noah's animals, like on the cradle I carved for you before you were born, sweetheart, that I had to sell, but better, you can tell me what you want, dragons and lambs and eagles and kittens – ' but she was disheartened by the memory of the cradle, her distress at having to sell it to Rosamund, what a waste of effort it had been, and she said, 'No, I'll do something new, I'll carve you a wheatfield, a flock of sheep, a herd of fine pigs being driven to market, downy hens with round eggs, we'll have a henhouse, and eggs for breakfast every day – '

Rain had seeped through the roof of their house on the hill. The bedding was damp. Elaine put the baby down on the floor and knotted the shawl which was soaked through from the rafters to dry – if the rain ever ceased. She shivered, chill to her bones now she'd stopped. Her hopes and dreams for the future evaporated. 'It's all make-believe, Samuel,' she said. 'That's all it is.' If only she had got some dry firewood here. And some food. In her elation over being given the shawl she had forgotten to bring bread, cake or cheese home from the kitchen at Cymberie. She hung up her wet skirt, lay on the drier side of the bed with the baby held tight against her for warmth.

5

Elaine stood in front of the plain plank door of Walter Vernon's house. Samuel, fed, washed, his hair finger-combed, was in her arms. The purple shawl was around her shoulders.

She hesitated. It was very neat, the house, the plaster and the timber frame lime-washed, the earth around it raked, the unglazed mullions sharply diamond-cut. On each side of the door grew thorny rose bushes, trimly pruned, but this late in the summer there were no flowers on them. The evening sun fell in over the tops of the apple trees and turned everything to gold.

'What do you think?' Elaine whispered in Samuel's ear. 'It's the stuff of dreams, isn't it? Look at that roof. It's made of pantiles, not thatch. Think how nice that would be, sweetheart, a house that's dry the whole year round, just imagine, poppet. And it's got a great chimney, so there must be a fireplace by which we can keep warm all winter long – it's worth it, don't you think? Last winter in the round house – you were too small to remember that, my darling. So cold it was. C-c-c-cold, my sweet heart.' She hugged him tight. 'I did my best to keep you warm, my dear.'

She stepped up on the stone step and knocked gently on the door. 'He hasn't got glass in the windows, poppet, but we can manage well without that, can't we? He does have shutters that we can close against the north wind and the snow. And see, his shop is here on the premises. You'll be able to help him there in the evenings when you come home from school, Sam, as soon as you are big enough, I'm sure you'll be an excellent mathematician in no time at all.' He'll be educated, he'll know how much to charge, what change to give, she thought. He will have a father, Walter Vernon will be a father to him as he said he would. All boys need a father as they grow up, they need a man to discipline them and set them an example. Sam will have an education and I won't have to worry about my debts because when Walter marries me he will become legally responsible for them. He'll come to some sort of arrangement with Mistress Margery. The debts won't be my problem any more, she thought. The only trouble is, I don't want to marry him.

She drew out a 'no' on the step with her toes, shifted Samuel on to her left hip. 'I'm not really afraid, Sammy, I know this is the best thing to do. I'll say to him, I've come to give you the answer to your question, and I'll kiss him on the mouth, straight away, like that, plonk, then he'll kiss me back, and we'll go and find a witness and plight our troth in front of him. That's all it takes to get legally married, sweetheart, it's as simple as that. No need to mess about with the church. In half an hour your future will be secure.' She knocked harder on the door.

An old woman opened it almost at once: she was stooped and all in black, gap-toothed, hair hidden under a close-fitting black cap. 'Shop's shut,' she snapped, and slammed the door.

Elaine didn't know what to do. I can't just leave, she thought, not when this is so important, and she knocked again. The door swung open, the woman peered around the edge. 'You still here? What d'you want?'

'Please, mistress, is Master Walter Vernon in?'

'What d'you want him for?'

'I'd like a word with him, if you please.'

The woman glared at her fiercely, then turned back into the house and yelled, 'Walter! Here!'

'Coming, Mother!' And from the shadows inside the house stumbled Walter Vernon. He'd taken off his ruff and undone the top buttons of his doublet, his stockings fell wrinkled around his ankles; he was obviously relaxing for the evening. He stooped to tug at one stocking ineffectually, went to lift his hat and realised he hadn't got it on. His straight mousey hair fell lank to his drooping shoulders. 'Mistress Elaine,' he muttered. 'I wasn't expecting you.'

'I – I was just passing by,' she lied.

'That's no reason to interrupt good folk's peace and quiet,' snapped his mother.

'You – you asked me a question the other day, Mr Vernon.'

'A qu-question?' He ran his hand desperately through his hair, making it stand on end. He was shaking his head at her.

She was perplexed, didn't know what to do. But she had worked so hard at screwing her courage up to this point that she couldn't back out. 'You asked me to marry you, sir.'

'Him marry you, you brazen hussy?' shrieked his mother. 'You're all the same, you filthy money-grubbing girls. Marry you indeed! My Walter'll do nothing of the sort. He's the son of a saint, his father was burnt at the stake. He's destined for greater things.' She stepped over the door step, peering short-sightedly. 'You're that filthy murderer's widow, aren't you, from up north? My God, I wouldn't share a house with you if you paid me ten shillings a week! I'd never know if I'd be alive to wake up in the morning. Get out of here right now!' And she slammed the door fiercely.

Crows rose cawing from the trees. Startled by the noise, Samuel began to cry. 'Sssh,' said Elaine, 'sssh. Be quiet.' She jogged him up and down in her arms. She didn't move from the doorstep; she couldn't believe what had happened, she was sure Walter must return and open the door to her.

But he didn't. He didn't even argue with his mother; she would surely have heard his voice if he had been arguing. The house exhaled a bitter silence through the unglazed window bars.

She bit her lip, raised her hand to knock on the door again, stopped herself. What should she do? She didn't know. She'd had this scheme for their future fixed in her head, she felt blank and confused now.

In the end she just turned away and headed back up to her house on the hill. What else could she do? Tears of humiliation stung her eyes; but soon she was walking more easily than she had in days, she felt as if a great weight had lifted from her shoulders, her body was two stone lighter, she was floating on air, she had wings on her heels. 'We wouldn't marry Walter Vernon if he was the last man on Earth, would we, poppet?' she said, cuddling Samuel tight, swinging round and round with him in her arms.

Walter stepped away from his mother into the shuttered dark of his shop. All around him was the warmth of wax, the sweetness of honey. He stood with the tip of a finger on one side of the scales on his counter. He pushed down, watched the other side rise up.

In one bowl he placed his filial duty to his mother and his dead father, in the other his moral duty to Thomas Fisher's widow. What was it that Christ said, in the English translation of the New Testament locked in a chest under his bed? Leave your father and mother and follow me, was that right?

When he took his finger away the bowls of the scales came to rest level and even. But he knew that such a compromise wasn't possible for him; he had to choose one side or the other. He fell on his knees on the earth floor and tried to pray for guidance, his forehead against the oak of the counter. 'Oh, Lord,' he said. But all that came into his head was the terrible scene in the ale-house with the stranger who was known to be out hunting down Puritans lying there dead. A knife in his belly. Blood everywhere. Men crowding over him: the glisten of wet eyes, stubbled faces shiny with sweat in the weak taperlight. The stink of blood and of ale. Stickiness on his hands and his cuffs. The click of the latch as the door opened and another stranger came in.

Blood on his jerkin that his mother had washed out.

6

I am an arrow, Elaine thought, striding to work at Cymberie along the crest of the low hills, forest to each side, farmland visible between the tree tops. I am an arrow, I am a ball in mid-flight. Unanchored, in transit between home and work. For this brief moment I am just myself, independent of the people I have left, independent of the people I am going to. I exist without any purpose. I am self-contained; an island. I am on a journey. I am accountable to no-one, I owe no-one anything, I have no duty to anyone, I love no-one, I am frightened of no-one, I am just myself. I am free.

She stretched out her arms in the sun and began to run, relishing her freedom.

'Show me, please, sir. I want to write *Thomas*,' Elaine said. Sir Richard was seated in his black woollen gown in the armchair by the open casement; she was kneeling beside him. It was another still day, the sky hazy, the heat comfortable to his old bones.

'You work it out. What do you think the first letter is?'

She put her tongue to the front of her mouth. 'Tuh,' she said, and wrote it.

'No, the capital form,' he said, and she wrote T.

'O,' she said, 'as in lop, and swan, and mop.' She concentrated hard, mapping out the two semicircles of the open sound, linking them together.

'*Em*,' said Richard. 'Do you remember how that goes?'

'Like waves on the river in the wind,' she said.

'Write it then.'

'*Uss*. How do you make that sound?'

'Think. Analyse it.'

'A *u* and an *s*?'

'*A* not *u*. Show me. That's right. Who is this Thomas?'

She sat back on her heels, hitched her hair back behind her ears. 'He died,' she said. 'He was my baby's father.'

'You were married?'

'Yes.'

'You never told me before that you were a widow, Elaine.'

She didn't want to talk about herself. She gazed down at the floorboards; noticed a knot in one like an eye. She imagined it was a giant's eye, watching her from the past, watching her from the day the oak had been felled. It knew all about her.

'I should have guessed,' he said.

She put the parchment down on top of the eye so it couldn't see her any more.

'We have this thing in common,' he said. 'You have lost your husband, I my wife.' He put his hand on hers.

She pulled it away. She said, 'Let me read to you now.'

'Shall I find you a new husband?'

'No.'

'It would make life easier for you.'

'I don't want one.'

'Nor I a new wife.' He was crying, tears on his cheeks.

She couldn't comfort him in this. 'Listen,' she said, picking up the book beside her. 'This is the story of the Americas. *In the south, it is said, in the region of the high-peaked mountains lies a great city the walls of which are built entirely of gold. The city is so high that it is always surrounded by cloud: otherwise the flash of the sun on the gold walls would blind you. It is guarded by dragons with great wings, the bones of which rattle as they fly, making a deafening sound – '* She read slowly, remembering and interpreting the letters, putting them together to make sense, enunciating the words with great care. She concentrated hard so that the things she didn't want to remember slid out of her mind.

Reading made her head ache, but it felt good, as if she were stretching muscles inside her brain that she hadn't used before. When she had first started carving it had been the muscles in the backs of her hands that had ached, her head had felt newly alive. Invigorated; almost reborn, as if carving were a new life. Perhaps that was what learning was: putting on layers of possibilities, layers of new lives, as if they were clothes, enriching yourself. Bodices of knowledge, pearled ruffs of delight. She yawned suddenly, widely, unexpectedly.

'You are tired?' He was sometimes so attentive to her.

'No.' She began to read again. '*In the forests roam creatures that are half bird, half cat, with hooked beaks and golden eyes as wide as goblets, feathers black as night.'*

Through the open window came the clicking sound of hoes scraping on stones. Now he could walk a little, Richard had glanced outside. Three days ago he had seen how the formal garden he designed had been left to go wild, and he'd summoned Glascocke the head gardener who came in grovelling, stinking of sour ale, twisting his hands together. The old man raged at him: is this how you behave the minute my back's turned? You have a job you're paid to do, man, get on with it or I'll dispense with your services. *My wife*, Glascocke had pleaded, *she's ill, I have to look after her.* A pox on your wife, Richard had said; get on with your job or you and your wife will both be sleeping under the stars. Glascocke was down there in the garden now with two underlings, they were hoeing the grass and weeds from between the stones, rhythmically, scraping back, lifting the hoe forward, scraping back, backs aching, sweat dripping from their red and weathered faces – and Elaine knew she belonged with them, she was less than them, she was a murderer's widow, she didn't belong in this fine cool room with the books she loved with the words that conjured up new ideas, that carried her to strange places –

'*Parrots of jewel colours dwell in the emerald jungles; they are reputed to live for more than a hundred years.* That parrot – ' she said, and stopped.

'Show me,' said Sir Richard.

'What?'

'Show me the word you can't decipher.'

'I was thinking of the parrot in the portrait.'

'What portrait?'

'The portrait of your family downstairs.'

'What about it?'

'Is the parrot in it still alive?'

'Ysabelle took it when Ann died.'

Ysabelle was his daughter, Elaine knew. She lived in Wales, twelve days' travel away, in a draughty stone castle with her seven daughters and her red-bearded husband Bryan who was very quick with a battle-axe, to the peril of his neighbours' goods.

Shoosh, shoosh went the birch brush on the stones outside. Elaine stood up to look. 'They are sweeping up the weeds,' she said. 'The garden's looking much better.'

'Have they filled the lake?'

'It is part full from the rain. They've scrubbed the bird lime off the statue.'

'Soon I'll be able to go outside again.'

'The stairs – 'The stairs would be like a great mountain to the sick man.

There was a long silence. Then he said, 'I wonder if

Gabriel has seen that city, the one you read about, the one with the golden walls.'

'He is sailing in the Americas?'

'He didn't take anything when he left. Just his own things. Nothing of Ann's, nothing of mine. I tried to give him a fine compass that I have. He wouldn't take it. He held me to blame, you see, for the accident, he thought I should have prevented his mother from riding Durendal, he thought I should have stopped her from jumping that hedge.' His eyes glistened with tears.

She touched his hand with hers. He turned his hand over and clasped it. 'I'm an old fool,' he said. 'I need to sleep.'

She sat by him while he slept. If I was an arrow in flight on my way here, she thought, now I am an arrow that has reached its target and is at rest. A target stuffed with thorns. I can't ever forget this man beside me was the judge who condemned Thomas to death.

I'm living an illusion, I'm pretending this is truly a soft target, a straw butt, a safe landing here on these three mattresses piled on top of each other on the greatest bed in this rich house with its carvings, portraits and books, its paintings, silver and carpets. Nothing to do at this moment but sit here. What could be better? What could be more comfortable?

I am no longer an island. I belong with other people; I fit into a pattern of giving and taking, of dependency and support. People – islands spinning together, like cogs in a clock, so that Cymberie can function. Grating against each other, sometimes. Sir Richard the axis, the axle on which we all revolve. How dependent I am on him, for food without which Samuel and I couldn't survive; for the expectation of being able to escape the debt-trap I've found myself caught in; for the hope that one day

I'll be able to live the sort of life I want to. Making my living by carving. I don't think I could live without hope. When hope's gone, what's left?

His teaching me to read – that's making my life richer, opening up future possibilities for me.

She looked down at the sleeping man, his grey head on the white pillow beside her: his gentle breathing. Easy now, soft and regular; not as it was when she first came. There was a wisp of colour in his cheeks. She felt she ought to hate him for Thomas's sake. She shouldn't feel compassion for him, or gratitude to him. She shouldn't feel a sense of triumph at his slow continuing recovery. She touched his cracked lips with her little finger, but he didn't stir. You've depended on me for your survival, she thought, just as I do on you. I don't know what use I am to you now. Do you still need my milk? I say you do but I doubt it.

How lonely you are. You refuse to see your friends. There are few other people you can trust. Glascocke and Mistress Phillis, they have treated you as if you were dead already. Master Nathaniel is fine. He is loyal. He has gone to his parents' house today but he has left a stew cooking for you. I will go down and fetch it when you wake.

Yet when you seemed about to die even Master Nathaniel laid a bet on the time of your death, with the others. No loyalty is complete.

She had decreed that Sir Richard was fit enough to sit up for meals now. Joseph Chibborne the carpenter had made a small trestle table from chestnut wood, which stood against the wall. He had finished it only yesterday and the newly-cut wood smelled good. She stooped to sniff it: her hands itched to hold a carving chisel again. Joe Chibborne was one of those men who used to come to the chamber, pull up a stool and sit watching her nursing his master when his life hung on a thread

She pulled the table over in front of one of the casements, set the armchair by it so that Sir Richard would be able to look out and see the oaks that grew beyond the garden. What a massive, heavy green they were; a few yellow leaves at the top because it was the end of August now. That made seven weeks that she had been coming here; how much longer could this continue? She dreaded the time that must surely come soon, when Sir Richard would no longer need her, when she would have to resume her former life. How would she make money then? If only Thomas hadn't sold his chisels …

The thought of leaving Cymberie terrified her: she loved its order and security.

The gardeners had gone. The neat paths, the lake with its statue, the knot of box hedges, the lavender borders lay quiet. A bonfire of heaped weeds drizzled upward smoke. Robins pecked the disturbed earth between stones, searching for worms.

She placed a silver plate and a goblet on the table, his knife at the right, and went down to the kitchen. Her hand caressed the banister; her eyes scanned the now so-familiar wall paintings that she loved for the odd details that perhaps no one else had seen: the mating rabbits half-hidden by a bush, the hound running away from a shouting cook to a bitch with puppies, a loaf in his jaws; the golden-haired woman playing the virginals while a boy in the hunting scene above lay on his belly to drop a spider between her breasts.

The kitchen was empty, the oak table scrubbed and bare, the log fire ashy. The yellow sun fell in the cobbled yard outside. A dog dozed in its warmth, flat out on his side. On one of the windowledges a ginger cat snoozed. In the stables a mare whinnied. Doves pecked between the stones; maybe someone had thrown breadcrumbs out for them. Or maybe they were searching for small insects. Ants. Did doves eat ants? Ants would relish the warmth of the stones. On an afternoon like this the winged ants, the males and the young queens, would swarm up from their nests and take flight. Dark wings in the air. Clouds of them.

A wasp buzzed in through the window, settled on the table, probed at the boards. Perhaps there was a scrap of honey there, not wiped away after Nathaniel's last cooking session. Elaine turned the tap on the ale barrel and filled a jug, relishing the warm malt-and-spice smell, blew hard at the wasp which had settled on the lip; it flitted off and sucked the drops that had fallen on the flagstones. I must have a word with Joe Chibborne, Elaine thought, tell him we need a new tap for this cask, one that doesn't drip. I can't think why Nathaniel hasn't mentioned it to him.

She lifted the top off the hay box and using a cloth took out the lidded iron pot, couched in the crook of her left arm. Carrying the jug of ale and a ladle in her right hand, she climbed the stairs to Sir Richard's room, the heat of the pot seeping through the thick fabric. She set down the jug on the table; folded the cloth to form a mat under the pot.

'Elaine?' said Sir Richard, stirring. 'Is that you?'

'Your dinner is nearly ready, sir,' she said. 'I just have to fetch the bread and custard.'

When she came back he was sitting up in bed. 'There are strawberries too,' she said. 'Harry Tuck sent them over. His servant says they are the last in his garden. And he said that his master is pleased to hear that you are recovering, and wonders if you are yet well enough to see him.'

'Oh, Harry be damned. Why can't he leave me alone? Help me, Elaine.' She held his gown for him while he slid in his arms, supported him as he crossed the room. He was looking pleased with himself. 'I am getting stronger, though,' he said. 'Give me those strawberries. Damned fine fruit he grows.'

She set the bread at his right hand. She lifted the lid of the pot and ladled a portion of stew on his plate. 'Tear me some bread,' he said. Then as she turned to leave he reached out and gripped her wrist. 'Don't go,' he said. 'Eat with me.'

'Sir?'

'Get yourself a plate from the court cupboard. Pull up a stool and sit with me. I have never liked eating on my own. Take what you want, I have enough.'

He released her and she spooned a ladleful of stew on her plate. She tore off a chunk of bread and dipped it in the sauce, let it absorb the liquid and lifted it, sodden, to her mouth, with her finger scooped up the drip that ran down her chin.

'Nathaniel is a good cook,' he said.

'Yes.'

'Here, have a strawberry.'

'Thank you.'

'Where do you usually eat?'

'In the garden.'

'There is plenty here for both of us.'

She perched nervously on the edge of the stool, with her knife cut a chunk of meat, lifted it to her mouth folded in the bread. She felt awkward, uncomfortable. This wasn't where she belonged: not eating face to face with her master.

'I haven't dined alone with a woman for so long,' he said.

Elaine was silent. I am just a servant, she thought.

'You need to dress better,' he said. 'You could wear a more becoming bodice. You are not an old woman yet.'

'I dress as is right for my station, sir.'

'You always wear the same skirt.'

She looked down at her plate.

'Do you have just the one skirt, Elaine?'

That was no affair of his. 'I keep myself clean, sir.'

He watched her; she kept her eyes lowered. 'Where are you from, Elaine?'

'I don't belong in this village.'

'Do they make things difficult for you, because you're a stranger?'

She lifted her head; turned to look out of the window. 'Your garden looks good now, sir, have you seen?'

'You don't ever talk about yourself, Elaine.'

'It's not what I'm paid for, sir.'

'If I give you two shillings, will you tell me your life story?'

She hesitated. Two shillings would be very useful. Then she said, 'No sir.' She couldn't. If she were to tell him about herself, about what had happened to her, she would have to admit to herself that frightening dichotomy, that dual identity Sir Richard held in her life: on the one hand, the generous solitary widower whose life she had saved, who provided her with an ordered existence and taught her to read, and on the other the arrogant, merciless judge in a gown trimmed with dead beavers, who had ordered her innocent husband to be hanged. She needed to keep the two Richards separate in her head; she could not accept that they were the same person or she would go mad. She said, 'I can tell how much better you are feeling by the way you are beginning to be interested in things outside of yourself.'

'What do you need to hide from me, Elaine?'

'Eat the last of the strawberries, sir.'

'I could have you tortured until you tell me.'

She stared at him: was he serious? His face was straight, but she couldn't believe he meant it.

'I could have your fingernails pulled out one by one, I could have you whipped with an iron scourge.'

'Would you like another spoonful of custard, sir?'

He picked up his spoon, tasted a spoontip-ful, nodded. 'I'm so glad Ann appointed Nathaniel cook – he makes custard like no other man – smooth and cool in your throat – it slips down so easily –' He was getting tired. He leaned back in his chair, closed his eyes.

She took the spoon from his hand and fed him. Every time she touched his bottom lip with the spoon he opened his mouth and swallowed. 'You're like a baby bird, sir,' she said.

He opened his eyes. 'You don't see me as a torturer then, Elaine?'

She couldn't help smiling at him. Then she clinked the spoon against the empty bowl. 'Now for the final course,' she said.

'What's that?'

'Sweetmeat of fried rat and toad's piss.'

He grinned at her. 'I know what's due to me,' he said. 'I know what the last course is.'

He went back to bed for this. It was the most comfortable place. She soaped her breasts, rinsed them in the tepid water in the silver bowl, settled beside him, pulled his head toward her. 'This is ridiculous now, you know,' he protested.

'It's effective, sir. It's making you better.'

Late in the afternoon he took off the ornate key that he wore now on a blue cord round his neck and put it in the palm of her hand. She frowned at it. 'It's the key to Lady Ann's chest,' he said.

'I know it is.'

'Open it, will you.'

She got off the bed and knelt on the bare boards, undid

the padlock and lifted the heavy lid, smelled again the orange peel and elecampane roots.

'Right at the bottom it'll be,' he said. 'It must be twenty-seven years since Ann last wore it. She put on weight after Gabriel was born, it never fitted her again. She was slim as you when we married. Maybe not quite so thin.'

She waited for him to say more, but he didn't. 'What is it you want me to look for, sir?'

'It's a turquoise silk bodice embroidered with wide-open pink roses: the stamens are tipped with pearls. Green stems twine up the front. She wore it with green sleeves. I loved her in it –'

She found and unfolded the boned and quilted, heavily embroidered fabric. It was creased, smelled stale, needed to air. He wanted her to put it on. She took off her own bodice, laced this one over her shift. It fitted perfectly.

'Her shift was lower cut,' he said. 'I could see her breasts.'

She hadn't pinned sleeves into the bodice and the coarse linen arms of her shift, with the elbows worn thin, were exposed.

'Get some sleeves,' he said abruptly, as if he were disturbed by the sight.

She pinned in an orange pair, quite roughly, not with the pins close together as they ought to be. He must be remembering his wife wearing this, she thought.

'That's good,' he said. 'It looks fine with that plain skirt.'

'Too fine for me.' She started to unlace the bodice.

'What are you doing?'

'I'm taking it off.'

'Why?'

'So I can put it away.'

'Why do you want to put it away?'

'What do you mean?'

'It's a gift. I want you to have it.'

'No. That wouldn't be right.' She looked down at herself, stroked the shimmering fabric, admired the colours that in the darkness of the chest hadn't faded, touched the pearls. 'Are these real, sir?'

'Would I give you real pearls?'

She didn't know the answer. She was perplexed; she didn't understand why he wanted her to have this. 'Why, sir?'

'What use is the bodice to a dead woman? Much better that you should wear it.'

'I love it, sir, but –'

'Close the chest and lock it. Give me the key.'

Elaine stood still in the beautiful bodice, toes clinging to the bare floorboards, her hair a dark fuzz around her head. She was clutching at a bedpost because she felt so insecure. The slam of the chest lid, the click of the padlock had tipped the balance of her relationship with Sir Richard, had cast her on a foreign shore where the old constraints were gone and anything might happen. For him to give her something that his dead wife wore at her age: what could that mean?

'Come here,' he said.

Then he took her right hand and kissed the tip of every finger.

'No,' she said. One thing that had disturbed her about nursing him was the way it occasionally made her body yearn for the pleasures of marriage. She had defined it as *missing Thomas*. Sometimes it had made her belly ache with longing, made her go all moist inside. She had tried to pretend it didn't happen. Now it was happening again –

'I can do anything with you,' he said.

'No,' she said. 'No, I'm not your possession.' She bowed

her head, fumbled with the lacing of the bodice with clumsy fingers. The bow was knotted, she tugged at the ends, it was getting tighter, it was so awkward, she had to get this loop undone.

'Please,' he said, his voice anguished.

She was startled, looked up to see that he was crying, his face was wet with soundless tears. 'Oh don't,' she said, and grabbed the linen towel she used to pat dry her breasts, thrust it at him. He mopped his face. She finished wriggling out of the bodice, laid it neatly on top of the chest, stooped to stroke the bright lustrous silk of it, then turned and pulled on her own worn patched thing. How shabby it felt after Lady Ann's beautiful effort.

He was watching her. 'Elaine,' he said, 'Ann made that bodice herself. Before we were married. She wore it on our wedding day. It took her months to make it. She sat in her cold Northumbrian castle by a window overlooking the sea, sewing her neat stitches in the eastern morning light, spiking the stems in the westward garden in the late afternoon, adding the pearls by candlelight.'

'Ysabelle,' she said. 'Your daughter, wouldn't she...?'

'Ysabelle can't wear it, she's vast and in a perpetual state of increase. After seven babies –'

'Gabriel,' she said.

'He doesn't have a wife.'

'But he will marry.'

'Why? He can have as many women as he wants without. I don't want one of his whores to have Ann's work. I'd rather you had it. Count it as my thanks for your care.'

How businesslike Sir Richard was now, how rational. She felt a fool for having misinterpreted. 'I –'

'Take it.'

'Are the pearls real?'

'Of course not. They're only beads. The garment has no intrinsic value.'

'Then thank you, sir. It will give me great pleasure to wear it.'

'Let me see you in it again before you go.'

She didn't look back when she left him for the night; didn't see that he was crying once more.

She wore the bodice as she walked home across the common. She was a speck of pink and turquoise brightness flitting through the green monotony of the woods, a butterfly. The colour energised her, it made her feet light and dance, the richness of the fabric empowered her, the bones dug into her belly so she had to stand straight like a lady. 'Lady Elaine,' she said, standing tall on tiptoes, arms stretched out to the sides as if she were balancing on a tightrope.

She met a merchant with a packhorse who doffed his hat to her; she met a pedlar who carried his goods on a yoke who begged her to buy; she stepped out of her way to where woodcutters coppicing chestnut trees were taking a break in their rough shelter thatched with leaves; they offered her beer and she tipped back her head and drank from the pitcher; one of them put his arm around her and she kissed him on the lips and released herself, laughing. It was good to feel desirable again. To feel a young man's stubble prick your cheek.

She went to the churchyard to show Thomas her bodice. She stood at the foot of his grave. 'Look, Thomas,' she said. 'Isn't it pretty?'

Then sharp in her head came the image of Thomas's body being tossed half-naked into his grave. 'My lovely Thomas,' she cried, thinking then of him lying beside her in their bed when they were first married, her snuggling up to his warm side, caressing him, waking him, rousing him, him stroking her belly, sliding himself into her. Such utter fullness and completion. Utter contentment.

Then the bodice tripped another memory into her head, from the time when they were walking south side by side; it was a gibbet on a lonely stretch of moorland; a chain creaked, a rope slapped against wood in the wind. There was a figure clothed entirely in a hooded gown of black feathers. 'Think how warm it must be, a feather gown like that,' she said to Thomas. 'Do you think it's silk-lined? Shall I gather feathers and make you one?' She had been naïve, she didn't realise what it was. Thomas tried to strike out across the moorland, but the ground was boggy, they had had no choice but to keep to the stone path and walk right by. As they drew close the feathers flapped up in a black cloud that wheeled overhead, cutting out the sunlight, cawing: they were crows. And on the gibbet was what remained of a hanged man, gobbets of flesh hanging from his bones, entrails dangling – foxes and wild dogs had leapt up and torn at his feet, his legs and his belly, hawks had pecked out his eyes. 'Don't look,' Thomas had said, and walked between her and the gruesome, stinking sight.

And now, she thought, what remains of you, Thomas, my dear love? Worms burrow between your ribs, earthworms twine through the bones of your hands that were so strong, and held me. Hands that carved, that built a house. Dust fills your skull in which once your brain was lodged. Ants nest in it, perhaps, their busy-ness a mockery of all your thoughts that throbbed there. Thomas –

It's my fault you died, Thomas. I could have done something. What I did, it wasn't right, falling on my knees in front of Sir Richard like that as he left the courtroom, clutching at his legs, getting in his way, sobbing, weeping. His gown fell around me so I was suffocating inside its lining of slaughtered beavers. He swore at me. His harsh voice. Someone kicked me aside. What I did, it wasn't the right thing to do. I needed to do something else. I needed to be rational. Sir Richard, when you know him, Thomas, he's not unreasonable, he's a nice man …

All of a sudden hatred filled her, hatred for Lady Ann's beautiful bodice because she didn't know how else to define what she hated, she tore at its laces, she struggled out of it, she crumpled it and hurled it in the hedge, a kind of gaudy silken flower it stuck there among the prickles, stemless, to fade in due course in the sunlight and the rain. She turned away and pulled on her own worn, patched bodice, hating herself too for wanting to be pretty and admired and carefree.

And then she stepped away from Thomas's grave. She went up to the hedge and painstakingly unpicked the silk garment from the thorns. A few threads were pulled, in spite of all her care; she sat on the grass and smoothed the fabric over her knee, persuading the caught threads back into place the best that she could. She folded it neatly, lengthways, and tucked it out of sight inside her own bodice, so that it was held up by the waistband of her skirt. Just to know that it was hidden there gave her courage and reassurance; she had another self she could put on if she wanted to. There can be happiness, she thought. There is a future.

Back at the round house on the hill, she laid Samuel on the bed and picked up a stick. 'We can't forget your father, sweetheart,' she said. 'Look, I can write his name.' She scraped *T h o m a s* into the gravel floor, concentrating, tongue between her teeth, taking care to form each letter right. She went outside and scored the letters of her husband's name deep into the sandy soil that lay beneath the gravel. *T h o m a s*. I'll always care about you, Thomas, she thought defiantly. I'll avenge the injustice of your hanging. I swear this. I swear it to you.

The low sun that had filtered through the cloud filled up the letters of his name with shadow.

Samuel started to scream. She put him to her breast but he pushed away. He fought against her; he wanted a cup of cow's milk, like he had at Mistress Margery's. No, Samuel, drink properly, she said, there's a good boy. Don't be so lazy. She sat down on the bed in the half dark and held the back of his head firmly in her right hand, forced her nipple into his mouth with her left. He latched on this time and began to drink greedily. She could feel his teeth now. Soon she would have to wean him. She dreaded the loss of that intimacy, his dependency on her. 'Everything changes, Thomas,' she said out loud. 'Nothing ever stays the same.'

Sir Richard stood alone at the top of the stairs. It was past midnight and he wasn't carrying a candle, but enough indirect moonlight came through the tall narrow windows either side of the entrance door for him to see well what he was doing.

Silence from the closed doors behind him. The whole of Cymberie, apart from himself, was asleep.

The stairs fell below him. The height of them made him dizzy; he was perched at the top of a cliff, he was on the topmost branch of a great tree. He wished he had a better sense of balance. His illness had left him with the constant feeling, when he was on his feet, that he was swimming, or flying, or falling. 'I will get better,' he whispered.

He slumped down on the top step, clung to the banisters. He said out loud, 'I am Richard Brullant Belvoir, knight, master of Cymberie.' His illness had stripped him of his identity, it had made him a shadow of himself. When he had found himself weeping when he saw that girl in Ann's bodice he had realised how much mental strength he had lost. 'Ann, I'm not a maudlin old fool,' he said out loud. He had said, in the cobbled yard at the back of Cymberie, 'You're not riding Durendal,' and she had laughed and bent forward to stroke the great stallion's neck. She was forty-three but her hair was still fiery red, she was slim as a girl and her skin was white without benefit of ceruse; he'd still adored her. 'You try and stop me,' she'd said, and dug her heels into Durendal's flanks. He'd sprung away, a chestnut streak, tail like a flag, off at a gallop, veering into the deer park across the late winter grass. She had been riding astride like a man, she wore spurs on her boots, her skirt billowed. The sheer exhilaration of that moment had repeated itself over again and over again in his head; as had the desolation of finding her with her neck broken the far side of Stony Field hedge. Her head at that terrible slant, her body curved like a comma. The great horse had been waiting for her to get up, tramping the soft ground with his iron hooves, breath misting the cold air, saddle empty and reins trailing.

'You killed my mother,' Gabriel had accused him, standing in the hall thin and straight, his handsome face pinched with grief, two thin panniers of his belongings at his feet.

Just down there by the front door was where he had stood. When Richard closed his eyes he could see his only son whom he loved and admired and respected, whose exploits with women made him laugh. He was wearing his court clothes, his black and white doublet and stockings embroidered with spangles, a velvet hat with a tall green feather, leather gloves, a short cloak lined with fur. He was looking at his father with intense hatred in his eyes.

Don't go to sea, Gabriel, Richard had been begging in his head, with his whole heart; I'll give you anything you want if only you'll stay. You can have all of my land, you can have Cymberie. Just stay. Please. But he hadn't said one word aloud. He had just stood there, proud and silent, in the hall. Wondering if Gabriel could possibly be right; whether he was indeed to blame for Ann's death. Feeling the loss of his son as a second bereavement.

Gabriel had opened the door. Outside stood Durendal, caparisoned in royal blue velvet-trimmed harness and saddle, Glascocke, on foot, clasping the reins. 'Give me a hand, man,' said Gabriel, and together he and the gardener buckled Gabriel's meagre luggage on to the stallion that stood there quiet as a lamb. When he'd finished, and mounted, Gabriel had raised his hand to his father in farewell. Richard hadn't responded. Wordlessly, he had turned and stalked straight-backed to the small side chamber off the hall. His refuge.

It was there that he was going now. He couldn't do it in the daylight. Elaine would demand that Nathaniel carry him downstairs in his arms. How could she not understand how utterly demeaning it was to lose power over your legs, to have to trust one's body into the arms of another man, as if one were an infant again? Or else she would stand over him and insist, just tell me what you want and I will bring it to you. But his side chamber was sacrosanct, no-one was allowed there except Mistress Phillis on Fridays to clean it; Phillis knew she was not allowed to touch his papers, and she could not read, so his privacy was always preserved.

He longed to be human again, rather than merely alive. To busy himself with his concerns, make sure that they were going on well. There must be correspondence waiting for him, he was sure. Letters that had been put on his table because he was too ill to read them.

He slid down a stair on his bum. He was dizzy. 'Not as dizzy as by daylight,' he whispered, 'it's better in the dark,' and he slid down another step, adjusting his hold on the banisters. Thump on his bum. Another step, another. How many were there to go? This hall was so tall. The paintings were ghostly in the moonlight, the pallor of flesh glowed, faces and hands leapt out at him from the dark. Fourteen, thirteen. That boy, he had Gabriel's face: Fitzherbert had painted the boy with the sheep with Gabriel's face, how had he never noticed that before? More faces: perhaps the faces were all of people he knew. They pressed in on him, demanding, who am I? Who am I?

Glascocke was under the apple tree with a basket.

Ten, nine and now he was head-height from the floor, all he had to do was not lose his balance.

The floor tiles were cold under his feet. He hadn't thought to wear slippers, or stockings. He pulled himself upright by the newel post, clung to it as if it were a dear friend. The bottom of the hall was all in darkness, but he knew it so well, had designed it himself and had it built on the ruins of the abbey that Henry wrecked. The modern features – the octagonal entrance tower, the great windows with glass in, the magnificent chimneys – blended with the old. These beautiful tiles he had found covered in cowshit when he first came to see the place; that fellow Nabbott had thatched over this part of the ruin to use as a dairy. He soon got rid of the man. Fitzherbert had made a good job of the wall paintings. Philip Windebank hadn't been so expert with the wood-carving. He came well-recommended, but there was a coarseness about his work that didn't please. A pleasant young man, though. He had given him a letter of introduction to Alessandro in Venice, in the hope that the contact would be constructive. His and Ann's marriage bed was Italian made; now that was a nice piece of work.

His fingers touched the door in the dark, ran across the linenfold panelling to the latch and depressed it. The great hall was full of direct moonlight falling in from the south on to the long table, the wooden benches, his and Ann's armchairs at the head. The warm smell of wax rose from the polished wood, which gleamed. Silver threads glinted in the tapestry of the deer at the fountain.

And to the right was the small arched door. How well he knew this. His hands felt for the latch as if they had a memory of their own, his head ducked as he entered, his feet stepped down automatically.

This room had once been, maybe, a private chapel. It had an original, undamaged stone window in three segments, gothic-arched. The moon shone in through the leaded glass he had had fitted: the plain thick greenish panes and in the right hand section the stained glass of a shepherd holding a lamb. The shepherd had a halo and you'd have thought he was Christ if it weren't for the fact that he was in present-day doublet and hose that cast a red glow on the table immediately below.

He let go of the wall, stepped warily across the floor, let the back of the armchair take his weight. Thankfully he slid into it. It had been a marathon getting here. He was so tired. He laid his head on the table, on the pile of papers. He felt a crick in his neck, a pull at the base of his spine. He closed his eyes. His right hand fingered the feather barbs of a quill.

7

'Don't fight me, Sam. I'm sure we're late.' Elaine caught his dimpled hand and pulled it through the armhole of his shirt. 'You're growing too fast, sweetheart, that's what the problem is. Look how tight this is. I'll have to knit you some more shirts for the winter. We don't want you catching your death of cold, do we, mousekin?' She lifted Sam up and blew a raspberry on his tummy, and he got a fit of the giggles and she laughed too, tickled his chest. 'I'll tell you what we've got to do, my lovely, and that's fetch more rushes to patch the thatch. If Mister Vernon had kept to his word, we wouldn't have to, would we, poppet, we'd be living in clover in a nice watertight house and I wouldn't have to go to work and I'd be able to sit down all day knitting you fresh bellibands. We could have walked north to see my family and tell them about you and Walter. My mother'd swoon over you, she'd knit you up some shirts in a trice. She's so good at knitting. Your uncle Nicholas, my brother, he's a shepherd, he's always giving Mother baskets of wool he's gathered from the hedges. Keep still while I put on your tailclout.'

Elaine still had an overslept feeling as she wrapped her purple shawl around them both and stepped out into the morning drizzle. She knelt by the spring to drink a few handfuls of water, then hurried on. I've got to work out a plan of campaign about Walter Vernon, she was thinking, however much I don't want to marry him, he's too good a chance to miss. It's obvious he'd like to marry but he's completely under the thumb of his mother. Bad-tempered old witch. What in heaven's name did she mean about his being the son of a saint? She must be demented. I've got to find a way of getting round her.

Sam grunted and heaved and then there was a stink from his tailclout and she stopped to rinse it in the stream. 'You filthy piggy,' she said. The rain was getting heavier; she hooded the shawl over her hair and round to envelop the baby.

The church clock struck seven. It was such a dark morning, that was why she was late. And because she couldn't get to sleep for hours last night, she couldn't stop brooding on things. She couldn't stop worrying. All her fears for her future had circled endlessly, repetitively around in her head, over and over, making no sense, coming to no conclusions. She hadn't been able to control them; they had tired her out.

In at Mistress Margery's gate. No babies in the garden today; they were all indoors. In the hall, crawling on the rushes that covered the earth floor. A floppy-eared hound licked the bum of one of them. Margery had lit the fire in the hearth and was busy stirring a great cauldron of watery porridge for her charges.

Rosamund was standing there gossiping to her, jiggling her little Helen up and down in her arms. It was she who spotted Elaine first. 'Ho, look at my fine lady,' she said, 'all tarted up in her best purple shawl. Oh no, forgive my mistake, it's only that slut who lives on the hill. Mistress Elaine Fisher.'

Elaine could see trouble coming; her heart sank. Gently she kissed Samuel's curls and set him down on the floor. 'Be a good boy,' she murmured. 'I'll come for you as soon as I can.'

'Well?' demanded Rosamund.

'What do you mean?'

'Where did you get that shawl?'

'My mother wove it for me.'

'I've never seen you wearing it before.'

'I keep it for best, mostly.'

'Why are you wearing it today, then?'

'It's raining. Haven't you noticed?'

'You're lying, you are. That shawl's far too good for a girl of your sort. If it was truly yours, you'd have sold it, wouldn't you, for food? It stands to reason – it must be worth a bob or two. I bet you've stolen it from that old man at Cymberie, haven't you?'

'I'm not a thief.'

'You've tricked him out of it, then, haven't you? You sneaking creature. Big boobs on a skinny frame – there's a lot of men that fall for that. That shawl's not the only thing either, is it? Will Bartlett, he was buying a meat pie last night, and he speaks up, he says to me he's seen that woman whose husband was hanged, up on the common delicate as a fairy, all dolled up in a fancy bodice. Blue with pink flowers, a proper lady's bodice, he said it was. I've never seen you in that. I thought you'd only got your green one and that brown one you're wearing. That's all I've ever seen you in. I suppose you'll say your mother sewed that bodice for you, too.'

'I don't know any Will Bartlett.'

'Well, he knows you.'

'He's making it up.'

'Mistress Elaine,' said Margery sharply. 'If you are indeed receiving gifts from Sir Richard Belvoir, they are due to me.'

'What?'

'We agreed I'd receive all your payment for nursing the old man in settlement of your debts.'

'Not gifts, though. We never said anything about gifts. Gifts are different. They aren't pay, they're a kindness. If Sir Richard did ever give me a present, it would be mine.'

But Margery was implacable.

Elaine had no idea how to win her round. 'People give

presents as a sign of friendship,' she tried feebly.

'Sir Richard Belvoir a friend of the widow of a murderer? Is that what you're saying? You expect me to believe that? You better get this into your thick head, girl, if you get any gifts from that old man you hand them over to me immediately! Otherwise I'll get you clapped in debtors' prison and you'll never see your child any more. Give me that shawl.'

'No. It's mine.'

'Give it to me.'

'But it's raining.'

'Hand it over.'

What else could Elaine do? Her hands were slow as she unwrapped the shawl from her shoulders; it was like a second skin, a part of herself she was unpeeling, it hurt physically as she relinquished it into the older woman's rough-skinned paws. Vaguely, she was aware of Rosamund smirking in the background. She thought wearily: is the butcher's wife going to buy the shawl off Mistress Margery as soon as my back's turned? But she didn't really care. The shawl that had made her feel so good was gone for ever. It was irretrievable.

She turned away; she couldn't bear to face the pair. She touched the top of Samuel's head as she left, but he ignored her, was intent on banging a wooden spoon on a pewter plate. If only there were some justice somewhere in this world, she wished.

On the common the wind had risen. It rushed, it sang. The air was full up with the roar of it. The clouds ripped open, showed slashes of blue. Full-leaved trees tossed and creaked and swayed. Oak twigs broke off, littered the path with green, stray leaves tore and fell. Acorns pattered down like hailstones; trees shed waterdrops like giants' tears. A hump of grey cloud shot out rain that pierced Elaine's bodice and her shift and chilled her. I've got to walk faster, she thought, if I walk faster I won't get cold. But her legs were slow and leaden and her feet were heavy, mud and leaves clung to her skin, gravel pricked the soles of her feet. She had run out of courage. She was thinking: what's the point? Nothing I do can ever be of any good.

'Where've you been?' stormed Mistress Phillis. She was standing in the back doorway, yelling out into the rain. 'Why do you have to be late, girl, this morning of all mornings?'

'For heaven's sake, let me in.' Elaine was beyond caring if she upset the woman. She pushed past her, shook herself vigorously, her hair, sleeves and skirt, to dry herself out a bit.

'I didn't ask for a shower,' Phillis snapped.

'What's the matter?' Dust from the stone floor clung grittily to Elaine's wet feet; she rubbed her right sole against her left shin to clean it, glanced along the cave of the corridor to the kitchen where she could see five men, Nathaniel, Glascocke, Joseph Chibborne the carpenter and a couple of others whom she recognised by sight but whose names she didn't know. They were talking together, self-immersed, a buzz of excitement about them as though something terrible had happened. 'Sir Richard's died?' she asked.

'Worse than that,' said Phillis. 'He's gone mad. He's completely out of his mind.'

'He's nursing a pistol against his chest,' said Nathaniel.

'He's got a sword across his table,' said Joe Chibborne, 'the hilt just by his right hand. By God, its blade looks keen. As if he's been sharpening the damned thing all night.'

'I saw a dagger buckled under his gown when he shook his fists at me,' said Phillis.

'He says he'll kill us if we touch him,' said Glascocke.

'How did he get hold of the weapons?' Elaine, shivering, had wedged herself close to the fire; the back of her skirt was starting to steam. She wiped the drips from her hair from her face with her sleeve.

'He keeps them under lock and key in his side chamber,' said Joe Chibborne.

'What in heaven's name did you take him down there for, Elaine?' said Phillis. 'This is all your fault, you stupid girl!'

'Where is this side chamber?'

'You know damn well!'

'I don't. I've never even heard anyone mention it before.' Elaine's thoughts were chilled and slow, weighed down with her own problems. It was an effort to step outside herself, to focus on this new situation. Her mind was heavy; she didn't want to do it. She blinked, swallowed hard. 'Nathaniel,' she said, 'where is the master?'

'He's out of his mind, Mistress Elaine. Don't you go near him.' That was Glascocke.

'I don't believe he'll hurt me.'

'He's raving mad. He could do anything.'

'Where is he? In the room next to his chamber?'

'Downstairs. In the small room off the great hall.'

'Downstairs? How did he get there?'

'You helped him, you stupid fool.' That was Phillis.

'He won't pay any heed to us,' said Nathaniel. 'Maybe you'll be able to calm him. I've never seen him as gentle with anyone as he is with you. Not since his wife died, anyway.'

'I haven't been in here before,' Elaine said in the great hall, stopping to take in the long waxed table, the benches and tall glazed windows, the fine tapestries that trembled in the draughts.

Rain beat on the glass; outside the storm went on. There was an overcast darkness that presaged winter.

'He's in there,' Nathaniel said. He gestured at a small open door.

She stepped toward it.

'Take care. Some demon's got into his head. He's gone completely crazy.'

'Wait here for me. I'll talk to him on my own.'

'Call if you need help.'

Down the step was a small room like a chapel: a table beneath the pretty window, like an altar. It was strewn with a muddle of papers, some in heaps, some screwed up. The gleaming blade of a long sword was laid across them. The hilt was right by Richard's hand; he was in an armchair that was backed up against the wall. He was clutching a pistol close to his chest. Firearms were something she'd never come across, except in stories of knights' adventures; all she knew about them was that your adversary pulled the trigger and bang, a bullet came out and you fell down dead. She crossed herself. 'Good morning, sir,' she said cautiously.

'Get out.'

'What are you doing here?'

'Leave me alone.' He raised the pistol in the air and pointed the black hollow of the barrel at her. His hand was shaking, but his aim was centred round about the area of her heart.

She stepped forward, opening her arms, showing her hands were empty.

'For Christ's sake, get away from me!' His voice was anguished.

She came on forward.

'This pistol is loaded, Elaine.'

'I don't care.' She was suddenly, absurdly, sharply attracted by the sheer simplicity of being shot. 'Shoot me then.' For the moment she didn't care about anything or anyone. Death would end the necessity to struggle on, to fight to pay off her debt, to make her house habitable and to clothe her son. The struggle against lying, deceitful people. I won't have to make any effort any more, she thought. I can rest, she kept thinking, I can rest. She didn't think of Samuel at all, what would happen to him.

She kept walking toward Richard. She was watching his eyes, thinking his eyelids would quiver as he pulled the trigger, thinking that they would be the last thing she saw before she entered the next world. Hell or heaven, whatever.

His green eyes: they met hers steadily. She stared at the wide black pupils; the little red veins that coursed across the whites. She got closer and closer to them. They will be the end of my world, she thought.

She caught her foot in a fold of cloth. His gown. As she tripped she slammed her hands over her ears, expecting the roar of the pistol.

But there was no great sound. She had fallen somehow half-kneeling into his lap. Head against his warm belly, breathing. He must have put down his pistol; he put his two arms around her stiffly. 'Why, Elaine, why? What's the matter? Why do you want to die?'

She was sobbing. She couldn't answer.

He stroked her damp hair tenderly. 'Elaine, you too? There is so much loss in this world.' He scooped her hair aside and gently rubbed the back of her neck.

A movement in the doorway caught his eye. He looked up and saw the vast figure of Nathaniel hovering there. He reasserted himself. 'Get this bloody woman off me, man,' he said. 'Her clothes are dripping. Tell Mistress Phillis to put dry clothes on her. Then send Joseph Chibborne to me. I need him to build me a stronger cupboard in here. Things have disappeared. My dagger with the garnet sheath; there's no sign of that.'

'Yes sir.'

'Nathaniel.'

'Sir?'

'Bring me breakfast.'

Nathaniel put ale and sage, butter and bread on the long table. Sir Richard sat at the head in his armchair. 'Sit on my right,' he said to Elaine when she came back in clean starched shift, skirt and bodice, all tied round the waist with a length of thin cord because they were much too big for her. Her face was washed clean of tearstains; her wet hair was bundled up in a cloth. When Nathaniel started to leave Richard said, 'Stay. Eat with me. It's a travesty of the old days but –'

Joe Chibborne sat on his left. Richard gave him instructions about the cupboard he wanted him to build. It was to be six foot by four, and nine inches deep, made of thick oak, with solid lock and hinges. Elaine cut crustless fingers of bread, spread them with butter and chopped sage, held them up to his mouth. He opened and swallowed, automatic as a young bird. His eyes closed now and again with weariness, his head nodded. She wondered how long he had been awake.

She gazed around. It was so small, this group of the four of them at the head of the table in the great space of the hall. 'What were they like, the old days?' she asked.

Richard didn't answer; his head had fallen forward, he seemed fast asleep.

'We used to have feasts,' said Nathaniel. 'There were days of great feasting when Lady Ann was alive. All the local gentry would come. Such grand clothes there'd be, the gleam of silks and velvets by candlelight, the sparkle of gold and silver threads in the embroidery. Great diamonds on men's broad hands; round pearls gleamed on women's breasts. Minstrels sang up in the gallery. They'd dance to the music of flute, viol and tabor. The sway of skirts, the chatter, the laughter –

When he stopped speaking all they could hear was the sad beat of the rain on the window. The creak of the bench as he shifted his weight. 'It's so quiet now,' said Elaine.

'Lady Ann's death put an end to every jollification. This room hasn't been used since. Sir Richard has done no entertaining. When he was well he used the parlour across from this, that was my lady's favourite room. It's much smaller, and faces the garden. The windows catch the evening sun in the summer. Such beautiful sunsets you can see from there. Orange, and red. He'd have a log fire in the hearth, apple wood, she always loved the smell of the smoke.'

The next day would be the first day of September. The year was turning. Soon would come cold and dark and the necessary lighting of fires. The shorter days. The long nights. How Elaine dreaded that. She thought how Lady Ann's feasts would have kept the fear of the winter away.

'There used to be a great celebration here every Michaelmas,' said Joe Chibborne. 'Cymberie was famous for its Michaelmas fair. People came to it from miles around. But it's been a sad season these last two years. No fair, no singing, no dancing. No drinking. Just a hangdog queue of tenants standing in line to pay their rent.'

'And a quiet queue of workers come to collect their pay,' said Nathaniel.

'I've never heard of workers being quiet on pay day,' said Elaine.

Joe Chibborne glanced at his master to check he was still

asleep; jerked his head toward him. 'It's him. They're frightened of him. When Lady Ann was alive all was fine. He was always a bit sombre and a scholar, head in his books, but she brought lightness and gaiety here when she came. Cymberie came to life when she was its lady. And then he lost her and his son in one fell swoop. He blamed himself for both. He's had a sour face on him since then.'

'So there's no celebration at Michaelmas at all now?'

'It's just a day like any other.'

She looked at her sleeping master, and bit her lip, and sighed. 'He'll get a crick in his neck if he sits like that any longer.' Gently, supporting his head, she tried to straighten his shoulders so he was leaning against the chair-back.

But his eyes snapped open, his hands, white-knuckled, gripped the arms of the chair. 'What are you doing?' he demanded.

'Nathaniel's going to carry you upstairs so you can sleep more comfortably.'

'I can walk,' he insisted. He pushed himself up from the chair and leant heavily on her arm to totter the length of the great hall, out on to the tiles of the little hall. His gown caught between his legs; he tugged it free. 'I can manage, see?'

'Shall I fetch your slippers, sir?'

'You think I'm not capable of going barefoot like you?'

But the soles of her feet were hard, broadened, dirt-engrained; his were thin-skinned, and he flinched at the cool of the tiles, at the sharpness of a small stone brought in on someone's shoe. 'Let Nathaniel carry you up the stairs, sir.'

'I can manage.'

He was out of breath by the fourth step, sat to rest for a while. 'Are you sure you don't want help, sir?'

'I got down these damned stairs on my own; I can

damned well get up them too.'

He sat again on the seventh step, hauled himself up and on to the tenth. 'Stop hovering, damn you, girl! You're making me nervous.'

She sat just below him on the stair. 'What were you thinking of, sir?'

'Thinking? What in heaven's name do you mean, thinking?'

'Down there, in your side chamber. With the pistol close to your chest, the sword laid across your papers.'

'I was checking my weapons. Making sure that they're still in good condition.'

'The others – Mistress Phillis – the men in the kitchen – they thought you would attack them.'

'More fools them.'

But once he was back in bed, in his great fourposter, his gown hung on the back of the door and his head couched on the pillows, when he was fed and replete and she was sliding off the bed, fastening her shift, stretching her arms, sure he was securely asleep, and she was just stepping across to the court cupboard to pick up a book, he opened his eyes suddenly and said, 'I was fighting this.'

'What?' She didn't understand.

'All this.' He gestured vaguely round with his arm. 'I wanted to kill –' He hesitated.

'To kill?' She filled the silence.

'I'm not a competent victim, Elaine. I don't have the patience to be. I'm a fighter. I wanted to kill my illness. To be in control. Elaine, I'm worn out with being ill. I've had enough. I'm ready to move on to the next world.'

'You're getting stronger every day. Climbing the stairs – that was a real achievement.' She didn't want him to die: she needed him here. 'Set yourself a target, sir. Michaelmas – that's four weeks away. At Michaelmas you'll walk downstairs on your own, you'll receive your tenants' rents, you will pay your workers their wages. And you'll order a feast for the evening, a feast and dancing in the Great Hall. The gentlefolk from the houses around here will come –'

'And what'll they do? They'll pansy up to me and say, oh we're so sorry about Lady Ann, such a tragedy, how you must miss her! And they'll pat me on the shoulder and ask if I have any news of Gabriel. Oh, it's Ann and Gabriel they loved, not me! That dratted boy – you'd think he could have written me a letter once in all this time! *Bad news travels,* is how I console myself. No news and he must be all right. I haven't talked to most of my neighbours since the day of the funeral, Elaine, I've given them a wide berth, they must think of me as a miserable recluse, I don't want to see them.'

'Then invite your tenants, and people from the village, sir. It would be good for Cymberie to be filled with the sound of music, the rhythms of dancing. It's not natural for a big house to be so quiet.'

He closed his eyes, neither agreeing nor disagreeing. She watched his face for a few minutes, then crossed to the court cupboard and picked up the book about the Americas, took it to his table and put it down. She had caught sight of her reflection in the big silver plate and she unbundled her hair from the cloth, combed it through with her fingers. It was only marginally damp now. She glanced across to check he was asleep, picked up his horn comb and teased it gently through the long tangles of her hair, fanned it across her shoulders to fully dry. Painstakingly she picked every one of her hairs out of his comb so he wouldn't know she'd used it. There was no confusing his and hers: hers was such a dark brown next to his grey.

She picked up the book, looked at the front where there was a map on which were drawn all the strange countries the writer wrote of; a printed boat slipped across the sea in full sail, a cherub with puffed cheeks blew it along. The boat's course was marked with a line which she traced with her finger. She imagined the lonely bays that it had sailed into, the crescents of white sand overhung by great trees, gaudy birds perched in the branches – crimson, blue and yellow-feathered – she imagined herself alone in the boat and the boat beaching, herself climbing over the side into a blue sea that was warm, that lapped around her knees (she would have to hold up her skirt so it didn't get soaked; her bare legs were very white). Her bare feet as she stepped on the shore would make clear prints in the sand. A bluebird would fly down and sit on her shoulder, a jaguar would come from the undergrowth and rub against her legs, she would stroke its rough coat and it would purr –

'How are you at mathematics?' Richard said from the bed.

She didn't answer; she was so lost in her reverie that she couldn't think what he meant.

'Can you count?'

'I can count to a hundred, sir.'

'Do you know your numbers?'

'One two three four –'

'No, you fool! Can you read numbers that are written down?'

'No, sir.'

'You'll have to learn. Come Michaelmas, you'll have to help me with writing down the payments and receipts. I've never employed a steward – I like to do the accounts myself. Keeps me in touch with who's who and what's going on. Helps to stop the cheating. Swindling beggars, a lot of them are, if they get half a chance. Ann used to say: you're not the centre of the world, Richard, why not get someone else to do it? But that has never been my way. This year, though, I'm so damned weak, I'm going to need help. I know I can trust you. Damn stupid, I can count on the fingers of one hand the people I can trust –'

He was in danger of becoming self-pitying. She said, 'I'll bring the sand-box, sir.'

The sand-box was what she had often practised the shapes of her letters in, paper being so expensive. Drawing her index finger through the damp sand full of shell fragments that clung to her skin. Copying *Elaine*, the letters of her name, the edges irregular and crumbling. Richard said the sand had been brought from by the sea, which she had never seen but liked to dream of. A great pond or lake without further limits, eternally blue, save when storms and bad weather tossed it grey and dangerous.

'Pass it here,' he said, sitting up in bed. 'I use the new numbers, not the old Roman ones. There is less scope for confusion. There are ten shapes that you need to learn. Nought, one, two, three, four –'He drew them down the left side of the box. 'This is nought,' he said, 'it means nothing at all. Write it after a one and the two make ten.'

She didn't follow what he meant, but she thought how handy it was to have a nought, which didn't exist in the old Roman system of writing numbers. It so well expressed the income on which she had to survive at the moment, with Margery creaming off all of her earnings. She inscribed a whole boxful of noughts; though there were twenty of them, they still added up to nothing at all.

'Very good,' said Richard. 'Now try the ones.'

They were simple enough. The twos were a back to front C underlined, the threes like a capital E. Fours were a strange boxy shape. 'Four, four, four,' she said as she repeated them, impressing the shape in her head.

Last night she had again asked Mistress Margery to explain how much she owed her. Margery had sighed and complained and eventually got out her counting cloth and shuffled the tokens on it at great speed. The sums hadn't made sense. 'Show me again more slowly, please,' Elaine had begged. 'You're too stupid to understand,' Mistress Margery declared. But the counting had been so quick, with Margery's red hands covering the tokens, that Elaine had wondered if Margery truly knew how to use the counting cloth herself. However, with Richard's new numbers written down in permanent ink on paper, Elaine was sure she could make her debt fixed and definite, and so ultimately repayable.

'You're quick to learn,' said Richard.

'It interests me,' she said.

'Rub the fours away. Pass the tray. Try five now. It's like this.' When he had drawn it he brushed the sand off his finger on his white shirt: the shell fragments glistened, caught in the weft of the linen.

The five was not dissimilar to an S. Carefully she traced it out. The hollows in the sand filled with soft shadow. She tucked her hair behind her ears and concentrated. After she had filled the sandbox with fives she took the piece of parchment she had used for practice and laid it on his table, sharpened the quill with a knife and dipped it in the inkwell. *Elaine*, she wrote first, sideways round the edge of the writing she'd done before; and then *012345* and *543210* and *£5. 3s. 4d.* God forbid that Mistress Margery should ever claim she owed her that much. She wondered how to write farthings. Sir Richard would tell her; he had fallen asleep at the moment, he was gently snoring. *3f* she wrote. She had black ink on her index finger, she spat on it and went to rub it on her skirt and remembered she had on Mistress Phillis's skirt, that she mustn't get dirty. She dipped her finger in the basin of water and made a fine white lather with the spice-scented soap. A bubble formed between her finger and thumb; she opened the window and blew it out over the neat garden. A shimmering globe that the rain soon smashed.

The ink had left a blue stain on her finger which she couldn't get off. Mistress Phillis's clothes and skirt were baggy and cumbersome. Maybe her own would be dry now. She'd go and see.

In the kitchen she let down the rack and tested her linen against her cheek for dampness. It was warm, almost ready to wear. The hem of her skirt was muddy, but the mud would dry and then brush off. She changed her clothes there by the fire and took Phillis's garments back to her.

The housekeeper was slumped on her stool like a dormouse asleep, chin on her chest, curved paws on her darning, dropped needle swinging silver from its thread. Rain slashed against the arched window; neat snores issued from her broad nose. Quietly Elaine folded the bodice and skirt and laid them on a stool. Now to go back to her numbers –

'Hey,' said Phillis, 'where do you think you're going? Hang those things up. They've got to air. I don't want them stinking of sour milk.'

She'd caught Elaine on a raw nerve. It was something the girl worried about; that and smelling of baby sick and shit. You couldn't help them getting on your clothes, not when you were looking after a baby. 'The master never complains of my body smell,' she said defensively.

'He's got other things on his mind, hasn't he? You're not telling me he still needs a wet-nurse. Pretty tits you've got, haven't you? He's a randy old sod, he is. You'd have thought he'd have grown out of it, but men are such simple creatures. They only ever have one thing on their minds.'

'No –'

'Come on, I wasn't born yesterday. I've seen how his eyes follow you round the room. I saw how you twisted him round your little finger this morning and got him to give up his weapons when Nathaniel and I couldn't do a thing with him. I've seen you and the master cosying up over a book. What do you want to learn to read for? Just to get close to him, I know. Well let me tell you this, my girl, Sir Richard is a man who knows the rightful order of things. Whatever devious evil schemes you may have in your head, he'll never marry you, he'll never take you for his mistress. The moment he's well enough to be back in his right mind, he'll send you packing!'

'My God, you think I'd ever want to be lover to that old man?'

'It would be a roof over your head, wouldn't it?'

The rain stopped. The evening was fine. Waterdrops hung from the undersides of twigs; the low sun glittered in them. Many birds were singing. The sky was pale blue, washed clean. Elaine collected Samuel and carried him down by the river. The mud on the lane squelched between her toes, it was slippery beneath her soles, she had to watch her balance. The long grass at the sides was bowed down with wet; the seeds had long been shed, the stalks were bleached and dead. The river was brown and turbid, fast-flowing. Green leaves, a few broken twigs were afloat in the current. She crossed the stone bridge, her feet curving the cobbles.

'Here we are, Sam,' she said, and she stooped to sit him against the trunk of an oak rooted in moss and in gravel. 'You stay there, be a good boy.' She tucked the hem of her skirt in her girdle. She took out her knife and walked down and stepped in the shallows among the tall rushes. She bent to cut them, laid them flat on the bank. She mustn't cut too many; they weren't heavy, but they would be awkward to carry. She plaited a few together and used those to tie the remainder in a fat bundle which she shouldered on her back. That way the weight would not be too much to bear, she hoped.

Picking Sam up was difficult. The first couple of times she tried she almost lost her balance and toppled toward him. 'Oh come on, Sam,' she said. 'Can't you stand up and jump up in my arms?' As if he could. He flopped forward on to his tummy, seized a handful of gravel and stuck his hand in his mouth. 'No, Sam!' She dropped the rushes, grabbed him and jabbed her finger in his soft mouth, feeling for stones. 'Sam, that's not food!' Two small sharp stones covered in spittle. 'You horrible creature.'

Maybe if she fed him he'd be easier to manage. She unlaced her bodice and shift, sat with her back against the ridged bark of the oak, put him to her breast. For once he didn't fight. And nursing him calmed her. She smoothed his blond curls and ruffled them up on end, ran her finger round the curve of his ear, caught his dimpled hand and stroked it. She glanced at the bundle of rushes, compared them wryly with the substantial slate roof of Cymberie, the red tiles of Walter Vernon's hall-house. She thought about what Phillis had said, her accusation that she was trying to trap the old man into a relationship. Such nonsense. She was just doing a job, and learning as much as she could on the way. This is the only love I'll ever feel now, she thought, love for my son, and she kissed his head.

How calm the valley was. Sleepy meadows, hedges full of calling birds. In a bend of the river, in the shallows where the bank was trampled by cattle going down to drink, two swans were washing in the brown water, their pure whiteness sharp as a knife against the muted late summer colours. They splashed themselves, they shook their heads. Their long necks. Waterdrops flew off, rainbowed by the low sun. They ducked beneath the water and shook their wings, they preened themselves busily. How graceful you are, Elaine whispered after them as they sailed away upstream. How serene you are.

The sun fell behind a clump of trees on the low hill to the west, tipping the tops with gold.

A young girl, five or six perhaps, with her dark hair all in a tangle, came barefoot over the bridge. Five geese waddled in a row behind her. She stepped down into the shallows where the swans had been, and the geese followed her and drank: how sinuous their necks were as they bent them, how the sun glinted in the waterdrops that fell from their beaks. The girl whistled, and walked back over the bridge, the geese trailing obedient behind her. She didn't notice Elaine.

Under the arch of the bridge was shadowy as a deep cave. A flash of colour, vivid green and blue, darted from it upriver: a kingfisher. Its bright pure colour lit up the world.

No damselflies. Earlier in the day the brilliant blue damselflies, the heavy-bodied dragonflies danced here. But not now; the sun had sunk too far.

'Twilight soon,' she said. 'We must get home, Sam.' She detached him from her breast. 'Come on, my fine boy.' She left him under the oak and carried the bundle of rushes to the bridge, balanced it on the parapet, went back for him. 'If I still had my shawl, Sam, I could bind you to my chest, this would be easy.' Holding the baby, she shuffled her arms into the rush straps she had made and heaved the bundle up on her back. Her knees buckled with the weight. I should have picked them on a dry day, she thought, but I need them now. I'll manage. She clasped Sam to her chest. At least your weight will counterbalance that of the rushes, she thought.

But it was a long walk back to the round house. Her shoulders ached, her arms ached. She felt a little dizzy. One foot after the other, lift it up, put it down, lift it up, put it down. That was the way to get there, methodically, plodding on, Samuel's head nodding against her chest, he was sleeping, she was weary, she was sleep-walking – up the hill toward the village – on the level it would be better – up the hill past the pigs, the orchard with its ripening apples – she'd skirt the village, she wouldn't go in, she had to get to the other side, to the track up into the wild land where she lived – she hadn't come this way for a while.

Hammering.

It wasn't in her head. It was where the bramble patch had been, such fat blackberries at the beginning of August, globules of purple juice bursting to stain her lips, her chin, her fingers. And now it was cleared, bare trampled earth, not mud, this place was gravelly, stony like where she lived, and it wasn't humming with bees any more, it was full of the scent of newly-felled elm, it stung her nostrils, went to her head, the framework of a house was going up there, elm new-sawn, the ends of the great timbers cut to square mortices and tenons and pegged together, just two rooms, you could see the skeleton of it, all bones, with a high-pitched roof, how sharp you could smell the new timber, and the candlemaker was there, Walter Vernon was there with a hammer in his hand, he was holding out his hands in welcome with the hammer still in them. No, not a hammer, a wooden mallet. 'Mistress Elaine,' he said.

This was the first time she had seen him since that fiasco when she'd gone to his house to say she'd marry him. Since then, whenever she'd thought of him she had envisaged him with his stockings round his ankles and his stringy ash-white legs exposed, peppered with black hairs. No, she didn't want to talk to him, couldn't think what she might say. She didn't meet his eyes. She turned her head and plodded on.

His footsteps hurried after her. 'Mistress Elaine!'

She couldn't go any faster, not with all that weight on her back, that and the baby.

'Mistress Elaine!' He had caught up with her, he was walking beside her now. Striding easily beside her. Something had happened to him, there was a greater confidence in his walk. But she didn't want to know why, she kept her head averted.

'The other day,' he was saying.

She concentrated on the deepening shadows in the well of the lane between the hedges. She watched for a twig that might make her trip, a sharp stone that would make her stumble. Samuel was slipping down; she heaved him up against her chest.

'Mistress Elaine, listen to me. The other day –'

She wished she weren't weighed down with the rushes and the baby. If she weren't she could run faster than him, she was sure. She could drop the rushes but then she would have to cut and fetch more another day and she was almost half way home, her job was more than half done. It wouldn't be fair if she had to drop the rushes to get away from him. They weren't secure, in any case; she could feel the bundle slipping down her back.

'Mistress Elaine, I'm building my mother a house. I've told her she's got to move out. She doesn't want to go, but I've insisted that she must. When she moves out, Mistress Elaine, the candle house, I'll be living there on my own. I'll be free then, Mistress Elaine, to marry you. My mother won't be able to stop me. I'll be able to do what I believe is right. For the first time in my life she won't be telling me what to do. I'll be myself. You have taught me courage, Mistress Elaine, you have given me strength. It's because of you I'm building this house. In order to put things right. It is the only way to ensure justice is done.'

She was too weary to try to make sense of what he was saying. She bit her lip and tried to carry on. But she had no strength left. She stopped for breath, straightened her back and a strap on the rushes broke, the bundle slithered to the ground behind her. 'Oh ...' she sighed.

'Let me help you.'

She glanced at him. A pale blue ruff he was wearing with matching cuffs. He was still holding the hammer. It looked strangely familiar. 'That beetle,' she demanded fiercely. 'Where did you get it?'

'What?' He didn't understand.

'That mallet, that hammer, where did you get it?'

'This?' He looked down at it, confused.

'Yes.'

'Why?'

'Tell me where you got it from.'

'I bought it a few days ago up at St Bartholomew's Fair, in Smithfield. I was selling my candles there. I did pretty well, I can tell you, made a good few bob for myself. You won't be financially uncomfortable if you marry me, that's for certain.'

'That beetle,' she repeated. 'Tell me where you got it.'

'Humfrey Howarde, that's the fellow's name who sold it me. He trades in old tools – chisels, saws, that kind of thing. Travels round from fair to fair, like I do. I often see him. I liked the look of this mallet so I bought it off him. He wasn't eager to sell it because it was breaking up a set, but it's crafted nicely, it's got a good feel to it, I knew it would come in useful. I've been using it to make sure the pegs the carpenters put in to hold the frame together are properly home. I can't stand shoddy workmanship.'

'Let me hold it.'

'What?'

'That hammer.'

'Take a rest, Mistress Elaine. You look weary. Sit down for a bit. Let me hold the baby for you.'

'No.' She swung Samuel round to her side, let her hip take his weight, kept her arm round him protectively. 'That mallet – let me see it.'

'It's just an ordinary hammer.'

It was just the beetle Thomas had made himself for hammering in the chisels in the initial work of each carving. Cutting straight into the raw wood to find the blurred shape that he would refine and define until it became an angel, a heron, a goddess or a monster. He had made that beetle. He had made the handle to fit the exact dimensions of his fist. When she took it from Walter Vernon, when she held it, it was almost like putting her hand in Thomas's. Clutching the round warm wooden handle that was just an inch longer and wider than her own fist. Thomas had carved it from a tree that had fallen in her father's orchard. The sweet curves of the grain: she traced her finger along them. Look at the lizard curled round the top of the handle: his mark because he couldn't read or write.

She longed to carve again, to lose herself in her and Thomas's craft. To feel the chisel cut into the hard wood, the pale woodchips falling around her feet, to bring out the beauty of the grain, the growth rings, all the years of a tree's growth becoming clear and sinuous, the wood smooth, without splinters, and strokeable – she wanted the people who saw her carvings to run their hands over them, to finger the warm wood and say, oh this feels like stroking my lover's skin – to touch the hair of a creature at a pew's end and smooth it as if it were a lazy cat in the sunshine – she longed to create something new, to see things in a new way. What my carving is, she thought for the first time, why I love it is, it's a search for perfection in this world where so much is difficult and wrong and people are so fallible. It is the only way I can achieve any sort of perfection – a satisfaction. I have made this: look.

She ached to hold a chisel again. It was a physical pain she felt in her wrist, in the muscles of her arm, the palm of her hand. How could she ever get Thomas's tools back?

Then a sudden thought struck her. 'The Michaelmas fair,' she said.

'What?' That was Walter.

'There always used to be a Michaelmas fair at Cymberie.'

'There did indeed. What about it?'

'Sir Richard – he's much better – nearly better – he wants to hold it again in thanksgiving for his recovery. Down in the deer park.' How easy it was to invent facts when you wanted something very much.

'I haven't heard anything about it.'

'He only decided today. There will be jugglers by the lake. Music and cock fights. A play. You must come with your candles. Sell them. Invite other people. That fellow Humfrey Howarde – he must come with his tools. Ask any other tradesmen you know.'

Walter Vernon hesitated; he seemed uncertain whether to believe her or not. 'There certainly always used to be a fair at Cymberie,' he said. 'It was one of the best.'

'It's going to be wonderful again,' she assured him. 'Speak to anyone – Nathaniel – Joe Chibborne – Mistress Phillis – not today, ask them tomorrow, they will tell you all about it.'

'I was planning to go to London, but I would certainly be glad not to have to carry my wares all that way. The question is, will enough people go to make it worthwhile?'

'Of course they will. You must tell everyone about it. If you like, I will marry you right then and there on Michaelmas day by the lakeside. That is, if you will give me a wedding day gift of carving chisels.'

'A gift of chisels?' He sounded incredulous.

'A set of carving chisels in a leather roll, that's what I want, marked with the same lizard mark as on the handle of this beetle. They used to belong to a friend of mine. Humfrey Howarde must have them, if he had this.'

'You are a strange woman, Mistress Elaine. It's because you come from the north, I daresay. We will learn to understand each other.' He put out a hand to touch her hair, wary as if he were about to touch a snake and was uncertain if it were a harmless grass-snake or a venomous adder.

She backed away. Her face was filmed with sweat and very white. Her eyes had dark rings beneath them.

He let his hand drop. 'The rushes, Mistress Elaine, shall I bind them with rope for you?'

'If you please.'

'What are they for?'

'To mend the roof of my house.'

He straightened up, the rope in his hand. 'There's no need to do that. It's only a few weeks till we marry.'

'But your mother –'

'I will make sure this house is finished by Michaelmas. I will light a fire to dry it out as soon as the plastering is done, and carry all her things across so she can move straight in. My candle house will be lit and waiting for you and the baby to come home to after the fair. I'll get a new mattress for the bed in the solar. A crib for the baby. There'll be nothing to stop our marriage. I look forward to it.'

'Yes.' She wondered if she ought to kiss him, but he was

keeping his distance and didn't seem to expect it. She shook her head slightly. Her thoughts were cloudy and muddled. She wondered vaguely if she were going down with a fever. She hoisted Samuel on to her hip and concentrated on picturing the round house on the hill, on putting one foot firmly in front of the other. Step by step she would reach it.

This bed. It was so comfortable. Not soft. It was quite hard. But it was where Elaine belonged. It felt right. Lying on her back she could see stars through the holes in the roof now. She felt a little light dew on her skin. It was cool and refreshing.

Samuel lay quiet against her side. How well he fitted there. Made for the space. He would have to sleep on his own in four weeks' time.

Tomorrow, there would be that matter of her lie about the Michaelmas Fair to attend to. She didn't know what she would do about that.

She didn't need to worry about tomorrow now. She could enjoy her present contentment.

She was very tired.

The sky was blue-grey. It wasn't deep night yet. That bright star there, was it Venus?

In the candle house Mistress Vernon sat in her black on a bench, lace pillow on the table in front of her, the sharp flames of the three candles reflecting in the gaudy glass beads on the bobbins. She rubbed her eyes wearily. 'This work is hurting my eyes more and more,' she complained. She laid one bobbin across another, fixing the pattern of a bird's eye with the fine white thread.

'Don't do it at night then. There's no need, Mother.' Walter had shed his day clothes, he was wearing a loose gown with felt slippers and was seated in a wooden armchair, feet up on a stool, hands clenched on the ends of the arms. *Honour thy father and mother*, he was thinking. Well, his father was long dead. The house he was building for his mother was good; he was pleased with it. She didn't yet know it was for her. She thought she was going to live for ever in this house where she had been since the day that she married. She would be better off in the new house. Not so much housework to do. The small cubes of the rooms would fit close around the simple, repetitive pattern of her days.

It would be strange to have a new woman in this house where his mother had presided all of his life. What foods would Elaine cook? Maybe they would eat northern, foreign food that was not to his taste. He would have to instruct her. He would have to lay down the law, make sure that she conformed to his routine. The child too; the baby would doubtless bawl and crawl around the place, disturbing his peace and quiet. But this thing must be done. It was an obligation on him.

He got up and went outside, by the light of the half-moon strolled in the garden. Pale moths fluttered round his ankles. He opened his gown to piss against an apple tree. An owl shrieked. This is justice, he thought. This world we live in is cruel and by its very nature unfair, but what I am doing is the best simulacrum of justice I can achieve. Always I try to do what is right.

He knelt in the grass and put the palms of his hands together to pray.

7

'Are you coming to the fair?' Elaine asked Rosamund. They were standing outside Mistress Margery's gate. It was a sunny morning, the sky blue, the air washed clean by yesterday's rain, the grass sparkling with dew. In the garden, on a mat of rushes, plump bare-bottomed babies crawled and cooed and lolled and chuckled. 'Ah, love them,' said Rosamund, ostentatiously adjusting the fine purple shawl she wore over the coiled plaits of her blonde hair.

'You won't want to miss it, I'm sure,' Elaine said thoughtfully. For the moment she wasn't concerned about the theft of her shawl; she had other things on her mind.

'What are you talking about?'

'The Michaelmas Fair at Cymberie. Has your husband booked space for a stall yet? They'd nearly all gone by yesterday evening.'

'There's no fair at Cymberie. There hasn't been one for a couple of years.'

'You mean you haven't heard? Sir Richard has reinstated it in celebration of his recovery.'

'What? The old man's better?'

'He can walk up and down stairs now.'

'Huh. That means I've lost a whole guinea in bets on the time of his death. My husband is going to be livid.'

'Why don't you take a stall too then, to give you a chance to recoup your losses?'

'That's worth thinking about. If I had a hot-meat stall at the fair, I'd be able to make a tidy bit. Late September, there's that nip to the air, people are always hungrier then. It's getting colder already, don't you think? This morning I felt very chilly. Aren't you cold without a shawl?' She drew it closer round her chubby face, making sure that Elaine couldn't avoid noticing it.

'I'm fine,' Elaine says steadily. 'I wouldn't wear that colour purple though, if I were you. It doesn't go with your ruddy complexion at all.' She turned away, began to stride along the puddled lane.

'Wait!' Rosamund came running after her. 'I want to know more about this fair. You tell whoever's arranging it that I want a pitch, will you? Mind it's in a good place though, next to the play or the cockfight would be fine, not stuck out somewhere on the edge of things, I'd never pick up any trade there.'

Elaine stopped, turned back. 'You'll have to pay for it.'

Rosamund fumbled in her purse, offered a sixpence.

'That's not enough.'

'Think of all the bread you can buy with that.'

'I'm not short of bread any longer.'

'Oh, very well, you can have your shawl back if you want. I don't want it, you're right, it's a horrible colour. Ralph, my husband, he said to me as I came out this morning, what do you want to wear that terrible colour for?' She was unwrapping the shawl as she spoke, she flung it at Elaine. It fell on the surface of the lane, trailing a corner into a puddle.

Elaine picked it up. It smelt of raw meat, Rosamund's trade; it was stranded with coarse blonde hairs. She couldn't bear to put it on immediately. She folded it carefully, laid it over her left arm. 'You'll have to give me the sixpence too,' she said.

'No.'

'To pay for the pitch. I have to give it to Master Nathaniel.'

'Oh, very well.'

Elaine took the silver, slipped it in her pocket.

'Make sure you give it to him. Don't cheat me, or there'll be trouble.'

Elaine turned her back.

Crossing the common Elaine kilted up her skirt, shook her purple shawl free of its folds and took hold of two adjacent corners. She lifted it high and ran, leaping over the puddles, the shawl flapping, flying free like a celebratory pennant behind her, the rain-washed air cleansing the fabric, her heart thumping, feet mud-stained, legs swallowing the miles. Drips from the wet trees pearled her hair, darkened her shoulders. Her mouth ached from smiling.

'Oh no,' said Nathaniel. 'You think I don't have enough to do?' Red-faced, he was standing square at the far side of the kitchen table, broad-shouldered and tall, his great hands resting on the scrubbed surface. In front of him crisp loaves were steaming, the hot yeasty scent rising into the air that was scalding hot from the high-stacked log fire. A cauldron was boiling; steam misted near the ceiling.

Elaine hesitated, not sure how to convince him. She pleated the edge of the shawl nervously, looked up again. 'Think how good it would be for Sir Richard's spirits,' she murmured.

'Are you out of your mind? He can only just slither out of his bed and you expect him to go to a fair?'

'No, not that. But if he knows it's going on – if he can hear the music in the distance, and the laughter, the sound of the crowd enjoying themselves, that's bound to give him pleasure.'

'What in heaven's name has led you to believe that our mighty master cares a groat about anyone else's happiness?'

'If we invite musicians to the fair we can get them to come and play up at the house as well.'

'Music was always Lady Ann's joy, not the master's.'

'If it reminds him of past happiness it will surely aid his recovery.'

'More likely to drown him deeper in the doldrums, if you ask me.'

Elaine hesitated. She knew she had to win Nathaniel round if there was to be any chance of the fair going ahead. How could she persuade him to back the idea? He was an expert cook: could she get at him through his love of cooking? 'After the fair, when it gets dark,' she suggested tentatively, 'we'll have a Michaelmas feast here in the great hall. What do you think? Venison pasties and quail, a dish of larks and roasted capons, gingerbread, some of your delicious custard.' He didn't respond. She studied his face: sweat was dripping from his forehead into his eyes. He rubbed it with the floury back of his hand, leaving white tracks. She tried to convince herself that his expression had softened a little, that he was looking more amenable. 'We'll have some sort of entertainment for Sir Richard,' she coaxed. 'A play, maybe, or dancing. The musicians can earn a few pence at the fair, and then come on up here. Sir Richard will be able to manage the stairs easily by then. He can sit in his armchair at the head of the table in the great hall and fill his proper role once again.'

'You talk to him about it.'

'I –'

'For Christ's sake, why do you think he cancelled the Cymberie fair? Because of Lady Ann, because of the pleasure she took in it, because of how much she loved it. He couldn't bear to contemplate it without her there beside him.'

'Perhaps reviving it might help him overcome his grief?'

'It can't be done unless he approves it. I'm not paying for any musicians out of my wages; I'll tell you that for nothing. And who's going to authorise the extra expenditure on food if it's not him?'

After the heat of the kitchen the entrance hall felt chill. Elaine stood still within the gaudily-painted walls, flexing her toes on the cold tiles, rubbing her right hand up and down one of the banisters. I didn't think this through, she kept thinking, this idea of the Michaelmas Fair. I did it too much on impulse. I can't ask Sir Richard about it; I daren't. It's none of my business. I'll have to tell Walter and Rosamund the fair's been cancelled.

But she kept thinking of Thomas's beetle with the lizard carved on the handle; how snug it felt in her hand. The longing to get her hands on his carving chisels possessed her, her hands ached for the feel of them, she wanted them more than anything else in the whole world. She needed the tool-seller Humfrey Howarde to come to Cymberie with his stock of tools, for there was no way she could get away, she was tied by the demands of nursing Sir Richard.

The penalty, of course, the price she would have to pay for them, was marriage to Walter Vernon. But however she herself felt about that, it would give Samuel a father, and security. If anything happened to her, her son would still have a home. It was very reassuring to know that. And they would have a watertight roof over their heads, food in their mouths, in the hall-house that smelt of candle-wax. Simple things; but they mattered so much.

Women survived unhappy marriages. She knew her contentment with Thomas was rare. She could learn to give up her independence, to submit herself to Walter's will, to do his commands. She could accommodate herself to him. She would learn to take small steps, shrink her spirit deep inside herself.

She wished she understood what motivated Walter. He

was not at all attracted to her physically, as far as she could tell. Nor was she to him. She was sorry about that; she missed the intimacies of marriage. She woke up aching for them some nights, dreaming she just had to reach out to rouse Thomas beside her. 'I can manage without love,' she said out loud to the portrait of the Belvoir family over the mantelpiece. 'But Thomas's chisels, I want those. They're all that really matter. They're all I truly care about. I must have them.'

'What in heaven's name is the matter with you today, Elaine?' demanded Sir Richard. 'You can't do the most elementary arithmetic. Why have you put fourteen in the pence column? You know as well as I do there are twelve pence in a shilling.'

'Yes sir.'

'For God's sake! Pull yourself together, girl. I want you to do my accounts for me. You can't get away with that sort of slapdash laziness.'

She bit her lip, rubbed out the fourteen in the sand-box. 'Sir, it's a shilling and tuppence, but I don't know where to put the shilling.'

'Put a one under the line in the shilling column – there. You add the two and the four. What's that?'

She stared numbly at the figures.

'Well?'

'Sir, I don't know what to do.'

'Come on, woman. I've never thought you stupid before. Add up the wretched numbers.'

'It's not that, sir. I've told people in the village that there's going to be a fair at Cymberie this Michaelmas, and –'

'You what?'

'I said there'll be a fair at Cymberie at Michaelmas. I've told people in the village and they're coming. Rosamund Smith is having a hot-meat stall, Walter Vernon's going to sell his candles, and others –'

'Why did you tell them this?'

'I thought it would give you pleasure, sir.'

'Give me pleasure? A great cacophony on my doorstep?'

'Down in the deer park, sir, by the lake. You'll hardly hear it. Except that we – Nathaniel and I – we thought you'd like a feast here in the great hall in the evening.'

'You thought I'd like a feast?'

'Yes, sir.' She paused, searching for inspiration. Finding it in a letter on the table. 'As a way of repaying your friends, sir. They have been so generous while you have been ill, sending you gifts, asking after you. You owe them something in return. What could be better than to invite them here?'

'Crowds of people cavorting round getting drunk, generally making a mess of the place?'

'It would get your debt to them all paid off in one go, sir.'

'You've gone mad, Elaine.'

'It would be a celebration of your recovery, sir.'

'What?'

'Cymberie's so quiet, sir. It's a lovely house. It needs people in it.'

There was a long silence. Richard stared out of the window at the distant trees. At last he turned back to her. 'Elaine, you are always surprising me. That's exactly what Ann used to say. It's made for feasts and festivals, this house, she said. She loved it here. An unsociable old bear, she called me.'

Elaine sat with her hands demure in her lap. In the end, when Richard didn't say any more, she asked, 'Does that mean you don't mind, sir? Does that mean we can hold the fair?'

'You can do it for Ann's sake. So long as I don't have to concern myself with it. I never did before.'

'You just have to sit at the head of the table at dinner time, sir.'

'Oh, very well.'

'Will you give me a list of your friends I should invite, sir?'

'Tomorrow. I'll do it tomorrow.'

'Will you sanction the extra expenditure, sir?'

'If you'll concentrate on learning how to do my damned accounts so that I can collect the rent from my tenants and not be cheated.'

He went back to bed and rested. She applied herself hard, head down, hair falling forward over her face, finger tracing the numbers in the sand. She kept on taking the sandbox over to Richard. 'Is this right?' she'd say. 'Have I got this sum right?'

'For God's sake,' he'd reply. 'Leave me in peace. Can't you see I'm exhausted?' But always he would prop himself up on his elbow and draw the sandbox toward him and say, good girl, and set her another sum.

By the end of the morning she was getting all her sums right: not a mean achievement when she had learnt to write her numbers only the day before. 'You've done well,' he said.

'That just proves it.'

'What?'

'Nothing.' She was thinking about how when she had first got in debt to Mistress Margery she had kept putting the woman right about the amount of money that she owed her, but Margery had shouted and screamed at her that she was a useless fool, a misbegotten cretin of a northerner. Northerners never knew how to add up, God was her witness, she'd said. 'Thieves you are, all of you,' she ranted. 'The iniquity of it! When I think how much I've put myself out to help you and your baby and all you can do in return is to try and cheat me out of what you owe me!' And she'd thrown her apron over her head and howled in noisy distress. Elaine had been low after the birth of her baby, she was confused, she clung to the only person who had ever given her aid. She began to believe that northern numbers must indeed be deviant in some way, and utterly wrong: now here was Richard telling her that she had been right all along.

'Go down to the side chamber off the great hall and get some paper. I want you to practise with a pen. No, help me up first. Then go and tell Nathaniel and Mistress Phillis and Joe Chibborne and Mistress Winifred to come here at once, will you?'

At the mention of the feast and the fair Phillis came to life. She squared her shoulders, stood taller, projected her bosom and rubbed her fat hands together in pleasure. 'Now, sir,' she said in a businesslike way, 'I'll engage the musicians from over in Ulting; they play a pretty tune, they'll make everyone kick up their heels. Who are you planning to invite, sir? They will need to sleep here. I must get the spare blankets washed.'

Of course, Elaine thought, sitting out of the way by the window, Phillis had been engaged by Lady Ann who loved feasts and celebrations; she must have been dying of boredom under her master's reclusive regime. No wonder she had been so bad-tempered. Nathaniel, too, became enthused, he started talking over the details; and Joe Chibborne chipped in now and again. There were some old booths from past fairs kept in the far stables, he said; he'd check how sound they were and repair them if necessary.

Elaine detached herself from the wash of their voices. She stared out at the statue's reflection shimmering white in the lake among the spiky-petalled water-lilies; at the blue sky flecked with clouds chased by the brisk west wind; at the trees that were turning – more and more yellow leaves at the tops. She had a clean sheet of paper in front of her but she wouldn't touch it while the others were there in case someone distracted her and she made a blot; she needed to concentrate so hard when she was writing. Now and again she overheard a phrase of their conversation: *Timothy Huggins has a damn fine cock.* Or *Talk to the priest. The choir will sing.* And she wondered just what she had put into motion.

She pictured a little scene down by the lakeside. It will be like this, she thought: herself and Walter Vernon isolated on the slope among the brightly-clothed throng. The two of them thin and tall and soberly clad. He would hold her hand limply in his and ask if she agreed to take him as her husband. *Yes*, she would say, looking down at the ground. *I am content.* Then he would intone: *I do before these witnesses take you Elaine to be my wife.* And that would be that. They'd be married. Humfrey Howarde would be their witness; he would be all in black, he'd wear an apron and a bowler hat. However much she didn't want things to change from how they were at the moment, she knew that they must. And that would be the end of her life at Cymberie.

When the others had gone, she picked up Richard's knife and sharpened the quill, dipped it in the inkwell and carefully traced out her name at the head of the paper. Elaine Fisher. The letters were firm; they didn't reveal her self-doubt. In figures small as she could she started to write out sums and to solve them, her precision and accuracy, the attention she gave the task keeping the future at bay.

Propped up on the pillows of the great bed, Richard opened his eyes and watched her intense concentration for a while. 'This fair, Elaine, it will make you happy?'

'What do you mean, sir?'

'You will enjoy the fair? You won't want to die any more?' He held out his hand.

She got up and crossed the room and took it. 'Sir,' she said softly, 'I won't want to die. And neither will you, I pray.'

'I can't answer for that. My hurt is so deep.' Then he smiled and said: 'If you are to be my clerk and sit beside me on rent-collection day, you can't wear those ragged clothes.'

'There's nothing wrong with my clothes, sir. I keep them clean and mended.'

'You think I don't have any pride? You think I want people to say, *there's a man who will go in velvet and beaver but is too mean to clothe his servants as befits their proper station*? Here, take this key. Summon Mistress Winifred, then open my Lady Ann's chest.'

No, Elaine thought. She didn't want him to give her clothes when Mistress Margery was bound to get them off her and sell them to Rosamund Smith to taunt her with. But how could she explain? 'Sir –'

'My God, Elaine, I know that tone of voice of yours so well! Don't argue with me! It's I who have to look at you! I can't stand those faded earth-colours that you wear. If I choose that you should wear silk you will.'

'Sir –'

'Fetch Mistress Winifred.'

The embroideress was out in the garden, on the stone bench in the arbour. The vines above her were weighed down with great bunches of green grapes. She liked to work here because the light was good, even when as now the sun was hidden, the sky heavy with clouds. She'd put aside the silvergilt embroidery on the crimson velvet of her master's funeral pall; she was now embroidering his coat of arms in the corner of a thick cream blanket, using wool thread this time, in a big-eyed needle.

'Mistress Winifred!' Elaine called.

She looked up. 'Huh, it's you. A fine job you've landed me with, you and your dream of a fair. You know what I've got to do? Mark all the best blankets. Mistress Phillis has got it into her head that everyone who comes to stay on Michaelmas night is going to ride home with their bedclothes.'

'They've all got odd ideas. The master's decided I have to be dolled up in fine clothes for the occasion as if I were some kind of an ornament. He told me to fetch you.'

'I've got twenty blankets to mark! I can't do anything else as well.'

'He said you must come.'

Mistress Winifred sighed, and stuck her needle in the blanket, stood and folded it up neatly, tucked the frizzy red curls at the side of her face under her cap and waddled flat-footed toward the house. 'Do this, do that,' she muttered. 'I don't know. People have no idea how busy I am. They don't understand the work that I do; they have no idea how long things take. They –' She grumbled on, all the way into the house and up the stairs. But once in Sir Richard's chamber she curtsied deeply and stood silent, plump hands folded over her belly.

He was sitting up in bed. 'Elaine, here's the key,' he said. 'Open the chest.'

She unlocked the padlock and lifted the heavy lid. The moth-deterrent smell was weaker than it had been. 'Sir, I will have to put in fresh elecampane roots.'

'Let me see.' He stood up and slid his arms into the sleeves of his gown, shook it down round his ankles. She carried his heavy chair over to beside the chest and he sat, leaning forward to study the fabrics that lay at the top as if they were a complex puzzle. There was a kind of avarice about his eyes, and secrecy, as if he were greedily drinking in memories that he didn't want to share. The clothes reminded him, perhaps, of a summer day in the past when he and Ann had ridden out side by side across the deer park and made love on a bank in the dappled shade of trees, cushioned on moss; or of a winter day when she had come indoors pink-faced and lovely out of a blizzard and he brushed the heavy snow from her hood and her shoulders. It melting at their feet. Pooling around them as they kissed.

The two women watched in silence. 'Sir,' Elaine said in the end, 'all I need is a new bodice. I can get the material from the weaver's if you will give me the money.'

'No. These clothes – there's no point in keeping them now. Having them here – it won't bring her back – she won't come back to wear them. Better to get rid of them. That dark green bodice, Elaine, the colour will suit you. It is sober, quite clerk-like. Ann wore it with ruby-red sleeves. Those, there, I think. Put it on. Winifred, do you have your pins? You must alter the garments so they fit Elaine well. I will not have her dressed as a peasant when people come to the house. You must wear shoes, too, Elaine. There are her boots, somewhere, and some slippers –'

Such soft slippers, made of calfskin, dyed bright green. Elaine sat on the floorboards to pull them on. Thumb in the heel; they were a tight fit. 'My feet have grown broader with going barefoot all these months,' she said with regret. It was a token of the loss of an innocence that could never be regained. Like the scar of Thomas's chisel in the palm of her hand, which would always mark her.

'They will stretch if you wear them,' said Richard. 'You and Ann – your feet are much of a size. There is an ivory collar made of lace. There. It will need starching to freshen it up. Those cuffs go with it. And that skirt, the green linen, that will do very well. You will look most clerk-like. Those couple of shifts – you might as well take them. You can patch where they're stained under the armpits. There's a blackwork one somewhere. Damned expensive it was. All that fine embroidery. What in heaven's name did you get that for, Ann? I said. No-one will see it. – I'll know it's there, she said.'

Winifred said, 'Stretch out your arms,' and launched herself at Elaine with her pins. She took tucks at the sides of the bodice, lifted the seams at the shoulders to make the bust fit better. Put darts under the bust to make the fit exact and flattering. Was careful to keep the armholes the same size so the sleeves would lace in snugly. She tied on a farthingale, checking how the skirt fell over it.

'You are a few inches taller than Ann, Elaine, for I can see your ankles.'

The tops of her feet were brown from the summer sun, from all her walking. Her face was lightly tanned even though she had plaited reeds to make herself a wide-brimmed hat. She looked like a peasant, not a lady.

'Now you can read and write,' he said, 'you must wear those clothes whenever you are at Cymberie, as befits my clerk.'

'Yes, sir.' She took them off slowly, cautious of the pins, and Winifred gathered them up in her arms, to take them away to sew and to starch and to iron.

Elaine put her old clothes back on. Richard went to bed, and she sat beside him. The day had grown dark now; rain beat against the thick greenish panes of the casement. She watched the waterdrops run down the glass like tears. She saw how coarse the linen of her shift was, noticed the dirt engrained in the hem of her skirt.

After a while she said, 'I'll read to you.' She laid his head gently on the pillows and fetched the book of the Americas. *In the darkness of the forests great serpents slither on their smooth bellies*, she read. *They are the measure around of a fat man's thigh, and they shimmer with scales as brilliant as any gem. It bodes a man well to beware should he step out of the shadows into a patch of sunlight: those serpents coil there in the heat, gaining strength, always ready to strike.* She stumbled over some of the words.

When Richard was fast asleep she got up. Lady Ann's chest was still open and she saw a grey hooded woollen cloak that had come to the surface when the other clothes were taken out. It was an old thing, much patched and darned. It had to have been put in there by mistake. He'll never miss it, she thought. And if he were awake and I asked him, he would give it to me happily, I know that he would. I need it to keep off the rain as I walk home. If I get soaked to the skin I have no way of getting dry at home. The rain's that heavy, the purple shawl won't be sufficient; and I don't want Margery to see it again. I can tell him tomorrow I have taken it.

She put the warm cloak around her shoulders and closed the chest, slipped the padlock into the hasp and clicked it shut; tucked the ornate key under his pillow, beneath his sleeping head.

9

Strangers began to come to Cymberie. Elaine met them on the track across the common land. Some were alone, bowed beneath heavy packs upon their backs; they trod wearily on the short grass that was soft under their sore feet. Silent as ghosts they went, leaving their green footprints in the grey dew. Good day, Elaine would say, and they would incline their heads a little in reply.

Others came in groups: musicians played rebecks, drummed tabors and sang; men carried fierce cocks in cages made of plaited willow. Cockadoo, the cocks crowed boldly, louder than any native birds, showing off their bright feathers and red combs, their lustrous throats. Go home, Elaine wanted to shout to all of them: go back home, Cymberie fair isn't till Michaelmas. She couldn't understand how word about it had got out so quick and spread so wide.

By the end of two weeks there was an encampment down by the lake in the deer park. *All those people,* Richard kept grumbling, hands clenched on the ledge of one of the gallery windows with a view to the south. *Disgusting.* He ordered a long privy to be built over the stream where it ran away from the lake so the visitors wouldn't kill his fish with their shit and their piss. Women came to the camp as well as men: two whores in particular Elaine noticed, who, decked out in doublet and hose, haunted Nathaniel's kitchen on wet days and pestered him for pies. How curvy their long legs looked in their knitted stockings! How extraordinary it was to see the shape of the lower half of a woman's body revealed like that! Their wool doublets were unbuttoned half way to their navels, the coarse fabric prickling the fair skin of their breasts. Turning it red.

Elaine flitted about in her green skirt and the velvet bodice with the ruby sleeves, glad of the dignity they gave her, that made newcomers to Cymberie treat her with respect. There were many new servants. Nathaniel had engaged boys from the village to help him, and an old man whose job it was to turn the spit. There was an influx of dairymaids who busied themselves making butter and cheese. Mistress Phillis directed a flock of women who scrubbed floors, turned and aired the mattresses, chased cobwebs from the ceilings and polished wood and silver. All day their voices burbled and chirruped through the rooms of the great house that Elaine had only ever known quiet.

'For God's sake, shut that damned door, keep out that filthy noise,' snarled Richard from his table by the window.

'Yes sir,' she said. She had brought the rent books up from his side chamber and was painstakingly going through them. Last year he had made many mistakes: charged some tenants too much, others too little. She wasn't always sure that she could read his writing correctly; she got him to check her figures. When it came to a deficiency of fifteen shillings in one account, he explained, 'Last year I had lost heart. I had run out of the courage one needs to survive the routine of everyday life.'

'You are better now, sir.'

'Yes.'

She knew how ill he was still. Half an hour was as long as he could sit up; after that he needed to lie down and rest for a while. He hadn't been downstairs again. She kept trying to make him feel better. 'This year,' she told him, 'as a thanksgiving for your recovery, it will be proper for you to be generous and not to demand the rent arrears.'

'You think so, do you, madam?'

'Yes sir.'

'Oh, very well. It will be less effort, anyway.'

He was engrossed in going through a pile of correspondence that had arrived at Cymberie when he seemed very close to death, which had been placed on the table in his side chamber and then forgotten. There were several letters from Philip Windebank who had done the woodcarving in the hall, whom he had recommended to work with Alessandro in Venice, all pleading for money. *I cannot live as befits an Englishman in this strange land,* the boy complained. Then after a couple of months there had come a letter to say that he had embraced the Catholic faith and married a stonemason's widow. *We agree very well,* he said, and *I work all day in her yard. I find I have a greater affinity for marble than for wood. I remain very grateful for your help and support, but I will not be returning. Your obedient servant –*

There were complaints about Richard's non-attendance at his parish church; fines he must pay. A letter from a friend who was drawing up a map of the whole of the region, asking if he might stay at Cymberie for a month. That had arrived way back in June. 'Did he come?' asked Richard.

'I don't know,' said Elaine.

'I will write and let him know that I am well.' He picked up his pen.

Elaine's green velvet bodice remained firmly laced. 'Let's put an end to this farce,' he had said brusquely a dozen days ago.

'What farce?'

'You know.'

'It wasn't. I made you better.'

'Well.'

'So shall I go home, if you've no need of me now, sir?'

'I need you to stay on as my clerk,' he had told her. 'You're someone I know I can trust. You may be ignorant but you learn quickly.' And here she was, full of all the bustle of doing the accounts and helping with the organisation of the fair.

Her soft velvet bodice was like bright armour, making her strong for each day, bestowing authority on her. When she said to stallholders in the drizzle on the green grass by the lake, 'You will have to pay a fee of two farthings,' they paid up without a murmur. She went down there every day, always watching out for a tool-seller by the name of Humfrey Howarde, but he never came. She bit her lip, swallowed her disappointment, filled up the leather purse she carried with the stallholders' halfpence and took it back to Richard. As she climbed the long stairs between the brightly painted walls, the flock of women cleaners with polish cloths in their hands, bums in the air, parted and stepped aside to let her pass. The velvet bodice even had an effect on Nathaniel and Mistress Phillis, who knew her so well; they treated her with more respect, almost as if she were a lady.

She didn't wear the bodice back to the village. Each evening she took it off in the apple store that was one of the stone rooms close to the kitchen, and hung it to air from a hook in the ceiling between the wide slatted shelves that were still empty; the apples had not yet been gathered in. She did the same with her green skirt and farthingale. You will not take my new life away from me, Mistress Margery, she thought. I won't let you.

She placed the green slippers side by side in the centre of the floor. Her bare feet were stained with the calfskin dye and the dirt from the roads. She went home in her worn old clothes, covered with the grey woollen cloak she had taken from Lady Ann's chest. Somehow she had never succeeded in telling Sir Richard about taking it. She had planned to, but to do so had felt awkward, like an admission of theft, a violation of the complete trust that he seemed to have in her. And there had never been an opportune moment for her to put it back – he almost never left his room, and when he did she had to accompany him.

She loved the grey cloak. Though it was worn, patched and shabby with many moth-holes in it, there was a gentle lambswool softness about it, and a faint legacy of the scent of roses clung to it and enveloped her when she swung it round her shoulders. She belonged inside it. It granted her invisibility as she silently crossed the common, hood up against the slight breeze that had settled into the east and made the dawns and dusks chill but the days sunny and cloudless, as warm as if summer had never passed.

Those late September nights were frosty and clear. When she went to bed in the round house on the hill she folded the cloak around herself and Samuel, the soft fabric lapped up to their chins, keeping them warm. She watched the stars through the holes in the thatch, she stared at them till her eyes ached. The night sky was a dark cloak wrapped round the Earth; through the moth-holes in it she could glimpse the fiery brightness of Heaven. Twinkling, shimmering pinpoints of light. On a planet, somewhere, perhaps Thomas survived. Maybe Lady Ann. The stars were her friends. She didn't want a roof on her house. She loved to lie there. Samuel snuffled in his sleep, snug against her side. The stars circled, they wheeled from east to south to west. Andromeda and the Pleiades, the seven daughters of Atlas. She seemed to watch for hours. She didn't know when she was asleep and when she was watching. Dew settled on her face, pinched like frost. She was at home here. She didn't ever want to leave.

She began to make a regular detour south of the village on her way to collect Samuel each evening. Down where Walter Vernon's mother's house was springing up among the emergent shoots of new brambles. A red brick chimney climbed like a hefty oak through the skeleton of green timber, became octagonal and twisted above the ridge of the roof. The rafters were webbed with battens that would bear the small tiles stacked to one side. Great bundles of hazel twigs waited to be woven through the framework of the walls, and then daubed with clay.

When the house was complete Walter Vernon's mother would move into it, and he and Elaine would marry. She stared up at it, thinking, I will have to sleep in his hall-house where I won't be able to watch the stars from my bed. His tiled roof will weigh down on me, I will feel all the mass and the weight of the wood and the tiles hanging above me, they will oppress me, I will lie flat as paper between the two sheets. The marriage will turn me into a ghost of myself; I will become a grey shadow that slithers out from beside him into a dull world without books or writing, no interest or challenge, a world of boiled cabbages and always the smell of the wax, bubbling beeswax will permeate the house, it will cling in my clothes and my hair.

Maybe my marriage to Walter won't be so bad, she thought, I will have my chisels after all, I can carve. But she feared that she wouldn't have the heart for it. Maybe I will lose courage, she thought, as Richard did. Walter will expect me to help him with his business, he will expect my days to follow the selfsame pattern as his mother's. He may disapprove of my carving, he may not like the noise or the mess. On the other hand he will make a good father for Samuel. A boy needs a good father. The two of us will have food and shelter. I don't think he will beat me. What more could anyone want of life?

Oh, Cymberie, of course. But living there wasn't a possibility. The old man was bound to die soon, and then she would have no place there.

Could the new house of Walter's possibly be finished by Michaelmas? That was less than a week away. How close that seemed all of a sudden, their marriage impending. Could she delay it?

The house had to be ready and Walter's mother must have moved into it before their marriage could take place.

The house was right on the edge of the village. No other houses overlooked the site.

There was no-one around. No person, anywhere.

Elaine touched one of the great bundles of hazel twigs in the garden with the tip of her finger. It won't be too heavy, she thought; but when she tried to lift it she found that it was, and she had to cut the bands around it and divide it in two to carry it, one half at a time, down past the sweet smell of the ripe apples in the orchard, past the field full of pigs to the bridge. She rested each half-bundle on the parapet, and then shoved it over the edge, into the middle of the river. She watched the splash, watched the twigs separate as they drifted slowly downstream.

The next day she took a basket from Cymberie and on her way home filled it with roof tiles from the pile at the side of the unfinished house and bore it, taking the weight on her hip, down to the bridge. She balanced the basket on the parapet and lobbed one tile at a time toward the sunset. It was a calm evening; there was a light mist. No sign of the swans. *Splash* went the tiles; silver spray flew up from the dark river water.

It was only as she hurled the last tile toward the sinking red ball of the sun that she noticed the goosegirl with her flock down among the rushes in the shallows. Pale face turned upward toward her. Elaine swallowed her shock and waved, turned her back and hurried away up the hill. Will the girl tell her mother? she worried. Will the mother tell Walter? Will Walter change his mind about marrying me?

My poor baby. My Samuel. He needs a father.

Margery's garden was deep in shadow when Elaine reached it. Sunflowers hung their seed-laden heads, russets were dark baubles on the apple branches, tall hollyhocks rustled together, gone to seed and dry as old women. The stone path was cold under Elaine's bare feet, the frost on the grass nipped at her ankles. She lifted the latch and went straight in the cottage without knocking.

Margery had taken off her cap and her grey hair fell lank over her black shoulders. She had pulled up a stool to the fire and sat with her feet in the ashy hearth, scrambled egg in the earthenware bowl in her lap. She was dipping into it with a crust of bread. 'What are you doing here?' she demanded.

'I've come for Samuel.'

'What?'

'I've come for my baby.' Elaine glanced round the room. 'Where is he?'

'You took him hours ago.'

'No I didn't.'

'You did.'

'I never did so.'

'Stop your teasing, Mistress Elaine. I checked the garden to make sure all the babies had gone, and Samuel wasn't there.'

'He's not in here?'

'Use your eyes, can't you? Can you see him?'

'Where is he then?'

'You took him.'

'I didn't.'

'Well then, God knows.'

'The strangers …' Elaine was trembling; she held on to the door post for balance. 'There are strangers everywhere, coming for the fair – do you think one of them took him?'

'If a stranger came in the garden, the dog would have barked.' Wearily Margery pulled herself to her feet, set her bowl on the table, shuffled her feet into her boots. 'Caesar wouldn't let anyone who shouldn't take one of my babies. I swear it, on my mother's life. Samuel must be in the garden. I must have missed him.'

How big the garden was, all of a sudden. Swimming in shadows. Elaine stood and scanned it. Every cabbage had a baby's curves, every gooseberry bush concealed a child within its prickles, every rustle of dry leaves was a token of life. She ran up and down the paths. 'Samuel! Samuel!' Wood smoke: she coughed. There, under the bench in the rose arbour, a blur. She ran to it, knelt down and grabbed it – but it was a cloth that had been dropped and forgotten, a damp cloth that she let fall from her hands, and she stood there, eyes aching into the twilight. 'Samuel!'

'Where are you, my boy?' Margery called.

'He's not here, I tell you.'

'He's playing hide and seek with us, that's what it is. Sammy, Sammy, you little tinker, where are you?'

Dry leaves rattled. Elaine was so scared. *God please. Sweet Mary please. Find me Sammy.* Let not some misadventure have befallen him.

'He's such a crawler, Sammy is, I've never seen a baby like him for crawling. He could have gone miles. Sammy, you come to your mother right now, don't you make her fret.'

Holy Mary mother of God please – 'He's not here. He's gone.' Her voice was very hoarse.

'Caesar! Here, boy. Where are you?' A tremble of panic in Margery's voice. 'The butcher's bitch is on heat, that's the trouble, he's been wandering, he's likely to be round there. Caesar!'

The skinny floppy-eared hound slunk from his kennel at the side of the house. 'Now, I don't suppose –' said Margery.

But Elaine was there before her, kneeling, sticking her

head inside.

An oval pallor. A lightness as slight as petals on a moonless night: foxgloves, or wild roses.

'Well?'

Elaine reached in with shaking hands. 'Samuel? Sweetheart.' His hair, all damp, his cheek, his mouth, she felt them – she slipped her hands under his armpits, pulled him out. 'Samuel.' She held him tight in her arms, she rocked back and forth on her knees. He was damp, he was warm from being snuggled up to the dog. 'Samuel, I thought you were lost. Samuel, Samuel.' He was all that was important in her life. He was her belonging; he was her everything. *Thanks be to God. Thanks be to God. Thanks be to God.* She wrapped him in the grey cloak.

'I will always do what is best for you, my sweet heart. This is my fault – I shouldn't have dawdled home. I won't rebel, ever again. You scared me so, poppet, I thought something had happened to you, my love. Don't worry, sweet heart, I'll look after you. I will always do what is best for you, my sweet heart.' In all this world, he was the only thing that truly mattered to her. She kissed his eyes, she hugged him. He began to scream.

10

More and more strangers came to Cymberie along the track across the common. Their voices mingled with the wind in the trees, you could hear them clear in the lulls in the breeze. Singing and whistling snatches of songs, the low tones of gossip, laughter and anger. The strangers were bright colours glimpsed between branches; sharp twigs snatched at their clothes and trailed threads of scarlet, cinnamon and orange as markers on the way. The quiet lane of which Elaine knew every tuft of grass and every stone was changing: she felt a stranger there herself, walking along clouded in her grey cloak.

Horses' hooves made sharp prints in the soft earth. Every frosty night leaves would fall to obscure them, the yellow heart-shapes of the silver birch, the golden hazel, the crisp chestnut leaves. Down in the hollows the horses churned up the mud so the lane was impassable on foot and everyone had to step up on the mossy bank or pick their way through the trees, hands protecting their faces so the twigs wouldn't catch their eyes.

Sometimes at dusk deer would come and bend their heads, silent as shadows, to drink from the hoof prints.

'For God's sake, what does that damned woman want to come here for?' demanded Sir Richard. He was in his little side chamber; Elaine had encouraged him to come downstairs to it this morning, hoping the change in his routine would help him grow stronger.

'Let me write this down before I forget it,' said Elaine, working beside him at his table; and she added yesterday's sevenpence to the column of receipts of rent from the stallholders at the fair. 'What are you reading? Is that the letter the messenger brought?'

'Is he still here?'

'I don't know.'

'Go and find him. Bring him to me. I'll give him a message to take back to Ysabelle. He must tell her I won't see her. I know what it'll be like if she comes. *Father, you can't live in this great place on your own,* in that sweet honey voice of hers. *Not with all its sad memories for you.* Oh, I nearly picked up a stool and smashed her over the head with it last time she came. She made me so angry. Why won't she accept that I'm happy here? It would be hell on earth for me to live with her and her daughters. The racket they make. Bla bla bla all day long. Their high-pitched voices on and on. Their lutes and their virginals. Cynthia on her harp. You've never heard anything so awful. And that terrible husband of hers. My God, he's a savage, he still goes rampaging round chopping off people's heads with his battleaxe!'

'Is Ysabelle on her way here?'

'She's staying with a friend in Hatfield. How do you suppose she heard of the fair, way down in Wales?'

'Perhaps you're worrying unnecessarily, sir. Cymberie is a big house. It can accommodate her without any inconvenience to yourself.'

'I don't want the damned woman here!'

'She is your daughter, sir.'

'I don't want to see her.' He was very pale; his distress was making him sweat.

'Sir, you don't have much family.'

'Don't taunt me with that!'

Elaine picked up a pen. 'Your father is still not fully recovered, and requires complete peace and much solitude,' she read as she wrote, 'as a consequence of his severe illness.

However, he anticipates your arrival with great pleasure, and hopes you will honour him by presiding beside him at the feast on Michaelmas night.'

'It's useless. She always speaks her mind. I've never found any way of keeping her quiet.'

'Don't worry.' Elaine put her hand on his arm. 'I will stand guard over you, sir.'

'Give the letter to me. I had better countersign it. Take it to the messenger now. Then tell Mistress Phillis to come to me. She'll be delighted Ysabelle is staying. There was always the complicity of the three of them against me. Ann, Yssy and Phillis. It's strange how one forgets these things. But I want Yssy in the rooms at the far end of the gallery, not anywhere near me.'

After he had rested, a simple meal at the small table upstairs, by the open casement. Chicken pie, apple fritters, custard. The autumn air had a damp feel to it. Richard shivered. 'It's as if the world were moist with tears.'

'You should come outside in the garden, sir. It's warm in the sun.' The fresh air would make him feel better. Perhaps that was his problem, being shut up too much in the house. She felt powerless, not knowing what to do for the best for him.

'Tomorrow. I'll do so tomorrow.' He was tired now. He went to bed. 'Stay with me, Elaine,' he said.

She picked up the book of the Americas and sat cross-legged beside him on the blankets. But for once she didn't want to read. She lay down beside him, on top of the bedclothes, head on the pillow next to his. Her world was changing and she was afraid of what might happen. She wished she could turn time back. Her breasts ached to feed the old man, to have that simple need and tenderness. That clear-cut role. That certainty that she was doing right.

It was all her fault, this stupid business of the fair. A ridiculous impulse that had escalated way beyond her imagining. It had grown its own momentum, independent of any organisation. All you had to do was say the word *fair* and people flocked from far and wide. They wanted to get together, to break out of the routine of everyday life. Especially at this time of year, with the approach of winter and the shorter days, the cold and the shortages of food that were bound to come, they needed to have a good time before it was too late.

But the fair hadn't worked how she'd hoped that it would. Walter's friend the tool-seller Humfrey Howarde hadn't come. And if he did – well, so what? Even if she had Thomas's tools, she couldn't ever recapture the simplicity and happiness of her life with him. Carving couldn't do that for her.

She had changed: she had become another person.

The door to Richard's room was slightly ajar. Through it slithered the faint buzz from the fair. Come, it whispered, come, come and see.

Elaine couldn't resist. As soon as Richard was asleep she slid off the bed, pulled on her slippers and hurried downstairs and out of the kitchen door, down the hill toward the deer park. Such a ferment of people there was beside the lake; from above, they looked like a restless bubbling soup. Bright caps of carrot, lettuce and beetroot, doublets of dull turnip, earth and cabbage-colour all rubbed against each other. She herself was in her clerk's velvet bodice with the ruby sleeves; she was carrying a purse to collect any rents that were due.

Such a cacophony of voices! The noise fizzed around her. The yells of the men surrounding the cockfight, that was the loudest for the moment; someone was shouting the odds, others were screaming on the bird they'd backed. A play was about to start; a horned devil in scarlet was prodding the audience into place with a pitchfork. *Who'll buy my fine pies?* went the baker. *Who'll buy my hot meat?* sang out Mistress Rosamund over her brazier. *Pigs' ears and faggots, hot lamb chops.* A staggering drunk mistook what she was offering for sale and made a grab at her full breasts, and she slapped him around the face with such force that he ended up on his back in the grass, staring up at the sky.

Such a pretty sky. A constant pale blue. The good weather had settled now it was past the time of the equinox. 'A half penny if you please,' Elaine said to a man towing eight half-grown hogs attached to a rope. 'That is, if you're wanting to sell them.' He paid up without demur; she put the coin in her purse. 'How far have you come?' she asked. 'Fifteen miles,' he said. 'I want to get a good price for my pigs.' 'Let's hope this weather lasts until the end of the fair,' she said.

Over at the edge of the crowd the butts had been set up and twenty or so men, with a cask of ale to hand, were testing their skill in a leisurely way. They were mostly middle-aged; the youngsters despised the longbow as old-fashioned. Tomorrow there would be a formal contest; Richard was offering a fine brown and white cow as a prize.

The booths that offered goods for sale were set up in a double row beyond the lake. Such pretty things they had to offer – wooden dishes, pewter goblets, bowls and cauldrons. There was a metal-mending man. *Knives and POTS*, he went. *Knives and POTS. Knives and POTS. Hot pippin pies, hot* went a woman with a basket lined with a white cloth. A man who claimed he'd travelled to China on the back of a camel unwrapped a length of yellow silk when Elaine approached, and poured it over her outstretched arms like water: how she loved it, how she yearned to possess it! She would make a bodice out of it, she thought, a bodice of yellow silk embroidered with buttercups with gilt stalks, if she could borrow some of Mistress Winifred's threads. If she took money from the safe in the side chamber she would be able to pay for it. 'No,' she said, 'no, I can't,' and he gave her a stick of cinnamon for free, cinnamon from beyond Arabia, he said, *I trekked across deserts to get it*, and she rubbed the dry twist of bark between her fingers, tore it apart and sniffed at the rough interior of gold sand and sailing ships cutting through blue waves, a froth of white at the bows, salt sea, young men in gold earrings up to their eyebrows in adventure, bringing home riches; and her own life was so restricted and trammelled that she wanted to say, *let me come with you, the next time you go. I can dress as a man.* But her attention was caught by Walter Vernon; his candles were spread out on an unbleached blanket laid on a trestle table and customers were crowding round, admiring his wares, and buying them. This must be a good time of year for him, she thought, with people thinking of the dark winter nights lying ahead. She waved to him, but he was so preoccupied that he didn't notice. He was wearing his mauve ruff, the one that suited him best. He's not such a bad man, she thought, seeing him fill his leather purse with pence.

A sweetmeat-seller offered her a gooseberry lozenge from the tray that he carried and she let the opaque jelly melt in her mouth, wishing just one didn't make her want more when she couldn't afford them. Then she saw a new arrival, an old man carrying a creel on his back. He took his place at the end of the row and she steadied the basket as he slipped his arms out of the straps. 'That's heavy, grandfather,' she said, and he grunted and turned away, trampling his pitch flat, shuffling his feet over the grass. Then he spread a length of red fabric, a ragged rectangle the colour of dried blood, on the ground.

'What are you selling, grandfather?' she asked.

'What's it got to do with you?' He was a skinny old man,

face lined and weather-beaten, but he was agile in spite of his evident tiredness. He busied himself in pulling the fabric straight, ensuring that it was flat.

She stooped to help him. 'This is strange cloth,' she said. Above the smell of the old man's sweat it stank of fusty saltiness. 'It's very thick. Where did you get it?'

'None of your business.'

'The fair is my business. It's my job to collect the rents.'

He glared at her. 'A woman collecting rents, heh?'

'That's right.'

He gestured down at the cloth. 'I didn't steal it, if that's what you're thinking. They gave it me when I was working in the boatyard in Maldon. It came off of the *Susan* when she was wrecked. That's no use to us, they said, it's too small to be any use. You take it if you want it, they said.'

'It's a piece of a sail?'

'Yes ma'am.'

She slipped her finger through the hole in the corner where the rigging must have been threaded. It fitted like a wedding ring. She thought of the map at the front of the book of the Americas, the sketch of a boat speeding along and the West Wind puffing out his cheeks, filling the sails. She remembered the story of the city of gold, imagined the red-sailed boat becalmed in a blue bay fringed with green trees. The rhythmic shush of the low surf on the shore. A whale out to sea, a shark. Spotted jaguars slinking through the shadows. Their growls; their teeth.

'The *Susan* was supplying the London trade,' said the man. 'Taking hogs to the city.'

Elaine sighed, recalled to the real world. 'It'll cost you two farthings to sell here,' she said.

'Walter Vernon said he'd pay for my pitch.'

'What are you selling?'

'Nothing to interest you, lady.' He pulled packages wrapped in worn cloth out of the creel, laid them on the scrap of sail, started to unwrap them. 'Tools, you see. Axes. Saws. I've got a good sharp cutlass for cutting firewood.' He tested the edge with his thumb. 'Excellent, this cutlass is. The best you can buy. Feel that for sharpness. You won't get a better blade on a cutlass than that.'

Elaine took the cutlass and ran her finger lengthways along the edge, feeling for the slight burr of the metal on one side that would mean it had not been properly sharpened. But the blade was clean and sweet; this man knew what he was doing. 'Are you Humfrey Howarde?' she asked.

'What's that to you?'

'Do you sell carving chisels?'

'Woodworking chisels. Ones that will cut a tidy dovetail or mortice and tenon.' He unbuckled the other satchel, pulled a straight-edged chisel out of one of the sleeves. 'Ah,' he sighed, 'now here's a beauty. She's not been used in a while, that's why she's rusty, but sharpen her up and she'll cut like a dream. Your husband will be pleased if you bring that home to him, mistress.' He was obviously in some doubt as to her status, balancing her fine dress against her country accent.

'I'm looking for one set of chisels in particular. They're all inscribed with the mark of a lizard on the handle.'

'You've heard tell of those, huh?' He stared at her appraisingly. 'Now they're fine tools, my lady. I've had those quite a while, since November last. That's ten months, and I've not found the right purchaser yet. No-one who appreciates their quality and is able to pay a good enough price.'

'Let me see them!'

'I don't have them with me. They're not the tools for

country yokels.'

'You do have them, though?'

He nodded.

'How much do you want for them?'

'They're not cheap.'

'Walter Vernon will pay.'

'Wally will pay?'

'He has promised me them as a gift on our wedding-day.'

He stared at her. 'Wally is marrying you?'

'What's wrong with that?'

'Nothing, lady, nothing. I just never put him down as the marrying kind. I wish you both the best of joy.'

'Keep those chisels for me, won't you? I'll tell Walter you have them. Don't sell them to anyone else!' The chisels were a lightness in her heart, a longing that drove her to the candlemaker's stall.

'Walter,' she kept saying. 'Walter.' But he was intent on a sale, he was laying a bundle of a dozen candles in the basket of a maid in a scarlet bodice, he was joking with her; she was giving him a piece of silver, which he slipped in the purse at his waist.

'Walter,' Elaine said, but he still didn't see her. 'The very best wax,' he was saying to an old crone in black, 'gathered from hives up on the hill, where they've stood in the full sun all summer long. The best quality wicks, twisted from flax that's grown two feet tall in its meadow. These are the finest of candles, mistress. They will light up your winter, they will make it as brave and gay as the summertime.'

'Not at that price they won't,' went the old crone, starting to shuffle away.

'Wait,' said Walter. 'Maybe we can come to an

agreement –'

'Walter,' said Elaine.

He heard her that time, glanced round and held up a hand to quiet her, continued with his spiel. 'Come now, Mistress Hoxton, I'll throw in an extra candle for the same price.'

Thomas's chisels were an unrevealed secret, an undiscovered treasure that Elaine kept hidden in her heart; the chisels were a promise that was a gloss on this golden day, a hope that buoyed her up, made her feet light as she climbed through the fair.

'Good day,' people kept saying to her. 'Good day, Elaine. Good day, Mistress Fisher.' And she smiled and said good day back, good day Mistress Grace, good day Winifred, good day Master Robin, good day Joe, good day –

She took a square of the quince cheese that someone offered her, a comfit from a tray. Sugar on her lips, sweetness in her mouth; sweetness all around in her belonging once more: she was no longer an outsider, she had a function in this community. She was accepted now

Under the arch into the cobbled yard of Cymberie. A man was there splitting logs, his bare back to her. *Crash* he went down with his axe into the dull lichened trunks. He heaved the axe high and his muscles tensed beneath his skin; his skin was polished with sweat, it gleamed in the sun, *crash* he split the trunks neatly to show the bright heartwood inside, to release the raw wood smell. Elaine paused to watch him. When I have the chisels, she was thinking, looking at the strength of his shoulders, itching to carve them, I'll start with a great baulk of oak, I'll need a broad shallow blade to get that smooth rhythm to the wood –

When I have the chisels, she thought suddenly, I won't have Cymberie any more. I won't be here. I will be a dutiful wife in a small hall-house that stinks of wax. I will wash, I will cook, I will sweep the floors and sew, I will help my husband with his tasks. I will kneel to pray beside him. I will bring up my son. The only time I will be free will be late at night, and then the hammering of the beetle on the chisel head would wake them. I will be limited to making little things that I can hollow out of the wood in silence, with a small chisel. A doll, or a puppy, or a hen. Toys. A spinning top. A clothes peg to pin the washing.

The rich abundance of Cymberie overwhelmed Elaine as she stepped up out of the sunshine into the dim corridor. All was ready for the feast. Every one of the storerooms was full. The local cheeses made from the milk of cows that grazed on the rich pastures of Cymberie had been augmented with huge round Rochford cheeses and the Canvey Island cheese that came from the hardy sheep that grazed the marshes. In the fish room gleaming salmon were strung from iron hooks by cords of plaited grass, and full pails of green-finned Walflete oysters overflowed on to the damp flagstones. In the next room hung the carcasses of three sheep, two cows, four pigs and a deer, the raw flesh sweet-smelling and sickly; fat flies crawled over the skin. In another room the air was heavy with spices, cinnamon and cardamom, caraway and cloves, and late wasps lolled across the mounds of white muslin and poked their tongues into the sugary dishes beneath. Lazy. Sleepy. Greedy.

The kitchen was sleepy too. The sun slanted in the windows on to the flagstones. The great fire in the hearth had caved in on itself. *Shoosh* it went as a glowing log subsided. Sparks glittered orange for a few seconds, then died.

'Nathaniel,' said Elaine. He was sitting at the table, head bowed, and, filled with sudden affection for him, she came up behind his broad back, touched his shoulders and ran her hands down his arms to clasp his wrists. 'Almonds,' she said, releasing him. 'I thought you were asleep, with your head forward like that, but you're peeling almonds.' His strong thumbs with their floury nails were sloughing off the brown skin; the moist creamy nuts piled up in the stone mortar.

She went round the table and pulled up a stool to sit opposite him, started to help. 'Where's everyone else?' she asked.

'I've sent them down to have a look at the fair.'

'You're not going down yourself?'

'Mistress Ysabelle is coming in the morning. She loves my cheese and almond tart. It's been her favourite dish since she was little.'

'Is that what you're making now?'

He nodded.

'You're pleased she's coming then?'

'Look on the ledge and see if David's brought in today's eggs.'

There they were, brown and curved, warm in an earthenware bowl in the sunshine. Downy white feathers clung to them, stirred in a waft of air from the open window.

'Not that coverlet!' screamed Mistress Phillis from the room at the far end of the long gallery. 'For heaven's sake! Not for Mistress Ysabelle! What are you thinking of?'

Elaine paused at the top of the stairs, hand on the round top of the newel post, as the black-clad housekeeper hurtled toward her, a bundle of dark dornix crumpled in her arms, veered sharply into the room where the linen was stored and emerged a few moments later, laden with heavy folds of gold-trimmed brocade. As she hurried back to Ysabelle's room the sunlight that fell through each window of the gallery made the ivory fabric gleam and glisten. Glisten and shadow, glisten and shadow.

Richard's room was spiked with the scent of the soap that Elaine used to wash her breasts with. This afternoon it had been lathered into a froth of white on his chin, and Joe Chibborne was drawing a razor through it. Richard was leaning back in his armchair by the window, where the light was strongest. At the click of the latch he flicked his head toward the door, but seeing it was just her he turned back. 'For God's sake, watch what you're doing, man,' he said. 'I'm made of flesh and blood, not wood.'

'Please keep still, sir,' said Joe.

Elaine sat tidily on a stool, hands in her lap, and waited patiently for him to finish and slap gin on Richard's chin and bow himself out with his implements. Then she stood up. 'You look very smart, sir,' she said. 'Your beard is neat and trim.'

'The damn fool's nicked me,' he grumbled. He pushed himself up from the arms of the chair, clung to the court cupboard as he glared at the reflection of his pale face in the silver plate. 'Look at that.'

'It's only a tiny cut, sir.'

'I just wanted to make myself decent for Ysabelle. Otherwise I'll never hear the last of it. *You're letting yourself go, Father*, she'll say. *Come back to Wales and I'll look after you properly.* Heaven forbid! Elaine, look in that chest, will you? The old one with the iron binding – you'll need the key. Here. There's a dark grey gown there made of silk brocade. It's quite respectable, not like the shabby black things I've been wearing. Get it out and hang it up somewhere to air. I'll wear it tomorrow.'

Elaine undid the lock and lifted the lid. The contents of the chest were coloured severe but the fabrics were sumptuous. Her hands felt their way through the fine wools, slippery silks and a soft menagerie of fur trims and linings as she searched for the grey brocade. That was not plain grey, either; when she pulled it out gold threads sparkled in the pattern. How beautiful it is, she thought, how rich, so different from everything in the world in which I have grown up; and she looked over at the old man whom she had nursed and pulled back from the very cliff-edge of death and thought how little she knew him; thought how it was habit, the repeated pattern of their days, that had built this bond, this kind of affection between them, that had made her come to care for him. Yet she was still uncertain of him.

'That's the one,' he said. 'Ysabelle won't tell me off if I wear that.'

'Sir, may I go now?'

'Is it time already? Yes, if you wish.'

As Elaine went down the stairs she thought how she would be in good time for collecting Samuel. She pictured him crawling among the cabbages in Mistress Margery's garden: she would like to paint that: there was something about the way the curve of his bum echoed the curve of the cabbages that made her laugh. And here on the stair wall was a space where she could paint him, that empty buff patch over beyond the apple tree, where the invention of the painter had for once seemed to desert him. Or maybe his scaffolding hadn't been adequate and it had simply been too difficult to reach. Maybe she would summon up her courage and ask Richard's permission to paint Samuel in. After the fair was over; when all the fuss had died down. Though he would probably point out that Samuel was part of her life story, and nothing at all to do with Cymberie.

Perhaps, after they were married, Walter would let her paint the bare walls of the candle house. Maybe she could carve angels and paint them white, like gulls, with gilt eyes, and fix them to the rafters above her and Walter's bed. Their marriage would need all the blessings it could get. She wondered how Walter felt about angels. Did he condemn them as pure Catholic superstition? Would images of angels be banned in his strict faith?

Down in the shadowy hall, she gazed up at the family portrait hanging over the fireplace. Belvoir father, mother, son and daughter all stared out from the frame, stiff-lipped, stiff-clothed. The only emotion that was manifest was Richard's love for his wife. There was no indication of the tensions that exist in every family; everything was perfect. But that perfection had all came unstitched. At this moment Lady Ann was six foot underground, Gabriel was bobbing about in a fragile craft on a tempestuous sea, Richard was mortally sick and Ysabelle was on her way here to drive him mad. Yet he loved her; that was clear from the care he was taking over his appearance. He wanted to be esteemed by her.

Elaine thought of her own parents, of how she hadn't been in touch with them since she left home, how they didn't even know that Thomas was dead and they would be thinking – because they were always optimistic – that no news was good news, and she and Thomas were prospering together, getting commissions, being well paid.

When she went back to see them with Walter beside her, what would they say? Her father would approve of him, she was certain. *He has sound business sense*, he would say, and nod sagely. *Just the right kind of fellow for you to marry.* He hadn't been that keen on Thomas. He's a kind man, and handsome enough, he'd conceded. He's a good carver. But you need to marry someone more down to earth, my dear. Someone with their feet securely on the ground.

Almost as if he had known then what Thomas's fate was to be.

Thomas had never told her of the holes in the soles of his boots. It had only been when he was hanging from the scaffold that she saw them.

A rattle of the latch on the front door made her jump. The creak of the hinges as it opened even more so. This door was always kept locked. But perhaps Mistress Phillis had drawn back the bolts and turned the hefty key in anticipation of Ysabelle's arrival.

A sliver of north light fell through the doorway, to be part-blocked by a thin figure pausing between the door and the jamb, then shut out with the whisper and creak, the thud and the click of the door closing. Just the dull light from the tall narrow windows to each side of the door, then. A man silhouetted against the light, his face obscured by the shadows.

TAKE OFF MY MOTHER'S CLOTHES.

How sharp the man's voice was. How full of hate.

TAKE THEM OFF, I SAY.

She opened her mouth but before she could utter one word his hands had seized the wrist of her left ruby sleeve, he was wrenching it off, the pins were giving. Pricking. She moved to hit him with her right hand but he grabbed that sleeve in his left, slapped her face hard with his right. She reeled back: how it stung! She kicked out at him but couldn't make contact, almost overbalanced. That sleeve came off too, he was so strong, the pins pricked her, sharp, sharp – then he grabbed the lacing on her velvet bodice, his fists tore it out – he swung her round, he grasped the back of the bodice, she stumbled forward as he pulled it off her – oh, he hurt so – he was trampling the pretty fabric underfoot. 'You thief. You whore.'

'I –'

He grabbed the waistband of her skirt, seized the ties. He was so strong. She had thought she was strong but she was powerless in his grip. 'Let me – undo it,' she gasped, but no, he had to do it, with hands desperate with rage. She lost her balance and fell. The skirt came away in his hands, he pulled it from under her, leaving her splayed there on the old, cold tiles with her shift rucked up so he could see the swell of her white belly, the dark vee of her hair, but he didn't touch her again, he didn't care about her, he was sobbing like a baby into the bundle of torn clothes in his arms.

She was slithering backward, tugging her shift down, she had to get away from this madman and she kept slithering back, without whimpering, nothing to attract his attention, back to the kitchen, her eyes fixed on the mad fellow's grief; she touched the doorpost and pulled herself upright, clinging to the oak frame, she lifted the latch and she was through to the kitchen's blessed warmth and low sunshine, how strange it was, the sameness now, it was empty, thank God for that. She lurched along to the apple store, the fragrance of the apples now gathered in tangible in the air as an ointment, a balm, and she pulled down her own clothes from the hook and trembling put them on. Lady Ann's calfskin slippers she left square in the centre of the room.

'In heaven's name, what's happened to you?' asked Mistress Margery. 'Come on in, girl.'

Elaine didn't understand how she had reached the door of her cottage.

'Was it a man?' said Margery.

Elaine couldn't answer.

'The state of you,' said Margery. 'Take off your clothes.'

'No.'

'I'm not going to hurt you.'

'No.'

'I make an ointment from marigolds. It will help the bruising.'

'I can't pay you.'

'Haven't I always helped you when you truly needed it?'

'Yes.'

'Well then.'

Elaine lay on Mistress Margery's bed that smelt of sweat and of piss and the old woman loosened her clothes and, filling her palm with ointment from a jar, rubbed her skin, soothing long strokes down the length of her body, the prickle of the rough skin of her hand, the softness and soothing, the scented rubbing that lessened the pain and the shock –

'Don't go to sleep. You can't sleep here.'

Elaine stood by the door with Samuel in her arms. She was shivering so much that Margery wrapped her own shawl around her. 'Give it back in the morning,' she said. 'Did you forget your grey cloak?'

'Tomorrow –'

'What?'

'I don't know what to do tomorrow.'

'Who did this to you?'

'I don't know.'

'Was it Sir Richard?'

'No.'

'Who was it?'

'I don't know. I never saw him before.'

'You have to go to work tomorrow. We all do. Without

work we can't survive. Tomorrow is Michaelmas. It will be an easy day. Plenty of people around. You will have nothing to fear.'

A new moon. Elaine saw it as she climbed the path to the round house. A white cloud of a crescent skew as a cradle as the sky turned red in the west.

'Samuel, Samuel,' she said, rocking her body as she sat on the gravel with her back against the house wall. She undid her bodice and put him to her breast. She could still do that, in spite of the bruises. She crooned over him: '*... was all my joy ... was my delight ... my heart of gold ...*'

Her voice broke on a sob.

11

Cold dawn. Soft light filtered through the roof, the doorway. The sleeping baby was snug against Elaine's chest. She needed to piss. She slid away from his warmth, bare legs out from under the sheet, chill.

Venus was still bright in the western sky. The sky grey blue. Her body was stiff from her injuries, it hurt when she moved. Gravel was sharp underfoot, it prickled like small pins.

She squatted a little way behind the house. Her piss steamed.

Cold. Shivering, she picked her way down to the spring and stripped off her shift, scooped up handfuls of water to rinse herself clean of the man who'd attacked her last night. The water, coming from underground, felt warm. It couldn't wash off the dark marks of her bruises.

If Walter offered to marry her today she would do so even if she didn't get her chisels. What she wanted was security. Food, a roof over her and Samuel's heads. No one daring to attack her, because she would become a respectable woman. A Puritan preacher's wife, soul clean as linen long-boiled and dried in the sun. But Walter's mother's house wasn't yet completed. She remembered herself tossing the roof tiles one by one into the river. The swing of her arm; the grittiness of the clay in her fist. The splashes they made. Silver in the brown water, as if they were dashes of hope. The goosegirl's face turned upward to her like a pale lily flower at the riverside. The memory was distant as a dream. Did Walter know of it? Had the goosegirl told him?

She ran up naked to her house, shaking her arms to dry herself. There was one bruise in particular that made her gasp, on the back of her ribs on the right side. 'It'll get better,' she panted, grabbing a clean shift; one that had belonged to Richard's late wife, pulling it over her head. She wrapped Margery's warm shawl around herself and woke Samuel to feed him. 'Oh, you lazy bones,' she said, flicking his feet to keep him awake, as she had had to do when he was newborn.

When she had washed Samuel she dressed herself. Her own bodices were very worn. She wished she still had the velvet bodice with the ruby sleeves. Sir Richard will be angry if I dress shabbily, she thought, today of all days. Michaelmas day. I will have to meet Ysabelle, protect him against her. I will have to support him at his feast, in the presence of his neighbours. How can I dress shabbily for that?

She brushed the dried mud from the hem of her skirt and tied it on. She lifted her mattress and took out from beneath it the turquoise silk bodice Richard had given her, that Lady Ann had quilted and embroidered with pink roses and pearls for their wedding day. It was creased; Elaine laid it on the bed and stroked it with the palms of her hands, admiring the workmanship, trying to smooth out the last of the snags in the fabric from when she had thrown it in the graveyard hedge. The pearls at the centre of the flowers – she was sure they were real, although Richard denied it. How could they be just glass, and so lustrous?

Her old sleeves looked like sacking next to the bodice. She had no choice but to pin them into it. Once she had put it on and laced it up, she covered it with her own bodice, not wanting thieves to see it, and hooded herself with Margery's shawl. She carried Samuel to her cottage. 'Thank you for your kindness in lending me the shawl, Mistress Margery,' she said, returning it.

'How are you this morning?'

She shrugged her shoulders. 'I will be late tonight,' she said. 'I have to attend Sir Richard at this evening's feast.'

‘If I have to buy cow’s milk for the baby, that will cost you extra.’

‘Of course. You are not going to the fair yourself?’

‘I don’t believe in throwing my money away. How late will you be?’

‘I’ll come back as soon as I’ve put Sir Richard to bed.’

‘Any time then. Folks who don’t care about the cost of a candle don’t keep to the hours that God appointed for waking and rest. If it’s after dark, don’t bother coming. I’ll be sleeping, and Samuel can sleep beside me. He’s an easy child.’

‘I’ll come first thing to feed him.’

‘He’s ready for weaning. He drinks cow’s milk fine from a cup now.’

Elaine touched her breasts. ‘It’s just I –’

‘The same for all of us. We all want to feel our children need us.’

How strange the woods were that day. Bursting with people clad in their best clothes. They slid between the half-leaved trees like bright shadows, laughter like birdsong, boots crunching the dead leaves; they converged on the track, all heading for Cymberie, some alone, but most in small groups. Families with little children carried piggy-back, old women with empty baskets and coppers jingling in their pockets, ploughmen whose backs were bent as if their boots were still weighted down with the thick mud of the fields, a choir whose chins were newly-shaved and criss-crossed with cuts – *Gloria*, they went, *in excelsis deo* – gangs of boys who ran, and played tag, and dawdled, and young women gossiping in low-cut bodices tarted up with ribbons and laces. All out for a good time. Singing and laughter. Some drunken shouting in spite of the early hour.

There were so many people that Elaine felt invisible. Her

attacker wouldn't be able to single her out in this crowd.

The stiffness caused by her bruises eased with walking, though the bruise on her back was still painful.

All she knew about her attacker was that he was tall. He was tall and thin, and wore rings. She had a deep scratch across her right forearm where one of his rings had caught her. He had been wearing a short cloak. But his face had been against the light and she hadn't been able to see it. He hadn't smelt drunk.

What she remembered most about the attack was her own powerlessness in the face of his strength and aggression. The fear, and the pain.

There came a strange noise. A kind of buzzing. A Michaelmas swarm of bees? What was it? She strained to identify the sound; she'd never heard it here before. A noise curling up the hillside from down by the lake – distant music, maybe? It must be serpent and hautbois playing. Yes, there was the beat of the tabor.

One of the young women stopped abruptly. 'Listen,' she said.

'The fair!' whooped another, and they all picked up their skirts and started to run. Taking the left fork where the track divided, the quickest route to the deer park.

Elaine ran too, feeling safe in their company, down the track and scrambling over the gate in the hedge, veering across the long grass, holding her skirt high, the cold dew numbing her feet, across the open land, no sign of a deer anywhere, pelting under the standard oaks that cast such long morning shadows, down to the campsite by the lake: the blue smoke of wood fires rose in the chill air, the crisp scent of frying bacon. The young women hurried toward the musicians, but Elaine ran on to the line of stallholders.

Humfrey Howarde was asleep, curled up in his blanket,

his creel beside him, but Walter Vernon was already busy setting out his stock for the day. She stopped still, panting, and watched how careful he was, how everything had to be neat; and then he became aware of her presence and looked up. 'Mistress Elaine,' he said.

'Walter.' She didn't know what to say then. He was wearing his mauve ruff again, his hair was combed, he was looking quite decent. Like a man you wouldn't be ashamed to be married to. It was unreasonable to feel reluctant. 'Walter, you said – you mentioned – you know – today –'

A couple of old women wandered over and started fingering his stock. 'How much is this candle?' one of them asked.

Walter looked at Elaine; he looked at them. He mentioned a sum.

'Lord have mercy! That's downright robbery. I'll have a word with your mother - '

'Well, let me think, maybe, seeing as it's you, Mistress Alice, maybe –' He was holding out a hand to detain Elaine. 'How about six for two halfpence? Elaine, wait – '

She could just make out the tall chimneys of Cymberie through the thin mist, above the treetops, at the top of the hill. I should be there now, she thought, Sir Richard will be waiting for me. 'Walter, I've got to go to work, I just need to know when –'

'Not today,' said Walter. 'The house isn't finished. They haven't given me all the roof tiles I ordered. There's a great hole in the roof still – I can't move my mother in. I'm not a free man yet. Will you be content to wait until next week? Everything will be fine by next week.'

'Two halfpence,' said the old woman. 'What kind of joke is that?'

'Next week,' said Elaine, her heart lifting. 'Next week will do very well.'

'Now if you throw in this couple of little candles as well, if you include them in the price –'

'I certainly won't,' said Walter. 'Do you know how long it takes to –'

Elaine stretched out her arms in the mist and flew up the path to Cymberie. A week's reprieve: her body felt lighter, her bruises all healed, she was floating on air. She soared, she wheeled, and in no time she'd reached the back door. She went in the corridor.

'Get more logs!' Nathaniel was bellowing from the kitchen. 'You fool, you dolt, don't let the oven get cold!'

Old Egbert who was one of those who had been called in to help in the kitchen limped out and, passing Elaine, stuck a finger up in the air in the cook's direction, and she laughed and entered the apple store; she unlaced her old bodice and took it off, perched on the edge of one of the shelves to dry her feet with it; and then she pulled on her calfskin slippers, hung up her bodice to dry and shook out her skirt as she strolled into the kitchen.

'What are you looking so pleased about?' snapped Nathaniel. 'Quick, pass me that cloth. Careful, don't get grease on your pretty bodice. You've got dead leaves in your hair, do you know? Here, take Sir Richard's breakfast up to him. God knows where Geraint has got to. The boy's disappeared. Gone down to the fair I daresay. I'll give him a taste of my belt when he gets back. There's so much to do.'

'You've got golden leaves in your hair,' said Sir Richard. 'Kneel down.' He patted the side of the mattress and she knelt on the broad floorboards as if she were praying. She rested her forehead on the edge of the bed and he slowly, gently picked out the leaves, careful not to pull. 'Oak and hawthorn,' he said. 'Such lovely leaves.' He cupped them in the bowl of his hands. 'They are like fishes,' he said.

'Sir, I've brought you your breakfast.'

'I don't want to eat. I'm waiting for Ysabelle.'

'Let me get you dressed.'

'Like gold fishes,' he said, lifting his hands high and letting the leaves fall to the sheets so autumn came to the house. 'I asked Gabriel if there were truly fishes of gold in the rivers of the Americas. I said, Gabriel, I don't understand how that can be because surely they would sink, gold being so heavy. He said, it is only a legend. He said he has climbed into the mountains and never seen a single gold fish in those turbulent rivers.'

She thought: the old man is wandering in his mind again. Maybe the last few days have been too much of a strain. She smoothed his hair back from his forehead. He wasn't hot; he didn't have a fever. 'Sir, you must eat, to keep up your strength. You want to be fit for Ysabelle.' She stood by the bed, held the goblet of ale to his lips and tipped it until he was forced to sip. 'This will make you strong, sir.' She cut his bread into small squares and fed it to him slowly.

He wasn't interested; he traced his finger over her breasts along the embroidered stems of her bodice.

'Concentrate,' she said.

'Ann wore that as my bride,' he said. 'She never wore it after Gabriel was born.'

'Two more squares of bread and you can leave the rest.'

He swallowed them dutifully. 'I think Ysabelle will come about midday,' he said.

'Plenty of time to get you dressed then, sir.'

'It's the first time you've worn it since I gave it you. I wondered if you had sold it.'

'I wouldn't do that, sir.' She rolled up her sleeves and washed his face and hands, under his arms, his private parts. She dressed him in his shirt, his ruff, his doublet, hose and breeches, the gown of grey brocade.

'I won't sit up yet,' he said. 'I want all my strength for when the children come.'

'Let me comb your hair, sir.' His thin hair. She combed it slowly, gently, rubbed the back of his head the way that made him relax.

He leant back against the pillow, looked up at her. 'Is all well with you, Elaine?' he said. He was frowning.

'Why do you ask, sir?'

'That dark bruise on your arm. That scratch – it's deep.'

'I fell on my way home yesterday, sir, and bruised myself a little. That's all it is.' How calm she could be when she was with him.

Before noon there came the rattle of hooves on the stones and a great knocking on the front door. 'Is that her?' demanded Richard.

Elaine opened the casement and leaned out. 'It's just a messenger, sir.'

'Help me up, Elaine. She'll be here soon.'

He sat at the table by the window. She closed it to keep out the slight chill, piled logs on the fire to warm the room. He asked her to bring his papers; he wanted to look busy when his daughter arrived.

She brought him pens and an inkhorn too but he didn't touch them, just kept staring toward the blank trees of the common, the autumn trees like waves, all browns and yellows and golds, the colours muted by the mist. 'She'll come soon,' he insisted.

'Sir –' She was worried about how tense the old man was. It couldn't be good for him. She reached out for his hand and stroked it, wanting him to relax.

'Stop that,' he snapped.

And then there she was. Ysabelle, his daughter. The mist had suddenly lifted and she was riding sidesaddle out of the woods in a skirt of sky blue satin, bodice and sleeves of white silk embroidered with yellow, her hair piled up beneath a green hat with a tall scarlet feather. She was mounted on a glossy black mare. The reins that she held in her gloved hands were attached to a bridle trimmed with scallops of scarlet velvet, as was her saddle. Behind her came a sober maidservant on a grey pony, and a train of six menservants in black, each girded with pistol and dagger and walking beside a mule laden with baggage. At her side rode a tall thin man on a great chestnut stallion: an armed guard, Elaine thought at first, because there was a wide-awakeness about the fellow, he sat very straight and he turned his head this way and that, looking at the house and the lavender beds and the marble statue's white reflection in the pond; he pointed out the entrance tower to Ysabelle, and she nodded and laughed, and put her hand on his arm with a gesture of such familiarity that Elaine asked, 'Who is that man, sir? Is he her husband?'

'He's Gabriel.'

'Your son Gabriel?'

'Yes.'

'But I thought he was –'

'He came home last night. Help me. I want to greet them at the door.'

When Elaine glanced at Richard she saw his face was transformed by his love for his children. His eyes glowed, his pasty skin was flushed with colour, all his skinny angularity was softened. She felt a stab of jealousy; she'd thought he cared a little for her.

His eagerness gave him strength: he grasped the table and levered himself to his feet; he almost ran to the top of the stairs. Elaine had to hurry to keep up with him so she could steady him if he needed it.

Down in the entrance hall the front door was already standing wide open, light flooding in to illuminate the painted walls and the family portrait, the worn floor tiles, the slope of the stairs. An array of maids and menservants were lined up in welcome, Winifred and Joe Chibborne, Glascocke and several others, and Mistress Phillis and Nathaniel were stepping side by side over the threshold, there were raised voices and joyful greetings, the neigh of a horse. Richard stopped two steps from the bottom of the stairs, almost as if he was afraid, grasping the banister, and then Ysabelle came, whip still in her hand, and she said, 'Father,' and ran up and embraced him, and his lip trembled and his eyes started to water. She put her white arm around his grey waist and led him into the parlour at the foot of the stairs that had been Ann's favourite room, where he had never once been in all the time of Elaine's coming to Cymberie. A fire was lit in the hearth and the room was homely, a red carpet spread along the table and the sheen of highly polished silver, cushions on the armchairs, books on the shelves and glazed casements here too, a view over the garden to the west –

'Sit down, sit down,' said Richard, lowering himself into a chair. 'Nathaniel, bring tint. Our returned wanderers must need refreshment.' But there was a jug on the table already and Nathaniel was pouring the red wine into goblets, adding sugar and offering it to the three. Like a trinity they sat in their ornate carved armchairs, hands clasping the talbot heads on the ends of the arms. Elaine hung back, feeling awkward and out of place.

But Gabriel jumped up and offered her his seat.

'No,' she said, and shook her head, too surprised to explain.

He persisted. 'You must be one of my cousins,' he said. 'You look so familiar. I know I've seen you before. I've been away a long time, though, and I'm sorry, I can't remember your name.'

'Elaine Fisher is my clerk,' Richard said. 'She's no relation of yours. She has been invaluable to me during my illness. Pull up a stool for her, Gabriel. Here, beside me.'

It was the effect of the turquoise and pink bodice she was wearing, Elaine realised; it was because of that that Gabriel has assumed she should be treated with respect. She crossed her arms across the front of it and sat silent, a little back from the semicircle of the others, listening to the brother and sister vying with each other at story-telling.

Ysabelle's stories were all of her daughters and the life that they led in their castle – hide and seek on the battlements and music practice in the great hall, and Cynthia waking at dawn on midsummer morn and lugging her harp up the steep stairs to the highest turret, there to greet the longest day by playing like an angel. 'An angel indeed,' beamed Ysabelle. 'The most beautiful angel in the whole world, her golden hair tumbling round her shoulders. The peasants stopped work in the fields to listen. The very sheep stood still and strained to hear –'

Ysabelle's hair was mid-brown. Her brother's was fairer, cut short and brushed fiercely back from his face. He had a high hairline starting receding, a widow's peak. His face was weathered by the sea winds, his eyes were creased at the corners from staring into vast distances. He talked about having docked at Plymouth and given his men a few days ashore before they sailed up to London and there unloaded the Good Adventure and began to dispose of the goods they'd brought home, which comprised gold bars as well as strange fruits and vivid-feathered parrots in a great cage that the Spaniard from whom they liberated them said was modelled on one belonging to the Emperor of China. 'Oh the girls would love a parrot!' Ysabelle exclaimed and Gabriel told her he hadn't found homes for them yet, and promised to keep them the best pair. 'Did you bring monkeys?' she said, and he said no, but he had brought a velvet pouch full of emeralds, and Ysabelle leant forward and said: *That ring on your left hand*: and he said *This*, touching the massive rectangular-cut emerald with its shoulders moulded of gold in the shape of sea-monster's heads with sharp horns: 'Yes,' he said, 'I acquired this from the captain of a Spanish vessel that had stuck fast on a reef off some deserted island – he gave it me in exchange for a tow off the coral – but his boat was holed and it sank to the bottom.'

Nathaniel came in then with a platter of radishes, and Elaine had to stir herself from dreaming of white-tipped waves breaking beneath a blue bowl of sky and frantic sailors rowing for their lives to a tree-rimmed land; she had to fetch silver bowls of water and calmly place them on the table for them to wash their hands; and when they sat and dipped the radishes in salt the topic of conversation switched to Cymberie, and Ysabelle told her father that the place was too much for him now and he must come and live with her and the girls in their castle in Wales, she wouldn't brook any resistance, she said; and Elaine looked at Richard and saw how this meeting had drained him and how exhausted he was, barely strong enough to eat, and she butted in softly and described how well he managed his land, how he let out all of it except for the deer park and enough of the demesne to provide for the needs of the house, in order that the estate should not be demanding to run. 'Simon Pascall is in charge of the meadows and pastures, and makes sure they are evenly grazed,' she said. 'George Noke cares for the orchards.'

'You seem to know all about it,' said Gabriel. 'How long have you been working for my father?'

'Since July,' she said. Then, because she was uncomfortable with his attention focused on her, she went on to detail the various tenancies, taking refuge in the solidity of field names and rents. Drayton Palmer had Nether Ravens and Thistlie Field and Holy Oakfield; he kept pigs on Crows Lawn and grew rye in Weastefield. Peter Wentworthe farmed the Spring and Stubbes Pasture and Halborow Meade, and John Brodbury farmed Great Meads and First and Further Ley and kept cattle in Bog Field when it dried out in the summer and the grass was long and lush, vivid with purple knapweed and blue damselflies.

'My God, that brings back memories,' said Gabriel with a smile that made Elaine think: how alike you are, you and your father. 'Do you remember, sir,' he went on, 'how you made me walk all round those fields with you? I was only little; my legs ached so much when we got back home. *You must understand your land*, that's what you kept saying to me. *You must understand the land if you are to farm it well.*'

'It was a waste of time,' said Richard. 'I couldn't make you care about it. You always were a stubborn child.'

'Those field names still make me feel at home, all the same. You have pounded them into me, sir, they are part of my being.'

'Would you – will you stay?' Richard's voice was naked with longing. Elaine flinched, knowing he was laying himself open to be hurt. 'Your mother and I, when we bought the old friary and its lands, we stood under the oak trees at the fringe of the wood and we said, this will be a place we will pass on to our children. We built this house with that in mind. Money was tight at first, but we did it for you.'

'I sail for the Americas again in January, sir. It's all fixed. We've secured the boats and we have most of the financial backing we need. I have an appointment with the company of Goldsmiths next week; that should see to the rest. Maybe when I return in two or three years' time I'll settle down, who knows?'

'I have been very ill this summer, Gabriel. I – it has made me aware of my own mortality.'

'For God's sake, sir, do you think I'm unaware of mine? You live in such cushioned comfort here, you forget what the real world is like. How do you think I've been living? All the fighting I've done – those terrible fevers that haunt the Indies – they run wild on board a small boat! I brought only a third of my original crew back with me to Plymouth. They were such good men, the ones that I lost, I mourn them still –'

Nathaniel came into the room with two boys, and they set on the table dishes of pottage and spit-roast beef, bacon, cabbage, pork pie, turnips, quince cheese and custard. 'Well,' said Ysabelle comfortably, 'let's feed you up now, Gabriel.' She carved the beef with her amber-handled knife, pricked the slices with the point and piled them on her brother's plate.

Elaine helped Richard to a small portion of bacon and some custard. But he was not interested in his meal, he was pursuing his own line of thought. 'Do you want Cymberie, Gabriel?' he asked.

'What do you mean?'

'You can have it now if you want it.'

'No, no, don't give up the place, I'm happy as I am.'

'How about when I die?'

'For Heaven's sake, sir! This meal is a celebration, not a wake. You're in no danger of dying yet, that's plain to see.'

The old man had eaten nothing. Elaine dipped the tip of

her spoon in his custard and raised it to his mouth but he smashed her arm down on the table. Custard spattered everywhere. His children didn't comment. She bit her lip, didn't complain.

Later he went to bed. She hung up his ruff and his gown and when she turned round his eyes were closed. 'They won't stay long, sir,' she whispered. 'They'll soon be gone and life will be back to normal. Don't distress yourself over them.' She dipped a corner of the towel in the silver bowl, carefully wiped the custard from her bodice.

All afternoon the music of the fair entered the house. It sang up the slope from the lake, it twisted between the mullions, it throbbed in the floorboards, sprang in the joists. Elaine could feel it through the thin soles of her slippers.

Closing the casements couldn't keep it out. The great bed shivered. Richard muttered in his sleep. Elaine didn't leave him. Ssh, she said, ssh. She started to read to him from the Book of the Americas. *Trees of infinite magnitude and variety grow in forests that are perpetually green. They have the capability to protect the native peoples, not only by providing them with nourishment, and shelter from the terrible heat of the sun at noonday, but also by furnishing them with remedies against the diseases that infest these parts: the fierce fevers, monstrous headaches and racking sicknesses. The dried bark of certain trees...*

Elaine heard a shuffling sound and when she raised her head she saw Gabriel leaning against the open door, arms crossed, ankles crossed like a crusader's on a tomb, his short cloak swinging from his shoulders. He was watching her as intently as if she were a strange alphabet he was trying to decipher. She thought: that cloak you wear, the horned emerald ring on your finger, was it you who attacked me last night? She shrank away from his gaze, cast her eyes down at the book, began the sentence again: *The dried bark of certain trees...* She stopped, unnerved, licked her lips. The silence between them lasted some while and then he said, 'Do you know that you read with my father's accent? But when you talk you have a northern accent.'

She offered him the book. 'Will you read, sir?'

'What's the point? My father's asleep.'

Sound asleep now. She brushed the old man's hollow cheek with her finger, stroked his thin hair.

'Are you and my father lovers?'

'No.'

'Have you ever been?'

'No.'

'Does he give you presents?'

'Sometimes.'

'Did he give you that bodice?'

'Yes.'

'Has he ever given you clothes of my mother's?'

'Yes.'

'Last night, was it you in the hall, when I came in?'

She wanted the incident never to have happened. 'I don't know what you're talking about,' she said.

'In the dusk I thought you were my mother. I thought I'd put my grief aside. Seeing you – it – grief welled up inside me, it was like a great wave. It drove me –'

The dried bark of certain trees... she repeated again.

'Do you have a lover?'

'No.'

'You're so beautiful.'

'You have a reputation as a man who likes women.'

'It's a pleasant way to pass an afternoon.'

She looked down at the book in her hands.

'My chamber is just along the gallery.'

'So?'

'Come and I'll show you.'

'Show me what?'

He leant forward and kissed her ear. His starched ruff rasped her neck, his stubble prickled her cheek, his breath tickled, his lips were dry and warm. She wanted suddenly to reach out to him, to grasp him, to love him. But she jerked back. She had her pride; she wasn't a whore. 'Why don't you go down to the fair if you've nothing else to do?' she said.

'Will you come with me?'

'No.'

'My father's asleep. You're not needed here. Come with me.'

'No.'

'Come, Elaine.'

She shook her head fiercely, eyes downcast.

'Very well. I'll find someone else.' He turned away and she heard the stairs creak as he went down them. The latch of the front door clicked open; the door slammed. She closed the book and dropped it on the bed, ran along the gallery to the small room at the end with its view over the cobbled yard and the lane leading down to the lake. She was barred in by the mullions (no glazed casement window here) and she pressed her face against the sun-warmed wood to see as well as she could.

Into the yard were riding a man and a woman in velvets and furs, on dappled horses; a boy ran from the shadows to hold their reins. They would be here for tonight's feast, no doubt. And here came Gabriel, tall and so good-looking in his weathered way, slinking round the side of the house: obviously he had seen the guests but didn't want to get trapped into polite conversation. Elaine watched him stride easily down the lane until he disappeared from sight. Under the oaks. Into the vast noise and throng of people at the fair.

It's strange, she thought, how, if I hadn't been overwhelmed with the desire to possess Thomas's chisels, the fair would never have happened. I invented it. It all started so lightly, on an impulse. I told Walter about it. It was a lie, but he believed me, and it escalated from there. Look at all the people it involves now. Look at the holiday it has created for them. A celebration before winter.

A play was in progress. Adam and Eve on the back of a cart. She listened to Adam scream as God tore a rib from his side.

She couldn't resist going into Gabriel's chamber. She touched his pillow. His shirt of fine silk was folded under his sheet. She lifted it and smelt it. Sweat and sunshine. She held it against her face.

In the evening the music came into the house. It began with a blast of trumpets that rattled the windows, eased into waves of viol, lute, serpent, hautbois and the pulse of the drum, that washed up the stairs to lap at the sill of every chamber door: come *on*, they summoned the guests preening themselves by candlelight in front of steel mirrors. Come *on*, it's time.

Down the stairs washed the wide skirts, the spangled silk stockings that glittered in the glow from the high-banked log fire; diamond and pearl-ringed hands slithered down the banister; the shimmer of gold thread and cloth of silver filled the great hall as the guests from the big houses of the neighbourhood stood around and chatted of this and that while drinking deep from gleaming goblets, until the brother and the sister came down late and side by side and led them into a slow pavane: skirts and cloaks swung, hand touched hand, feet barely lifted from the dance floor –

Upstairs Richard was perched on the edge of his mattress, grasping the bedpost. He'd been sitting like that some while. Elaine said gently, 'Sir, they are waiting for you to take your place so the feast can begin.'

'I have had such a pain in my chest, Elaine.' He was ashen-faced, dark smudges beneath his eyes.

'I'll tell Ysabelle and Gabriel you're not well enough to preside at the table.'

'No.' He shook his head. 'I can do it. Help me, Elaine.'

She pinned his ruff, eased his grey brocade gown over his other clothes. He had to keep resting for breath. 'Sir, let Gabriel take your place at the table.'

'I'm not dead yet.' He pulled himself to his feet, the gown falling round his shaky legs.

'Sir, it would be better for you to stay upstairs.' But she so much wanted to be down with the music. It was calling her, her left foot was tapping, she couldn't stop it.

'Rings – can't look like a damned pauper –' He fumbled through his keys, held out an iron one with a triple-feathered head. 'The cupboard in the panelling –'

She'd never seen inside this before. The recess was piled deep with leaves of parchment; on the top shelf was a leather casket. She reached it down.

He unlocked it, opened the lid. 'My eyes, Elaine –'

'It's not your sight, sir. It's getting dark.' She lit the six candles on the court cupboard, held two close to him, saw the casket was lined with velvet, some kind of blackwork embroidery in the lid. Was it embroidery or writing?

He picked out a large square diamond, an egg-shaped ruby, a purple garnet, and slid them on.

'Careful,' she said. 'They're loose.' He had put them on the fingers he had always worn them on: but his hands had grown so thin during his illness that the rings were bound to slip off. She pulled them off and pushed them on his middle fingers. 'There, sir. That'll be better.'

He studied the effect. 'Looks wrong – no good –' He fumbled through the remaining jewels, picked out a caul of gold net and pearls. 'Wear this. Your hair –'

She hadn't thought to make any attempt to tidy herself. Swiftly she combed her hair, scooped it up and hooded it with the caul, checked her reflection in the big silver plate. The candles flickered light and dark shadows across her face, glittered in the caul, recast her as a lady. She turned to look at him and he nodded; but she felt uncomfortable, dressed too fine for her station. 'I'll put the casket away, sir – do you want this paper in the lid? It has your name on it.' It wasn't embroidery, she'd realised; it was parchment with his writing on it.

'My name, my wife's name, my parents' names, my grandparents' names – the dates of all my loved ones' deaths – I've put them all down here. Elaine, I charge you with this task: when I die, add the date of my death to this paper. Then I will be at peace with those with whom I belong. I don't belong in this world any more, Elaine.'

'Sir, you're not going to die. You'll soon be better.'

'Don't lie to me, Elaine.'

She didn't know what to say. She turned to put the casket away, turned back. 'Listen to the music, sir, doesn't it make you want to dance?'

'Promise me, Elaine. Add the date of my death to that list when I die.'

'Sir, we must go downstairs.'

'I want to join them. I want to be with my family.'

'Ysabelle and Gabriel are downstairs. And your friends. Here is the cupboard key, sir. Come, let me take your arm. Lean your weight on me.'

Side by side, slowly, they descended the steep Darien of the stairs toward the front door, which someone had left ajar. Step by step into the nip of the evening air, the heat of the orange glow cast by the log fire. She tucked her arm under his to support him; her body absorbed the tremors that shook him.

A portly man in a blue velvet doublet, just adjusting his purple satin breeches, shouldered the door wide open and looked up.

'Harry!'

'Richard, by Our Lady! Good to see you up and about again! How are you, old friend?'

Elaine detached herself into the shadows as the two men moved to embrace each other. Harry thumped Richard on the back so heartily that she was afraid he'd fall over. 'My god, you look well, old fellow! I heard you were knocking on death's door but you don't look like it now. You look like you could gallop ten miles. Oh, it's good to see everyone at Cymberie again, my friend. Like the old days. The parties you used to hold then, you and Ann. The hunting. Christ. The stirrup cup that fellow of yours made. Powerful stuff. Never got the recipe off him. What did you hide yourself away for, old man? We've all missed you. The times I've ridden round and that fellow of yours, Nathaniel, is it, he's told me you've ordered no-one was to be admitted to your chamber. No need to be a recluse, old boy, no need, much better not, tragedies happen to all of us, we all understand, old friend, but not the way to cope with things, shutting yourself off from everyone, not the way at all. It's good to see you. So good.'

In the fireglow Richard's thin ill face was suffused with pleasure. He went to speak, but croaked; coughed to clear his throat. 'Harry –'

'Come on in and take your seat, old boy. Everyone will

be delighted to see you.' Unostentatiously Harry took Richard's arm and supported him around the dancers to the head of the table. 'There we are, old man.' He settled Richard into his armchair, then flopped heavily down beside him. 'I daresay you haven't been down to the fair, have you, old fellow? One of the best I've been to in years. I congratulate you. Excellently arranged. Plenty of entertainment. I won two guineas on a Chelmsford cock. Beautiful fellow he was, great comb as scarlet as sin –'

Elaine hovered behind the two men, unsure what to do, uncomfortable among all these fine people. Sir Richard would be safe with his friends and family around him. He didn't need her. She hesitated, wanting to ask his permission to leave, but unable to interrupt Harry Tuck's flow of words.

The pavane came to an end. The dancers curtseyed and bowed and, laughing and gossiping, jostled to wash their hands in the bowls of rose-scented water, to dry them on the towels and seat themselves at table. Elaine sidled out, close up against the south-facing windows. Through the thick glass she could see the sharp roofline of the kitchen and a round oak in silhouette against the darkening sky. She wondered if she could go home, whether Ysabelle would be willing to put her father to bed.

'Where are you going?' That was Gabriel; he'd noticed her.

'Home.'

'You can't do that.'

'There's no need for me to stay.'

'For God's sake, the party's just beginning! Come and sit down!' He seized her hand and she had no seemly choice but to follow where he led her.

Just down the table from her master. She kept looking toward him, checking that all was well with him, finding reassurance in concentrating on him. Servants brought in platters of oysters and salt beef as a precursor to the meal, and she watched him help himself.

'Stop worrying about my father,' said the man at her side. 'He'll be fine. Do you want mustard with your beef?'

His hands were broad, long-fingered, deft to help her. The nails chewed short. Lace cuffs frothed white over his tanned skin: wavelets on to golden sand. The sea-monster horns of his emerald ring reared up like a young bull servicing cattle. 'Don't you scratch people with that sometimes?' Elaine asked, smoothing its prongs as if that would make them lie down.

He shrugged his shoulders.

She itched to pull up her right sleeve and challenge him with the scabs on her arm, but she couldn't in the formal company she was in. 'You must miss your mother,' she goaded him.

'Last night,' he said quietly, 'at first glance, in that light, when I came in the door, I thought you were her. You must understand that. You wore her clothes, you are the same build as her, you had that same stance there in front of our family portrait; how she loved to look at it, as you were doing – we are all kept safe there, in the fence of that gold frame, unchanging, she used to say, we are preserved against any accident of fate: but yet time opened the gates and we were set free, Ysabelle to her Welsh warlord, I to prance around at court, her to her love of riding, as if she sought to outpace her approaching age by galloping with the wind in her still-red hair. I loved her so. A wild thing. And then you turned and I saw that you were not her. Your hair was dull brown to her red, your face passive to the bold energy of hers. I – when I saw you it was like a storm in my heart, a great wave of grief, a flood of anger that broke the dam-walls of restraint – anger possessed me – I never knew grief still possessed me. I thought I was safe. I thought I couldn't be hurt any more. I'm sorry if I hurt you.' He put his hand on her thin wrist. 'Did I hurt you badly?'

'My arm hurts,' she said. 'And my back. It's bruised –' But suddenly her physical pain seemed slight against the hurt that she had inadvertently caused him. 'It's much better now,' she said.

'You're sure?'

'Yes.'

He hesitated. 'You're telling me the truth?'

'Of course.'

He said, 'I – I find it difficult accommodating myself to living at Cymberie. I live in such a different world now.'

'What do you mean?'

'I don't belong here. My boat – the Caribbean sea – it's a different game.'

'Tell me about it.' She looked up at him, observing for the first time the vulnerability that lay behind the green sheen of his eyes.

Oh, he told it fine. His stamping ground was the chessboard of blue ocean checked with green islands, where he constantly had to pit his intelligence and strength against the other players. Violence was no part of his game plan. 'Death comes too easily out there already,' he said. The pawns that he had to capture were gold bars and treasure.

'Do you mean that you're a pirate?' she said.

'The Spaniards have no right to the wealth of America,' he said. 'There's no moral reason why it should belong to them. They have stolen all their riches from the native peoples whom they mistreat. Everyone has to earn the right for things to belong to them.'

'Have you earned your right to Spanish treasure?'

He laughed then; told her of his seizure of the *San Fernando* in a bay north of Cartagena in the dead of the night. 'We rowed around the headland, the eight of us,' he said, 'in a small boat. Muffled oars. We didn't speak. Bare scrap of a moon. White foam on the black rocks. Fish rotted on the shore. The breeze wafted us the scent of the watch's tobacco. We cut the anchor chain. Iron clunked, waves lapped against the hull. We clambered up loose ropes. The watch were drunk.'

'Go on, don't stop.'

'It wasn't difficult. We penned them in the captain's cabin. No alarm was sounded until the *San Fernando* was well out in the bay. Where I could get a crew of my own men aboard, and sail her out of the bay.'

'How?' Elaine was trapped by his tale: intent, forgetful of herself. Gabriel was very like his father, of course. Was it that, or his storytelling, that explained why she felt so at ease with him?

'Your handsome brother's lost none of his charm, by the looks,' boomed a woman's loud voice suddenly from the far side of the table. Ysabelle was sitting there with a band of women of her own age, obviously old friends; they'd been gossiping about husbands and acquaintances and drinking freely. 'Who's that girl Gabriel's got his beady eye on this time? Arthur Stracy's daughter, is she?'

'Will you take some of this baked venison, Elaine, or some apple fritters?' Gabriel offered gravely.

She reached out with her knife and helped herself. 'Go on,' she said. 'Go on with the story. What happened then?'

It was silent, what happened next, lost in the hubbub in the hall. Sir Richard, face flushed red, slumped forward on to his plate.

Harry Tuck put his arm around him. 'There, there, old friend,' he said to his recumbent head, and tugged him upright by the shoulder, and rubbed his temple clean of mustard. 'A little tired, are you, Dick?' He spoke more loudly. 'Or hot – it's so hot in here with this press of people. I can't stand it myself. Let's get out of here. Hoi, Gabriel!'

In an instant Gabriel was there beside him, slipping his arm beneath his father's shoulder and hoisting the old man to his feet with an ease that made Elaine think, he's done this before, in battle, for his men, when they've been wounded by an arrow, or by gunfire; and Harry Tuck was supporting Richard on the other side, and Sir Richard was dragging his feet along between the two of them when he regained control of his legs and his head came upright, and he grunted, ' A bloody puppet, is that what you think I am?' Elaine, swinging her feet over the bench to get to them, heard Harry mutter, 'Come on, old man, you can't die in front of an audience, it's not done,' and Richard said, 'I can die how I damned well want,' and Gabriel said, 'What in heaven's name are you two arguing for? There's no need to die at all.'

Then they were in the entrance hall and Nathaniel was marching through from the kitchen bearing a roast swan on a charger, and, seeing the state of his master, he thrust the swan at Elaine who faltered under the weight; he swung his skinny master up in his arms like a baby and carried him up the stairs. Elaine bore the swan through to the table and, when an elderly woman clutched at her arm with a bony ringed hand and demanded how their host was, she said he was fine, a touch of indigestion from the rich food, that was all, and she hurried after Nathaniel, running up the stairs behind him, pushing past him through the chamber doorway to fold back the bedcovers, Gabriel on her heels and lighting the candles, Harry Tuck still down in the hall, hesitant about intruding.

'Lay him on his pillows,' Elaine said. 'I'll make him comfortable.'

Richard half-opened his eyes. 'Damned fuss,' he grunted.

'Sssh,' said Elaine. 'Don't worry, sir. Rest yourself. A good night's sleep will put everything right.'

'The swan,' said Nathaniel. 'Where is it?'

'I'll take your shoes off, sir.'

'Where did you put the damned swan, Mistress Elaine? It's taken me hours to prepare it.'

But she was thinking just of her master, didn't notice when Nathaniel set off in search of the swan. 'There, that's more comfortable, sir. Let me unpin your ruff. Now I'll put your rings away.' She slid them from his fingers, tugged the gold and pearl caul from her hair (*don't*, whispered Gabriel, stretching out his hand, *you look so pretty like that*), put everything away in the casket which she locked in the wall. Gabriel lifted a strand of her loose hair when she turned back: 'It's so long,' he said. 'So soft.' He let it fall.

She said: 'See. I'm putting the key under your father's pillow. No one can accuse me of stealing.'

'I wouldn't accuse you.'

'Well.' She proceeded to gently divest the old man of his clothes, leaving him in his shirt because he was quietly moaning.

Then all of a sudden he was vomiting, his shoulders heaving, his thin body convulsed with retching. She cleaned him up swiftly without comment; but it was odd sick, with what seemed to be traces of old blood mixed in the fragments of his meal: old brownish blood that stank of rust. 'Something you ate,' she said. 'I'll leave the bowl here in case you're sick again.'

'I'll look in on him later,' said Gabriel. 'Come downstairs with me now, Elaine.'

'I'll stay with him until he's fully asleep.'

'I'd better go down or people will talk.'

She sat on the bed, leaning against the pillows, waiting

for the old man to settle. She'd done this so many times. But this evening was different because downstairs the band had begun to play English dances, and the quick rhythm of them was getting into her feet; she couldn't keep it out. The floorboards were shaking, the bed shook. Her feet itched to dance. Don't let the music disturb you, she whispered to Richard, and tried to be calm. But she wanted to join in the dancing. It was a part of herself that she'd forgotten, a part that belonged to her childhood and her courtship with Thomas (though he'd never been a good dancer, was always a few steps behind), a time when the world was simple and full of certainties, with clear allegiances and no shortage of food, and she yearned to go and join in, to recapture the past, but she couldn't because she had to stay with the old man, and she had in any case no place in the hall, no reason for being there; all her reason was with Samuel and she had to get home to him, had to get home –

And then the old man was asleep and she pulled the coverlet up to his chin. 'Goodnight, sir,' she whispered. 'God keep you safe. I'll be here in the morning.'

Before Elaine could go home she had to change into her old bodice, which was hanging in the apple store beyond the kitchen. But as she stepped through the entrance hall a thin figure emerged from the shadows and grasped her arm. She started, terrified, remembering the attack on her there the previous night.

'Don't be afraid.'

'Gabriel?'

'Trust me, Elaine.'

'I –'

'Elaine, come and dance.'

'No. I have to go home.'

'Nonsense. It's early yet.'

'I must.' She was thinking of Samuel.

'You can't leave the party already.'

'I must go.'

'Come on. One dance.'

'No.'

'Just one little dance. Five minutes, that's all. What difference can five minutes make?'

Five minutes in the candlelight shimmer on vivid silks, soft velvets, glitter of spangles, sparkle of jewels and the scent of sweat as the company joins hands in a circle: stamp, stamp your green slippers to the beat of the drum rhythm strong in your head, side step and kick to the centre, never mind your last night's bruises; you've forgotten the steps it's been so long since you danced and you're a little behind. Gabriel guides you into the star turn, four of you with right hands raised to the centre and you're circling behind a stranger whose short cloak flies out and brushes your breasts, and Gabriel has his free hand lightly on your waist at the back, he's directing you, the comfort of that touch of sureness in a room full of strangers, and into the promenade holding his hand, the drum all the time beating faster, faster, faster …

The music stops. Gabriel still holds your hand. You laugh at each other. Other people are getting a drink. You can smell the ale on their breath as they come back to grasp your hand, pull you into the circle that's forming. You're not yourself, you're part of the pattern and the surrender is sweet, the drum rhythm starting again and promenade and turn …

'I have to go,' Elaine said suddenly, pulling away.

'No, stay and dance.'

'I must get home.'

'You can sleep here the night.'

'Nonsense. All the rooms are full.'

'There's space in my bed.' He looked down at her, resting his hands on her waist.

She put a finger up to his lips. 'I have to go home. My parents –' It was so easy to lie.

'I'll keep you company.'

'No. It's not far. I'm fine on my own.'

'It's a dark night.'

'Do you think I'm a woman who's afraid of the dark?'

'A fine gentleman I would feel if I left you to go home alone.'

She couldn't think of a way to avoid his company. And she wanted him. She wanted him so much. *Thomas, it's been so long*, she thought. Thomas, would you understand? I miss your body so much. What Gabriel did to me last night, it was a mistake. He won't do it again. He won't hurt me.

So she let him lead her by the hand out the front door, crossing the lawn, bumping into each other. Kissing. His stubble was sharp against her face. Oh, the young man smell of him, laughing under the stars and the slip of a moon. How long since she'd laughed like this?

Their eyes became accustomed to the night. He started playing with the lacing of her bodice, undoing the bow.

It was past the hour when she always fed Samuel. Her breasts were full. Milk rose to her nipples, spilled over on to her shift. No, she thought, no, not when I want him so much –

'No,' she said.

He tipped her face up to his. A proper kiss, tongue in mouth. Oh, she wanted him. But her shift was wet with milk that even now might be soaking through her bodice. He was pulling her toward him, not letting her hold herself away, and all she could think of was milk stains on the cornflower blue satin of his doublet: how they'd ruin the fine garment, how he might demand compensation that she'd never be able to pay.

'No.'

'Yes.'

'No.'

'Come on.'

'I can't.'

'You're no virgin, Elaine, I don't believe it.'

'It's not that.'

'Come up to my bed.' His hands were linked loosely round her neck, arms resting on her shoulders.

She could just see how fondly he was smiling at her. She ducked suddenly and ran.

'Elaine!'

She sprinted across the lawn, into the shelter of the lane.

'Elaine!'

He was coming after her, made slow initially by his surprise. She raced on. When he started to gain on her she vaulted up the mossy bank, in under the trees. The holly tree, the hiding-place holly tree, surely that was near here?

Branches whipped at her body. She covered her face with her arms. The dead-leaf rustle, the snap of twigs would be a giveaway that would surely lead him to her.

A darker mass rose up before her. Solid as a bell. On hands and knees she crawled in. Sharp leaf prickle in the palms of her hands. Clawing at her head and her back.

Once inside, she kept still. Still and silent. Only the thud of her heart, trying to bound out of her chest. She hooked her arms around her knees, sat still and listened for him.

'Elaine! Elaine!' He was blundering around. She could tell where he was by the crunch of the leaves. 'Elaine, what did I say wrong? I didn't mean to frighten you. Let me see you home,

Elaine, please. Elaine, Elaine – '

The sound of his lost voice retreating was picked up by the owls. *Twoolaine, twoolaine...*

When there was no sound but the owls and the bark of foxes, and intermittent rustles that had to be fox or badger, Elaine crept from the shelter of the holly tree and made her way back to the track. Above her head restless twigs shivered against stars that as the night wore on became sleepy with mist; what little light there was, was dulling. It was so dark. She stumbled on an unevenness in the path, thought that in bare feet she'd better be able to tell where she was stepping and she slipped off her calfskin slippers, walked with them in her hand.

How cold the earth was. Cold and wet. Better to walk on the moss which though it oozed moisture was soft and warmer. Were living things always warmer than inert objects? She thought of rocks that were heated by the summer sun and how good they were to lie on, how their warmth soaked into your back. There were no rocks in this southern land.

She came to the village and walked between the dark houses to Margery's gate, beyond which lay her cottage that was a hump of darkness. She knocked softly on the door. 'Mistress Margery?' She tried the latch but the door was bolted on the inside. She pictured the woman curled under her blankets and snoring with her own dear Samuel a pink comma snug against her side, in a room warmed by the ashes of the dying log fire. It was so cold out here.

She felt so alone. She wanted to feed Samuel, to have that affirmation of the value of her existence: him at her breast; him depending on her. How can one claim any value for one's own life? she thought. Isn't it only in interaction with others that our lives become worthwhile?

She was weary; her body felt heavy. Her bruises were aching intensely: perhaps because of the exertion of dancing, or the walk home. She sat in the arbour, on the wet bench. The dew was heavy, it fell in occasional drops from the rose to her lap, to the shoulders of her turquoise bodice. She fingered the pearls on the tips of the embroidered stamens. She didn't want to go home. The house on the hill seemed suddenly intolerably lonely, and the solitary walk there in the dark unbearably long and perilous.

The mist had risen and the stars were now so bright that they seemed certain, like a home. There was Orion, there the Plough, there the Great Bear. They were as familiar as fields.

There was the North star that guided Gabriel across oceans.

The stars were far, far off.

She was accustomed to watch them through the hole in the roof of her and Thomas's house.

Mistress Margery's house was a home because Samuel was in it.

Cymberie is a home but I don't belong there, she thought. Tomorrow I will be there. Tomorrow – She pictured herself assuming her role. She would cross the lawn to the great house and walk round the outside to the kitchen, enter by the old corridor, stop in the storeroom to put on the clothes that fitted her for her post. Her skirt, her sleeves, her bodice, the green slippers.

I am still wearing my work clothes, she panicked. They are stained with milk, they will smell sour tomorrow. She thought of Gabriel, how that would disgust him. She didn't want him to think her a slut.

She picked her way along the stony lane to the centre of the village, past the low houses that were sleeping humps of thatch. A dog barked; a cock crowed, out of time. An owl called and another answered from some distance away. The cows that by day were pegged out to graze the green were shut up for the night; likewise the goats. The shutters were closed on the inn; the sign of the Bell hung still on its hinges. The village was lonely and quiet as if no-one lived here.

Enough light fell from the thin moon for her to see the wooden pail perched on the wall of the well. She lowered it gently until it splashed; she jiggled the rope to make sure it would fill. Then she wound the pail up, the handle creaking, the effort of turning it catching the bruise on her back.

That strange phenomenon of water coming up warm from underground. She bathed her hands in it, than let it stand until its brimful surface was smooth as a mirror and she could see the moon in it. She shivered. She knew that once her clothes were wet she would be colder than she was now; but if they were to be dry by the morning she had to wash them. She wished she had her shawl with her.

She took off her bodice and gently rinsed the silk. The water was pure; it wouldn't hurt the fine fabric. Then she loosened the waistband of her skirt and pulled her shift off over her head. How cold the night was on her bare skin.

Even in the thin moonlight she could see the dark milk patches on the linen; she dipped them in the water, rinsed them well, wrung them as dry as she could. The creases won't matter, she thought, they'll fall out as soon as I wear it again.

When she lifted her eyes she saw a light coming toward her along the lane. It trembled and flickered, kept on towards her.

Will o' the wisp. Goblins. The Black Dog with yellow eyes wide as trenchers and a great mouth with sharp teeth, that would open and swallow her up. Munch her into mincemeat.

All the tales that her father'd told her, all the legends that she'd laughed at from the security of her family hearth, tumbled into her head. She shrank away, clutching her shift over her bare breasts. This was the Black Dog incarnate, coming and coming and coming one-eyed toward her: should she stand and face him, or run?

'Elaine.'

The Black Dog could speak? It knew her name?

'Mistress Elaine?'

'Walter?' Was that his voice?

'What are you doing here so late?' He was carrying a lantern, she could see that now, it lit up the belly of his black doublet, the underside of his mauve ruff, the tip of his long nose, the fringe of pale hair beneath his tall hat.

'Mistress Elaine, what has happened to you? Why aren't you dressed?' He put the lantern, and the thick book that he carried in his other hand, down on the side of the well; he unclasped his cloak and moved to swing it round her shoulders, stopping when he saw the dark bruise on the white skin of her back. 'Who has done this to you? Who has hurt you, Mistress Elaine?' He explored the bruise gently with the tips of his fingers. It was the nearest he had ever come to a caress but it made her flinch.

'I – it's nothing. I fell over.'

He took her hands and pulled them toward him so her shift no longer covered her breasts. She looked down at the ground, and shivered. She hated him looking at her. It was the cold, and her fear, they had made her weak. This is my husband-to-be, she said to herself. She longed for some sign of tenderness. She wanted him to love her.

He touched her ribs. 'You are bruised here as well,' he said. 'Who did this to you?'

She felt violated by his touch, slipped her shift back over her head, tightened her skirt, crossed her arms across herself. 'I fell over, I told you.'

'Did he do worse to you than this?'

'What do you mean?'

'Did he…?'

'There was no-one.'

'Put my cloak around you. Make yourself decent.'

The warm folds smelt of wax. 'All it was, was that I was washing my clothes at the well.'

'At this time of night?' He didn't believe her. Then he said: 'You can sleep in the barn. It will be warm there, and no one will bother you. I would give you my bed but my mother won't permit that you come in the house.' He held the lantern up. 'There – now you can see where you're going.'

In the lantern light every stone in the lane had a dark shadow, a chiaroscuro of wrong and right. She put her hand on his arm but he shook it off. She stubbed her toe: 'You'll have to wear shoes when you're married to me.' Her eyes stung with tears. She was very tired.

'Climb this ladder.' He put her hands on a wooden rung and she climbed dutifully. Cows shuffled in the dark of the barn; she smelt their warm breath, the acidity of their urine, the sweetness of the hay. 'There's a wide ledge up there. You won't fall off.' He picked up his lantern from the earth floor and left her.

Prickle of hay stalks. She wrapped herself in his cloak to protect herself.

Thin slivers of starlight crept through the cracks between tiles, between the mullions of a high window. The rafters of the barn were the slant of old trees that sheltered her. She pillowed her head on her arm and slept.

Walter blew out the lantern and stood in the garden in the stillness of the apple trees, in the sweetness of the ripening fruit. He let the peace of this place where he had always lived sink into his bones and calm him. *This night will change my life*, he was thinking. He took off his hat, clasped it in his folded hands. 'Lord,' he said.

At the meeting he'd come from, at the barber's house, the gift of tongues had fallen upon him, and he had spoken unchecked, unhesitatingly, of the wickedness of Cymberie fair and the folly of men's pursuits and trivial amusements when the single thing that mattered was to live rightly and win the love of God. Browne himself had been there, and had asked him to deliver one of the sermons at their next Prophesying. A sermon on repentance, it was to be. The honour of it burned a warm pride in his chest, that he, a simple candlemaker whose sole reading was the Bible, should be perceived as having attained a level of faith and understanding worthy of being of use to others.

And then, coming home, he'd seen Elaine Fisher at the well, she who was a living reminder of his fallibility and imperfection. There she'd stood, bare-chested as a wanton, fair-skinned as an angel, her ribs still visible from her time of near-starvation when he'd not dared approach her in case anyone guessed from his so doing his terrible sin: his complicity in the lies of drunkards in order to save his own skin. Letting her husband be hanged for a crime he himself had committed. How many hours he'd spent on his knees in penitence for that.

There she'd been, half-naked by the well, her skirt slipping down her hips like some mermaid's tail. For the first time she had stirred desire in him. When he was a boy he'd felt desire. Jone, fourteen, with swelling breasts with pink nipples that she exposed for him to kiss when he gave her a groat. She didn't let him do more. When he fumbled at her skirt she'd slapped him hard and said, you marry me first. You bring her home over my dead body, his mother had said. She's trouble, you keep well away from her. You've a lot to live up to. – None of the girls he tried were any match for his mother, and he soon gave up, except for the occasional quick coupling in a field in spring. It had been so long that he had almost forgotten what desire felt like.

He'd watched Elaine from a distance before he began to court her. Watched her get thinner and thinner. He had hoped it would be the Lord's will to take her from this earth, and set him free from his obligation to her. But when she got her job at Cymberie where there was plenty of food, he'd known that wasn't to be, and he had realised that he had to marry her, that being the only way in which he could protect her. Courting her, he'd known how utterly inept he was. He had felt low as a slinking cat bringing a gift of a dead mouse or frog to appease its owner. He didn't know how to woo her – and there by the well he hadn't known how to express his desire.

And he'd been shocked by those terrible bruises. And confused: he didn't know if they were real. Had someone beaten her, or kicked her around? Or were they spiritual symbols of the suffering she'd undergone?

Bruises always fade, he mused: it is still possible to make good her life. They would marry, yes, he and she would marry: he would work hard and see that she and her son lacked for nothing.

But that was in conflict with his calling. *Follow me* our Lord said. And here was Browne asking him to deliver a sermon on repentance to hundreds of his fellow-men so that he might aid them in coming to the true path of God. Holy work indeed. But work that would put his own life at risk. Wyatt had drawn him aside and was urging him to take ship with him to the Continent where they could both practise their faith in greater freedom.

'Can't you see sense, man?' Wyatt had said. 'Your own father was burned at the stake for his beliefs. What did he achieve by that? Nothing of any lasting value. It's our task to build the kingdom of God on Earth.' Wyatt was suggesting that they set sail across the ocean to the New World and found a community there where they might worship in peace in the true way, free of politics and the dictates of monarchs. How he longed to do that, with no compromise.

In their new world they would build houses of the local trees and roof them with reeds; they would build a plain church that would be free of all the wicked idolatry that was the inheritance of this land. There'd be no statues of saints, no paintings, no fine robes, no altars: just purity of faith. They would take communion hand to hand.

They would catch silver fish in the river and net strange birds in the branches, plant corn and harvest great golden fields of it to the glory of our Lord. It will be a new Eden, he thought, a perfect place. I will be Adam and Elaine my Eve, Samuel our little child. The sea will lap against the shore and the same moon rise above the horizon as rises here. We will pray with the salt breeze threading partings in our hair. We will take cattle and poultry with us, we will be like Noah repopulating the world after the Flood. Our new world –

We just need to find it.

Our Father, let it be. Walter knelt in the wet dew to pray.

Elaine burrowed deeper into the hay, pulling his cloak tighter around her.

12

Elaine sat dangling her legs from the hay loft, picking pieces of straw out of her bodice and hair. Two horned cows in the shadows gazed at her as they tugged at the hay in their manger, trailing long beards of it which they slowly ingested. She threw off Walter's cloak and yawned and stretched, jumped down and slid past the cows, smoothing their warm flanks. 'I've got to go,' she told them; but the barn door was barred on the outside. I'm not waiting for Walter to show up and open it, she thought. I have to get on with my day.

She kilted up her skirt and clambered up the beams to the high window, sending a couple of hens that were nesting in the hay clucking off in alarm. She squatted on the window ledge, looking down the lane to the church tower, the hands of its clock ticking round to work-time. Some cottages were astir, smoke drifting up from their chimneys, bacon burning on a griddle. A boy yawned under a yoke carrying two pails from the well, stumbling sleepily as he passed by; and then the low sun touched the mist in the valley, and Elaine let herself down from the window, dropping the last few feet to the grassy bank, then running, first to the well to find her green slippers, and then to Margery's cottage in a village now full of gold light.

Leaves turned to bronze and amber. Dew pearled on grass and hedge, on the coarse cabbages; on the rose thorns of the arbour, drops condensed and dripped. The door to the cottage stood open and Mistress Margery was there, kneeling to light the fire, turning her head at the sound of Elaine's footsteps on the path. 'That son of yours is a good sleeper,' she commented.

And there he was, in the dirty-sheeted hollow of

Margery's bed, swaddled as if he were still little, and damp with pee. 'Samuel,' she said softly, and at the sound of her voice he opened his eyes and began to scream.

'Sssh –'

Then he was sucking hungrily away at her breast, and Elaine, her bodice and her shift unlaced, her damp hair slicked back, was singing *Summer is a-cumen in* while Margery, the fire lit, busied herself sweeping the room. She stopped a moment, resting her hands on the broom handle. 'Look at you,' she said, 'out without a shawl. You'll catch your death. You foolish girls, you'll never learn.' She picked up her own shawl, and laid it across Elaine's shoulders. 'You had a grand time last night, no doubt,' she said, 'in all that finery.'

'This isn't my bodice,' said Elaine, afraid Margery was going to demand it. 'I have to give it back. They lent it me for the feast.'

'More fools them. They should have known you wouldn't know how to care for it. Look how you've puckered the silk.' She pulled it deftly between her rough fingers, flattening it. 'Was it Ysabelle who lent it you? She's a good girl, I nursed her myself. And that terrible brother of hers, before her. Don't you have anything to do with Gabriel, my girl. Babies follow in his wake like gulls the plough, and one child is more than enough for any single woman.'

'I can look after myself.'

Margery snorted. 'That's what they all think.' With a fierce swish of the brush she drove the dust out the door. 'Just watch yourself, that's all.'

The trek across the common to work again. Elaine was happy that Samuel was well settled for the day. There would be nothing to make her late for him tonight.

The bruise on her back hurt a little, but she'd slept well in the barn, was looking forward to reaching Cymberie. She started thinking of Gabriel, hoping he hadn't taken offence when she ran off last night. She wondered when he would be setting off on his travels again. He won't stay long with his father, she thought. He's too impatient.

Drifting toward her came bands of villagers who had had such a good time at the fair that they hadn't made it home last night. Dozy they were, quiet as ghosts, damp-clothed and sleepy-eyed, padding along with baskets of bread, candles and bacon hooked on their arms, or sporting new leather belts, or taking peeks at folds of cloth that would be just the thing to cut and sew into new sleeves, or a pretty bodice, or a fine doublet; or they were ignoring the thumps of live chickens in a sack on their back, or the squeals of a piglet under their arm. Some of them knew Elaine by sight; they nodded good day.

Then she walked out from under the shade of the great oak and there stood Cymberie in front of her. The red brick block across the dewy grass. The high twisting chimneys above the steep slate roof. The blue smoke escaping into a sky that was becoming bluer by the minute as the rising sun burned off the mist.

How many blessings this house has held for me, she thought. It has been a magic place, a cornucopia spilling out gifts. Food: that was the first thing, the simplest thing, when I was starving. Bread and cake in my mouth. A full belly. The energy it gave me when I was so used to being weary.

People too. Solid Nathaniel in his kitchen – the way he has accepted me has been another blessing. Sir Richard in his chamber – it's so strange that, in spite of everything that's happened, my nursing him has created a closeness between us, a kind of friendship, even though he's a knight and I'm no more than a vagrant. Even though – well, what's past is past. You can't live without closing your eyes to one thing or another. And he has taught me to read and to write. I enjoy that so much. He has made me his clerk – that's a post that usually only a man would hold. Oh, and other, subtler things. The way he understands me when no-one else does. He understood when I wanted to die. As I understood him. We were a comfort to each other. We are. Grief our bond. I was too perfunctory with him last night. That was Gabriel's fault.

Gabriel Belvoir is another kind of blessing. He both makes me feel desirable and fills me with desire. Will he be here today?

Her feet were muddy from the lane and she rinsed them under the pump in the deserted yard, pulled on the green calfskin slippers. The horses in the stable were restless, and a cock crowed from the top of the midden. Where is everyone? she wondered, and she thought, they'll still be sleeping off the excesses of last night.

The kitchen table was piled high with the debris of the Michaelmas feast. She cut a slice of almond tart and a piece of cheese, and munched them; chased a buzzing fly from the carcass of the swan; spread the muslin cloth across the table to protect the food. The scarlet beads hanging over the edge clinked against the table legs in the draught from the window, like little bells. Later Nathaniel would basket up the remnants of the feast and get someone to carry them to the village and distribute them to the poor.

She poured herself a glass of ale and drank it. Someone had mended the tap on the cask.

The whole house was so quiet: like a ghost world. All the guests and their servants must still be sleeping; the Michaelmas celebrations must have gone on long after she'd left.

Nathaniel must still be in bed. It wasn't like him to skimp on his duty. She cut a thin slice of day-old bread, another of cold ham, for Sir Richard to break his fast with; put them on a pewter plate to take up to him, filled him a goblet of ale.

At the top of the stairs she paused. I could go to Gabriel instead, she thought. No-one would know. She put plate and goblet down in a window embrasure and stepped softly along the gallery to his closed door, stood outside it and pressed her ear close to the smooth oak, listening for noises within the room.

There was no sound. He must be asleep, she thought. I could lift the latch and go in. Just for a minute, perhaps. See him sleeping there. Eyes closed, breathing gently; a smile on his lips: that's how he'll be, in his nightshirt of fine silk, his hair ruffled round his face. He'll be dreaming of exploring new lands. New seas. A pyramid of a mountain on an island clothed in green forest.

I could go in his room and slither in his bed beside him. It would be good. So satisfying. She stretched.

She lifted the latch.

A bang, a loud crash came from behind her. What was it? Perhaps one of the guests knocking something over in a drunken stupor. Or was the noise from Richard's room? She jerked round, sprinted along the corridor, shoved his door open. The bed was empty, the sheets rumpled, the blankets pushed back. Dry blood and bile on his pillow. 'Where are you, sir? Are you all right?'

He was on the far side of the bed, kneeling in front of the iron-bound chest in which his best gowns were stored. He was dressed just in last night's white shirt. Bare knees on the hard floorboards. 'Damned lid …'

She pitched down beside him and grabbed his left hand. 'What've you done, sir? Why is your hand bleeding?'

'Leave me be!'

'Let me see. The lid fell on it, did it? It's very heavy, that thick oak.'

'Stop fussing, woman.'

'I'll bandage your hand, sir.'

'Why in the name of all the saints are you so late? I've got to get dressed to say farewell to my guests.'

'Sir, there's no hurry. They're still in bed. Nobody is moving round as yet.'

'Got to get dressed.'

'Calm yourself, sir. Let me help you up. I'll bandage your hand and then I've brought you ham and bread – eat a little and you'll feel much stronger.'

'I want my damned gown!'

'Sir, I'll get it for you. Get back into bed first. It's cold this morning, you'll catch a chill in just your shirt.'

'For God's sake.'

'Sir, please –'

'You do as I damned well say! What do you think I pay you for?'

'Sir –'

'My gown – the black damask with a beaver lining – give it me!'

'Let me help you back into bed first, sir.'

'I'm not a child, dammit. Do as I say – otherwise you can leave. I don't employ anyone who disobeys my commands.'

'Put on this old gown, sir, for the moment. It'll keep you warm.'

'No. The beaver –'

She propped the lid of the chest against the wall and stared into the dark confusion of fabric inside, that reeked of orange peel. 'Beaver, sir.' She dipped her hands in, feeling through the layers of smooth satins and ornate brocades, the coarse wools for the warmth of fur. She was frightened; Sir Richard had never been so angry with her before.

'Sir, is this it?' But it was a velvet doublet.

'You fool –'

'The beaver must be further down, sir.' But she was thinking of Lady Ann's chest, how her blue shawl with the silken tassels had been missing from it; this gown of his, which sounded so fine, might well be missing too. What would he do if she couldn't find it? Her fingers felt numb.

'God's sake, girl.'

She became more methodical, taking his clothing out of the chest item by item so she couldn't miss anything, laying each piece of fine fabric, each silken glisten or damask whorl on the floorboards. 'Beaver, sir?' she asked him.

'God's sake, girl –'

'What's this?'

'Bear, you fool. I don't want to wear that.'

She continued to empty the chest. He stayed on his knees, watching intently, nursing his bleeding and bruised left hand against his chest; it was staining his white shirt red. Then at last there was a gown that seemed to match his description. 'Sir?'

'That's the one. Help me up, Elaine. Something's wrong with my damned legs.'

She heaved him up. 'You're tired, sir, I expect.'

'Not dead yet. Damned thing – put it on.' He was clinging tight to a bedpost to keep himself upright.

'Let me change your shirt first, sir. And bandage your hand, or you'll get blood on the gown.'

'Always felt good in it – need to feel good –' He held out an arm. 'Help me – help.'

She slipped a sleeve of the gown on him, supported him

while he put in his other arm, squatted down to shake the hem so the ample fabric fell wide and free. The chevrons woven into the damask shimmered in the morning light; the lustrous fur lining draped in full-length panels at the front. It was a richness which his thin body barely inhabited; he was just a stick inside it. But it made her remember –

'Well, Elaine?' He wrapped his bleeding hand in his shirt and raised his gaunt eyes to stare at her. 'Well?'

She had backed up against the window, hands behind her on the sill, the thick glass haloing her hair with greenish, sickly light. Her eyes were dark pits, her mouth an open O.

'Handsome, yes?'

'No – no.'

He was standing without support: tall, dignified, judicial. 'Elaine, what's the matter?'

She stared at him. The gown he was wearing was the one he had worn when he condemned Thomas to hang by the neck until dead. The courtroom scene flowed vividly into her head. The guards were dragging Thomas away and she was falling in front of the judge. She was clutching his stockinged knees. His long gown was falling around her, enveloping her, swallowing her in its dark beaver lining. Dark and distress.

'I look good, Elaine, yes?' he demanded.

She couldn't speak. She was lost. It was all blackness inside her. Emptiness. A great void. She closed her eyes.

'Elaine –'

She was falling, she was being sucked down. A whirlpool, Charybdis, she was spinning, water was closing over her head –

'Elaine, what's the matter?'

It was the man who had ordered her innocent husband to hang who was talking.

'Sweetheart?'

You can only keep your eyes closed for so long, some time you have to open them, you have to stop pretending –

The blackness: it was too much. She couldn't absorb it any more. She had to turn it away. She forced her eyes open. She was still clutching the windowsill, leaning back against the glass so the leading creaked. 'You killed him,' she shrieked.

'What?'

'Murderer,' she screamed. 'Murderer!'

'Elaine.' Richard staggered toward her, white and stricken-faced.

'Murderer,' she repeated. She couldn't let him touch her, not when he'd done that to Thomas. The leading behind her burst, a pane of glass crashed to the path below. Sounds, now, from outside, the bell on a cow –

'Elaine,' he said. 'Sweetheart.' And then he lost his balance. He pitched face down on the broad floorboards, his arms crumpling beneath him.

'Richard, no!' All at once she had forgotten everything, he was all there was in her head, she was thinking just of him, this old man with his thin hair, she was rolling him over, pulling at his shoulders, tugging at his hips. Richard, she was saying, Sir Richard, Sir Richard. His nose was grazed, she leant forward to wipe it better with her sleeve.

But something stopped her.

As if there was suddenly a great distance between them.

Uncountable miles.

She knelt back. 'Sir Richard. Sir.'

He didn't give any sign of acknowledgement. He was looking surprised. Wide open eyes.

He was different. This was different. She didn't know what to do.

'You are leaving me, sir?' That long lonely journey beyond the realm of the body, where we all must pass. That's where he was going. She was certain of it.

She took hold of his uninjured hand. He didn't respond. She wasn't sure if he was breathing.

His hand was cold. 'You're very cold, sir.' She covered him with a blanket; she fetched a pillow for his head. He gave a kind of groan. 'Sir –' She stroked his cheek, she smoothed the hair back from his forehead.

She became aware of someone watching her and looked up. It was Gabriel. 'I heard you cry out,' he said. He was wearing just his silk shirt. His white legs were peppered with black hairs.

'I think your father's dying,' she said. Then when she looked down again rusty blood was dribbling from his nose and open mouth.

'Oh, sir,' she said.

13

Elaine was at home. Home in the house on the hill. It was mid-afternoon. Nathaniel had brought her here because something had gone wrong with her breathing; she could draw breath only in great shuddering gasps.

She was alone. Samuel was in her arms. It had been such a strange day.

She could breathe all right now.

It was so quiet here. She had never known it so quiet.

She sat outside with her back against the wall of her house until the rain began.

Sssh, it whispered.

It's my fault, she thought. My fault for saying *that* to you, sir. I'm so sorry. You'd have been fine if I'd never said that. The shock of it, that's what did it. But I couldn't help it. The past was too strong for me.

I'd have made you strong again, sir, if you'd let me. I would, really. I'd have made you better. You'd have been fine. I did it before, I could have done it again. I'm so sorry. It's my fault.

Why did you go and leave me? I would have made you better, really I would. If you'd've let me.

At some point Gabriel came to see her. She saw him silhouetted in her doorway, thin as a spear thrust in the gravel. He stared all around. He stepped into the house although she didn't invite him. He took her hand between his, but there was something wrong with her senses, she didn't feel his touch. She could see his mouth opening and closing, she could tell that he was talking, but she couldn't hear what he said, it didn't form into words, it didn't connect in her head, what he said.

She thought, I have lost everything.

She said, 'Your father's dead.'

She didn't tell him that she had killed him.

He sat on the bed beside her, he stroked her hand. She held herself rigid.

'You're still shaking,' he said.

Another time Nathaniel and Joe come. What were they doing here? This wasn't where they belonged.

They brought baskets of bread and apples, a ham, a cheese and a great jug of milk. They kept moving, they kept circling around her.

She was numb. She was still.

Maybe she had turned overnight into a clock face and Nathaniel and Joe were the clock hands. They revolved around her, but they couldn't touch her.

Nothing can touch me, she thought. Things have touched me too much, and now nothing can touch me.

When they left her a fire was burning in the house, logs stacked beside it. Elaine sat by it, hands looped around her legs. Her shins started to redden. Then she sat on the bed with Samuel on her lap and held the cup to his lips and he gulped down the milk with great eagerness. She was glad of the milk because her own had suddenly dried up and Samuel sucking at her empty tits had been making them sore.

She found that after the men had left, when she lay on her back on the bed she couldn't see the stars. An eyelid of fresh rushes had closed shut over them. The dew and the rain couldn't fall on her any more. She pulled up the clean sheet, the warm blanket up over her shoulders.

Walter came. He said, my mother's house is finished. We can marry whenever you wish.

She looked up at him from the bed and said, *Not now.* She couldn't see his face against the light but she imagined his disappointment like a heavy fog and to dissipate it she added, *maybe next week.*

He said, now that you have lost your employment at Cymberie you need to marry me. You have no other means of support.

'There's something broken inside my head,' she said.

'You have to be practical about this,' he said.

'I will feel better next week,' she said.

'It's dark in here,' he said, and he put a taper to the tall candle he had brought her. She rolled on her side and stared at the flame for hours.

One morning she got up and fed Samuel with milk from the cup and wiped the white dribbles from his chin, and then she went outside and picked up a stick and wrote *Thomas* in the gravel. She couldn't remember the letters at first, because of this awful heaviness in her head, and so she wrote *Elaine* which she was sure of. Then she added *Samuel*, and *Elizabeth*, which was her mother's name. Then she wrote *Richard*, stared at it, bit her lip. The names looked all the same. She went back in the house and put on Ann's green slippers and came out and shuffled the names up together. Slither of the little stones under her feet.

'Samuel, don't eat the gravel,' she said.

She thought, we are all made of sand and stones.

Mistress Margery came. It was strange to see her here, away from her cottage. She brought a caraway cake and milk in a jug.

'Thank you,' said Elaine.

Margery was puffing and red-faced, out of breath from climbing the hill. 'How are you now?' she said.

'Well.'

'Such a shame that your job at Cymberie has come to an end. How will you manage?'

Elaine didn't answer.

Samuel plucked at the hem of Margery's skirt. She picked him up in her arms. 'There's my fine boy,' she said. Then she said, 'Elaine, will you read this letter of mine, if you please?'

'Very well,' said Elaine.

It was a piece of paper that had been unfolded and refolded many times, so that the ink was fuzzy along the creases. She ran her finger under the lines, decoding the writing. The letter was from Margery's son who was in a debtors' prison. He thanked his mother for the money she had sent him, and told her how he gambled it on a sure bet, a cock called Roy with purple feathers at his neck. But some evil chance befell him. The cock was killed and the boy lost every penny that he had. He had no money for food now. Would his mother send him more?

'I paid the priest two farthings to read that letter,' said Margery. 'I have paid you nothing and it still says the same.'

'I'm sorry,' said Elaine. She looked around her and the turquoise bodice hanging from a twig in the wall caught her eye. 'Here,' she said, taking it down. 'It's all I have that I can give you. Maybe you will be able to sell it. I don't have a job now, I'm not working, I can't pay you any more.'

'Don't worry about it,' said Margery. 'This will settle our debt.' She put Samuel down on the bed and folded the bodice neatly into her basket. 'God be with you both,' she said and left.

Elaine sat blank at the end of the bed, her hands gripped

tight between her knees, her feet pressed hard to the floor as if they had taken root. She longed to have the bodice back. She wanted to hold it for ever against her cheek, the silk soft as goosedown, the pearls like tiny pebbles printing in her skin.

Walter came again. He stood in the doorway and said, 'Mistress Elaine, when shall we marry?'

She didn't answer.

He kept standing there. 'You have to marry me,' he said.

Wearily, she got up to face him.

'I have to put things right,' he said.

She tried hard to pay attention to what he was saying.

'It is my duty,' he said.

She couldn't make sense of it.

'I have made the way smooth,' he said. 'I have built my mother her own house and now we can marry.'

'Um,' she said.

'Look.' He gestured with a long thin arm around the house. 'This is all you have,' he said. 'This tumbledown place. You have no job, no money, no means of support. I will provide comfort and security for you and your son.'

The headache that had weighed on Elaine since Richard's death intensified as she concentrated. 'I could live with you as your sister,' she suggested.

'No. People would say we were sleeping together. We would be tried before the church courts.'

Again she was silent. Her hands twisted together nervously.

He sat heavily on the side of the bed, looked down at his lap. Samuel was fast asleep, close up against the wall, he gave a little belch.

Walter swallowed and said, 'Last November I was with

friends at the inn. There was a fracas with fellows from the next village. I killed the Puritan-hunter accidentally. I was defending myself with my knife; someone pushed me. My friends told the watchman it was the stranger who'd done it. They said it was Thomas Fisher, your husband. I didn't have the courage to confess it was I. I was afraid of dying. Why should I be hanged for what was an accident? But that's the law.'

She stared at him. She couldn't make sense of what he was saying. Her headache was like a helmet with the visor closed so she couldn't see out. It was leaden, very heavy.

'I wish this had never happened,' he said. 'But things are as they are. I am trying to put them right. Please. I believe in justice.'

She rubbed her eyes, which were so dry they were stinging. 'No-one can ever put things right,' she said. 'It's not possible.'

He said, 'I have put my life in your hands.'

But she didn't want it.

Then, sometime later, another day, perhaps, Nathaniel was there again. His hands were empty, scrubbed clean. No flour under his nails. He wore a black cloak, was tidily dressed. 'Come with me,' he said.

'No,' she said.

'You have to come.'

'Why?'

He was silent and she could hear the church bells tolling, the sound brought to her from the village by the south wind. They were ringing to make the devil flee away from a departing soul. 'No, Nathaniel.'

'Yes.'

'No.' She buried her face in her hands.

'Elaine, he would expect it of you.'

'You don't understand. It's all my fault.'

'He was an old man. It was his time to die.'

'No, no. My fault.'

Nathaniel lifted her by the hand to her feet. She felt dizzy. 'No one could have done more for him than you did, Elaine. Now you must say farewell to him.'

'No.'

Nathaniel wrapped Samuel in a baby shawl of soft wool which was somehow there in the house. He carried the baby, guiding her with his hand on her elbow; all the way down the hill and along the lane, into the village and past Margery's house and the well, right up to the church. He stood her at the foot of the tower and trusted Sammy into her weak arms and left her, among a crowd of others whom she recognised were there by the warm stink of ale on their breath, the smell of their sweat.

Six black horses bridled in velvet and plumed with tall feathers came to a stop in the lane, their harness jingling. One of them farted. On the cart that they were pulling rested a coffin draped in a pall cloth of crimson velvet embroidered with gold: wheat, a sheep, an apple tree, a stag on a path, Sir Richard's coat of arms. The talbot. Elaine recognised them all, thought of Winifred in the garden embroidering them. She didn't need to ask whose funeral this was.

Six men carried the coffin into the church. They were cloaked in black, wore deep hoods that hid their faces. One of them was Gabriel; she saw his ring. He didn't see her. The others were guests who had been at the Michaelmas feast. They weren't used to walking in step. 'Left, right, left,' called Harry Tuck after a false start. The coffin rested on their shoulders; they linked arms underneath it. Their faces were pressed hard against the side of it. One man was shorter than the others; the coffin tilted intermittently down at the feet. It was obviously heavy but it must have been the weight of the oak that made it so because Richard was so very thin.

Elaine squeezed into the end of a pew at the back of the church. Someone made room for her. 'A sad day, Mistress Elaine,' he said, and glancing up she saw it was Joe Chibborne. 'Yes,' she said, and pressed Samuel who was still sleeping, couched in his shawl, tight against her chest. She was aware of the brightness of the church, the autumn sunshine slanting through the clerestory windows on to walls that had been whitewashed to wipe out the vivid scenes of the paintings that had ornamented them for a hundred years or more. Carved kings clutching shields loured down on her from the closeboarded roof of the nave. She smelt the sweat of the people pressed around her, the ale and pickle on their breath.

The pall-bearers entered the church and *I am the Resurrection and the Life* chanted the priests and the clerks in their white from the door to the light.

Elaine began to weep. She couldn't stop. Tears glistened on her cheeks, her chin. All through the service she wept, her sobs a descant to the psalms and prayers, and she didn't know what she was weeping for, or whom, she was just overwhelmed with grief, for Richard, and for Thomas who had been denied these rites, for whom she had never allowed herself to weep; for her own aloneness.

She couldn't stop. *The Lord helpeth them up that are fallen* sang the choir. 'Chin up,' whispered Joe beside her. 'Don't let the old boy down.' But she kept on weeping and she felt in the end a sense of release. She was letting them go. Letting them both float up into the aether that all spirits inhabit.

14

The church bells were ringing again, on and on without stopping: not the sombre tolling of the day of Sir Richard's funeral, but solid notes of rejoicing that cascaded and sang in the southerly breeze across the fields and into the bare woodland, piercing the walls of the house on the hill, within which Elaine was folding her and Samuel's clothes into the sheet on the bed; she was tying up the four corners to make a bundle for her back. She rolled up the flock mattress, tied it with plaited honeysuckle vines, stacked it a little way away from the house, together with the blanket and clothes. She had been crying and her face was taut with dried tears; she rinsed it in the tepid water of the cauldron, then tipped the pan so the water soaked into the gravel floor. She put the cauldron outside with her cup, fastened her knife and spoon to her belt.

'We've nearly finished,' she said to Samuel, and she threw the heap of kindling on the fire so it flared and crackled and orange flames licked high to dispel the shadows in the house.

She took the axe and whacked the joints of the bedframe that Thomas had built until it fell apart. With a long side-piece she poked the fire to make it crackle angrily and the flames leap higher; she piled the rest of the bedframe, and all the dead wood that she had stacked at the side, into a pyramid around the flames. They caught light in seconds.

It was so hot in there now; sweat was running into her eyes. 'Pretty, isn't it,' she said to Samuel, wiping her forehead with her sleeve. The centre of the fire was a fiery furnace of scarlet and orange, the wood was caving in, and with each fall the flames flared higher, they were licking the inside of the house roof now and she grabbed Samuel who'd begun to cry and backed up with him against the hazel wall that she had built with Thomas.

'It's so hot,' she said, shielding her baby's blond curls from the flames with her hands; and the rushes on the roof caught and crackled and sizzled and she laughed out loud; and sparks fell, one landed on the back of her hand and the roof started to collapse and she gasped and ducked quickly and she was out of the doorway, she was standing on the gravel hilltop in the blue November morning and the bells were still ringing and flames poured through the walls and the roof and flared like a beacon into the pale air: she was clutching Samuel and was half-laughing, half-crying: don't cry, Sammy, she was saying, it's good, it's an ending, we're beginning again, we're setting out on a new journey, a new adventure –

But her feet were reluctant to take her. She stayed rooted to the spot watching her and Thomas's house where she'd been so happy, happier than she'd ever been in her whole life, watching their house disappear.

And all the time the bells kept ringing, the bells rang over and over and over again like a headache. 'We must go down to Walter Vernon's house,' Elaine said, and she hitched the bundle of clothes up on her back, and stood there clutching Samuel.

'A new beginning,' she said, and kissed him on his smoky forehead. The fire was slow now, it had entered the phase of ash and smoulder. Logs turned white, their surface crazing, embers glowed. 'I didn't think it would be as quick as that,' she said. It hadn't taken long, that demolishing of all her certainties and dreams. And now she was adrift.

She kissed Sam's ear. 'We don't have any choice, my boy,' she said. 'Let's go to the candlemaker's house.'

Down the hill Elaine went; down that familiar path. She knelt among the fallen leaves at the edge of the spring to quench her thirst, cupped water in her hand for Sam to drink. 'Sweetheart –'

On she went, down the path she'd worn through the woods, to join the lane to the village. Samuel whimpered at her side and '*ssh*' she said, '*ssh*,' and 'we'll make a scholar of you, little one, you'll see, Walter will pay for you to go to school and all will turn out for the best;' and she shivered in the rising wind that had turned to the west and numbed her mind to her fears of what her world would be like once she had stepped across the threshold of the candle house: 'It'll be good, Sammy, won't it?' Never mind the marriage bed, herself and Walter lying side by side cold as marble figures on a tomb, never mind the necessary disciplining of herself to a stranger's whim, that loss of identity she would suffer: 'It'll be good, Sammy.'

The wind was driving cloud across the sky now. She was afraid it might rain and all their clothes be soaked, and she started to hurry along between the bare hedgerows. And all the time the bells were ringing their counterpoint to the brisk rattle of the dry oak leaves, to the whirr of a woodpecker's bill in a birch, to an unseen ploughman's loud 'Whoa' travelling in the clear air and then his 'Go on, walk on,' followed by the jingle of harness and harrow. 'Steady,' he went; and then she heard the noise of a galloping horse in the lane, that unmistakable vibration pounding toward her, going fast by the sound, faster than any plough-horse, and she stepped to one side and seconds later it raced past, a tearaway chestnut under a figure in blue who was spurring it on.

Then 'Whoa,' shouted the rider. 'Whoa, boy.' And when the horse had slowed he turned it and came back on his tracks; he leapt down and, holding the reins, went straight to its head.

'Good boy,' he said, stroking its muzzle with a hand heavy with a sea-monster emerald ring as it stamped restlessly. 'Quiet, Durendal. Quiet. Quiet. Elaine.'

'Master Gabriel, sir.' Astonished to see him, she still managed a half-curtsey.

'I saw a fire on the hill,' he said, brushing his fair hair back from his forehead. 'I was afraid for you – I wondered if it was your house ablaze.'

'It was, sir.'

He looked at her gravely. 'You are well, none the less?'

'You can see that I am, sir.'

'You are not hurt at all?'

'No, sir.'

'I didn't recognise you at first glance. Those bundles – your clothes – you look like a vagrant.'

'I am moving house, sir.'

'You are leaving the village?'

'No.'

'Well, give me your bundles. Durendal can carry them for a while. He's no packhorse, but then neither are you.' He strapped Elaine's bundle of clothes and her mattress to Durendal's saddle.

They walked on some time in silence, Samuel sleeping in the support of her shawl. They were awkward, neither knowing what to say to the other.

'The weather's changing,' he said in the end.

'Yes,' she said, then a while later: 'The bells have stopped ringing at last. What were they ringing for?'

'It's the seventeenth of November. The anniversary of our noble queen's accession.'

'St Hugh's Day,' she said. 'They always used to ring the bells to celebrate that back home, until the change in the church.'

They had fallen into step with each other, side by side, him leading Durendal by the reins. He said, 'Your baby's not too heavy for you to carry?'

'No – no, I'm used to his weight.'

'When I met you at Cymberie, I didn't know you had a baby.'

'No. Yes.'

'What's his name?'

'Samuel.'

'He looks a fine lad. Let me carry him for a while.' He touched the child's hair; his hand brushed her breast.

'I can manage.'

'His father?'

'He's dead. It's nearly a year ago that he died.' Then, wanting to change the subject but not knowing what to say, she managed, 'I'm sorry about your father.'

'I never knew how well he was loved,' he said, 'in spite of that filthy temper of his. People were so kind.'

They were walking through the village now, past Margery's cottage where Margery and Rosamund stood gossiping in the garden, and stared after them open-mouthed. Past the well on the green where cattle and goats grazed to the jingling of the bells round their necks. A great horned beast lifted its head to stare brown-eyed after them and set tinkling the old Sanctus bell that it wore, that its owner had bought after the queen's reformation of the church. Children set down their pails of water to watch them, or stopped skipping and stepped to the side of the lane to let them pass; old men in gardens leant on their hoes and gazed; women bringing in washing that had been spread on hedge and bank to dry paused in folding their sheets, and grandmothers who sat spinning in doorways put down their wool and let their tired fingers rest, eased their backs as they set their minds to embroider gossip about what their new lord was doing walking beside the stranger, that foreign girl from up north, the murderer's widow with her baby.

Gabriel led Durendal into the lane that went past Walter Vernon's house; it was the shortest way to Cymberie. Elaine's feet dragged: *Not this way* is all she could think, dreading reaching the candle house. But Gabriel was unaware, off in his own thoughts: 'Elaine, I'm in a dilemma,' he said.

'Yes, sir?'

'I'm all set to sail to the New World in the New Year – the *Adventure* will be ready and provisioned by then. The trouble is, I don't know what to do with Cymberie. My father left it to me in his will, and I don't want to sell the place, though it can't be run at much of a profit, now he's got rid of so much of the land, but – well, I suppose I'm attached to the damned house. I find I dream of it when I'm travelling – I just need to find myself in a tight spot and I dream of Cymberie, the cool hall and the room where I've slept all my life, the gardens, the orchards and pastures, the deer park. Childish though it may seem, I don't want to lose that comfort. I need to know that Cymberie continues to prosper.'

The candlemaker's house was just round the next corner. Elaine could already see the neatly pruned branches of his apple trees over the hedge. She visualized Walter standing in his doorway waiting for her in his mauve ruff, his thin hair neatly combed, his arms folded across his chest. She wondered who the witnesses to their marriage would be, and if they would be standing waiting beside him, or if they'd be seated at the table in the hall, gossiping over tankards of ale.

Gabriel resumed: 'I've just been to see a young man whom Harry Tuck recommended to me as a competent steward to care for the place while I'm away. But there was something –

you get a feel for men when you're a ship's captain, you know whom you can trust – I felt uneasy with him. He was too eager to please. If he had no backbone, what would he do when I wasn't watching? – Elaine, I know my father trusted you completely with all the business of Cymberie, and – for all that we were always at odds, I respected his judgement –'

There was the candle house with its pantiled roof that would keep her and Samuel dry over the winter, its walls that would keep them warm –

'I know that you are familiar with the land and the tenants, I know you can read and write and are accustomed to keeping records.'

There was Walter himself on his doorstep. A new blue ruff he was wearing.

'Elaine, will you be the steward of Cymberie while I'm away?'

She stopped stock-still. She couldn't have heard him right.

He stopped too, and addressed her directly. 'I'll pay you of course. I don't expect you to do it for nothing. Eleven marks a year: that's what I offered Harry Tuck's nephew. It'll be a condition of service that you have to live at Cymberie; I don't want an absentee steward. I want someone who will care for the house and ensure that it doesn't go to rack and ruin. I want to have every confidence that Cymberie's walls will be waiting to welcome me back when I return.'

'I understand that, sir.'

'I know you can't make up your mind at once. I don't expect that. But – if you're not willing, I'll have to employ Harry Tuck's nephew and hope for the best, and I need time to train him up, so I need to know soon. The devil of it is that he has a house of his own over at Hornchurch, which his wife isn't willing to leave because she's expecting her first child, and her parents live nearby.'

'I'll do it, sir.' A sprout of absolute joy burst from a seedcase deep in her chest.

'What? Are you sure?'

'Yes. On one condition.' She was looking up at him; she was radiant.

'What's that?'

'That I can take up employment immediately.'

'What, now?'

'This hour, sir. This minute. This very second. Please.'

'You understand I will be away, almost certainly, for two or three years. You are happy to undertake to remain as steward all that time? You need to consider the matter, I think. You should discuss it with your family.'

'No, sir, no. I know it's what I want to do.'

'You're a young woman – a pretty one, too. What will you do if a man asks you to marry him while you are my steward?'

It's slipping away, she thought, this chance is slipping away. He's going to change his mind any minute. Her eyes were fixed on Gabriel's face, but she was imagining Walter walking down his path to claim her. 'The witnesses are waiting,' he might say. Then there'd be no escape. 'I will wait for you to come back, sir, I swear. I won't fail in the duties you give me.'

'You are so earnest, Elaine.'

'I love Cymberie, sir.'

'Well, if you are sure –'

'Thank you, sir.' She put her free hand round his neck and stretched up to kiss him hard on the lips. She had to do it. She couldn't stop herself. He was her rescuer, her angel-in-disguise; she just adored him. She was smiling so much her mouth ached. The corners of his eyes were creased with laughter-lines.

Walter was standing on his doorstep, waiting for Elaine.

He had been waiting since noon; that was when she had said she would come. He had invited Turney the barber from Baddow and his friend Wyatt from Blackmore to be witnesses to his marriage, because they were Puritans as he was. They were within doors now, poring over the first epistle of St Peter. *You also, like living stones, are being built into a spiritual house* – how good those words were. How well they expressed the purpose that he felt in his life. Elaine too would learn to be a living stone; he would teach her. Though at this moment he was ashamed for her, compelling his brethren to wait around like this; it was mid-November now, and they would certainly have to walk home in the dark. This was not how he would wish his wife to behave. Because of her lateness he had had to go to the butcher's to buy pies to feed his friends. He had moved his mother into her new house yesterday: 'You'll be sorry,' she'd told him as he wheeled her goods, her mattresses and lace cushions, her pillows and clothes, her high-crowned hats, her pans, sooty cauldron and all along the lane in a barrow: 'You'll be sorry, my boy, that you shoved your mother out of the way like this. Disgraceful it is.' – 'Mother, I've done it for the best, the candle house is now too big for you to manage. I …' – 'Men are all the same. They are always bewitched by a pretty face.' – 'Mother, how many times do I have to tell you, Elaine is quite plain. It is her simplicity of dress and modesty of demeanour that have attracted…' – 'Nonsense!'

When the small group of man, woman, child and horse rounded the corner, Walter didn't immediately see Elaine. What he noticed first was the beautiful chestnut stallion with his gleaming coat and royal blue velvet-trimmed harness, and a bundle of washing tied behind the saddle, which seemed so out of place; then he noticed the weather-beaten man whom he recognised as Gabriel Belvoir, the late Sir Richard's son, who had a strong look of his father: he was dressed very effetely in a blue satin doublet and a brief flyaway cloak that was utterly useless as a source of warmth, and a tall hat with a curled ostrich feather which would give him no shelter against the weather; and then Walter saw the woman whom it was clear that Belvoir had just kissed, for she was taking her hand away from his shoulder, and blushing, and her eyes were naked pools of adoration, and there was an air of happiness, no, joy, about her that was so utter, so complete, that only a trollop or a bawd could feel it – and because she was so different from the Elaine that Walter thought of, whom he labelled *unfortunate victim*, he could not recognise her.

And when he did, he was shocked, he wanted to turn his back on her, have nothing to do with her. What good could come of their marriage, if she was prepared to kiss another man on the way to her wedding?

But he was bound by his duty; he knew it was his task to educate her: he must forgive her. 'Elaine,' he called loudly. 'Elaine Fisher.'

She showed no sign of having heard him. Belvoir was taking her child from her. She was putting her foot in the stirrup; she was hauling herself up into the saddle; she was seated astride, showing her bare legs, her green slippers. Belvoir was reaching her baby up for her to hold. The baby was crying. She pulled down her skirt. Belvoir took the reins and led the beautiful chestnut stallion on down the lane, out of sight.

Then all was quiet in Walter's world: just the thud of the horse's hooves on the soft earth, and distant children's voices, and the rising wind in the branches. A pigeon cooing. But in his chest there was a strange turmoil, a mix of anger and humiliation, and of relief that Elaine was walking of her own free will out of his life, and that maybe he need no longer feel any responsibility for her.

The wind was in the apple branches, they rubbed and creaked against each other. The hedges sighed. The wind eddied and sang around the house, it stirred Walter's ruff and he felt suddenly lighter, as if he had wings, as if the wind was the breath of God and it was lifting from him the guilt that had obsessed him since the murder in the inn the year before. He dropped on his knees, there in the garden, in his best stockings. 'Thanks be to you, oh Lord, always and always. Thank you for this mercy.'

Turney couldn't understand why Walter was filled with joy. He spread his hands wide on the table in front of him, showing the dried blood under his nails. 'Your bride has been seduced by a man who is renowned as a libertine,' he said, 'and you're content with that? You're not going to attempt to bring her back to the path of righteousness, even though what awaits her must be certain poverty and ruin? When he's had his pleasure with her, Belvoir will cast her off, have no doubt.'

'But if that's what she wants –' protested Walter.

'Women are weak,' said Turney. 'They need to be brought to see the error of their ways. Give her a good hiding and she'll soon know where the right path lies.'

'Better,' said Wyatt, 'to place this whole matter in the hands of God, and let our Lord bring things to their proper conclusion.' And the three men bowed their heads over the table where they sat, and prayed together for a half an hour or so.

'Our Lord has a purpose in all things,' said Wyatt, taking Walter's hand as he bade him farewell. 'Maybe he is setting you free to come to Holland with me.' He picked up his walking stick and kissed his friend on the mouth.

15

Elaine was climbing the hill to Cymberie. It was cloudy and the wind was cold; she pulled her shawl tighter around herself. Samuel was snug against her chest and sleeping.

It was strange to be on the back of a horse. The motion was rocking; she felt insecure. A little queasy. The view was different, she could see further from up here. And the leaves were all fallen; the fat trees were skeletons now. There was the oak at the edge of the lawn, there the white statue in the mid of the black water that the wind tossed into waves crested with pennants of spray. 'Sir, I want to get down.'

Gabriel steadied Durendal, brought the horse to a stop.

There was the house she had thought she would never see again, that solid block of red brick with its slate roof and octagonal entrance tower, the tall chimneys that trailed smoke to the sky. 'I'm afraid,' she said.

'Give me your baby then. I won't drop him.'

He took the child and she slid down from the horse's back, stumbling and half-falling to the ground. She swiftly righted herself. There was earth in the palm of her hand and she looked at it queerly.

'Have you cut yourself?'

'No. No. Just a slight graze.' She brushed her hand on her skirt and held out her arms. 'Let me take Samuel. You look so awkward holding him.'

'He's a bit damp.'

'Babies often are.'

They walked along the path to the main entrance, that Elaine had never entered by before, stood on the top step by the oak door with its arched moulding. Gabriel rang the great bell that hung there: the sound clanged out across the gardens and deer park, into the house. They waited.

She said, 'Are you sure of this, sir?'

'I've taken on more staff. One of them should come. I can't imagine why my father ran this place with so few people.'

That wasn't what Elaine had meant. She had meant: do you truly want me to be your steward? She felt so uncertain. So unsure of herself. She was thinking: maybe I'll have forgotten how to read. I haven't seen a book in six weeks, and it's only a short time ago that I learnt my letters. Maybe I'll have forgotten my figures, maybe I'll have forgotten how to add and subtract. How can I be a steward if I can't read or write? She began to trace out a two, a three, a four, a five with her toe on the stone step. With Sir Richard not here, who will tell me if I am making mistakes? she was thinking.

Gabriel rang the bell again, more fiercely; and a minute later a young lad, one of those brought in to help at the time of the fair, came running, skidding round the side of the house. 'What kept you?' Gabriel said angrily. 'You'll have to learn to be quicker than that. Here, take Durendal, rub him down and put him in the stable.'

'Yes sir.'

The entrance hall when Gabriel lifted the latch was almost the same: the cool ochre and red tiles, the heavily carved staircase, the wall paintings that on this November day held deep shadows in spite of the tall windows by the door; the family portrait where the young Gabriel posed with a toy boat and no-one had died. But a high-banked fire breathed warmth into the cold, and garlands of dried hops and the wax polish on the wood filled the air with sweetness: the place had more of an air of being well cared for.

'Let's go straight through to my father's side chamber,' Gabriel said. 'I've been busy planning my next expedition and I've barely looked at the letters that have come. I want you to make a note of all letters that arrive, and reply to them for me. Everything needs to be done on a more formal basis. There's no full record of the wages people are being paid – nothing about yours, for example. I want all that written down. And I want you to make a full inventory of the estate.'

'An inventory?'

The door from the parlour opened abruptly: a broad bearded man in plum doublet and yellow hose, an ivory ruff, stepped out and said, 'Gabriel Belvoir.'

Gabriel wheeled round. 'Benedict! You're here already!' The two men embraced, clapping each other on the back.

'Wild horses couldn't keep me away. I've had enough of life on land; I'm itching to be back at sea. I see you've been busy.'

'What? Oh, her. No. It's business, my friend, just business, I assure you. No more than that. Mistress Fisher was my father's clerk. She's just agreed to be steward of Cymberie while I'm away. Look, I've arranged another meeting with the Merchant Taylors' Company on Wednesday, can you come? I'd welcome the support of your golden tongue.'

'So this fine little fellow isn't yours?' Benedict Pole said, chucking Samuel under the chin and setting him crying.

'Good Lord, no. Benedict, how long have you been here? Have you eaten? I've obtained a new map, come and see. Woodville got it from a Spanish pilot he captured, it should be reliable.'

And Elaine was left on her own in the hallway. An in-between place, a kind of Purgatory. 'Ssh,' she said to Samuel. 'Be quiet, my dear one.'

What she longed to do was to go upstairs to Sir Richard. It remained a strong habit with her, it was where her feet naturally took her: she wanted it with all of her heart. 'But he's not there, my poppet. He's gone.'

A roar of laughter burst from the parlour.

The fire crackled.

A gong in the kitchen: what was that for? She wanted to go and see Nathaniel and hug him, feel his bear-arms a comfort around her. But, 'Suppose,' she said to Samuel, 'suppose I can't do it. What if I've forgotten how to read and to write, my little one? Then I'd be a useless steward. Let's go to Sir Richard's side chamber first.'

Through the hall, where the table was bare and bowls of clear water sat cool at the side for the washing of hands before the next meal. The tapestries shivered in the draught from the wind outside.

To the little door at the side, which swung readily open. 'Samuel,' she said. 'Listen …' She wanted to tell him about coming here and finding Richard with his weapons, his pistol and long sword and dagger. 'He wanted to die,' she said. 'I wanted him to kill me. But that would have been wrong. It would have been a betrayal of you.' She couldn't explain just how logical this desire had seemed at the time, the answer to all of her problems. It seemed nonsense now. 'I'm responsible for you, sweetheart. We are all a part of a pattern. It's a matter of understanding that.'

In the door, down the step. There was the table, the armchair where he used to sit, the books, the arms cupboard Joe built. 'It's cold in here, poppet.' She shivered.

There was no fire, no fireplace even. She didn't know why he had never had one put in. She wrapped Samuel in her shawl, folding it and tying the corners in rough knots so he was a warm cocoon with face and hands visible, and laid him on the tiled floor, giving him a pewter tankard to play with. She wondered if it was Gabriel who had left it there, if his lips had smudged the sheen of the metal.

She sat in the armchair and picked up a quill, sharpened it in the way that Richard had taught her. It was good to hold it; as if the feel of it in her hand, the way her fingers curled around it, the brush of the barbs on her palm, would help her remember how to write. She dipped the pen in the ink and began to doodle on a margin. *Elaine Fisher*, she wrote. *Samuel Fisher. Gabriel Belvoir.* 'My hand has a memory of its own,' she told Sam. He banged the tankard against a leg of her chair.

She picked a book at random from the several stacked there and let it fall open where it willed, then began to read, enunciating clearly, as Richard had taught her: *3. To know any time of day by the sun, and any time of night by the moon and the stars, take their altitude. Put the ring of your astrolabe by your right thumb...* Was this a book of Gabriel's? A book that told him how to steer the right course when he was sailing the great ocean? She looked up at the greenish glass of the window with its figure of a shepherd holding a lamb, and thought how strange it must be to be out of sight of land and adrift upon the heaving sea, and for the only points of reference to be the sun, moon and stars, which were always moving; and she thought how her own life was fixed by the solidity of trees and hills and earth and houses.

But her steward's duties would revolve around pen and paper and the recording of facts: she'd have permanent black inkstains from the quill on her thumb and fingers as her badge of office, she'd be confined to lines and columns that would offer security against the shapelessness, the randomness of life.

She reached for a thin book with no letters on the spine, the one in which the half-yearly accounts for Cymberie were bound. Here were the rents payable at Lady Day and Michaelmas, and the rent arrears, and the expenditure on wages and fodder all carefully detailed in Sir Richard's neat handwriting, the disbursements for hay, grain and beans full and complete up until the time when Lady Ann fell from the horse Durendal. Thereafter the accounts were fragmentary; maybe Sir Richard had not always had the courage to continue with them as he should. She ran the tip of her finger up the slopes of his letters, around the curves of them because they reminded her of him, she thought of his teaching her, she felt close to him then. Here were the accounts for the Michaelmas fair, his and her letters jostling against each other, his wavering because of his illness, hers rounded and childish because of her inexperience in writing. 'I don't know if I can do this if you're not here to guide me,' she said aloud. Here were three or four later entries in a firm hand she didn't recognise; was that Gabriel's writing?

Then all of a sudden she remembered Richard's leather casket that held his jewellery, and how on a parchment folded in its lid he'd written his and his family's names, all dead bar him. 'When I die,' he'd said, 'add the date of my death to the list. Do this for me, Elaine. Then I'll know for certain I am with them, and I can rest in peace.' Something to that effect; she couldn't be sure now what he'd said.

She had to do what he wanted. She jumped up, snatching Samuel up in her arms.

Elaine needed Richard's keys. She knew what they were like: five on a brass ring embossed with his seal: the ornate one to Lady Ann's chest, the plain one to his own, the feathered one to the cupboard in the panelling, the new one to Joe Chibborne's arms cupboard, and –

She thought: Phillis is in charge of all the keys of the

house. Surely she'll have picked up Richard's keys when he died, surely she'll have hung them up with the rest. Unless Gabriel took charge of them –

'Mistress Phillis,' she said at her door.

'You.' Phillis, perched on her stool by the window, pinned her needle neatly in the sheet she was mending in the last of the daylight, put her work aside. 'You are back, then.'

'Master Gabriel has asked me to serve as his steward.'

Phillis nodded. 'Nathaniel and I told him you can read and write, we said you had run Cymberie for the last month or so. We said you'd do the job well.'

'Ah.'

'We didn't want him to appoint a stranger who'd nose around and upset our business while he's away. Is this your baby?'

'Samuel.' Elaine gave him over into Phillis's demanding arms, and he started to cry.

'There, there, my sweet, now quiet, hush you then, it's your granny Phillis, you've nothing to fear, you come along with me, we'll go in the kitchen and find you a sweetmeat, my fine one, my soldier, we'll see what your uncle Nathaniel has in store for you there…' And off she went, bustling plumply in her dark dress with the ivory ruff, Samuel looking wide-eyed and silent back over her shoulder at his mother.

But she was examining the keys. The ones on hooks in the whitewashed stones of the walls were all too big; they were door keys. Maybe in there, she thought, looking at the little cupboard hung on the wall, and she turned its butterfly latch, swung open the foot-square door. And there they hung in the shadows. She was sure they were his. She lifted them down and folded them in the palm of her hand, fingers tight around them so no-one could see. She slipped into the kitchen, where Samuel was sat on the table with a wooden spoon in his hand, waving it at Phillis who had snatched some mashed-up fruit cake from his fist and was berating Nathaniel: 'You fool, you can't give a baby rich food like that.' Then out into the hallway. A detour to the little side chamber to fetch pen and inkhorn, then she ran upstairs to Sir Richard's chamber.

It was strange how, when she pushed his door open, habit, the familiar pattern of their former days, made her expect to see him still there. But his bed was stripped bare, just the bottom of the three mattresses left to cover the bed-cords, his blankets and coverlet washed and folded on top of it, his pillows naked of their cases.

The room smelt stale, and she opened the casement to let the fresh air in: never mind how cold it was outside. She felt such a sense of loss all of a sudden. 'Sir, I'm so sorry,' she said. 'I couldn't help it. Your gown. You shouldn't have worn it. It was Thomas. The courtroom. It brought the memories back. It was too much for me. You didn't murder… You did what you had to do. Because they lied. You didn't know they were lying – And you were doing so well. You were getting better. I'm sure you were. I'd worked so hard to get you better. You were stronger every day. And then – then – there wasn't anything I could do. Sir, I'm sorry. I'm so sorry…'

She squatted down, stroked the grain of the floorboards where he'd fallen. The wood was rough: a splinter stuck in her finger and when she pulled it out a bubble of red blood sprang to the surface of her skin. One of the boards was stained and she thought: it's dry blood from his injured hand, or vomit from his mouth, and she spat on the hem of her skirt and wiped until the mark came off. 'You didn't need to die, sir,' she said. 'Not yet. Not yet.'

Her eyes stung with tears; she rubbed them roughly with

her sleeve, crossed to the panelling and opened the little cupboard, took out the leather casket, unlocked it and tipped it on the mattress so its contents spilled out on the ticking: the three rings he'd worn to the Michaelmas feast, the square diamond, the ruby, the purple garnet, a couple of others, two seals with the family talbot on, a great sapphire and an uncut emerald, the pearl caul he'd given her to wear, a lump of amber with an insect caught for ever in the yellow stone.

And the parchment from the lid. She stared dumbly at his writing that she'd mistaken for embroidery the first time she'd seen it. *Ann Isobel Belvoir*; *Richard Brullant Belvoir, knight.* Drawn in careful pen-strokes. She thought again of his teaching her to read and write, the hours they'd spent heads bowed together. 'Sir,' she said.

'Elaine.'

It was his voice.

'Elaine.'

But he was dead. 'Sir?' Her voice trembled.

'Who were you talking to?'

'It's you.' Not him; Gabriel.

'Who did you think it was?'

Now she was looking at him, watching his lips move, his lips that were slightly plump for a man, she could tell the difference between his voice and his father's. They were nothing alike.

'Well?'

She shook her head.

'What are you doing?'

She looked down at the jewellery on the bed, the glitter of it on the ticking. 'I'm not a thief, if that's what you're thinking.'

'I didn't think it. Phillis vouched for your honesty. What are you doing?'

She showed Gabriel the parchment.

'Well?'

'Your father asked me to add the date of his death to this, when his time came. This is the first chance I've had.'

'You better do it then.'

She took the parchment to the table, sat in Richard's chair, dipped the pen in the inkhorn. She had to do it the best that she could. As she slowly formed the number thirty, three and nought (that nothing again; we all come to that), the letters of September, she thought of the sandbox and of practising her writing in it, she almost felt the sand beneath her fingernails once more.

Gabriel moved close, to look over her shoulder. He put his hand on her shoulder.

Instinctively she leaned back against him. Then she said, 'I have to write the year,' and sat forward. When she had finished she laid down her quill. 'I have done all that your father wanted,' she said. That part of my life is complete, she thought. I'm in my future now.

'You can be yourself now,' he said. He scooped up her hair and kissed the back of her neck.

Prickle of his short beard against her skin. Surprised, she laughed. It was so long since anyone had done anything like that. 'What did you do that for, sir?'

'Why do you think?' He leaned over her, rested his hands on her forearms and kissed the bridge of her nose.

'Hah, thought so,' called Benedict Pole from by the door. 'You can't fool me, Master Gabriel, I've known you too long. I know your taste in women.'

'Nonsense.' Gabriel picked up a strand of Elaine's hair and pulled it so it hurt. 'I was just explaining to Mistress Fisher that as my steward she'll have to take more care of her appearance. Like, she'll have to comb her hair. God knows when she last did it, it's all of a tangle. And she'll have to dress better, not like a peasant. What happened to that pretty bodice that you had, mistress?'

'I – I had to sell it,' she lied.

'I can't have my steward going round in rags. You'll have to dress to fit the part. Benedict, come and see this quadrant I've acquired.'

Elaine in a bedchamber of her own at Cymberie; the small one at the eastern end of the gallery. She'd expected to sleep in the loft above the kitchen with most of the other servants, but Gabriel said, no, there's no need for that. It was a small room with a four poster and a truckle bed, a large oak chest in which she'd stored all of her worldly goods: her mattress, her cooking things, her and Samuel's few clothes. It was barely half full. She liked, though, to keep everything beside her, knowing she would be able to move on at a moment's notice if she had to. She felt that impermanent. This present arrangement was too good to be true. She didn't believe it would last. 'I should have married Walter, Sam,' she said, 'for your sake.'

He lay in a cradle beside her. Had it been Gabriel's and Ysabelle's? It was carved with fields and trees, sheep grazing, a half moon on the hood. She'd rocked him in it and he'd lain bright-eyed and restless, wide awake at the strangeness of this new place, but she'd rocked him and kept rocking till he'd closed his eyes at last. Dark eyelashes on pale cheeks. Mutters in his sleep; a burp.

She lay awake in the strangeness now. She'd left the curtains of the bed open around her. She felt the house weighing down on her, the brick walls, the plaster ceiling oppressing her, the great oak timbers of the roof, the heavy, heavy slates. How strange to be sleeping under stones. The weight of the house pressed down on her and she longed for the airiness of the round house and its affinity with the woodland around it, letting in the breeze and stars and rustling, singing trees, hoot of owl and shriek of fox –

She couldn't hear a single tree. She got up and crossed the room and in the darkness pushed aside the window sheet and reached through the bars of the mullions to fumble the shutters open (no glass in the windows in this lesser room); she pulled herself up on to the sill and pressed her bare body against the coolness that breezed in. The moon, just past the full, cast shadows in, stripes of the mullions across her pale skin.

A knock at the door. She didn't answer but it opened. Gabriel stood there in his nightshirt, with bare feet and legs, holding a taper. The flicker of the flame distorted his thin face, his nose, his eyebows. 'Mistress Elaine? I came to see all's well.'

'All's well, sir.' She measured the distance to her shift which she'd hung up with the rest of her day's clothes because there still clung to it the residual smell of the bonfire she'd made that morning of the house on the hill; but Gabriel was stepping in front of it.

'You're not cold like that?'

'A little, sir.'

He came closer, held the taper near her. She pulled the window sheet across to cover herself. He touched her bare shoulder.

How warm his touch.

'There are goosepimples on your skin.'

'Yes, sir.'

Dust on the sheet made her sneeze. She could smell the wine on his breath. His sweat. See his prick hard, poking his shirt. She thought suddenly: that's what I want. It would be good. It would be ridiculous. It would be fun. 'Gabriel –'

'Let me make you warmer.' His voice was slurred. Gently he prised the window sheet free of her fingers, pulled it aside. He stroked her hips, the curve of her spine, cupped her buttocks, kissed her belly.

She stepped down from the sill, stood tall as she could in the moonlight, shook her hair behind her shoulders. 'Is there any way I could have avoided this?' she said. 'Did I have any choice?'

'I've never forced a woman yet.'

She laughed. 'You won't need to force me.' She reached up under his shirt to stroke his strong back. 'Today was meant to be my wedding day,' she said. 'Did you know that?' She ran her hand down to his crotch and caressed him.

He stepped back and ran the tips of his fingers along the moonlight lines on her breasts and her belly. 'Sweet tiger,' he said.

Elaine stretched in the deep shadows of the bed curtains, her arms and her legs; she wriggled her shoulders, arched her back, pulled up the blanket to prickle her chin. Her mouth ached with smiling; she licked her dry lips.

She hadn't heard Gabriel go. She'd slept so well; the best in months. Years it felt. She cuddled the pillow where his head had lain, sniffed it for the smell of him.

Squeaks from Samuel. She opened the curtain a fraction on the cradle side. Sweetheart, she said. He was lying on his back, waving his fists in the air. Sweetheart.

She put a dry clout on him and brought him into her bed, tried to cuddle him but he was having none of it, he romped on hands and knees away across the coverlet and rolled off. A few squawks of pain, and then silence; the door swinging open. 'Samuel!'

She jumped up, pulled on her shift and ran blinking into the gallery that was lit by the low sun of the winter dawn, saw her son crawling like a purposeful puppy in his shirt and belliband at full speed toward the stairs. 'No, Sammy, not there, come back!'

She caught him as he was about to roll over the top step, and snatched him up; glanced down and saw the front door wide open and Benedict Pole in fur-lined cloak and feathered hat outside soothing his restive mare; and Gabriel was just mounting Durendal. Full leather bags were hung behind his saddle. He wore a blue doublet, a red velvet hat, a short woollen cloak trimmed with some white fur, maybe ermine. 'Gabriel! Gabriel!'

But he was talking to Pole, they were joking together, laughing, and he didn't hear her; she was relieved, for it wasn't her place to call out to him like that. But where was he going? He'd told her nothing about his leaving Cymberie. She stood watching, clutching Samuel tight in her arms, until the horses turned and began to trot away, hooves crunching the gravel, and Nathaniel shut the great door, pushing the bolt across.

'You ask what's taken Master Gabriel away? More of this *Good Adventure* business,' sniffed Phillis. 'More like *Westwards into the Jaws of Death* if you ask me. I'll never understand what maggot's got into his head. Give me safe old earth anytime. I couldn't bear a heaving sea, never mind what treasures one might find. Here, Samuel, have a taste of this egg.'

He pulled it off the spoon and squashed it in his fist, pushed it in his mouth.

'Why didn't Gabriel tell me yesterday that he was going away?'

'Why should he? What business is it of yours?'

'I need to be told what I have to do as his steward.'

'You'll have to work it out for yourself.'

Elaine was sitting in Richard's side chamber, going through a pile of letters that were still sealed, opening each in turn. Here was one to Richard, dated a month ago, from an Abraham Smith of Lincolnshire: *Most esteemed friend, I pray this map may please you, which I place before you, that our mutual acquaintance William Bacon has devised. It is most accomplished, and he has written also a brief account of the history of this county. I know this is a subject of great interest to you because of the illuminating history you have written of your estates.* I never knew Sir Richard had done that, Elaine thought; how much I don't know about him. But all I can do is reply that he's died.

Here was a letter to him from the woodcarver turned marble sculptor who had done the work in the hall, inviting his former patron to visit him in Italy and order a memorial for his late wife. It needs a memorial for the two of them now, Elaine thought: and she put that letter aside to ask Gabriel if that was what he wanted for his parents.

Here was another thing, a bill. She dipped the quill in the inkhorn, shook it and started to write, addressing it to Ralph Gibson, churchwarden of the parish church. *Concerning your request for the payment of six shillings and eightpence for the levelling of the pavement necessary upon the burial of Sir Richard Brullant Belvoir in church, the fourth day of October last*, she began. She frowned. Surely that should have been included in the funeral expenses which Gabriel had listed as paid. She consulted the account book but he had entered the expenses as one lump sum, not itemised. She bit her lip, thinking; looked up at the stone window with its thick greenish panes. There was an underwater feel here in this side chamber. A calmness. A memory of Richard that soothed her, always.

It's probably best to pay the bill, she decided, as a matter of goodwill, if nothing else. There's no way I can check, and when Gabriel sets off for the Indies in a month or so, I'll be having to make decisions like this all the time. She wondered if Phillis had the key to the safe-box so she could have the money, and set off in search of her.

In the kitchen she found Joe Chibborne drinking warm ale with Nathaniel; he raised his tankard and said, 'Here's to your return to Cymberie, Mistress Elaine. Is this the little fellow who's softened Phillis's heart? How do you do, my little man? What cold hands you have, my boy. What's your mother been doing, freezing you like that? There, you come inside my jerkin. Warm up in there, my pet.'

'He's such a restless child,' said Elaine. 'I put him on a blanket but he keeps crawling off it. He wants to explore everywhere.'

'He's a proper boy. What he needs is a playpen, so you can leave him in the warm and he'll come to no harm.'

'Will you make him one, Mr Chibborne?'

'Give us a couple of days, mistress.'

And the days fell into a pattern of busy-ness. Samuel spent most of his time in the warm kitchen, petted and talked to by everyone who came in, fed titbits when he was hungry, given boiled milk when he was thirsty. Elaine, in the cold side chamber, her purple shawl around her shoulders, dealt with all the letters: she read them through, she wrote the replies painstakingly, tongue at the back of her teeth, her slow hand gradually becoming more fluent. Then she began a new page for wages in the accounts book, at the head of which she wrote *Elaine Fisher steward 11 marks per annum*. She added the names and occupations of all the other staff at Cymberie, but she wouldn't take their word for how much they earned, oh no, she wasn't that gullible, she waited to check the figures with Gabriel when he next came down. Lickspittle, spat Phillis.

Then, not knowing what else a steward should be doing at this quiet time of year, she began the inventory, listing the contents of each room in the house. She started with the parlour: *Item, a long table on trestles, item, three cupboards, item, four chairs, item, a long table covering of Turkey carpet, another of dornix, two dornix cupboard cloths.* And that affluent multiplicity of cushions that must have been gathered by Lady Ann, she put them all down: *six green cushions, six embroidered cushions, four large embroidered cushions, two dornix cushions, three woven cushions* – And on to the servants' chambers that were without questions like *books* or *clothes* that she didn't know how to answer, whether to list them or no.

When the weather changed and pale blue mornings became the pattern – a little mist, a light frost, a skim of ice on the pond – out she went in the garden with her pen, paper and inkhorn. *Item, statue of an ancient goddess, name unknown,* she wrote; *item, two benches mounted on lion's heads; item, six lead flower urns, one lead cistern.* She was cold and she went back inside to find her soft grey cloak still hanging in the apple store amid shelves studded and sweet with the fruit, there where she'd left it another existence ago, when Richard had been growing stronger and Gabriel was a thorn in her heel; but now Richard was dead and Gabriel had become her lover.

Out again, the cloak around her shoulders. She inspected round the dark side of the house under the hollies where piles of logs were stacked high for the winter, supported by posts driven into the ground, their cut ends like pale faces showing the rings of their growth, the timber sweet-smelling: *Item, firewood*; and round to the outbuildings where she listed the farm tools: *Item, scythes, sickles and hooks, pitchforks and spades, hooked yokes and head yokes, turf spades and wagon ropes, hay ropes and hay sleds, axes, muck forks and briar hooks.* She stopped to watch a cock, a shimmer of bright feathers, dip its beak in a puddle to drink, its tail feathers quivering; and then raising its head to swallow.

She liked her lists, felt as though they brought the estate under her thumb. The lists gave her existence a purpose. She checked the store chamber with its forty white candles, five quarts of honey and dozen drinking glasses, the brew house with its barrels and troughs, its tubs and small spade, the larder with its salting trough and sides of bacon hanging from hooks.

Each day she'd roam further away from the house, continuing her listing. Then in the early afternoon she'd go indoors. She'd sit on a stool to eat a pie or a bowl of pottage in the kitchen that was soft orange from the subsiding fire, and sooty-smelling, the air still warm from Nathaniel's cooking; and she'd chat to whoever was there, or sing songs to Samuel.

One day when she went in Phyllis told her, 'There's a parcel for you.'

'A parcel? For me?'

'For Mistress Elaine Fisher, steward of Cymberie, the messenger said. I told him to leave it on the table in the parlour.'

'What is it? Who is it from?'

'How should I know? Do you think I have nothing to do but mind your business?'

'Is the messenger still here?'

'He ate and drank and then rode on.'

'Why didn't you call me?'

'What need was there? The parcel will wait for you, it won't grow legs and run away.'

Elaine hurried through the little hall to the parlour: who's it from? she was thinking. Can it be from my mother? Has she heard somehow that I am here? Has she sent something for her grandson?

Low sunlight in the parlour. Stale air; coldness. The scent of polish. The scarlet Turkey carpet running the length of the table. And on it a bundle of sacking.

Elaine laid her book, pen and ink down on a stool and concentrated on her parcel. With the small knife hung at her waist she unpicked the stitches in the sacking. She looped the thread into a skein so that it could be re-used.

Inside the sacking was a wrapping of coarse unbleached muslin. Inside that was a bolt of dark blue grosgrain. She shook it out; saw how the ribbed silk caught the light.

She'd shaken a piece of paper on to the floor: a letter. *Sweet Elaine,* she read, *My steward must dress as befits her station – make use of this. I continue with my preparation of the* Good Adventure. *We have some difficulties with the supply of stout ropes, but I do my best to overcome them. Yours ever, Gabriel Belvoir.*

She draped the fabric over her arms, then over an armchair to see the effect. She held it close to her face and looked at her reflection in a silver plate on the court cupboard; thought how though it was severe it suited her. And it was much smarter than the worn-out clothes she was wearing. She carried it through to the kitchen, where Phillis and Winifred marvelled at it too.

'Well,' said Winfred, with her scissors and pins, measuring the length of it against her arm, 'I can easily cut a bodice out of this for you, as well as a skirt.'

'Don't do it in the kitchen,' said Phillis. 'You'll get grease and smuts on it.'

'It's too cold to do it anywhere else,' grumbled Winifred.

'Mistress Steward is entitled to some comfort,' said Nathaniel. He crossed to the window. 'Hey, boy!' he yelled out. 'A fire in the parlour, now.'

So it was that they sat in the afternoon like the three Fates spinning, Phillis and Elaine doing the hemming and stitching, Winifred the more fancy stuff, in and out with their needles in small, almost invisible stitches the long length of the seams, straining their eyes against the dark fabric, moving apart as the daylight died to work by the windows, till that light had gone and it was time to work by the tapers; and then they sat in the armchairs with their feet resting on cushions, close to the fire: and Samuel woke from his afternoon nap and had the run of the floor, and Winifred twirled one of her red curls and glanced slyly at Elaine and said, 'I suppose Samuel will have a little sister in nine months or so.'

'What do you mean?'

'We all know why Master Gabriel's given you this.'

'Why?'

'Come on, we're not blind.'

'I don't know what you're talking about.'

'Well, time will tell.'

The skirt and the bodice were finished in a week. Elaine tried it on and adjusted the darts in the bodice so it skimmed her breasts.

Phillis found a piece of lace for a ruff and pinned it in place.

'Ah, you look like a lady,' sighed Winifred. 'You never know what might happen.'

'What are you hinting at?'

'I suppose it would be too good to be true, him marrying you. Pure fairytale.'

Elaine combed her hair back, twisted it up in a knot on her head.

Gabriel came home. 'Hmm,' he said at the front door, short cloak damp with fog; tossing it to Phillis, his hat to Winifred, while Joe Chibborne led Durendal off to the stable. 'My God, Elaine, you look severe. I can't wait to take that outfit off you.'

'Sir, I thank you for it. It's very fitting for a steward.'

'I've got something much prettier in my bags. Nathaniel, get Joe to bring them to the parlour. Elaine, don't skulk away. Come and tell me what you've been doing.'

'Sir.'

She brought the account book and they sat side by side at the table, the arms of the chairs forming a barrier between them but their shoulders touching, and he told her the correct figure for everyone's wages, which he knew off pat, and she wrote them down carefully, nervous of making mistakes with him watching her so intently.

The fabric he'd bought, when he unpacked it, was a kind of woven tapestry, a creamy-coloured mix of silk and wool by the feel, perhaps a little linen mingled in, with silver threads running through it, and patterned with green and brown flowers and deer: oh, it's lovely, she said.

'You like it, do you,' he said. 'It'll look good with your fair skin. It's not fitting for a steward to wear, of course. Far too costly. But maybe it'll do for a mistress.'

It surprised her how easily she stepped into the role. The other staff pushed her into it, of course: Phillis took Samuel in with her at night so he couldn't be a hindrance. Joe made sure that the boy saddled up a quiet mare for her to ride beside Durendal when Gabriel was off inspecting the estate; Nathaniel cooked dinners rich in supposed aphrodisiacs, which they ate alone in the parlour. 'Do you like these?' said Gabriel, spearing an oyster on the tip of his knife, placing it gently in her mouth. He topped up her wine.

'Thank you,' Elaine said. She didn't fight it. She knew it couldn't last. Life had been hard for her a long time; she didn't have any great expectations of it. 'When will you leave me?' she said.

'I go to London the day after tomorrow.'

But he kept coming back.

'I mean, when do you set sail in the *Good Adventure*?'

'Mid January,' he said.

'A month and a half.'

A fire burned in the hearth in his chamber. He undressed her by it: her ruff, her bodice, her skirt, her shift. 'Your skin,' he said, stroking it, taking the hard nipple of her left breast into his mouth. In the late afternoon as dusk was descending they slid into the dark fold between his linen sheets. 'Sweetheart,' he said.

She would stay awake, him asleep beside her, late into the night, until the waning moon rose and shone in the window. She studied his face in the moonlight, loving the curves and angularity of it, imprinting it in her memory so when he was gone she would be able to carve every feature, every crease, his receding hairline, the widow's peak, the small scar at the corner of his left eye. He would be fast asleep and gently she'd lift the bedclothes off him, push them to one side, study his body: his wide shoulders and strong chest, the muscles of his upper arms, his clenched fists (he wore his emerald ring even at night; now and again it scratched her); his stocky legs that were short in proportion to his body, his long-toed feet.

'What are you doing?'

'Looking at you.'

'Why?'

'I want to carve you.'

'God, that sounds vicious.'

'I mean carve you in wood.'

'You do woodcarving?'

'Not now. I did. I was very good. But Thomas – my husband – he sold our tools.'

'Mean bastard. I'll buy you some more.'

'Wood-carving tools are very personal things. You need to know what you want.'

'Tell me what you want.'

She lay back, head on the pillow. The ceiling of his bed was for the moment obscured by dark shadows, but she knew it was painted with the legend of Jason's journey in search of the Golden Fleece, it was restless with little blue and green waves crested with white. Jason's small boat was fragilely making its way between the twin perils of the clashing rocks, the Symplegades.

'Go on – tell me what you want.'

'What I want,' she said slowly, 'is a particular set of carving tools with a lizard carved on every handle. It's a small lizard with big eyes and a twist in his tail.'

'Where can I find these?'

'Oh, you won't be able to. A pedlar called Humfrey Howarde had them last Michaelmas, but he'll have sold them by now.'

'You know one thing I like about you, sweetheart?'

'No. No, I don't know at all.'

'You're always surprising me.'

'Why?'

'When I said, what do you want, you should have said, a bucketful of diamonds and rubies.'

'Is that what you want?'

'No. Yes. That's what my patrons want, why they're prepared to back me. They listen to my honey talk of clumsy Spanish treasure-ships weighted down with gold, and dole out a pittance to provender my boat, then fill their glasses with fine wine and put their feet up while they await my return with their share of the booty.'

'What do you want?'

'Me?' He knotted his fingers behind his head and considered a while. 'To explore beyond the horizon,' he said softly. 'That's what I really want.'

'What do you mean?'

'Have you ever seen the sea, sweetheart?'

'No.'

'It's the most changeable element you can imagine. Sometimes it's a sheet of dull pewter under a glare of bright sky. Sometimes it's pure light, flickered by a million sun glances, dark clouds above. Sometimes it's solid obsidian, a slow swell under blue. Always, at the furthest limit of my sight, there's that horizon line between sea and sky. It lures me on as if it were a golden hook to catch a fish. I want to see beyond it – I always want to see beyond it –'

She reached for his hand, interlocked her fingers with his.

'Sweetheart,' he said. 'I hate the land. It's full of petty rigmaroles, hoops I have to jump through. People to kowtow to. But I shall be sorry to leave you.'

In the dark early morning she dressed in the skirt and bodice made from the fine tapestry fabric he'd brought her. The outfit was not quite finished; a side seam and the hem were held in place with pins. She didn't flinch as, when he embraced her at the door, he pressed the pins' sharp points into her skin. He put her hair back behind her shoulder, ran his hand down her cheek and over her breasts, patted her belly. 'You look like my mistress in that, as I said you would,' he said.

They kissed, melting into each other. He broke away. 'Sweetheart, I should have gone yesterday.' He turned to mount Durendal and ride him toward the dawn. Elaine climbed the stairs to Richard's chamber, sat in his armchair and watched the sky grow light above the trees. Somewhere under the bare branches of the woods Gabriel was riding, hidden. Her eyes ached from scanning the trees, searching for a flash, a scrap of the scarlet of his cloak.

Nothing.

Getting up to go downstairs and begin her lists again, she glanced at her shadowy reflection in the silver plate on the court cupboard: wondered how Lady Ann's caul of pearls and gold net would look with the tapestry bodice. She selected a key from the bunch at her waist and took out the leather casket from the panelling, extracted the caul and looped her hair up into it: but it was still too dark in the room for her to see her reflection clearly. She pulled off the caul impatiently and stretched it over her hands. How like the pearls her times with Gabriel were: glowing, round, perfect, complete. And few. Acres of emptiness lay between them: the spaces in the net.

He brought her presents. One time he gave her a small silver box. 'What's inside it?' she asked.

'Open it and see.'

She kept thinking of foolish Winifred and her fairytale idea of a wedding. How much she wanted the box to contain a ring: a promise of continuing love. But it was a tiny ship, small as a walnut shell, with rigging made from gold wire starred with sapphires, a ruby for its rudder, a pin on the back. 'A brooch,' she said.

'Shawl pin,' he said.

'Why have you given it me?'

'Don't you know that a ship signifies happiness? Isn't that enough? It's the greatest gift that I can give you.' He took her hand. 'Things don't have to be for ever,' he said.

On the night of the day that he left she pinned the ship to the front of her shift. She slept in the tent of her bed-curtains, lying on her belly, and in the morning the ship jewel had impressed a deep red print in the skin of her chest, just above her breasts. She rubbed the mark gently, wanting happiness to last for ever; set straight the bowsprit which had become a little bent.

16

Walter Vernon was kneeling in the churchyard; he was pulling out clumps of dead grass from Thomas's grave and tossing them to one side. The earth on the roots was cold and clung to his fingers. 'Your wife's forgotten you now, Master Fisher,' said Walter. 'She's left us both.' For the past week he had waited around hoping to see her here; but she hadn't come. 'I've done my best for her,' he said. 'But what can I do now that would be of any good? I can't rule her actions.' Gossip in the village was pernicious: it said she'd thrown herself at Gabriel Belvoir, that they bedded together at all times of the day, that she went round Cymberie half-dressed; that Belvoir was so obsessed with her that he couldn't leave her alone, and was always touching her in tender places, doing it in the garden, the parlour, the stables, the hall, all around the estate. Walter couldn't vouch for the truth of the gossip: but he did know that Belvoir was at Cymberie far more often than was his custom, and that Cymberie's order for candles had doubled. 'Master Fisher, I am leaving the village, I can't look after your wife any more.' He was taking ship to the Netherlands in two days' time. Maybe he would go on to the New World with Wyatt. He felt Elaine ought to go with him.

What had precipitated his decision to leave was the success of his sermon at the open-air Prophesying in Dedham the previous Sunday. It was received with shouts and acclaim. The people of the congregation tore their hair; they rent their garments and covered themselves in ashes. 'You have touched their very hearts,' Browne had said. 'They begin to repent already. You have done well, my brother.' How that had swelled his heart with pride, to have Browne, who was so high up in the Puritan movement, commend him thus; but, knowing that pride, this warm feeling of success in his chest, was a sin, he had prayed that God grant him humility all his long walk home.

And God had answered his prayer through his mother. 'You utter fool,' she ranted. 'Your wretched father was burnt at the stake for being too open in his beliefs, and here you go all set to follow in his footsteps and get yourself hanged. How can you take no thought for me? How can I bear losing both husband and son? Can't you see how I suffer? It's too much – I will go mad.'

'Mother –'

She had turned her face to the corner. She wouldn't speak to him. And then Wyatt had arrived and told him that he was taking ship for the Netherlands on the twelfth of December: would Walter go with him?

Yes, he had said.

'Ai! Now you're leaving me!'

'I will send for you when I am settled, Mother,' he had said.

'Ha,' she'd said. 'First you throw me out of my house and then you want me to uproot myself again for you.'

She was happy in her new house, he had thought; it was compact, easy to keep warm on these raw wet days, the garden and the short walk to the village enough to keep her busy and active. Her health had been better than usual this autumn. He couldn't take her to the New World; she would die from the strangeness of it. 'Mother, I will do everything I can for your happiness. But I can't stay.'

As for Elaine – he admitted his powerlessness, he could do nothing there. She would have to make her own future. That, inevitably, would be that Belvoir would become bored with her and throw her penniless out of his house. She'd be back in the same position she was in when her husband was hanged, except almost certainly with two or three children in tow. Women were fools; how could she possibly prefer a future like that to a safe, ordered marriage with him?

'There's no accounting for women, Mr Fisher,' he said to Thomas's grave, standing up, dusting the earth from his fingers.

'You're not the only one that feels like that, Vernon,' said a voice behind him; and Walter turned to see Ralph Gibson, the churchwarden, his leather jerkin dropletted with blood from his butcher's trade; and Walter vividly recalled seeing Gibson's wife Rosamund at the Michaelmas fair selling pigs' ears and lamb chops and showing off her full breasts in a way that had gathered young men to her like bees to flowers. 'But it's strange to see you here, man. I've been thinking I ought to be coming after you for failing in your regular attendance at church, which the law requires.'

'Why pick on me? There's others are much worse than me. What about Gabriel Belvoir? This is his parish church, but he hasn't been here since his father's funeral, I'll swear. And he's taken a widow-woman as his lover, all the gossip is of his incontinence with her, and what do you do about it? Nothing! You should be reporting him to the episcopal court for his behaviour, but you haven't lifted a finger. Think what a bad example he's setting. He makes our young men behave as wild as he does, our young women yearn to be bedded. You must do your duty and ensure that he does public penance for his sin. In church, as is proper, before the congregation, barefoot, in a shift…'

'Rumour says the widow-woman was due to wed you.'

'He seduced her on her very way to marry me.'

Gibson nodded. 'I should indeed bring this matter before the church court,' he said. 'Everyone turned a blind eye to his escapades when he was young, but now he is older, and master of Cymberie, he should behave in a fitting manner. I suppose you want vengeance on the woman too? You want me to report her to the court as well?'

'There's no need for that. Time will soon bring her to her knees in repentance. I offered her everything a reasonable woman could desire but she has chosen to go instead after a painted butterfly. Her summer will end soon enough, and her example will be the best lesson to every wanton. Once she's pregnant, the justices will send her back wherever she came from, as a vagrant.'

'I've heard that Belvoir had appointed her steward of Cymberie in his absence, and is paying her a man's wage.'

'Huh. If there's any truth in it, it must be a trick for him to get his way with her. It won't last. He'll soon realise what a fool she is.'

'Yet you wanted to marry her.'

Walter sighed, shrugged his shoulders. 'Women,' he said.

'Indeed,' Gibson agreed. 'But nevertheless, as for you – heed my warning, Vernon. We were boys together, but you must observe the law. You must attend the parish church every week, and take communion three times a year. I can't keep trouble away from your door.'

Elaine looked again at the parcel on the cupboard in the little hall. It was wrapped in canvas, the folds stitched together in a workmanlike way. It had been lying there since the messenger'd arrived with it last night. She had guessed at once what it was from its weight and size. 'Thank you,' she had said, taking it from his hands.

'I have to wait for your reply, mistress,' he'd said.

'I'll give it you in the morning.' She'd asked Nathaniel to feed him well; Phillis to give him a bed for the night.

She couldn't explain her reluctance to open the parcel. It obviously must have come from Gabriel; there might be a letter inside.

It was mid-morning and she still hadn't opened the parcel. She picked it up. I'll open it in Lady Ann's parlour, she decided; there's more space on the table in there. She crossed the little hall, glancing up at the painting she'd completed last week, that filled the empty space on the wall to the right of the apple tree. Samuel was up there, crawling among cabbages; a kennel in the background, a lugubrious hound peering out. It made her smile. 'For God's sake don't fall off that bloody scaffolding,' Gabriel had shouted at her when she was doing it, bumping his head on a cross-bar. Sometimes he reminded her so much of his father.

She opened the parlour door and put down the parcel on a corner of the table. An everyday green dornix cover it had on it today, not the fine carpet used when the master was here. She stood by the fire, rubbing her cold hands together; took a peek at Samuel in his cradle, under the arched angel wings of the Noah's Ark that she'd carved when he was just a bump inside her. It was only last week she had bought it back from Rosamund the butcher's wife. It was so good to have money of her own, to do what she wished with.

How well Samuel slept in the cradle. As if he knew it was meant for him. Only another few months, though, and he would be too big for it. She touched her belly. She wasn't feeling sick at all, so probably she was safe.

She had to open the parcel. December days were short, and the messenger had a twenty-mile journey back to London.

He wouldn't want to do it in the dark. She unhooked the bunch of keys from her waist, used the sharp teeth of the key to the weapons store to cut the stitches. She unfolded the canvas. Inside was a letter sealed with Gabriel's seal; and a great roll of tools, the leather dark, worn and creased. A touch of mildew on it.

Slowly she unfolded the roll along the table. So long since she'd seen it: an aeon ago. When she'd been a different person; unshaped.

All of Thomas's chisels were there: she took them out one by one. All lizard-marked on the handles. Long and short; slow curves and quick curves. All rusty-bladed and – she tested them against her finger – blunt. Thomas would never have allowed them to get in such a condition.

She selected the widest, deepest gouge and sharpened it on his stone, slowly, remembering what he had taught her. 'There, do it like that, at the same angle as it will be to the carving,' he'd said, guiding her hand. 'It's all one,' he'd said. 'Everything is a unity.' She tested the edge, smoothed off the slight burr, stropped the blade on the back of the leather roll. You could see where Thomas had done the same thing hundreds of times before. She was holding his gouge – *like holding your hand.*

She opened Gabriel's letter. *My sweet Elaine*, she read. *I sought out the gentleman you told me of, and hope this little thing will give you pleasure. All goes well. Pole will have the sails and ropes tomorrow. A good meeting with the Merchant Taylors. While passing down Three Needle Street on leaving them, I chanced to meet Harry Tuck. He warned me there is a fellow – a candlemaker or some such from the village, do you know him? - who is determined to have me brought before the consistory courts for my supposed incontinence with you. I don't have the patience for such pettiness – I won't dance to their tune. Can you imagine my standing in a parish church in nothing but a white shift, declaring my penitence for loving you? Rather I'd shout out the reasons that I love you and how our love is good; how my joy in you increases each time we lie together. To say I regretted that – never. No man of honour would. So, my sweet heart, I expedite my departure. The* Good Adventure *being almost in readiness, and the weather set fair, I intend to sail within the week. God guard you and keep you safe and well. Think of me always. If you have difficulties at Cymberie, consult my sister. Farewell, my sweet. As ever, your loving servant, Gabriel Belvoir.*

No.

No. I have to see you. Gabriel –

Elaine found herself in the kitchen. 'The messenger, where is he?'

'Here, mistress.' A thin man with yellow hair, a shabby jerkin, a pewter tankard in his hand.

'You must take me with you. We must go at once. I have to see him.'

The messenger wiped his moustache with the back of his hand. 'It's past noon, mistress. Too late to travel today.'

'No. I have to go now. Do you know where he is?'

'He was staying in Cheapside when I left him.'

'Fetch torches, Nathaniel, we will take torches. Saddle my mare. Your horse – Phillis, you must care for Samuel.'

'Why? What's the matter.'

'I have to see him. I have to see Gabriel before he goes.' How hard she had tried to keep him out of her heart, knowing his inconstancy, knowing how likely he was to die on his journey to the Indies. But he had branded inside her a sphere of affection that expanded every time she saw him. Kissed him. Held him.

Slept with him. Loved him. She couldn't help it. It overwhelmed her. She had to find him now.

How could she be driven by this absolute, illogical necessity? It drove her through the day and the village, into the town where people looked strangely at a woman clad in a shabby grey cloak that half-concealed a fine tapestry gown, with only a messenger to attend her, into the evening and the dark of the deep forest where – was it wolves howling? that strange noise – and the torches flickered their light on the bare trees and her mare shied at shadows, and stumbled, and the messenger insisted, 'We must stop.' And then there was the inn and the bed that she shared with two sisters – instant exhausted sleep and dreams in which she was still riding on and on; and then there was the first light of morning and waking the messenger: 'Come on! We've got to go!' And out on to the road and into London, so many houses, she'd never seen so many houses before, nor people, the streets were filling up with people, some coming in from the country bearing baskets of cheeses and nuts, others running to no purpose, some talking strange languages, and there was the grisly head of a traitor displayed on a gate, such a fine stone house, such a fine – And the roads were cobbled, or paved with limestone and flint, what a racket they made, the horses' hooves on them.

'Here's where he was staying.' That was the messenger.

But when he knocked at the door he was told Gabriel had gone.

'Where? Where is he? I must find him.'

'Wait for me here, mistress. I'll enquire.'

It hurt her to wait, she wanted to be active, she wanted to open every door, to search through every room in this great city, saying, have you hidden him? Is he here? But she knew if she went the messenger maybe wouldn't find her, and she forced herself to stand still, holding her mare by the reins, putting up a hand to stroke her now and again. The noise and the traffic bemused her, the carts pulled by six horses urged on by the whistles of carters and the cracks of their long whips, the coaches that carried fine ladies and their maids, flocks of geese and of sheep, trains of packhorses, they all made her head ache.

But at last here was the messenger come back again. 'He's gone to the coast,' he said.

'Let's follow him.'

'Tomorrow.'

'No, now.'

'The horses must rest.'

'I will go on my own.'

'It's not safe, mistress. We'll stay here tonight.'

'I – I was sure of meeting him here. I haven't brought enough money to stay more than one more night in an inn.'

'We will stay at my sister's then, mistress.'

A narrow house in a thin street that stank of piss. Elaine shared a bed with one of his nieces and his mother, shut up with them inside the confinement of the ragged, dusty curtains; how she longed for the solitariness of her old house on the hill. The niece was racked by a terrible cough that jerked the mattress and pulled at the blankets. The grandmother did nothing and Elaine couldn't bear the child's distress. *Ssh*, she said to the girl; *ssh*. She settled herself at the head of the bed and cradled the child's skinny frame in her arms, rubbed her chest gently until she choked up gobbets of phlegm; some clung to Elaine's hand, she had to wipe it off on the turnback of the sheet. At last the girl's breathing eased; Elaine could feel the calmer rhythm of it against her skin as she fell asleep. Tired, she slept too: the two of them tangled together.

The clatter of passers-by in the street woke Elaine before dawn. Stiff from sleeping at an odd angle, she gently lifted the sick girl to the centre of the bed without waking her. She pulled on her clothes over her shift, tied the grey cloak around her shoulders, feeling for the ship pin, checking it was still there, hidden inside it. She ran her fingers through her hair to tidy it.

'Come on,' she said to the messenger. 'Let's go.' After they'd broken their fast with cold ale (his sister had not yet lit the fire) they rode side by side out into the icy streets, breath clouding the air, paused at a cookshop and bought apple pies which they ate riding, crumbs spattering their clothes, heading out of the city into a countryside of bare orchards, nut trees and neat gardens of leeks and cabbages where a few men still worked, shielded by hawthorn hedges from the rising north-east wind that brought a deep chill from far off snowy lands.

'I don't like the look of this weather,' said the messenger, riding beside Elaine.

She pulled her cloak tighter around herself; she was numb with cold.

'We'll stop at the next inn,' he said. 'There'll be a fire there. You can have a sup of warm ale, and rest yourself a little.'

She was glad when they reached the place, and slid eagerly from her horse, stumbling from the cold.

'I'll take your mare,' he said.

'Thank you,' she said, handing him the reins, and went inside, bending her head because of the low lintel, in where the heat of the log fire made a warm fug. She held out her hands to the orange glow; toasted herself.

But the messenger didn't join her. Where is he? she wondered after a while, and went out to find him.

He wasn't in the yard, nor could she see any sign of her mare or his gelding. A vague feeling of foreboding began to swell in her chest. 'The man who was with me, have you seen him?' she called to a stable lad forking horse shit.

He stopped what he was doing, leant on his fork and shrugged his shoulders. She offered him a penny. That wasn't enough. She tried threepence. He looked at the coin doubtfully, then decided to talk. 'The fellow headed back to the City as soon as you were gone indoors, mistress. At a fair speed, too, as if all the devils in hell were after him. He was riding his gelding and leading the sidesaddle mare.'

'Thank you,' said Elaine. She bit her lip. How alone she felt. Betrayed and deserted. She didn't know what to do.

The icy wind bit into her. She pulled her cloak tight around her; in doing so touched the ship pin Gabriel had given her. And she knew at that second that the only thing she cared about in the whole world was seeing Gabriel again. Everything else was immaterial. So what if the messenger had stolen her horse; that was between him and his Maker. She mustn't let anger at him distract her from her purpose.

She set out again on the road to the coast. The morning ice was thawing; she kilted her skirt up, jumped over puddles and mud. She was happy to be walking again, one foot in front of the other, stretching her legs. The exercise made her feel good, it warmed her. She loosened her cloak; her hand brushed the ship pin again and she clutched it. Happiness, Gabriel had said it signified.

She worried about how she was dressed, was afraid that her tapestry bodice and skirt that she'd put on for Gabriel's sake would make her an easy target for thieves now she was on her own. In woods on a ridge, in the seclusion of holly trees, she undressed and turned her best clothes inside out so they looked shabby and sombre, put them back on like that.

She passed pedlars on the road, housewives with baskets,

a child herding a flock of geese. Good day, she said; good day they answered back. Toward evening woodcutters tramped past her, carrying their axes on their shoulders. Goodnight, she said. She came to the clump of woodland they had cleared, where the limbless trunks of great limes and oaks lay on the leafy earth like fallen giants. She perched on one to rest, drawing her feet up and looping her hands around her knees, feeling the damp soak in her skirt, smelling the sharp fragrance of the cut wood: thinking how the trees had been felled at exactly the right time of year, in the cold while their sap was low and the moon near full, and she thought how good they would be to carve, and stooped to drink from a spring that rose there.

The tree-felling had opened up a wide vista across the flat land below. Long shadows fell across it. Not too long now, Elaine thought, another night and a morning and I'll be there with him.

I'll take ship with him, she suddenly found herself thinking, I'll climb in his narrow berth beside him, the side of it'll be hard against my back, and he'll be warm, his arms around me, my head on his chest – and we'll make love to the rhythm of the ocean, this strange element that he knows so well and I don't at all, we'll keep hold of each other until we land in the Americas where dragons guard the city of gold and serpents slither brilliant as gemstones –

When she came to a village she bought bread and a pie, which she ate as she walked on. When she came to a barn she crept in the back of it and made a hollow for herself among the close-stacked stooks of barley, wrapped her cloak around herself and slept.

Today I will see him. She dressed with great care, turning her tapestry bodice and skirt out the right way, smoothing her skirt over her farthingale, adjusting her shift to show off her cleavage. She combed her hair with her fingers, left it to flow loose over her shoulders. 'I love to see the red lights in it catch the sun,' he had said.

She covered it up with her cloak and set off in the half-dark. In due course the sun rose and diffused its weak wintry light across the sodden fields, casting long shadows. The bare branches of the poplars shivered in the breeze.

Today I will see him. The thought buoyed her up, it made her feet skip along. Even so, it was not until mid-morning that she came to the sea. She stopped in amazement. She'd never seen it before. It stretched out in front of her like a vast animal, shapeless and restless. Its heartbeat was the rhythmic white-tipped waves, its breathing the suck and susurration on the sand. Silver spray. Constant noise. That salt smell. It was full of darkness and yet brighter than any thing she had ever seen before, flickering with a million pinpoints of light.

She stood on a low cliff among a crowd of onlookers, shielding her eyes from the sun. Out in the bay lay two ships, each three-masted, their silhouette the same as that of her ship pin. She released it from the inside of her cloak, cupped it in her hand to compare it. Yes: that same round nutshell shape, the same fragile bound forward of the bowsprit, the same tension in the rigging. She folded her palm around the precious thing, the pin pricking her skin.

A train of packhorses was just plodding off the beach; they'd left barrels stacked on the sand, over which a sailor stood guard against the gangs of children and young lads running around and shouting. White gulls wheeled overhead, wide-winged, and shrieked and soared. On the sea, boats with four oarsmen each side were ferrying the barrels to the ships; others carried passengers perched in the stern. The crew, Elaine supposed; they must be carrying the crew on board, perhaps they're leaving soon.

'That ship,' said Elaine to the old man seated on a broken barrel beside her. 'Is that the *Good Adventure*?'

'That's the *Dove*,' he said. 'The one further out, that's the *Adventure*.'

'Ah.' She stared at it. Such a small frail vessel to carry Gabriel that terrible distance into the west.

She picked her way down the sandy path to the beach. How alien she felt, not belonging here among all the busy-ness and scurry, not belonging with the crowd who'd come to watch for a bit of excitement. All she wanted was Gabriel.

And yet she hung back. This is his world, she kept thinking. She slipped back her hood to set free her hair, bit her lips to redden them. Tucked her hair behind her ears, pulled it forward again.

How gritty the sand. She found herself writing *Gabriel* in it with the toes of her boot, as if it were a writing-box.

There was someone in a scarlet cloak stood further down the beach, by the barrels. Could that be him? She ran toward him.

No. Just a man with a face like a fish, in this terrible confusion of people.

Gabriel! Gabriel, where are you?

She felt a touch on her shoulder and whirled round.

But it was only Benedict Pole in a blue cloak, a scarlet feather in his velvet cap. 'Why, mistress, what are you doing here?'

'Where's Gabriel? I've got to see him before he leaves.'

'He's all set to go.' He nodded toward the *Good Adventure* and even as she watched men crowded on to the deck like bees and swarmed up the rigging like spiders; the unbleached sails, released from their ropes, dropped and unfurled, caught the cold wind that swelled them, and the ship was off, it was moving, it was gliding like a swan toward the ocean. At every mast top fluttered the flag of St George. A dozen scarlet pennants flew out and snaked against the pallid sky, licking the westward air, tasting it eagerly. The craft looked so merry, so confident, so full of hope.

So small cutting through the choppy waves. So frail.

Gabriel. Gabriel. Gabriel. 'Don't cry, mistress. He'll be back in two or three years, God willing. He won't be able to keep away from your pretty face,' said Benedict. 'Mind, man, watch what you're doing with that barrel. Don't split it before it's even loaded. You there, give him a hand.'

Elaine climbed back to the top of the low cliff and stood there a long time, watching the silhouette of the *Good Adventure* grow smaller, diminish to a shadow and disappear from sight. Soon the *Dove* too raised anchor; her sails swelled, her pennants burst forth and she followed in its wake.

The crowd on the beach dispersed. Everyone was gone.

Only the bare horizon now, this dull emptiness. Elaine was a pillar of ice, of salt, of sorrow, alone on the cliff. Her eyes ached.

The twilight swallowed her. Stars appeared. The sky lit up, a brilliant shimmer.

Still the shush of the waves on the sand. This constancy. *Ssh, ssh.* Always and always. *Ssh.*

Elaine walked home past the ruins of a friary where only a few stones still stood one on another. She crossed a narrow stone bridge that friars had built two centuries ago. Her boots fell apart and she walked on barefoot on a path beside a river that chattered over small stones, that pooled in dull ponds where trout flicked their tails and nosed upstream. She walked under bare oaks and chestnuts with their branches pitched above her like the bright-striped roof of a tournament tent.

But colourless. Winter drained colour from everything.

Sepia rather. Brownish. The earth stained her feet. There was green moss on the side of a tree.

She trod silently along the earth path where thousands of people had trodden before, where thousands would tread again, on and on until the end of time. The fabric of her skirt whispered. The earth was a constancy. Always and always –

This is my element, she found herself thinking. The earth is my element as the sea is Gabriel's and that will separate us for ever.

Cymberie was sleeping. Not one candle in a window. Only the solid silhouette against the starry sky.

Gabriel would be guiding himself by those stars. There, the North Star, there, up high where he'd shown her as they stood side by side in the deep twilight on the knoll in Stubbes Pasture. They had made love there, couched on her grey cloak.

Prickles under her feet: stones, leaves. She had been walking since before dawn. Her thigh muscles ached. Her knees threatened to fail her.

How bitterly the wind cut into her, out from the shelter of the trees.

She let herself in the back door. The flagstones welcomed her feet: that familiar slight grittiness. She fumbled her way to the kitchen where the ash of the dying fire – those two or three glows of orange – permitted her to find a candle and light it.

Upstairs: she had to haul herself up by the banister. She was out of breath by the seventh step: had to stop and rest a while.

Samuel's cradle wasn't by her bed. Maybe he was with Phillis.

She stripped off her clothes. Paused to pin the ship pin to her shift. Slid between the icy sheets.

The morning saw her rising. It wasn't light. She washed in the icy bowl of water by her bed; soaped her feet with the Indies-soap and rinsed the earth from her skin until it came pale. She'd scratched herself on brambles and stones; she'd a blister under her big toe.

She put on a clean shift and coiled her hair, dressed carefully in the dark blue grosgrain of her steward's uniform. Her green slippers. She found the ship-pin on her yesterday's shift, fastened it to the breast of her bodice where the gold and sapphires shone.

She smoothed the sheets of her bed, brushing out last night's leaves, green moss and twigs that had clung to her feet and her hair. Pulled up the blankets, quilt and dornix bedcover. She was steward of Cymberie; she had to do her duty.

White light on the gallery; the snow she'd been expecting had begun. In Richard's chamber she glanced at the silver plate on the court cupboard and noted the dark shadows under her eyes. You'd say my hair was a mess, sir, she thought, and used his horn comb, then coiled her hair up again. Beyond his casement windows the snowflakes fell heavy as feathers from angel-wings.

Her legs ached, going down the stairs. Her whole body was weighed down with weariness. She didn't know what time she'd got back to Cymberie last night.

The fire was lit in the kitchen; Nathaniel was kneading dough on the table.

'It's smoky in here,' she observed.

‘A north-east wind. That always causes a downdraught.’

‘It was so cold walking home.’

Nathaniel had candles at each end of the table, and by their flickering flames she could see flecks of ash, or soot, peppering the glossy surface of the dough. He turned it in his big hands, compressed it, folded it in on itself so the flecks disappeared. ‘Did you see Master Gabriel?’

‘No.’

‘This wind will blow him along nicely.’

‘Yes.’

He kneaded the dough one more time and slapped it in a bowl, covered it with a cloth and set it by the fire to rise. ‘You’d like a mug of ale?’

‘Nathaniel, I didn’t want him to go.’

‘For God’s sake, woman, keep your tears to yourself. Here, I’ll heat this for you.’ He set a shallow pan on the grill under the window, added cloves to the ale, grated nutmeg in, stirred in a spoonful of honey. ‘There – drink that.’

The tankard warmed her hands. ‘I wish you’d seen the *Good Adventure*, Nathaniel. She looked so brave with her sails up, her pennants flying in the wind. As merry as a booth at Cymberie fair. But, oh, his journey is so long. God knows when he will come back again.’

‘Are you hungry?’

‘Yes.’ She sipped the last of the ale and put down her mug. ‘I didn’t eat yesterday.’ She walked heavily to the pantry where the bread was stored and lifted the lid of the crock; but it was empty. ‘We don’t have any bread, Nathaniel?’

‘No, it was stale. I gave it to Glascocke for his pigs.’

‘What? Nathaniel, no! You can’t waste good food like that. People are starving at this time of year. God’s my witness, I’ve been there myself, I should know. Give the bread to the poor.

Don't throw it away on animals.'

'What I do with food is my business.'

'No. I am steward here. I govern Cymberie. You'll do as I say.'

'So the master's love-puppet has a voice?'

'Don't you sneer at me.'

'You won't tell me what to do.' He turned away, he thumped angrily by the window. There was a crash as a bowl broke.

She bit her lip, knowing she'd been too abrupt. She didn't want to alienate him. She wished she wasn't so tired, she wished she'd seen Gabriel, she wished she could think clearly. She tucked her hair behind her ears. 'Nathaniel – I – please, Nat, you know I'm right. Think of the Lady Ann. Sir Richard – he told me how generous his wife was, how she used to take food round to the sick. Isn't that how Cymberie ought to be? Let's turn this house back to what it was, Nathaniel, let's make it hospitable again, it's been turned in on itself too long –' She tried to put her arms around him.

But he avoided her. 'You're the steward, Mistress Elaine. You make sure the land's managed properly, you see the rents are collected, the workers paid and the house well-maintained. But don't think you can boss me around.'

'Do you remember how you saved my life when I came here?'

He turned and looked at her, and maybe he saw the exhaustion in her face, because all of a sudden he bustled out to one of the larder rooms and came back with a chunk of cheese, a wedge of fruit cake on a plate. 'Eat that, girl.' He tossed logs on the fire, and the bark crackled as the flames licked them. A gust of smoke blew down the chimney. The two of them coughed.

Elaine hesitated in the cold entrance hall, wiping the stickiness of the cake from her lips with the back of her hand. Gabriel always had a fire here, and she wondered whether to ask the boy to light it, or if she should save the firewood. 'I don't know what to do,' she said out loud. She thought: there's no-one I can ask for advice.

White light from the snow fell in the tall windows, illuminating the Belvoir family portrait. Sir Richard, Lady Ann and Ysabelle; and young Gabriel, toy boat in hand, eyes already scanning the horizon.

'Cymberie is mine for the moment,' she told them softly. 'Isn't that strange?' She wondered: what will the future bring? Maybe in a year or so's time Gabriel'll have forgotten me and be back with a beautiful bride on his arm, a fine Spanish lady perhaps, all black hair and red satin bodice; or maybe he'll die of one of those terrible fevers that haunt the Indies, that he told us about, maybe his'll be an inglorious sickbed, below-the-decks death. Then the estate will be sold and I'll be out of work and penniless again, just Samuel and I on our own once again. I must make a good fist of my stewardship of Cymberie so I can find work elsewhere if I must. I must use this time for learning. I must make possibilities for myself.

She stepped down into her side chamber and found a letter addressed to Gabriel that had arrived yesterday. It was from Abraham Smith, his father's friend, expressing sorrow at Richard's death and commending his great learning. Elaine smoothed the letter with fingers numb with cold and went upstairs to his bedchamber, looked at the books gathering dust on the court-cupboard. You shared your knowledge with me, sir, she thought, you taught me to read; the rest I must work out for myself. She picked up the book of the Americas, opened it toward the end and read a paragraph: *In a cave among these great mountains dwell spotted jaguars whose eyes glow emerald in the night and whose talons will shred a man's flesh; and they come to lap at sunrise from a mighty river that flows sixty leagues between grey rocks.*

She thought of Gabriel confronting jaguars. You'll have your sword and dagger, you'll be safe. I will read this book every day, she thought. Reading will be a comfort for me. The words will be my friends.

She took a folded blanket from Richard's bed, shook it out and caped her shoulders with it, sat on the chair by the window, the Book of the Americas open on the table in front of her. *There is a temple where the dead kings are laid*, she began.

But the snow distracted her. She was so glad she had got home before it began. It was falling more lightly now; she could just see the trees of the common as a dull blur. There was a movement at the edge, where the track debouched to the garden. Horses. Four great horses, harnessed together. What were they doing there? She opened the window and leaned out, heard men shouting and the harness jingling, the crack of a whip.

The horses were pulling a sled. The snow obscured it so she couldn't quite see what was on it.

She closed the window, put the Book of the Americas back in its place and ran downstairs. Nathaniel and Joe Chibborne were bustling out of the kitchen, followed by Phillis who was carrying Samuel. 'Sammy!' cried Elaine, and the baby wriggled and almost leapt into her arms. 'Sweetheart,' she said, burying her cold face in his blond curls, but he'd caught the others' excitement and jerked on her hip, urging her to the door that was now standing wide open so they could see the strangers in their sacking cloaks, their warm breath misting the chill air. Snowflakes still falling.

'You've lost your way in this weather, good sirs,' said

Nathaniel.

'Damnation, this place isn't Cymberie?' The man had a Kentish accent.

'Cymberie? Yes.'

'We were charged to bring this.'

'A log? What have you brought a log for? Do you think we can't grow good wood of our own?' It was an eight foot long section of a thick tree trunk, stripped bare of bark and branches, the pale wood mud-flecked from its journey, and yellowish against the white of the snow.

'That's a fine piece of timber,' said Joe, running his strong carpenter's hands along it, wiping it clean.

'He said, take it to the front door. Surprise her.' The carter's hood was slipping back; he pulled it forward.

'Surprise who?'

'The steward, he said. Surprise the steward of Cymberie.'

'That's me,' said Elaine. She stepped outside and Samuel gurgled with delight, stretching out his small hands to the snowflakes.

'What's it for, I'd like to know,' grumbled Phillis. 'A useless great lump of wood like that, messing up the place.'

'Who sent it?' said Joe.

'Look,' said Elaine. At one end of the log, rough and a little lopsided, as if it had been carved with the dagger he wore at his side by a sea-captain resting his horse among felled trees in North Kent (in the same place where she had rested) while he hurried to reach his ship and sail westward, was a carved heart. Inside it the letters G and E were joined together. She ran her fingers over them. The wood was gritty as sand with shell-fragments in. It was a feeling she would love for ever. *He was thinking of me. Even as he was leaving he was thinking of me.*

She knelt beside the log. Samuel escaped her and

crawled in the snow, shoving handfuls in his mouth. Phillis tutted and recovered him. 'Get up, Mistress Elaine,' she said. 'The master's gone and that's that. There's no point in ruining your skirt. Such a fine piece of silk grosgrain .... What are you grinning for, mistress, I'd like to know?'

You crazy man, she was thinking, you crazy, crazy man to send it me. Her chest filled with warmth; never mind the chill of the day. You know me so well, you knew I'd love to have it.

'What are you going to do with it, mistress?' asked Joe Chibborne.

'Get up, Elaine,' said Phillis, yanking her elbow.

'Leave the sled here,' Joe told the carters. 'Bring your horses round the back to the stables and I'll call the boy to take care of them.'

'Come indoors and warm yourselves. You've had a long journey. Have a bite to eat,' said Nathaniel. 'We brew good ale here.'

'Get someone to light the fire in the parlour,' Elaine instructed Phillis. 'Joe, get men to help you carry the log in the parlour. Put it at this end, by the north window.'

'You can't bring a great log of wood in the house!' That was Phillis.

'The master sent it me to carve, and it needs to be kept in the dry. Joe –'

'Not today, Mistress Elaine. When the weather's more settled and the men can get up to the house. It'll take a few of us to shift a log that size.'

That afternoon, when Elaine had laid Samuel to rest in his cradle, she put on her old clothes. She borrowed Joe's wooden hammer and collected the leather roll of Thomas's tools that Gabriel had recovered for her. Then she went in the garden.

It was quiet out there, and cold. She was alone. Her ankles deep in snow. She tucked up her skirt. The trees of the common were lost in a haze, the contours of Cymberie soft with mist. No birds sang. The sun was obscured. Just herself and the wood: that great log. It was all hers.

She threw off her shawl, selected a wide gouge and picked a point at which to hammer it in. There; she'd made a beginning: a scoop, a curl that might be the start of anything. She knew that the shape she wanted was concealed in the wood. All she had to do was keep going and she'd find it.

Over and over again she went with the gouge and the hammer, breaking the quiet. Woodchips flew up, they sank in the snow.

In with the gouge. This is what truly matters to me, she thought. It's what I love. It's where I'm not confused.

The mist muffled the sound. Woodchips fountained up, they caught in her hair, in her ears, on her nose, in her clothes. A blister began to form in the palm of her hand.